Swing!
Adventures in Swinging by Today's Top Erotica Writers
Edited by Jolie du Pré

ISBN: 978-1905091-35-5
Paperback version
Published by Logical-Lust Publications © 2009

Cover image by Helen E. H. Madden, pixelarcana.com
© Logical-Lust Publications 2009

Swing! Adventures in Swinging by Today's Top Erotica Writers is a collection of works of fiction. The names, characters, and incidents are entirely the work of the author's imagination. Any resemblance to actual persons, living or dead, or events, is entirely coincidental.

All rights reserved. No part of this publication may be copied, transmitted, or recorded by any means whatsoever, including printing, photocopying, file transfer, or any form of data storage, mechanical or electronic, without the express written consent of the publisher. In addition, no part of this publication may be lent, re-sold, hired, or otherwise circulated or distributed, in any form whatsoever, without the express written consent of the publisher.

To all swingers, the world over . . .

Preface

You live one life. During your life you should set goals and work to achieve them. One of my goals as an erotica writer was to produce a quality swinging erotica anthology and now—here it is! This is a goal I'm very proud of, because as the title suggests, *Swing! Adventures in Swinging by Today's Top Erotica Writers* contains stories by some of the best erotica writers around.

Why a swinging erotica anthology? Swinging has been a part of my married life for a number of years. Like most swingers, my husband and I have a strong, successful union and also, a positive attitude about sex. Swinging is a pleasurable experience that enhances our relationship rather than takes away from it.

What is swinging? Swinging is non-monogamous sexual activity. Your partner may be present in the activity or he or she may be absent. The main thing to remember is that swinging is not cheating. Swinging happens with the consent of your partner.

Some people assume that swinging only occurs at swing clubs. Wrong. Some people also assume that swinging is only for straight, married couples. Wrong again. Swinging can come about in a variety of situations: at a swing club, at a home, with straight people, with gay people, and on and on. That's one of the things I love about *Swing!* It's a diverse collection.

There are 25 erotic stories in *Swing!* So sit back, relax and enjoy everything that *Swing!* has to offer.

Jolie du Pré
Chicago, 2009

Introduction

Swinging 101

I've entitled this section "Swinging 101" because it's the one-hundred-and-first attempt I've made to begin this introduction.

The first few tries were attempts to tell you, dear reader, all about swinging. I gave up on that direction after a dozen false starts because it occurred to me, if you're reading the introduction for this anthology, you've probably got a good idea of what swinging entails.

Then I started trying to talk about the "taboo" of swinging. The taboo of swinging is, I think, an important element in the whole swinging experience. What can be sexier than the idea that you're doing something naughty and forbidden?

The taboo is born from several sources: first and foremost being the connotations of adultery that are associated with swinging. The idea of adultery is anathema to most couples. Extra-marital sex often precedes the beginning of the end within many monogamous marriages. And yet there are couples—lots of couples—who swing and combine their happy marriages with all the various infidelities that would undoubtedly drive a non-swinging couple to the divorce courts.

While researching swinging for my last two non-fiction titles, I spoke with many couples who had been swinging for a long length of time and the general attitude seemed to be: *how can it be adultery if both parties in a relationship know what's going on?*

This rationale made sense to me. My understanding of adultery and infidelity involves one (or both) partners doing something without the other's knowledge. If Mr. and Mrs. Smith pop next door to have a four-way with Mr. and Mrs. Jones–all four of them sharing the experience and every one of them knowing exactly what the other is doing–has anyone really been unfaithful or adulterous?

I don't think so.

But that seemed like rather a long and laborious point to make at the beginning of an introduction, and there was no chance of my getting any good gags in there, so I abandoned that idea.

I contemplated writing about the taboo of promiscuity in general. Popular culture, from the Bible through to Harlequin Mills & Boon, has repeatedly insisted that monogamy, fidelity and chastity are the cornerstones of our civilized society. How can society continue to exist if there are swingers out there flouting the laws of morality by enjoying a diverse and alternative sex life? Surely, if these hedonists continue to live their lives by such a libertine ethos, the fabric of existence is likely to crumble, tear, and disintegrate.

But I dismissed that style of opening because it came across as being too heavy on irony.

I made a dozen attempts to write about how swinging works for some and doesn't work for others. I made a dozen more attempts to write about how the mechanics of swinging can vary from the soft swinging options of one tentative couple to the orgiastic hardcore experiences of another. But none of those ways into this introduction seemed to say exactly what I wanted to say. And, while all of those issues are pertinent to the stories in this book, none of those approaches seemed to stress the point I wanted to make.

It's taken a hundred previous attempts for me to realize that what I want to say can be summed up with the word "diversity"—and that's what I should be talking about in this introduction.

Aside from the unifying theme of swinging, the theme of diversity is common to all the stories in this collection. The stories in this collection contain interludes between men and women and women and men. There are stories involving couples and single women, couples and single men and couples with other couples. There are straight characters, gay characters, lesbian characters and bisexual characters. There are stories of solo performances, one-on-one exchanges, swapping, threesomes, foursomes and more. There are vanilla encounters, sweetened by the flavor of breaking a taboo, and there are harsh BDSM scenarios packed with punishing, painful pleasures. There are love and hate, pain and pleasure, doubt and certainty, elegance and vulgarity and upset and satisfaction. This anthology is, in short, a celebration of all the sexual diversity that is swinging.

The diversity in this anthology does not just extend to the mechanics of sex or the sexual predilections of the characters involved. It also extends to the division of fantasy and reality that plays such an integral part in the lives of most swingers. I've previously described members of the swinging community as ordinary people with extraordinary sex lives. The broad range of characters in this collection could be fairly described in the same fashion.

If you're reading this introduction prior to dipping into the stories, I can assure you that you're in for a rare treat. Jolie du Pré has managed to collect fiction from a talented team of authors (I'm unashamedly including myself in that number), and they've each approached the theme of swinging from their own specific understanding of the subject. Again, because everyone's understanding of swinging is slightly different, this means the theme of diversity is reinforced from each different perspective and with every variation in the authorial voice.

Jolie's story, *Before the Move*, exemplifies all that I've been trying to say about how diverse the experience of swinging can be for each individual.

There is a chasm of difference separating the two couples in Jolie's story. Their attitudes toward what they share show two opposite extreme ends of the swinging experience. The characters in Jolie's story are the epitome of ordinary people with extraordinary sex lives.

I've been told it's the job of a good introduction to introduce the reader to the forthcoming stories and authors—like the host at a party would introduce newcomers to those who are already in attendance. If that's what this introduction is supposed to do, then I'll do it in the time-honored fashion of all the best swing parties: *"We're happy to have you here. Feel free to leave your inhibitions behind you and make the most of all the wonderful experiences that lay ahead. I'm sure you're going to enjoy yourself."*

Ashley Lister
England, 2008

Contents

Preface
Introduction

Movements, by Michael Hemmingson	13
Bravery Has Its Rewards, by Jacqueline Applebee	24
Unpacking an Adventure, by TreSart L. Sioux	32
What We Do, by Emerald	48
The Twenty-Minute Rule, by Ashley Lister	60
The Gerswins, by Keeb Knight	69
Costume Party, by Sage Vivant	84
Plato's Retreat, by Karmen Red	93
John Updike Made Me Do It, by Donna George Storey	104
Initiation, by Rick R. Reed	116
The Best of Friends, by M. Millswan	130
Premises, by Lara Zielinsky	148
Just Desserts, by Tawanna Sullivan	161
Bob & Carol & Ted (But Not Alice), by M. Christian	170
Quick-Fix, by Jolene Hui	178
Careful What You Wish For, by D. L. King	186
Caught in the Act, by Beth Wylde	195
Check and Mate, by Jeremy Edwards	211
Ghost Swinger, by Amanda Earl	221
The Swing Set, by Rowan Elizabeth	229
The Party, by Neve Black	241
Our First Encounter, by Randall Lang	249
One Weekend in Toronto, by Claudia Moss	260
Dez Moinez, by Alicia Night Orchid	274
Before the Move, by Jolie du Pré	288

About the Authors
About the Editor
Acknowledgments
Other Logical-Lust Books

Movements
By Michael Hemmingson

I. SUITE FOR AN END TO A MARRIAGE

The first time I saw my wife fucking another man, she was by our Jacuzzi the night of The Party. I was fairly convinced it would be the last party we'd throw as husband and wife.

Actually, she was with two men. One was a fellow I didn't know and he was fucking her from behind—his large, hairy hands tightly grasping her hips in an attempt to control the backward thrust of her pelvis as if she were a wild animal. The other one (my best friend) had his dick in her mouth. She was taking this dick down her throat pretty deep, and he was no bigger than me. She never did that for me. Maybe she never liked my dick; and this is something I could believe, given the recent sour circumstances of our marriage.

"I don't think I'm in love with you anymore," she told me three months ago. I was trying to have sex with her. Her pussy was dry. Finally, she pushed my hand away and said she didn't want to. We hadn't made love in quite a while.

"What do you mean?"

"Is it hard to understand?" she said. "How can I illustrate it any better? *I don't think I'm in love with you anymore.*"

"I see," I said.

"No," she said, "you don't."

We tried the marriage counselor routine, and that only proved to drive us further apart, snickering at all the flowery, New Age suggestions the counselor was trying to sell us.

"What a fucking waste of money," my wife said.

Her name is Beryl, by the way.

Movements

Michael Hemmingson

* * *

I stood there, looking out the kitchen window, and watched Beryl fuck. The one who was my best friend, his name is Art.

I wasn't surprised. The night seemed to be heading for this. Beryl was on the war path to have sex with someone—other than me.

"I'm feeling frisky tonight," she said when she pulled me aside during The Party.

She was drunk. I told her so.

"So I'm *drunk*," she said, "and I'm feeling *good*."

I wasn't feeling good. "Thanks for the information."

"I just want you to know," she said, "that I might do something *wild*. I might do something *sexy*, and I don't want you to get in the *way*."

"I won't," I said.

"I don't want you to get in the way of my being *happy*."

"I won't," I said.

It started, I suppose, with her dance—or striptease. She put on some electronic music, the kind that gives me a headache. I don't know where she got this music. She began to dance, and had an audience of men cheering as she lifted her skirt and flashed her panties, and then she opened her blouse and exposed her tits. She had small, pointed, brown breasts. She was a tall, slender woman with long legs and tanned skin and straight blonde hair, a very appealing woman to many men.

"That's some wife of yours!" someone said to me, slapping me on the back.

"Yeah," I said.

Beryl had stripped down to her thong. Drunken hands groped for her. One pair of hands belonged to Art. Beryl giggled, ran out back, and jumped into the Jacuzzi.

Watching her fuck, I knew it was the hottest sight I'd ever viewed. It was better than watching a porno: this was real.

I wasn't the only person watching, either. Several men, some I knew, some I didn't, moved toward the threesome. I moved with them. We were all like mesmerized cattle.

* * *

Movements *Michael Hemmingson*

Two months ago, I was sitting in a bar with Art. We were on our fourth or fifth drink.

"I think Beryl and I are getting a divorce," I said.

"You think?" Art said.

"Probably. She doesn't love me anymore."

"*No.*"

"Yes."

"*No.*"

"She said this."

"Do you still love her?" he asked.

"I'm not sure," I said. "I think I do."

"What went wrong? You two used to be the happy fun couple."

"I'm not sure . . . I think she might be having an affair."

"You *think*?"

"I wouldn't put it past her."

* * *

When Beryl was done with Art and the man I didn't know, she started having sex with two other men. The Party was becoming something else. Other people departed—old friends giving me strange looks. Someone said, "You didn't say this was going to turn into an *orgy*." It was past one in the morning anyway, the time most parties start winding down.

Art, with his clothes back on, passed me.

I grabbed his arm.

"Hey," he said softly.

I just looked at him.

"We should talk," he said.

"Yeah," I said.

* * *

The Party was over, people were gone. Four a.m., I lay in bed, listening to my wife taking a bath. The door was unlocked. I went in. She stared at me. She was sitting in the tub, water and soap all around her. She started to say something; I held up a finger to stop her. I unzipped my pants and showed her my hard prick.

"Do you plan to do something with that?" she said.

"I have some ideas," I said.
"You look all worked up."
"I am that," I said.
"I haven't seen your dick that bulging and red since . . . since we first met."
I approached her, my body shaking. "Did you like fucking those men tonight?"
Softly: "You know I did."
"I could tell. I haven't seen you fuck like that since . . . since we first met."
She said: "Did you like me fucking those men?"
I grabbed Beryl's head. I was fast and she was surprised. I pushed her face into my crotch. I bunched up her slick wet hair in my fists, like I was angry. I was more horny than angry, or a fine line that crosses both conditions. She took my cock in her mouth. I wondered how many loads of come she swallowed this evening. Mine would be just another. Beryl pulled my pants down, grabbed at the flesh of my ass, yanking me forward, so that I was partially in the water with her, getting wet . . .

* * *

In bed, I asked her how long she'd been fucking Art. I knew that tonight wasn't the first time—the way they were with each other: that familiarity of the body. Beryl said, "For a while now."

II. SONATA FOR A NEW PHASE IN MARRIAGE

The three of us were in the Jacuzzi. This was inevitable, this had to happen; I knew it, Beryl knew it, Art knew it.
We'd had dinner. It was a quiet dinner. I savored every bite of the mushroom sautéed chicken Beryl had prepared, the scalloped potatoes that reminded me of being a child and eating mother's well-cooked meals. It was a warm night. Beryl suggested we relax in the Jacuzzi, drink wine. Art wanted beer. Beryl drank wine. We got naked, acting like excited, modest teenagers doing something daring and naughty, and went into the water.
It was a clear night out, a lot of stars.
I was also drinking wine.

Movements
Michael Hemmingson

"That's Mars up there." Beryl pointed at the sky, to a bright star with a red tint.

"Think there's life up there?" Art said.

"Mars? Or elsewhere?"

"Mars."

"Sure," she said.

"What do you think?" Art asked me.

"As long as they don't invade us," I said, "I don't care."

"I'm glad you're not mad," he said.

"I'm not mad," I said. "I keep telling myself I should be. But I'm not."

"It's good that you're not," Beryl said. "It means you're growing. It means you're moving in the direction I am, and that makes me happy."

Art waded through the water, to her direction. She giggled. He backed her against the Jacuzzi wall. They kissed. I sipped my glass of wine and watched him kiss her. I watched him lift her body up, sit her on the edge of the Jacuzzi, spread her legs, and go down on her. Beryl liked this. She ran her fingers through his wet hair and made familiar sounds of pleasure. I knew those sounds like a distant cousin one has fond memories of. She leaned back, propping herself on her elbows, letting Art work his tongue between her legs, his hairy hands rubbing her stomach and breasts. She looked at me and said, "Come here and stick that dick in my mouth."

I got out of the water. The hair on my body was matted, I was dripping. I liked walking about like this, my cock pointing the way. I crouched before Beryl so she could take me in her mouth as Art continued to eat her pussy, grunting sounds coming from his throat.

We then moved away from the Jacuzzi, to a lounge chair, where she sucked on us both: Art and I standing close, almost touching skin, Beryl going from one cock to another. I could smell Art's body. I could smell the musk from his crotch, and I wondered if I was emitting any odors he could sense. Needless to say, the smell of sex permeated the immediate air around us.

We took turns fucking my wife. Art went first. I wanted to watch them; watching them made me want her all the more.

"Whore," I whispered in her ear when it was my turn.

"Yeah," she said, "talk dirty to me."

Movements   Michael Hemmingson

When we went to the bed, Beryl wanted us both inside her at the same time. "One in my kitty," she said with a seductive voice, touching herself, "and one in my booty."

* * *

"I have hope for us," she said later.

We were lying in bed, alone. The sex had been good. I remembered a night, not a month ago, when we were in bed together, and she said, "We should just have wild sex right now, that'd solve all our problems," but neither of us could do it.

"That's good," I said.

"I really do." She kissed me.

I kissed her back.

"I feel so sexual, so alive again. I love you but I want to fuck more men. I want to fuck a *lot* of men. Will you help me do this?"

* * *

She could have done it by herself, or with Art, but she wanted me involved, and I wanted to be involved. And Art, of course, wished to be there too.

It started with the gang bang. Art made the arrangements for this, being the resourceful fellow that he is, getting the guys Beryl had fucked at The Party together for another go at it. There were nine of them in all, more than I had originally imagined. Had my wife really fucked nine men that night? I suppose so. Ten, including Art. Eleven, including myself.

If I ever thought that what happened was just a wild fantasy, or a dream, I have the evidence on videotape. It was, yes, Art's idea to capture this night for posterity. When he suggested it to Beryl, she got this wild look in her eyes and said, "Yes." I was beginning to know that look better and better. I wanted her to say no. I wanted her to say no because I liked the idea myself.

(A number of times, alone, feeling lonely, thinking of the life I once had, I will put that tape into the VCR, and watch. I will watch my wife fuck all those men in a single session, fucking them in every combination possible.

Others have watched her. Hundreds, thousands, all over the world. This is really what this story is about.)

* * *

It was Art's idea—again—to create a web site and place stills from the gangbang video on it. He created the web page, and allowed people to access it for free. In a matter of days, the site was getting thousands of hits. Art said this was a combination of posting stills to various news groups with sexual themes, and the help of a number of search engines.

After a month, he—or we—announced that the whole video tape could be purchased for $34.95.

In a matter of weeks, 2,000 orders came in.

First we were just some people doing kinky things, and now we were in business.

We were, I guess you can say, pornographers.

III. SOLO IN THE JACUZZI, WITH MEMORY

I was alone in the Jacuzzi. It was another clear night. That red star was indeed Mars. I stared at it. I wanted to go there. I wondered what sex life was like on Mars.

In the bedroom, in the house, Art and Beryl were fucking. He was fucking her in the ass when I had left, and came out here, turned on the jet streams, and sat in the warm bubbling water. And closed my eyes while looking up.

In the water, I thought about the two of them. I pictured his cock going in and out of her butt, the muscles of her sphincter contracting with each thrust. The more I thought of this, I started to become aroused. The image in my head was far more enticing than returning to the bedroom and seeing and smelling it. In my mind, I was the director, I was in control, and I made my own movie of the act.

I also pictured scenes from the night of The Party.

I touched myself. I had my cock in my hand, under the water, and I began to jack-off.

I watched my semen clump in the water, floating to the top, getting caught in a whirlwind of bubbles, spinning around, blending in with water and chlorine.

INTERMISSION: How We Met

I met her at the recital of an experimental cellist. He was on tour for his new CD. In the first half of his performance, he presented classical pieces by Debussy and Mozart. I had difficulty listening—I kept glancing at the blonde woman who was sitting alone, across from me in the small concert hall. She was wearing black slacks and a white cotton blouse. She kept looking at me as well. We talked during the intermission. Small talk: what do you think of the cellist? Oh, he's good. We sat together for the second half, and the cellist presented his own iconoclastic work, hooking his instrument to microphones, adding special effects, or playing along with a tape full of strange sounds. Towards the end, he did a manic solo and broke two strings. After, I asked the blonde woman—Beryl—if she'd like to go get some coffee. "No," she said, "but how about a beer?" Two months later, we were living together. Six months later, we were married.

IV. QUARTET

"We've been approached with a business deal," Art said on the phone. Beryl and I were both on separate phones in the house, different rooms, listening.

"Go on," she said.

He said, "There's this couple—here in the city—who have a successful on-line business. They do the same as us: sell videos and pix of them fucking, or the wife fucking some guys. Then they started to make and distribute vids of other couples. Acting as distributors, growing their business. You know? They came across our web site, and they want Beryl. I mean, they can sell five times the amount of videos we do. So they say."

"What does this mean?" I said.

"More money," Art said.

"More money," Beryl said, "sounds good to me."

Movements

Michael Hemmingson

* * *

This couple—Fred and Donna—invited the three of us to dinner, to talk about the possibility of a business venture. Art drove in his own car, and was late. Beryl and I were both nervous, and we didn't know why.

They had a nice, modestly furnished suburban house, not the kind of place you'd think a big Internet porn outfit would be located. Fred and Donna were also the kind of couple you might see at a PTA meeting—modestly and almost conservatively dressed, quiet, and friendly. They were in their late thirties, attractive, and unassuming.

Over dinner, we talked about our lives, not sex.

I wondered why I was here. I was expecting drugs, hard booze, triple-X love acts.

Fred suggested we go to the water.

They also had a Jacuzzi, but this one could fit ten people. It was very nice and spacious. Fred and Donna disrobed before us, and got in. Donna was a bit on the chubby side, but had a magnificent tan and silicone-enhanced breasts. Fred, I was quick to notice, didn't have a hair on his well-muscled body, and a dick that had to be ten inches long.

Art stripped and jumped in. Beryl and I took our clothes off, slowly, still uncertain, and joined the party.

We were all drinking Champagne, by the way. It always begins with some kind of party.

"You have a great body," Donna said to Beryl.

"Thank you," Beryl said.

"I'd love to fuck you," Donna said.

"I'm not bi," Beryl said.

"Too bad," Donna said. "But maybe Fred can fuck you. I like to watch him fuck other women."

"Sounds good to me," Beryl laughed.

"You got a look-see at his tool?" Donna asked.

"Oh yes," Beryl said. "I wonder if I could take it."

"It takes some getting used to," Donna said. "His cock is very nice."

"Yeah," Beryl said.

Art and I looked at each other.

"Let's talk business," Fred said.

"Let's," Art said.

"This past year," Fred said, "we've cleared three million in sales."

I almost choked on my Champagne. Beryl did.

"You're shitting me," Art said.

"No," Fred said.

Donna smiled. "We'll make more each year."

"Porn is the backbone of e-commerce," Fred said, "and the amateur market is in a boom. A huge boom. There are dozens, hundreds of people like us making a living off pleasure. We have something many people out there want."

"Intimacy," Donna said, "and love."

"This business saved our marriage," Fred said. He drew Donna close to him. They held each other. They kissed. "We wouldn't be together now," he went on. "It added. . . excitement. It delivered us from an absolutely dull life, the same thing day after day. You know what I mean?"

"I was ready to leave him," Donna said. "I wanted something more."

"We both did," Fred said.

"And we found it," Donna said.

Beryl and I looked at each other. I moved to kiss her. She kissed me. Art looked away.

"We like what you have," Donna said.

"We can get rich together," Fred said.

"I like the sound of that," Beryl said.

"Me too," I said.

Fred grinned. "So let's fuck and seal the deal."

We all laughed.

"Hey, buddy," Fred said to Art, "there's a camera in the house, and a light. Why don't you get it?"

Art nodded, and got out of the water. He looked lonely, walking away wet and naked. I can't say that I felt sorry for him.

Donna moved to me, and Beryl moved to Fred. I took Donna's large breasts in my hands and rubbed them. Her pink nipples were pointing at me. Beryl was stroking Fred's big dick and she said something like, "Oh my!" He sat on the edge of the spa, and Beryl did her best to take him in her mouth.

"You want me to suck your dick too?" Donna whispered. "What do you want me to do? I'll do anything, anything."

Art set up the camera.

Donna and I got out of the water to fuck. I had her on her back, her thick legs on my shoulders. She smelled strong of perfume. She reached up and bit my nipple as I fucked her. Beryl was still sucking on Fred.

"Hey," Fred said, turning to me with a smile. "I think I'm about to come in your wife's mouth."

Art didn't join us. As he operated the video camera, he jerked-off. He was now an observer. I could see it on his face: something was missing. He looked lonely and I didn't care.

V. EPILOGUE

Our hair was still wet when we got in the car. We were electrified. The sex had been good, the idea of success even better.

I touched my wife's face.

"We don't need Art," she said.

"I was thinking the same thing."

"Our marriage will work, won't it?"

"I hope so."

"We can be as happy and wealthy as Donna and Fred."

I wanted to say that we *were* Donna and Fred. We'd just made love to our mirror images, and it was caught on tape.

I started the car.

"Turn on the heater," Beryl said. "I don't want to catch cold."

I did, and as we drove, the warmth started at our feet, and moved up our bodies and to our faces. We were holding hands the whole way.

Home, our hair dry, we went into our own Jacuzzi and fucked in the water and under the stars, and there was only us, and it was very nice again, for awhile.

Bravery Has its Rewards
By Jacqueline Applebee

I said I'd be okay about things. I said that I would be brave, but as I stepped over the threshold of an ordinary-looking house in an ordinary London street, I wasn't so sure. The sounds of sex greeted me—I felt like an intruder, sneaking in while the owners were busy in the bedroom.

My husband Sean ushered me deeper into the house. The lighting was low, soft Jazz played at a discreet volume, and red and black balloons were scattered everywhere. The place looked decorated for a party, and really that's what this was—a swinger's party, with me as an anxious first-timer.

"I can't wait," Sean whispered. "You are going to have so much fun tonight."

I tried not to look at all the other guests, but I felt their eyes on me. Sean was showing me off, as he sometimes does. He swept the light wrap from my shoulders, just as we passed an older couple. The tops of my large breasts were visible in the low-cut dress I wore. The red cloth would probably match the color of my cheeks. I moved on quickly, but only managed a few steps before I felt Sean tug my hand back into his.

"Relax, Nicky," he said with a smile, his brown eyes twinkling with excitement. "You're beautiful—they just want to admire you."

I nodded, and squeezed the hand that lay in mine. I had come here because of my curiosity, because I had fantasized one too many times about what it would be like to be with another man while my husband encouraged us along. I had no desire to cheat, to play behind his back, because the best part of my fantasy was the knowledge that Sean could see everything, and become turned on by it all. However, fantasy is not the same as reality; I was never this nervous in my dreams.

Bravery Has its Rewards   Jacqueline Applebee

We had talked about things for some time, but tonight all that talk would be put into practice. Sean traveled a lot up and down the country running his own assertiveness training courses, and I knew he often found comfort in the arms of other women while he was away. I would never try to make him stop, and as long as he practiced safe-sex, then I was happy that his needs were being taken care of. Jealousy is a thing that used to bother me, but just knowing that Sean is never lonely or without affection when he is away, more than makes up for any pangs I might feel. We may want to have sex with others, but we are dedicated to our relationship.

"Where's the host?" I asked, after no one had introduced themselves as such.

"I'm sure you'll see our hostess in a bit," Sean replied, before nodding in the direction of a woman being groped by a man at the top of the stairs.

"Hello, Estelle!" Sean called out, and the woman waved at him enthusiastically.

"I'm so glad you and your lovely wife could make it, Sean!" Estelle responded breathlessly, and then returned her attention back to her friend.

The guests seemed to be a diverse mixture of people; there was a selection of ages and races too. I heard different accents, and even what sounded like German, being spoken. I smiled at that; it was good to know that swingers came from all different backgrounds. This went against the little I had researched about the lifestyle, when I knew I was definitely coming to the party. My short expedition onto the Internet seemed to reveal that swingers were only ever white, only ever middle-aged and middle-class. It was nice to know that the computer had got it wrong—instead of just one flavor, I could choose from a whole chocolate box of experiences. A gorgeous black couple inched past me, and it only reinforced the analogy—there were some luscious delights to be sampled.

We walked through the kitchen, and then out to the small back garden where a crowd had gathered. I watched a young man bent over a woman's lap. She spanked him to the rhythm of chants from the onlookers that surrounded them. They counted at a steady pace, their voices getting louder as they reached twenty-five, when everyone shouted out, "Happy Birthday!"

The man rolled unceremoniously off the woman's lap, and when he leapt up to more applause, he caught my eye. I smiled shyly at him, and

Bravery Has its Rewards   Jacqueline Applebee

then mentally kicked myself. There was no point in being coy—everyone here knew why everyone else had come.

Sean chuckled low in his throat; he'd seen me making eyes at the birthday boy. He angled us towards the young man as he slowly walked by. The wall of reality and outright fiction began to crumble as he approached.

"Happy birthday, Ray!" Sean called out, and Ray waved back with a smile. Just as Ray was about to move closer, another guest grabbed him, and pulled him away to where a birthday cake was being served.

"Come on, Nicky. Let's get settled," Sean said with a sigh, and he held my hand, pulling me back into the house. A man dressed in a maid's outfit met us half-way down a corridor. He carried a tray full of wine, and flavored condoms. He offered us a drink, and admired my earrings as we helped ourselves. I tried not to stare at the short ruffled skirt the smiling man wore, or at the stocking-tops that peeped out just below the fabric. Everyone else seemed to take things in their stride, but this was a whole new world to me. Of course I'd read about alternative lifestyles, and I knew a few gay men who worked in my organization, but I'd never socialized with them. It dawned on me that there was a whole section of people out there that I just didn't have a clue about.

I swallowed a mouthful of red wine, welcoming the blush of alcohol—the drink that I gulped quickly warmed me. I felt another source of heat as Sean swept his hand up my dress. The maid watched us intently for a moment, and then he winked at me, and continued on his way, leaving Sean to caress my thighs with gentle touches.

"Who was that maid?" I asked, as Sean's fingers ran along the lace edge of my knickers.

"That was Estelle's husband," he muttered into my neck. He kissed me lightly, but before I could respond, he stopped. "There will be plenty of time for that later."

In the front room, we paused to watch a woman being tied up by an able man whose hands moved with precision. He created a rope dress on the woman, using a single length of white rope to bind her, while accentuating her breasts, bottom and thighs. The pale lengths contrasted with her dark brown skin, and it was an impressive sight to see. The man then helped the woman to her knees, and proceeded to unzip his pants. I instinctively glanced away for a moment—he couldn't be doing what I thought, could he? The kneeling woman looked over to me as she opened her glossed lips. She sucked the man's dick into her mouth, and I was

Bravery Has its Rewards   Jacqueline Applebee

hypnotized by the amazing sight. Everything seemed to slow down as her full lips gripped him; I could see the veins in the man's wide dick, and the way the woman's mouth was being stretched with every swallow. The man above her was definitely enjoying himself.

"You like sucking cock don't you?" he teased. "Suck my cock, go on, you love this, you little slut. Suck it, suck it good."

After a few moments of his vocal encouragement, the woman withdrew, and looked up at the man sharply.

"Yes, I like sucking cock! Now will you just let me do it in peace?" she snapped, irritation clear in her French accented voice.

Sean and I both laughed discreetly at her brazen attitude. I was glad that she had told the man to be quiet. The woman went back to blowing the now-silent man with enthusiasm. She really was good at it. The man held her head as he jerked against her, and then froze as he came. Another man walked alongside, and helped the woman up. Together with the first man, they both untied her, and then they started stroking her gently. The threesome shared a big hug before looking over to Sean and me in a friendly way.

"She's the best cock-sucker on the South coast," the first man said as an introduction. "Yasmin is a real expert."

I looked at Sean hesitantly—I could almost visualize Yasmin with her mouth wrapped around his cock, while she sucked him like a professional.

"Maybe later," Sean replied to the unspoken question breezily. He sounded as if he were turning down a cup of tea.

The threesome linked hands and walked away, with Yasmin still naked between the two men.

"God, that was so tempting," Sean remarked, once they were out of earshot.

"Why didn't you go for it?" I asked, puzzled.

"Oh, I have plans for us," he said with a knowing look. I tingled at the thought of what might happen, and it was then that I realized, with some surprise, that I was no longer nervous. I supposed that after watching a live-action blowjob, I must have loosened up a bit.

"You're going to be okay, aren't you?" Sean asked. This time I had no hesitation as I nodded my head and squeezed his hand.

"Good girl. I'll be back in a bit." Sean scooted off. I wandered back to the garden, listening to the sounds of moans that rose above the jazz music. The garden was almost empty now, but someone had set up a table

Bravery Has its Rewards **Jacqueline Applebee**

groaning with food. With all the energy that would no doubt be expended this evening, I was sure that everything would be eaten.

As I helped myself to some cold sliced meat, a young woman walked up to me.

"Hi, I'm Natalie," she said, and popped a strawberry in her mouth.

"Nicky." I bit on a thin slice of beef, suddenly hungry.

"Is this your first time?" Natalie inquired.

"Am I that obvious?"

She giggled, before explaining, "No, it's not that. It's just that I'm sure I would have remembered someone as lovely as you." She ran a fingertip along my arm as she spoke. I willed myself to look at the colorful display of food, and I silently gulped the mouthful of roast beef that I had been chewing. My mind quickly processed Natalie's soft words and her gentle touch. "If you want some fun later, just give me a shout," she continued.

I nodded dumbly, willing Sean to come back. Natalie was very pretty, but I had never considered being with another woman before. I couldn't help but wonder what it would be like, and that made me feel even more like a fish out of water than I previously had.

"There's no pressure, but it's nice to see another Unicorn here," Natalie remarked cryptically.

"Unicorn?" Had I heard right?

"You know, another single woman at a swing party—we're as rare as unicorns," she said pointing between the two of us.

Natalie looked over my shoulder, and the woman who had spanked Ray stepped past me to hug her tightly. I took a gulp of wine and moved to a discreet distance, watching the two women kiss each other fondly. The kissing was soon followed by stroking, caressing, and enthusiastic groping. The older woman held Natalie's chestnut hair in a firm grip while they kissed, and that made something stir inside me—I loved being held tightly during sex, and I adored the feeling of being made to accept anything Sean would give to me. Yasmin and her ropes sure looked pretty, but it held little appeal, whereas Natalie being restrained by pure physical strength was a whole different matter. I longed to feel that, and I hoped that I would experience it tonight.

Sean reappeared a few moments later, with Ray, the birthday boy, in tow. I suddenly felt scrutinized as Ray looked at me with appreciation. Ray was a good-looking man with a mass of freckles over his face and neck.

Bravery Has its Rewards — Jacqueline Applebee

When he smiled his boyish smile, he didn't look twenty-five; he looked an awful lot younger. Was I making excuses to get out of this arrangement? I didn't want to have sex with someone younger than I, and in reality there was only a few years difference between us, but Ray looked just about eighteen— just about legal. I wasn't sure if I could go through with this.

"Why don't we go inside?" Sean offered innocently. As he spoke, I saw the happy, open look on his face, and I remembered why I had come here. Ray was a grown man, and I was an adult too—it was about time I acted like one and took responsibility for my desires.

It happened so fast. One moment we were all in the garden, but the next, we were upstairs in one of the large bedrooms. I undressed slowly, not to tease, but because my nerves had returned with a vengeance. Sean was the first and so far, only man to have seen me completely naked with the lights on, so as I stepped out of my knickers, I felt incredibly self-conscious. I knew my panties were damp; I couldn't hide my arousal beneath my shyness. I wanted this. I wanted Ray.

Sean sat on the edge of the bed, while Ray pulled me over. The silent man reached forward and stroked my face. I arched against his hand, but gasped as he dove down lower. My nipples hardened and strained towards him as he caressed me. My nerves slipped away, replaced by a warm yearning that grew in between my legs.

"She likes her nipples sucked hard," Sean offered the advice softly, and then he backed away, but I could still feel his eyes on me as Ray bent his head to my breasts. He kissed my nipple gently at first, but then the force of his mouth grew. I instinctively gripped Ray's short brown hair as the suction increased. Sean was right of course—I loved it. My legs opened wide, and in a smooth move, Ray wrapped them around his hips. I let him angle and adjust me, aching for him to be inside. Sean passed him a condom, and Ray slipped it on without hesitation. He winked at me before he drove all the way in, knocking the breath from my lungs with his powerful thrust. My head rolled back with the force of Ray's moves, and the action seemed to suddenly make everything clear in my mind—I realized why swingers loved their lifestyle so much. No two fingerprints are identical, no two bodies are the same, and no-one's sexual techniques are alike either. I suddenly wanted to make love with everyone in the building—I wanted to feel their differences deep inside my pussy. I wanted to feel all those unique hands on me, and all of those unique tongues!

Bravery Has its Rewards Jacqueline Applebee

My head jerked up at a soft sound; Sean had unzipped his jeans, and was now kneeling by the side of the bed, watching us intently as he fisted his cock in his hand. His honey-brown eyes were wide, and a look of concentration lay over his face.

"Give it to him, Nicky," he commanded, with a voice rough with lust. "Tell him what you want."

I looked from Sean to Ray, my whole world melting before my eyes. This had gone so far beyond a fantasy, it was unreal.

"Please," I begged, surprised at how desperate I sounded. "Please hold me tighter. Screw me harder."

I felt every ounce of muscle in Ray's lean body as he held me in a clinch. I was consumed, unable to move, and forced to be still in his iron-hard grip.

"You're doing great, baby," Sean encouraged. I tried to respond, but all my words had dried up. It was if the only thing in existence was Ray's dick slamming inside me—the heavy piston movements that generated ferocious heat. I felt myself at his total mercy. Ray began to grunt like a caveman at this point, with every shove followed by an animal-like sound. My clit was so full that it felt rock hard, and so sensitive that every brush of Ray's body made it twitch. I came, jerking in the restricted space, and Ray exploded seconds after.

"That was just amazing," he said breathlessly. "You are one hot lady!" He wiped his forehead for effect, but I could see the layer of sweat that drenched him; he was burning up too. Ray rolled over, and lay on the bed, looking exhausted but happy. Sean lay on my other side, and hugged me.

"Who's my brave little slut?" he asked playfully.

"I am," I responded in a sing-song voice. Bravery had never been so rewarding.

I noticed movement by the open door, and was too tired to even mind the group of people standing there.

"That was great," one of them said with an appreciative voice. "Happy birthday, Ray!"

Ray kissed the back of my neck, and whispered, "Let's not wait until next year before we do this again."

Sean's eyes lit up at that. I knew this party would be the first of many. Maybe next time I could get together with Natalie. Yasmin could blow

Bravery Has its Rewards   Jacqueline Applebee

Sean too. He'd like that. The possibilities for fun started to form in my mind, and I was so happy, I felt on top of the world.

When I had first arrived at this event, I had said I would be okay, but as I cuddled against Sean, kissing him with thanks, I realized that I was more than okay now. I was fantastic!

Unpacking an Adventure
By TreSart L. Sioux

"Trisha, did you find the coffee maker?"

"Not yet," I grumbled while rummaging through the cardboard box.

God, this move had been a pain in the ass! I never realized how much shit Kimberly and I had accumulated.

We had just moved from the hectic city to a remote little town in Kentucky. Both of us truly needed a change. Our relationship of ten years had become a little rocky from all the variety of stress in our lives and this was our final attempt to gain back what we had lost.

We wanted the passion.

The spontaneity.

Lust.

True love.

"I must have a cup of coffee. I can't function without one."

"I'll tell you what. How about I go into town and get us some? I noticed a cute little coffee shop on Main Street."

Kimberly started opening a box. "Oh would you, honey?"

"Sure. No problem."

Tenderly, she placed a kiss upon my lips. She really was the love of my life. I fell in love with her dark flowing hair and eyes as green as precious emeralds the moment I saw her in the park. Simply, we were meant to be and this move would be the ticket back to a strong relationship.

* * *

I decided to walk into town since it was a lovely day out. The fresh air was invigorating. This was so much different than living in the city. No cars honking or the smell of exhaust. I could hear birds happily chirping in the trees, and felt the sun shining down upon me from a blue sky.

Relaxation.

I made my way to the coffee shop. The aroma of beans brewing awoke my senses.

"Hi, can I help you?"

She was an attractive woman with blonde hair neatly pinned up. "Yes, two large regular coffees to go."

"Hey, you're new here, aren't ya?"

"Yes, we just moved in."

She smiled. "Welcome to our town. I'm Janice and part owner of the shop."

"Thanks."

"Katherine, come out here and meet one of the new folks in town!"

Katherine emerged from the back. She was even more attractive than Janice. Her long legs and red hair made me think of Ginger from Gilligan's Island.

"Hi, I'm Katherine."

"I'm Trisha. Nice to meet you."

"Same here."

Was it just me, or was this woman looking me over? Nah, I just needed my coffee intake.

"Ya'll moved into the old Johnson place, right?"

"Yes."

"That's a beautiful home. Katherine is co-owner of the shop," said Janice as she placed the cups on the counter.

"We love it, but unpacking is so unbearable."

"Where are ya'll from?"

"New York."

"Well, we're glad to have you here, and it was nice meeting you. I need to get back to work with the inventory." On that note, Katherine left.

"How much do I owe you?"

Janice smiled. "It's on the house."

"Thanks." I picked up the cups and headed for the door. Just as I was about to open it Janice spoke once more.

"Hey, if ya'll need any help unpacking just let us know. We'd be more than happy to help ya out."

Unpacking an Adventure   TreSart L. Sioux

"That's very kind of you. Take care." I really didn't know what to think of the two ladies. I mean, they seemed nice enough, but something bugged me. Was it the attraction I had for them, more so Katherine? Hell, why did I even assume they were lesbians? I knew I didn't need to think in this mode. I needed to concentrate on Kimberly and me.

* * *

"Wow, that's some good java."

I could tell Kimberly was in better spirits after taking the first sip. "Yes, they are very nice people."

"They?"

"Janice and Katherine. They own the coffee shop."

"Oh." Kimberly started to go through more boxes.

"Janice said if we needed help unpacking that they'd be more than willing to lend a hand."

"Oh, Trisha! She was just being polite. Who the hell would want to help unpack?"

For some reason, I felt that Janice had been speaking the truth, but decided to drop the subject.

"I don't believe it!"

"What?" I asked.

Kimberly pulled the coffee pot out of the box. "Figures," she said.

* * *

We'd been unpacking for a few hours when we heard a knock at the door. Kimberly went to answer while I continued working.

"Can I help you?"

"Hi, I'm Janice and this is Katherine."

"From the coffee shop?"

"Yes, we thought we'd bring you a house warming gift."

"Oh, that's very nice of you. Please come on in. I think Trisha and I could use a break."

The women came into the living room where I was placing knick-knacks on the mantel. "So we meet again," I said with a huge smile.

"Yes we do," laughed Janice.

Unpacking an Adventure **TreSart L. Sioux**

Katherine placed a cake on the table while Janice and Kimberly sat down.

"I'm going to get some drinks and plates. Is there anything you two would prefer?"

"Nah, we're not picky," said Janice.

I left the women in the living room and gathered up what we needed.

While in the kitchen my mind began to play tricks on me again. I imagined Katherine wearing black, silky lingerie, her cleavage showing, waiting for me to fondle. Oh my God! I had to stop! But I was finding it difficult. My sex life with Kimberly had gone downhill drastically. We hadn't even teased each other in almost a month. Plus, the last time we did, it was only a quickie. There had been no enthusiasm from either of us.

"Here we go," I said, returning. "I poured us each some tea. I hope that's okay."

Katherine reached for a cup. "It's fine."

I cut us each a slice of the cake and served. Katherine's hand gently brushed mine and I could feel my face flush.

"So, how long have you two owned the coffee shop?" asked Kimberly.

Katherine took a sip of her tea. "About four years. Janice and I have always wanted to open up a business in this town. We first started off small, just your basic coffees, but we've recently expanded."

"What do ya'll do?" asked Janice.

Kimberly and I looked at each other.

"Well, I'm a writer and Trisha is an editor."

Janice wiped the cake crumbs from the corners of her mouth. "Wow! That sounds exciting! What type of writing do you do?"

Kimberly had no hesitation. "I create adult novels."

For some reason, Janice and Katherine didn't seem shocked or appalled.

"Really? What kind of adult novels?" Guess that struck Katherine's interest.

"Lesbian novels."

Still neither of them seemed to mind.

"We'd love to read one," said Katherine.

"Sure. As soon as we get this place unpacked and I find them, I'd be more than happy to give you a copy."

Everyone laughed. I guess we all were beginning to loosen up.

Unpacking an Adventure — TreSart L. Sioux

We chatted for an hour about the town and the people. It seemed like everybody was pretty much laid back. Then, out of nowhere, Katherine asked the question.

"So, how long have you two been together?"

The room fell silent. I knew my face was turning several shades of red.

Kimberly poured more tea in her glass. "Ten years."

"That's wonderful! Janice and I have been together for seven and it just keeps getting better."

So they were lesbians! My pussy was fully awake now!

"Well, sometimes relationships can be hard, but other times they can be a blessing."

I couldn't believe Kimberly said that. I mean, we hardly knew these women and she was spilling shit out. I decided to change the subject. "Would anyone like some more tea?"

Janice stood up. "No thanks, we really need to get going."

"We appreciate you dropping by and bringing the cake," I said. Kimberly and I walked the women to the door.

"Ya'll feel free to stop by the coffee shop anytime," said Katherine.

"Thanks," replied Kimberly.

The women left and my lover and I were alone again, in more ways than one.

* * *

We unpacked a few more boxes and decided to call it a night. I thought I'd flirt with Kimberly to maybe loosen up the tension. "Would you like to take a shower with me?"

Kimberly sighed. "Not tonight. I'm just going to have a glass of wine and catch up on the news. I'll take one later."

I shook my head and walked up the stairs. Why wasn't she even making an effort to help save our relationship?

After unpacking boxes for most of the day, the shower felt wonderful. I lathered up my body, feeling refreshed and . . . extremely horny.

My hand slid down my smooth body and began to caress between my pussy lips. This had become a ritual for me. I slid a finger deep inside, feeling my walls contract and then release.

Unpacking an Adventure   TreSart L. Sioux

I couldn't help but think of Katherine and even Janice. I wonder what they liked in bed. Were they kinky? Plain?

My other hand ventured to my hard clit while I inserted two more fingers inside. I could imagine Katherine sticking her fingers in me. Was this wrong to be thinking of another woman touching in areas only meant for my lover?

I didn't care. All I wanted was to come, and I did.

After my shower I wiped the mirror clear of the condensation from the swirling steam. I stood there for a moment and stared at myself. Maybe Kimberly wasn't attracted to me anymore.

I guess I was average looking with my long brown hair and dark eyes, but for a forty year old my body was holding up pretty damn well.

I let out a deep sigh.

* * *

Kimberly was already in bed, reading the paper and sipping on a glass of wine. "I wasn't sure if you wanted a glass."

I slid in next to her. "No. Guess I'll just go to sleep unless you had something else in mind?" trying one more time for some passion.

"You've got to be kidding me! I'm exhausted from all the work."

I turned my back to her and closed my eyes. I guess it just wasn't my lucky day.

* * *

My dreams that night were extremely vivid. I was in a dimly lit room with several large windows and flowing curtains. At first I didn't see anyone, but from the shadows emerged Janice.

"I was hoping you'd show up."

"What? Why am I here?"

She didn't say anything else. Slowly, she walked towards me, her blue eyes inviting.

She removed the black robe revealing a body full of all the right curves.

Unpacking an Adventure   TreSart L. Sioux

The next thing I knew I was on a white covered bed with an assortment of flower petals. My clothes had been removed and Janice straddled my body. She smiled while her fingers played with my nipples.

Was this a dream? It seemed so real!

Janice slid down, her face so close to my pussy I could feel the heat from her breath.

Inhaling.

She was just about to lick my clit when . . .

"Trisha!"

I snapped awake from Kimberly shaking me. "Jesus, what?"

"You were fucking moving all over the bed."

I looked at the clock. It was a little after three in the morning. "I'm sorry."

"I'd like to get some rest!"

"I said I'm sorry!"

We both fell back asleep, frustrated . . . well, at least I was.

Dreams invaded again.

* * *

The room was the same except it was brightly lit. I looked around and came face to face with Katherine.

She stood before me dressed from head to toe in latex and leather. A whip was in her right hand and one hell of a large smile across her face.

Before I knew it, my clothes were off.

"Trisha, bend over the chair."

I was speechless. Here was this beauty in front of me, commanding to expose every inch of my flesh.

I obeyed. My ass was lifted up for her spanking pleasure.

"You so deserve this!"

She raised the whip, and in one swift move I felt the burning and stinging sensation across my ass cheeks.

"Let's do that again!"

Over and over until the only sensation I had was complete numbness.

"Now let me have some of that sweet taste of your pussy."

Unpacking an Adventure   TreSart L. Sioux

I knew she was close to licking my drenched pussy. Her breath just as Janice's was, only inches away.
"Damn it, Trisha!"
I jumped up in bed, startled from Kimberly shoving me.
"What?" I don't know why I asked. I knew the reason.
"Well, guess I'll go ahead and get up now and start unpacking! Looks like someone doesn't want me to get any sleep!"
I watched as she angrily got out of bed. This was starting off to be a great day.

* * *

Weeks had passed and we finally had everything organized. Needless to say, our relationship wasn't doing any better. Sure we had sex a few times, but neither of us was happy. Sex had become a routine instead of a desirable pleasure.
Kimberly had begun a new book, but often complained of writer's block. She said there wasn't any inspiration.
I used to be her inspiration.
We often frequented the coffee shop and quickly became close friends with Katherine and Janice. Although most of the time when visiting the shop, Kimberly and I went solo.
The rest of the folks in the small town were very friendly, but none of them quite stood out like our new friends.

* * *

"I'm going to the coffee shop? Want to come along?" I asked.
Kimberly sat at the computer smoking a cigarette. The only time she smoked was when creating.
"No. I'm busy."
I knew that was going to be her answer. I headed for the door.
"Damn it!"
"What?"
She slammed her hand down on the desk. "I have no creativity left in me."
I didn't even bother to reply. I simply left.

* * *

Unpacking an Adventure   TreSart L. Sioux

"Where's Janice?" I asked Katherine and placed my cup of coffee on the table.

"Oh, she's running around town paying bills."

I blew on the cup, enjoying the enticing aroma.

"How is Kimberly's novel coming along? We finally caught up with all that she has written and we are hooked!"

I laughed. "She is a great writer, but she's been hitting writer's block lately."

Katherine refilled another patron's cup then sat down next to me.

"Look, I don't want to come across as pushy, but ya'll really don't seem connected."

"Is it that obvious?"

Her hand reached across the table and gently caressed mine. "Yes, it is."

"Oh, Katherine, I don't know what to do. She's so upset with not being able to create, and for some reason I think she puts part of the blame on me. I know I'm not the perfect lover, but it's been such a long time since we had that spark."

She looked around the shop and leaned in. "Actually, I have an idea that might just help ya'll out."

"You do? What?"

"Ever swing?"

I know my jaw had to have hit the floor and collected what dust had accumulated from the day. "Excuse me?"

"Ya know . . . swap partners?"

"I know what you mean, but no."

Katherine sat back. "Look, I know it's not everyone's cup of tea, but think about it. Maybe ya'll need a little extra spice in your life."

"Oh, we need more than extra spice."

My mind began to race. I was attracted to both Katherine and Janice, but I had a feeling it would be the last stake in the heart of my relationship with Kimberly.

Katherine stood up as more customers walked in. "Give it some thought. You might be extremely surprised."

I stared down at my coffee.

* * *

Unpacking an Adventure

TreSart L. Sioux

Kimberly still sat at her desk with numerous crumpled papers surrounding her. "How's the creating going?" I asked.

She seemed in her own world.

"Kimberly?"

She snapped out of it. "Yes?"

"I was just asking how your creating was coming."

"Uh . . . actually a little bit better."

"Really? That's fantastic!"

She didn't say anything else and I felt it was best to just let her be.

* * *

The rest of the day I spent cooking a nice dinner. The aroma had to be getting to her. She had been at the computer for hours.

I was right.

"What do we have here?"

I smiled. "We have all your faves."

"So I see."

She placed a kiss on my cheek. Hmm . . . that was a start. We sat down at the kitchen table.

"Trisha, you really did a wonderful job with dinner tonight."

"Well, I knew you were having trouble writing. I just wanted to hopefully get some relaxation between us. I also bought your favorite bottle of wine."

"Excellent!"

There was a change in Kimberly. Not all the tension was gone, but perhaps there was some good to come.

* * *

We enjoyed the meal and wine. I must admit I was feeling a slight kick from the booze, but it was turning out to be a wonderful evening. I had no complaints. I wondered if I'd get lucky.

"Okay, I'm going to clean up. Why don't you go write? If you feel like it, of course."

"Trisha, sit down. I think we need to talk."

My heart sunk. This was it. She's going to dump me. "About what?"

She took a large gulp of wine. A big gulp didn't always mean you were thirsty. "About us."

"Okay, I'm listening."

"Look, I know this hasn't been the best of times for us."

Now I took a big gulp. "No, it hasn't."

"I'm just going to get right to the point. Janice visited me today and . . . well . . . she expressed something that might help us."

What the fuck? I thought Janice had been out paying bills?

"She brought up the subject of swinging. There, I've said it."

Okay, if you were in my situation . . . how far would your jaw have dropped?

"Hey, I know it's not something we talked about, but . . . well . . ."

I leaned in. "You want to try it?"

At first, she couldn't look me in the eyes, but eventually we locked. "Yes, yes I do."

I grabbed the bottle and poured my glass to the top.

"Trisha, what do you think?"

My lips touched the rim of the wine glass and swallowed. Gently placing the glass down, I simply said, "Yes."

* * *

Kimberly and I laughed about the fact that Katherine had come to me about the idea and Janice to her, but I know we were both extremely nervous and unsure how we would feel after the encounter. We decided the next day to venture to the coffee shop around closing hour, curious to know how all of this was done.

* * *

"Hey ya'll! How are you two doing?"

"Just fine Janice," said Kimberly as we all sat down at the table.

There was an energy shift within each one of us I couldn't explain. Janice and Katherine seemed so calm, while I felt a little uneasy. Was this what Kimberly and I needed, or were we about to make the biggest mistake of our lives?

"So, anything new going on?" asked Janice.

Kimberly laughed. "I would say a whole lot!"

"Hey, Janice and I don't want ya'll to think we ganged up on you. Just giving ya'll an alternative if up for it."

Kimberly stared out at the empty town. "I am."

Janice and Katherine turned their attention to me.

With confidence from within, I said, "I am too."

So began the new adventure.

* * *

A month went by with no action from the other women. Kimberly and I did make love a couple of times, and although not outstanding, it was a step up. All was calm until one particular night.

We had invited Katherine and Janice over for a game of Monopoly and drinks. A night I would treasure.

* * *

"Ah, you landed on Boardwalk! Show me the money!" I laughed.

"Okay you money thang," replied Katherine.

"This is a long game." Kimberly yawned.

"We can make it more interesting," said Janice.

"Yes, let's do. Trisha, if you land on one of my railroads in the next five minutes you have to come to bed with me."

I stared at Katherine in shock.

Just like that.

Fuck.

"Okay," I said.

Till this day I truly don't remember saying that, but I do recall Kimberly's look of agreement. Janice reached out and touched my lover's hand.

"I hit your Park Place . . . I'm all yours."

Kimberly's eyes lit up.

Let the games begin!

Needless to say in less than five minutes I landed on one of Katherine's railroads. The moment it happened, I felt a major rush of excitement, but also felt scared out of my mind. Right then and there we ended the game.

Unpacking an Adventure   TreSart L. Sioux

All of us went upstairs. Were we going to be in the same room? I had no idea how this was going to happen, but I did know extreme wetness was sliding down my inner thighs.

We walked into our bedroom. Katherine pulled me close to her, our mouths only inches apart.

"You're shaking."

"I know. I'm nervous." I said.

"Don't be."

I couldn't help but stare into her eyes. I was in my own world with her. I had no idea what Janice and Kimberly were up to but, right at this moment, I didn't care.

Slowly, she began to unbutton my blouse. Next were my jeans. Each article of clothing was gracefully removed until I stood before her naked.

Katherine's eyes left mine briefly to look over my body. God, I felt like I could come just from her stare.

"You have an amazing body," she whispered in my ear.

I can't remember the last time someone said those words to me. In the distance, I could hear soft moaning.

"Get into bed," she instructed.

I turned around and saw where the moaning was coming from. Janice and Kimberly had already shed their clothes and were on the right side corner of the bed. Janice was licking my lover's pussy while playing with her tits.

My God the view was really turning me on. I stood back for a second, quietly observing, when I felt Katherine's gentle touch on my shoulder.

"Come."

She led me to the bed and I slid in next to Janice and Kimberly. They too were in their own world. Katherine began to remove her clothing and as each item fell to the floor the anticipation grew stronger.

The scent of fuck and lust surrounded our bodies. Kimberly's moans grew louder. I looked over and saw that Janice had now inserted her fingers deep inside Kimberly.

I knew my lover and I knew she was about to come.

"Not yet," Janice said and stopped what she was doing.

"Oh God, please!"

"No, it's time for you to pleasure me."

Unpacking an Adventure   TreSart L. Sioux

They exchanged positions and Kimberly greedily began to lap at Janice's juices.

"Hey, you."

I turned my attention back to Katherine. Immediately, I noticed her ample tits were pierced with brass rings. She was completely shaven, giving me a perfect view of her glistening pussy. She straddled my body and playfully pinched my nipples. I couldn't help but reach out and lightly tug on the rings.

"I need to taste you, but first let me taste those lips," she said while running her fingers across my face.

Katherine leaned in and placed a passionate kiss with her tongue sliding in, playing with mine. I could hear Janice's moans becoming louder and louder until I knew she must have came. Moments passed.

"Kimberly, now it's your turn," Janice said.

Meanwhile, Katherine made her way to my tits, her mouth planted firmly on my nipple while her hand played with my other. Now I was the one joining in with all the moans. I knew Kimberly was having her pussy licked, sucked and fucked. Her cries of ecstasy became louder and louder.

"Do you want to watch your lover come?" Katherine asked.

"Yes," I replied.

"Then watch. I have other things to take care of."

I turned my head just as Kimberly began to shake, and before I knew it, Katherine's mouth was on my hot pussy.

Sweat was dripping off of Janice and Kimberly. Their faces flushed from the intensity. I began to concentrate on what Katherine was doing to me. Her tongue made its way back and forth on my clit while she easily slid three fingers inside, feeling my walls and wetness. My eyes closed and I equally met her moves.

Up and down.

Side to side.

What I once dreamed of was finally happening.

I knew without opening my eyes that Janice and Kimberly were watching, which was turning me on even more. Our pace began to quicken. Tiny twinges of pleasure were circulating throughout my body, but more so in my snatch. Katherine quickly removed her fingers and replaced them with her tongue.

"My baby is going to come," said Kimberly.

"Kimberly, go to her now," said Janice.

Unpacking an Adventure   TreSart L. Sioux

Katherine took her tongue out and began to rub my clit. "Yes. Make your lover come."

This was unreal!

Kimberly smiled and took her place. Her fingers played with my clit while she placed her tongue inside. That's all it took. The orgasm ravished my body in waves. Over and over I came until I felt like I was going to pass out.

I was a paralyzed woman in paradise!

A few minutes passed by in complete silence. I had to regain my composure, and when I did, it would be time to indulge in Katherine.

Janice and Kimberly removed themselves and sat on the loveseat facing the bed. They were ready for the final show.

Katherine leaned back on the bed, spreading her legs for all to see. I wasted no time straddling her. Giving back the passionate kiss she had given me earlier.

Our bodies were drenched with sweat, which only turned me on even more. I played with her tits and the shiny rings. At first it was a little strange sucking on them, but I quickly became used to it.

My tongue left a trail down her stomach and to her pussy. She let out a soft sigh once my mouth covered her clit, sucking slightly, then with more force.

Her hands ran through my hair and pushed me in as close as I could go. I placed my fingers inside her, hearing the sound of her wetness as they went in and out.

"That's it. Suck my pussy."

I could feel the stares of Janice and Kimberly. The view they must have: my ass and recently fucked pussy for both of them to see.

I concentrated on Katherine's needs, once again in rhythm.

"Yes, right there and don't stop."

That's exactly what I did. She began to move faster, her breathing becoming heavier. In a matter of seconds, she squirted her juices all over my hand and chin. I have never been with a woman who could do that.

Again, there was silence except for Katherine's heavy breathing. I sat up in bed and wiped the sweat off my forehead wondering what we'd do next. Should we thank them? Were they spending the night?

"That was wonderful," said Katherine as she placed a kiss on my lips.

Kimberly and Janice stood up and began to put their clothes on. Katherine and I did the same. Once downstairs we all hugged and wished

Unpacking an Adventure   TreSart L. Sioux

each other a good night. Kimberly closed the door after them and turned around with a big smile.

"Are you okay?" she asked.

I could still smell and taste Katherine all over my body.

"Oh yes." I said, returning the smile.

* * *

Katherine and Janice did save our relationship. Kimberly and I couldn't have been happier. Our sex life flourished. My lover's creation level soared, and I'm now actually running behind in editing.

I know. I'm sure the question in your mind is if we are now swingers. Well, the following week I got to find out what Janice tasted like.

What We Do
By Emerald

"Want to go to Boston next week?" Jackson had asked last Friday as he arrived home from work. His company had decided at the last minute that they wanted him to help staff their annual conference, held this year in Boston. Despite his warning about how busy he would be most of the time, I had agreed.

Now half asleep in our hotel bed, I watched his last-minute preparations for the first day of the conference. He shrugged into his suit jacket, looking palpably sexy, and marched around the room gathering the things he needed to take downstairs.

"Okay sweetheart," he said, coming to the bed with a smile to kiss me goodbye. "I'll try to make it up to see you during the lunch break."

Had I not been so sleepy, the smell of Jackson's aftershave coupled with the striking figure he cut in his black suit would have made it hard to resist pulling him right back down into bed with me. As it was, I found it was harder just to keep my eyes open.

"Okay," I yawned. "Have a good day."

Jackson whisked out the door. I glanced at the clock and saw that it was not yet 7:30. Falling back against the pillow, I closed my eyes again and didn't wake up until two hours later, at which time I stretched, rolled over, and pulled myself out of bed.

I ordered room service for breakfast and decided to try to get some work done. After two hours in front of my laptop at the desk in our room, I pushed back the straight-backed, armless, and rather uncomfortable chair and decided to go for a quick dip in the pool. Locating my bikini, I slipped it on and grabbed a sarong, padding down the hallway in flip-flops.

Entrance to the pool was only granted by walking through the fitness center, and I enjoyed the numerous mutual looks from the throng of sweaty, hard-bodied men as I wove through to get to the glass doors on the other side. I spent a half hour or so in the cool water before climbing back out to return to my work upstairs.

With damp skin and wet hair clinging to my shoulders, I stepped onto the elevator and pushed the button for my floor. The elevator stopped a few floors later on the floor where the conference was taking place. Several conference participants stepped on, their laminated name tags announcing their identities.

I smiled at each and looked back up to watch the electronic numbers climb, but not without having noticed the magnetic cuteness of one of my new fellow occupants. He looked younger than the average age of the attendees, probably mid-twenties, with the kind of unruly curls that never failed to make me salivate, especially when paired with a suit. I loved a man in a suit (this morning notwithstanding, Jackson still had to practically fend me off some mornings when I woke to find him tying his tie in front of the full-length mirror in our bedroom), and this kind of barely rumpled professional look—the illusion of formality topped by a mass of curls that was always just a little bit tousled no matter how much effort was made to control it as part of the otherwise meticulous polish—made me wet every time I encountered it.

Though he and another participant had been in mid-conversation when they stepped on, I had seen his glance rest on me. I heard them determine that they would go off to their respective rooms now and meet for dinner later. His colleague got off at the next floor. The elevator made a few more stops and eventually emptied out, leaving only the two of us.

I glanced at him again casually and smiled, noting his features more closely. He was tall, his eyes green beneath the mop of brown curls, his suit dark gray and very proper. His smile, as he directed it back at me, was flawless.

"Are you here for the conference?" he asked.

I smiled widely. "Did my outfit give it away?" I asked flirtatiously. He laughed as I answered, "No, I'm not."

"Cool. I am, obviously." He rolled his eyes and gestured at his name tag. His eyes sparkled as he looked into mine. "What are you here for then?"

As the elevator stopped, I met his eyes and said simply, "Fun." I paused as the doors opened, then broke eye contact as I turned toward them. "This is my floor."

"Mine too," he said and stepped off behind me. "Well . . . it was nice meeting you." His eager eyes took me in again as the elevator doors closed behind us. I smiled once more, and we headed in opposite directions down the hallway.

When I got back to our room, I was wet from more than the pool as I dropped my sarong on the bed. Mr. Young Professional was certainly a piece of ass I could get excited about—in fact, I already had.

I heard Jackson's key card slip in the door only moments later.

"Working hard?" he asked as he entered and saw me seated, still in my bikini, at the desk in our room staring intently at my laptop.

What I was actually doing was watching my favorite Green Day video on YouTube and thinking how much I wanted to fuck the hell out of Billie Joe Armstrong. Jackson approached and glanced at the screen as he bent to kiss me.

"Ah, drooling over Green Day again."

Green Day's status at the top of my "Bands by Whom I Would Most Like to Be Gangbanged" list was well known to Jackson. Had he had the means, I was sure he would have arranged such a scenario by now so he wouldn't have to hear me blather about it anymore.

I clicked YouTube shut and turned my body in the chair, missing my office swivel chair at home. "How's it going?" I asked.

"All right," he said, loosening his tie as he sat on the edge of the bed and reached for the room service menu on the nightstand. "Busy. I barely got away just now. I'm not sure how many days I'll be able to make it up during lunch." He threw me a regretful look as he opened the menu. "How's your day been so far?"

"Fine. I went to the pool this morning."

"So I see." He smiled at my brief attire with a wink.

"I met one of your conference participants today," I added.

"Oh?"

"Mm-hmm. In the elevator. He was very cute. Young, a little tousled—looked like a college frat boy playing dress-up."

Jackson snorted, aware of the effect such a look had on me. "Ah ha. Find something to keep you occupied while I'm so busy this week, did you?"

I smiled. I was glad he recognized so easily the interest at which I was hinting; though I knew his casual tone belied a true curiosity as to whether this was the case. And I understood that. I liked to know when he was planning to play too. In general, we let each other know in advance.

"It occurred to me. How do you feel about that?"

Jackson smiled somewhat ruefully. "Well, I like it better when neither of us has to resort to it simply because the other isn't available, but I can certainly understand the temptation. I just wish it weren't because I wasn't here to take care of you, myself."

"But you know it isn't, of course," I pointed out. I knew he knew that. "If you want me to be available just for you this week, I completely understand. It's no problem." It was true. It had occurred to me that he might want my undivided attention this week amidst his busy and somewhat stressful schedule.

Jackson smiled. "Thank you, dear, but no. It's fine." He handed me the room service menu and gave me a characteristic wink. "Though if you wouldn't mind maybe confining it to the day so you can be here when I get back in the evenings . . ."

As I'd suspected. "Of course darling. And I didn't even get his name. I might not even see him again." I went to the bed and kissed him, climbing on top of him in my still-damp bikini. Jackson eased back, running his fingers along my bare skin. His hands moved up and untied the strings of my bikini top. Then he flipped us over, pushing himself on top of me, and kissed me deeply. Lifting himself slightly to remove my bikini bottom, he undid his pants as well and slipped inside of me. I moaned, the smooth silkiness of his tie brushing against the skin between my breasts. He pushed into me deeply, slowly, my body rising effortlessly to meet his every thrust.

Then his mouth moved to my ear, one hand snaking around to the back of my neck and grasping my hair. I knew what was coming next; a hot jolt of lust shot through me as he began to whisper in my ear, "You can fuck whoever you want when you're here alone during the day, as long as you're ready to bend over and take my cock at night when I get back. You want to spread your legs for all those hot young colleagues of mine, don't you? I know you do. You like to spread the wealth of that hot pussy of yours like the little slut that you are."

I was panting, closer and closer to coming as Jackson pulled my hair even more tightly. He continued, still whispering.

"You probably want to come down and take over the seminar I'm leading this afternoon don't you? You want to walk right up to the front, strip that hot body naked, and watch all those horny businessmen in their suits line up to fuck you while I supervise. I bet that's exactly what you want, isn't it, Victoria?"

His words sent me over the edge, flying blindly into orgasm as my body thrashed beneath him. He kept pumping, faster now, my wetness all around us as he came into me, my hands still gripping his shoulders through the smooth white fabric of his shirt. He kissed me slowly before rolling off and rising from the bed. He glanced at the clock as he tucked his shirt back in and refastened his pants. Then he sat on the edge of the bed and touched my cheek, still filled with heat from our encounter.

"I have to run back downstairs sweetheart. I'll see you in a few hours."

I smiled blissfully, still breathless, and blew him a kiss. He stood and ran his eyes once more over my flushed naked body, then gave me a wink and headed for the door.

* * *

I slept in the next morning, ordering room service for breakfast when I finally rolled out of bed. Jackson was going to be busy all day and wouldn't be back for lunch.

"I'm going to try to cut out early tonight though and be back around five or so," he'd said as he'd leaned over to kiss me as I lay half asleep in bed. I'd opened my eyes and reached for his tie, stroking it lightly and wanting to pull him by it right down on top of me. Jackson had chuckled as he'd backed up, running his eyes over my breasts as the covers fell away from them. "I'm going to make dinner reservations for us tonight though. Is seven okay?"

At 6:00 that evening, I stood in front of the mirrors that made up the closet doors and applied a final coat of mascara. Jackson was due back any minute. He had called earlier to say he was stuck downstairs for longer than he'd thought he would be and would be up around now. I had on a new silver satin dress with a short flared skirt and my clear high heels that were high enough to make them look suspiciously like stripper shoes. I heard the key card in the door and turned to greet him.

"Don't you look fantastic," Jackson said, removing his name tag and dropping his room key on top of the dresser. He stopped to give me a hug and appreciate the view more closely. "I'll be ready to go in just a minute."

A few minutes later we walked down the carpeted hallway toward the elevator. I took his arm as we turned the corner and heard the familiar ding. "Hold the elevator please," Jackson called as we hurried to the open door.

Immediately, I saw my Cute Young Professional inside. His eyes lit up at the sight of me, then dimmed slightly as they moved to Jackson. I smiled widely at him as we stepped into the elevator, positioning myself right beside him so that I stood directly between him and Jackson. The other two occupants were busy conversing with each other.

I squeezed Jackson's hand and met his eyes. He raised his eyebrows. I sent a sly sidelong glance to Cute Young Professional and then turned my lustful gaze back on Jackson. Understanding the significance, Jackson followed my glance and then grinned at me. I suppressed the urge to giggle and saw Jackson look again over my head and nod, and I knew they had made eye contact.

"Here for the conference?" Jackson asked the object of my attraction, sidling over beside him without moving me any further away. "I'm Jackson Blake," he said, offering his hand and explaining his position with the company sponsoring the conference.

"Seth Harris," Cute Young Professional said somewhat uncertainly, glancing at me quickly before turning back to Jackson. "Yes, I'm actually just an intern, but my company wanted me to come for the experience."

They talked about their respective workplaces as the elevator door opened at the lobby floor. The other occupants exited. The three of us followed suit and paused in the elevator corridor.

"This is my wife Victoria, by the way," Jackson said heartily.

I stepped forward and shook Seth's warm hand. "Pleasure to meet you."

Seth seemed slightly uncomfortable as he smiled back and then looked back and forth between Jackson and me.

"Yes, she decided to accompany me even though I told her how busy I was going to be," Jackson continued with a smile. "They've got me working 10-hour days here. Lot of behind the scenes setup and staffing going on. I imagine it's not nearly so busy for you though, Seth? Maybe the two of you could get together some day while I'm off working?"

I barely smothered a laugh of surprise. Jackson loved to mess with people—including me. Seth looked nervous, which I found understandable, and said, "Uh, well—"

"I know Victoria gets pretty hot and horny all day up in our room all by herself. She loves fucking in hotels. Maybe you could stop by sometime when you're free during the day and take care of her."

This time the laughter swelled in my throat so much I had to cough to cover it up. Poor Seth looked like he was about to swallow his tongue.

Jackson smiled at him. "Our room is 719. Just call up during the day if you're interested." He offered his hand again, which Seth shook mechanically. "Nice to meet you."

I offered my hand too and gave Seth's a squeeze, trying a warm smile to snap him out of his shock. Then I turned and followed Jackson, leaving my Cute Young Professional standing dazed behind us.

"Very charming dear," I said dryly as we approached the revolving door that led outside.

"What? I was just trying to save you some work." Jackson said with a smile.

"Work?"

"The work of hitting on him yourself and trying to explain that it's okay with your husband if he fucks you. I know how you tire of it," Jackson said with a wink as I pushed through the revolving door. I turned to face him as he came through it right behind me.

"That's very thoughtful of you. I have a feeling, however, that you shell-shocked him into losing any interest in me. Further, he now knows exactly who you are and where you work. What if he says something to someone?"

Jackson scoffed. "What business is it of the company's how I run my sex life? Furthermore, don't underestimate the erotic allure of shell-shock, dear." He looked down at me and winked again as we stopped at an intersection to wait for the walk signal. I giggled and rolled my eyes. Jackson leaned down to kiss me, pulling me closer as his gentle tongue found mine. I knew the signal had changed as I heard people pass by us while we pressed closer together. Jackson's hands slid down my body, and I wondered if we would make it to dinner at all that night or turn around and go right back up to where we came from.

* * *

I felt Jackson's heat the next morning before I even opened my eyes as he reached down to kiss me. I blinked awake to find him head to toe in his charcoal suit and reached for him automatically.

"I can't right now baby," he whispered with a smile, grabbing my wrists gently as I pouted. "I have to go downstairs. Later," he added, kissing me. "I'll be back around seven. And I look forward to fucking your wet pussy when I get here." I whimpered and moved closer to him, nuzzling his neck along the stiff white collar of his shirt. "You can spread your legs as much as you want today for Mr. Young Stud if he calls, but make sure you're still ready for my hard cock when I get up here to pound you hard after a long day at work."

I caught my breath, feeling myself get wet. Humph. Now I was horny. Or hornier, I should say. He had been right about both things the night before—that I got hot and horny in the room all day by myself and that I loved fucking in hotels. I pouted again and nestled under the covers, wanting Jackson to come back and join me.

Reading my thoughts, he grinned as he gathered his laminated name tag and key card from the top of the dresser.

"Bye sweetheart," he said as he slipped his name tag over his head. "I love you."

"I love you too," I said sleepily, suspending my pouting for a small smile as he waved on his way to the door.

I rolled out of bed and decided to go to the lobby restaurant for breakfast instead of ordering room service. Emerging from the shower, I studied the contents of the closet and decided on a simple purple blouse and jeans. Once dressed, I grabbed my room key and headed down the now familiar hallway. As I rounded the corner to the elevators, I saw Seth waiting in front of them.

I smiled. He hadn't seen me yet.

"Well hi there," I said as I walked up behind him.

He turned, and his eyes jumped as he spotted me. I saw the eagerness in his expression even as he appeared unsure what to say.

"Hi," he answered finally, smiling. "It's nice to see you. Your, um, husband gave me your number so quickly the other night I didn't have time to write it down. And I forgot it in my . . . surprise."

I laughed. I could imagine. Despite his nervousness, I sensed sincerity as well, and I didn't doubt the authenticity of his story.

"Well fortunately for us these elevators seem to be all about our getting together."

Seth's breathing changed a little. I held his eyes with mine, all but pulling him to me physically as we stood several feet apart.

"Were you headed down to the conference now?" I asked. He was wearing a suit again—pinstripes this time. I wanted to rip it off.

"I was actually just going down to check out some of the vendor booths. Which can certainly wait," he added hastily, then blushed.

I stepped closer to him and reached up to touch his cheek. "You don't have to be nervous, doll. I just want you to take me to your room and fuck me while I wait for my husband to get off work tonight. Is that okay?"

Seth swallowed. There was silence for several seconds as I held his gaze. "Yes," he answered finally.

I smiled and linked arms with him as I turned in the direction I knew his room was. He fell into step immediately beside me, marching us down the hall to room 742. His key card slipped in the door. He held it open for me, and I stepped inside. He followed and fastened the dead bolt behind us.

"Wait a minute," he said in a low voice as he turned back to face me. "I don't have any condoms."

"I do!" I said with a grin, stepping over to the bed. I pulled one from my purse and held it up in one hand as I dropped the other to the buttons of my blouse, slowly undoing the top one. Seth's eyes dropped, and he inhaled deeply as he watched me work my way down, my fingers twisting each purple button until my blouse slipped off my shoulders and dropped to the floor. I was naked underneath.

Seth stared at my breasts, then crossed to me in one stride and grasped them with both hands, squeezing firmly as he dropped his mouth to mine. I was surprised by the heat of the kiss as I pushed against him, feeling his erection pressing against the pinstriped fabric that covered it. I reached up and pushed the jacket away from his shoulders, and he pulled it off without breaking the kiss, dropping it carelessly to the floor. I felt him step out of his shoes as his hands found my waist, hovering there delicately until I slipped my hand between us and ran my fingers up the hardness beneath his zipper. His hands grasped my waist harder, taking my breath away as I started to undo his pants. The pressure of his fingers on my flesh made me wet—an urgent grasp coupled with a nervous hesitation to move them anywhere else. And right then, I didn't want him to move them anywhere else. That desperate, pleading squeeze at my waist took my breath away.

Without thinking I pushed him down onto the desk chair just like the one in our room, ignoring the bed I stood up against. I wanted full leverage. I slipped the condom on and straddled him, wasting no time taking his cock deep inside me. His eyes closed, his head went back, and his breathless grasp went to my hips. My body slapped against his as I rode him wildly, my thigh muscles already burning with the urgency coursing through me to fuck him harder, faster, more. Seth's jaw clenched. I knew he was trying not to come, but I couldn't stop myself from bouncing up and down on his cock, pushing him deeper into me. He finally held me in place on top of him, his breath coming in short gasps.

"Stop," he whispered, and I slowed down enough to force myself to do so, my legs shaking like I was about to come. Which was prophetic of them, it turned out, because Seth stood me up and laid me back on the bed, climbing on top of me but not entering me. Instead he knelt above me and rested his fingers on my clit. I was so close to coming I cried out, and he moved them in a tiny circle, looking down to watch my pussy as it responded to his touch. I knew it wouldn't take much more, and I got louder as his pressure got harder until I came with a long yell, arching my back and grabbing the bedspread surrounding me.

Seth shoved his cock back into me and pumped hard, grunting as he came almost immediately. I smiled at his consideration, still out of breath and feeling the burn in my thighs. Seth stood back up and smiled at me almost shyly. I sent him a grin and hoisted myself off the bed, reaching up to kiss him before locating and re-donning my panties and jeans.

He watched me. "You're very beautiful," he said after a silence. I turned to him with a smile. He seemed to want to say more but stopped.

"Thank you."

He smiled and looked down. "Do you guys do this kind of thing a lot?"

I didn't have to ask what he was talking about. "Depends on what you mean by a lot," I laughed. "It comes up from time to time—no pun intended."

"Wow." Seth said it quietly, almost under his breath.

I slid my arms into the sleeves of my blouse and began buttoning. Seth glanced quickly at my flesh disappearing beneath the deep purple fabric. When I was done, I looked up at him. I felt a sudden flash of affection, and at the same time I felt a twinge as I observed his obvious uncertainty and hoped he hadn't felt belittled or pressured in any way. I stepped forward to hug him, and his arms opened immediately and found their way around me. I kissed him again and stepped back, deciding to offer some information I didn't always offer in these encounters.

"It's the way our relationship works. We don't always do the hitting on for each other like Jackson did for me this time," I said with a quick grin, "but it's just a part of what we do." I paused. "Thanks for doing this. I really enjoyed it." The words were simple, but they were sincere. I held his gaze as I said it. It was hard to know how Seth was reading the situation, but I really did feel appreciative that he had availed himself of something that to him obviously seemed strange and unfamiliar.

He blushed and said, "Yeah, me too. It was really nice meeting you."

I smiled again, satisfied, and wished him a safe trip home as he followed me to the door. There was a warmth between us, and as I gave Seth a final kiss there, he seemed more at ease than I seen him thus far. I headed down the hallway back to our room.

* * *

"Christ I'm tired," Jackson greeted me that evening as he strode through the door. "It's a good thing these things only happen once a year."

Wrapped loosely in one of the hotel's plush robes, I smiled and stood to give him a hug. "Why don't you take off your clothes and let me give you a back rub?"

"Why, how nice of you." Jackson smiled at me. "Hey, you're glowing a bit. Did you get banged by some young guy down the hall while I was gone today?"

I laughed out loud at his wording. "As a matter of fact, I did."

"Really? I can't wait to hear all about it." Jackson pulled off his tie. He advanced toward me, looping the untied tie around my neck to pull me to him for a kiss. "And are you still ready for my hard cock like I told you to be this morning?" he murmured against my skin.

"Always."

"Good." Jackson's mouth found mine, and the fire that only happened with him began to course through me. Wanting nothing but to be as close to him as I possibly could, I pressed hard against him. He responded by wrapping his arms around me, an embrace that was so much more than just the physical closeness of our bodies. I broke the kiss and moved my lips to his ear.

"I love you," I whispered. Jackson nudged me toward the bed, the words echoing against my own ear as he eased me out of the robe and gently laid me down, his fingers running over my skin with a fire that I knew only happened with me.

The Twenty-Minute Rule
By Ashley Lister

Lisa placed a hand on the guy's chest. Her fingers lingered there for a moment and she savored the tactile pleasure of caressing a stranger as she worked herself up and down. Unlike her husband, Larry, this man's chest was smooth and hairless. The skin was bereft of the tight clutch of scouring-pad curls with which she was more familiar. The flesh was waxed to a gleaming, frictionless finish—as muscular as Larry's chest—but different through a thousand subtle nuances. As her fingertips trailed across to his right nipple, she teased the hard, fat bead of flesh and smiled when he shivered. It was a moment she planned to recount in graphic and exaggerated detail when she and Larry were taking the slow drive home.

"Twenty minutes are up," she muttered.

With a conciliatory smile, and only a little regret, she pulled herself from him. The thick length she had been riding slid slowly from her wetness. A delicious tremor rippled through the muscles of her pussy as their bodies started to separate. She was aware of the condom's slippery egress from her sex and glanced down at her groin just in time to watch his sheathed cock flop, unsated, from her wetness.

His eyes were suddenly wide. There was an expression of dismay slapped across his features. "Twenty minutes?" he repeated numbly. "What the—"

"Twenty minutes," Lisa said again, still smiling. "I told you before we began." She was already standing and glancing around the dimly lit playroom for her purse and thong. The purse was easy to find. The thong was nowhere to be seen, and she dismissed it without another thought. Leaning over him, placing a leisurely kiss against his startled lips, she casually silenced his protests. "Thanks for that. It was fun." Her fingers

The Twenty-Minute Rule   Ashley Lister

trailed once more over the smooth muscles of his chest, seeking out the hard nub of his erect nipple.

And then she snatched her hand away.

With two swift steps Lisa was out of the playroom leaving the intermingled scents of sweat and sex, and the unspent stranger, as a memory behind her. Her heart continued to pound from the rush of arousal and adrenaline.

* * *

Outside, the night already had a tight hold on the gardens of The Fun Palace. It was the swingers' bar Lisa and Larry visited every first Saturday of each month and this party was as good as any other they had attended. A disco and TV room occupied the two main downstairs rooms with the TV room showing a constant stream of glamorous soft-core porn. Downstairs, in the cellars, were a dungeon and a wet-play room. Upstairs were two communal play rooms and three private rooms. On a good Saturday—and this was proving to be a very good Saturday—The Fun Palace could play host to more than two dozen couples and assorted singles.

Lisa thought there was no better way to celebrate the weekend.

Stepping into the chilly blackness, Lisa fumbled through her purse to find her cigarettes. She pulled out a Marlboro and then rummaged through the bag looking for a lighter that she knew would be lurking behind the condoms, lube, a mini pocket-rocket, two packs of tissues and . . .

"Light?"

As the question was asked a Zippo sparked in front of her eyes. A broad blue and yellow flame illuminated the darkness. Lisa took a moment to acknowledge that the voice was distinctly masculine, deep and powerful. Then she was sucking on the end of the cigarette and inhaling the noxious taste of the much-needed tobacco.

"Thanks."

"Not a problem."

The Zippo was snapped shut. As her eyes adjusted to the darkness, she was treated to the first sight of him. Tall, broad and conventionally good-looking, he held the remains of a cigarette in one hand. And it looked like he was wearing women's clothes.

She frowned.

He laughed.

"My wife's sarong," he explained, tugging sheepishly at the fabric.

He didn't need to say any more. Lisa understood perfectly. The UK's smoking laws had made it illegal for anyone to smoke inside a public building. Most smokers were complaining about the effect this had on their time in pubs and bars, and the quality of their experience in restaurants, but Lisa knew it was also having an impact on those smokers who attended swingers' parties. The nuisance of having to go outside for a smoke—regardless of the weather or the inconvenience—had meant she occasionally borrowed Larry's jacket to brave the cool night's chill. The man beside her was not the first one she had seen wearing something overtly— and unflatteringly—feminine. But she thought this was the only occasion on which she had seen a man wearing a sarong. Not for the first time in her life she thought: *This could only happen in The Fun Palace.*

"It suits you," she lied.

"Your outfit looks better," he murmured.

She glanced down at her naked body. She hadn't been able to find her thong in the playroom, and had written the underwear off as a sacrifice to an otherwise wonderful night. Reflecting on that detail, Lisa realized that her used thongs were a regular offering that she made to the Gods of the swinger parties. The fact that she was naked didn't trouble Lisa. She was justifiably proud of her figure and could see no practical reason to keep it covered up in the sanctuary of a party at The Fun Palace. Or even outside in The Fun Palace's gardens.

Not that they were fully outside, she allowed. The Fun Palace provided a sheltered porch for the convenience of smokers. The porch offered some covering from occasional spats of rain and was close enough to the main building so they could still hear the disco shrieks of ABBA trailing from the dance floor. If she had bothered to turn around, Lisa knew she could have stared into The Fun Palace and watched couples and singles cavorting to the music while she stood outside and smoked her cigarette. But, it appeared that this evening there were more interesting things to consider outside the main building rather than on the dance floor.

The smoker's gaze lingered over the slender strip of dark curls that rested above her mons pubis. The appreciation in his expression made her loins molten. His smile of approval glistened brightly in the darkness.

"Your outfit looks a lot better than mine," he murmured.

"Why, sir!" Lisa exclaimed with mock theatricality. "I do believe you're flirting with me."

"Only to try and get into your pants," he conceded.

She shook her head and drew on her cigarette. Holding her hands apart, exposing herself openly to him, she said, "But I'm not wearing any pants."

"Of course you're not," he agreed smoothly. He flicked his cigarette into the darkness and grinned. "How remiss of me to overlook that detail."

They laughed again.

Although the night was cool, Lisa wasn't troubled by the chill. Her bare flesh was dimpled by goosebumps but, after the sweltering heat of the playroom, it was a relief to be able to drink in the night's sweet air and allow her body's temperature to slowly descend.

She savored her cigarette for a moment longer and, from the corner of her eye, she cast a sly glance at the smoker flirting with her. The sarong looked ridiculously small on his large frame. It was a pretty outfit, designed for someone delicate and petite, she guessed. And it was wrapped so tight around him she could easily discern the shape of his slowly thickening erection.

A thrill of anticipation tickled down her spine.

The heat at her loins became more intense as she contemplated the idea of having this stranger outside, in the asexual environment of the designated smoking zone.

"You're here with your wife?"

He nodded.

"Where is she?"

"The last I saw of her she was heading toward one of the private rooms with a very attractive brunette."

Lisa nodded. She remembered seeing two women holding hands and heading in that direction. One of them had been a brunette. The intimacy between the pair had sired a blossoming curiosity in Lisa's sex that left her cramped with excitement and jealousy. If the two women hadn't seemed so involved with each other she would have been tempted to find out if they were interested in forming a threesome.

"Your wife's not letting you watch?"

"Not this time. The brunette's pretty nervous. It's her first time with another woman. I don't think she wants the extra pressure of knowing she's performing for an audience."

Lisa nodded. "I trust your wife's going to tell you all about it when you both get home?" Although she shaped the words into a question, she knew the answer before he said yes. It was the same way she and Larry enjoyed the parties: each going their separate way; each cultivating and collecting brand new experiences; then sharing those experiences as recollections and anecdotes that added to the intimacy of their lovemaking when they were again alone together.

"Not that I'm going to have much to tell her," he murmured. "I've been something of a wallflower this evening."

She made a sad face. Feigning exaggerated sympathy she made her expression mock-serious, stepped closer to him and continued to smoke her cigarette. "I hear you there," she admitted. "Aside from shagging a couple of guys in the playroom I've hardly had anyone look at me twice this evening."

"You're a veritable nun," he said wryly.

"I'm worried my virginity may have grown back," she joked and tossed her cigarette into the darkness. Stepping in front of him, she cast a meaningful glance at the front of his sarong and asked, "Would you like to help me break my vow of chastity, you poor little wallflower?"

They reached out for each other in the same instant. He passed her a questioning glance as his mouth moved toward hers, and she nodded enthusiastic encouragement. Their lips squashed together and she was treated to the urgent pressure of his tongue pushing into her mouth. The cool cotton fabric of his sarong slid smoothly against her body. As their bodies pressed together Lisa was made aware of his thinly-veiled erection: its length, thickness and heat.

When they finally broke apart both of them were gasping.

"Before we do anything else," Lisa began, "I have to tell you now: I work to the twenty minute rule. You don't have a problem with that, do you?"

"The twenty minute rule?"

"I never stay with any man for longer than twenty minutes at a party," she explained. "Twenty minutes from now I'm going to kiss you goodbye and thank you for your time, and then I'm either going to go and find my husband, or I'll find another man to spend twenty minutes with."

His fingers lingered against her bare arm.

The warmth of his touch was exciting enough to send fresh shivers directly to her loins. Her need for him was accelerating at a furious speed.

The Twenty-Minute Rule   Ashley Lister

And yet, his leisurely style made her resist the urge to melt for him. She found herself emulating his measured and unhurried pace as she savored the foreplay of touching, teasing and talking.

"I can live with your twenty minute rule," he agreed. Glancing at his wristwatch, frowning slightly, he added, "Although that means we'll be saying goodbye to each other at ten-thirty."

Lisa shrugged and pushed her fingers against his chest. Stroking her nails lightly through the folds of his sarong, gently scratching his chest and leaning in for another kiss she said, "That means we'll have to make the most of the time we have together."

He chuckled and leant toward her for another kiss.

As she tried to explore more of his flesh, pulling the sarong open and exposing his masculine physique, he drew her into his embrace. One hand remained on her arm, holding her firm and keeping her close. The other was behind her back, tracing the ridges of her spine, following a path downwards, and lingering over the swell of her right buttock.

Lisa shivered as their kiss continued.

His fingers slipped from her buttock and touched the crease of her sex.

She parted her legs slightly, so he had easier access. Inquisitive fingertips trailed against the moist split of her labia. As he gently stroked back and forth a surge of swelling need tickled upward through her body. Her clitoris throbbed as though it yearned for his caress. Her nipples, squashed against his chest, ached from the combination of excitement, greedy need, and lack of stimulation. Lisa pressed herself hard against him as they kissed, and she bravely resisted the urge to moan.

She lowered one hand to his groin and chased the shape of his erection through the fabric of his sarong. He was perfectly built for her needs: not so large he would cause discomfort but far from being small. She also noted, unlike Larry, this man had a foreskin rolled over the thick dome of his erection. Lisa had often thought that one of the joys of swinging, when married to a circumcised husband, was the pleasure she got from toying with a stretchy, sensitive foreskin. She reached beneath the folds of the sarong and wrapped her fingers slowly around his length.

He drew a long breath.

Gently, savoring the sensation, Lisa began to roll her fist up and down him. The sensation of having his foreskin travel back and forth was wickedly arousing. Feeling the tug of his flesh moving up and down with her hand, and watching his foreskin expose the purple flesh of his glans and then conceal it, she was almost consumed by the unfamiliar intimacy. The excitement had built quickly but with an irresistible force that made her long for more.

"Condom?" he muttered. He sounded as breathless as she felt.

Lisa snatched at her purse and removed one. Practiced expertise had her tearing the packet open and rolling the sheath down his length in mere seconds. The movement was so fluid it was almost professionally poetic.

"You want-?" he asked.

"Yeah."

"Here?"

"From behind?"

Incomplete questions, suggestions, and a communication based more on guesswork and shared knowledge of The Fun Palace worked best for both of them. Within moments Lisa was turned around, facing into the party as she held either side of the door frame. Her partner stood behind her; his hands resting on her hips; and his freshly sheathed erection ploughing purposefully into her sex.

His fingers gripped tight on her hips as he pushed forward.

The movement was slow, lazy and unhurried. The languid penetration seemed to take forever and allowed her loins to swell with the mounting thrill of excitement.

Lisa accepted his drawn out penetration as she stared into The Fun Palace. She had a clear view of the dance floor and saw Larry dancing with a blonde. The pair were clearly flirting—she could see that much from Larry's broad grin and the flutter of the blonde's lashes—but nothing more sexual seemed to be happening between them. She smiled tightly to herself and realized she was going to provide her husband with a lot of his evening's excitement merely by telling him of her own escapades at the party.

The idea fuelled a fresh thrill of arousal through her sex.

Deliberately, the man behind her began to slide his length from her confines. Lisa hadn't realized he had been taking so long to fill her. His slow, languid rhythm was infuriatingly exciting. She arched her back and clenched her inner muscles tight around him. As though retaliating, he gripped her hips more forcefully and then pushed back into her hole.

The battle, agonizingly slow and beautifully fulfilling, seemed to last forever.

He pulled back to the point where she feared his length would fall from her sex. Then he pushed inside with so much force it was like being freshly penetrated for the first time. The night air made his length cool. The chilly sheath was an icy caress against the heat of her inner muscles. And that sensation alone was enough to have her body hurtling toward a plateau of satisfaction.

Which made it all the more frustrating when he simply stopped.

"Why twenty minutes?" he asked.

The question was so unexpected Liza had no idea what he was talking about.

"Your twenty minute rule," he elaborated. "Why fix a time limit? And why, specifically, that particular length of time?"

Understanding finally washed over her.

She drew a faltering breath and tried to take her thoughts away from the thrill of what they had been doing to deal with the more pragmatic consideration of his question.

"Twenty minutes is long enough for me to have fun without devoting an entire night to one person," she explained. It was the usual response she gave when someone asked about her rule. "Twenty minutes is long enough for us both to have fun—and then move on and have more fun with someone else."

There were other reasons. The twenty minute rule allowed her a convenient and polite out if a prospective partner proved tiresome, incompatible or more demanding than she cared to tolerate. But Lisa chose to keep those points to herself.

The smoker seemed to ponder her response for a moment. His erection remained buried deep inside her. There was the slightest sway of his hips. He was no longer urging himself back and forth inside her. He was only reminding her sex that his presence remained there: stretching her muscles and filling her with a thick surge of arousal. His fingertips drew over her hips and moved up to her breasts. The tactile bliss of strange hands caressing her nipples sent a familiar spasm of pleasure flooding through her body.

Lisa bit back a moan.

"It's a shame we only have twenty minutes together," he sighed, "because, according to my watch, our time together is just about finished." Maddeningly, he began to slide his thick length from the centre of her sex.

The Twenty-Minute Rule — Ashley Lister

Lisa wanted to relish the sensation of his gentle egress. The muscles of her pussy walls tightened around him, as though they were fearful of releasing their prize. Without hesitating, Lisa whipped a hand behind her and clutched his left buttock—holding him in place.

"Just this once," she whispered softly, "I think we should restart our twenty minutes from this point."

He hesitated.

When he spoke, she could hear the triumphant smirk in his tone. "Really?"

"Twenty more minutes," she confirmed, sliding back onto him. She held her breath and tightened her hold on his rear as his length filled her. Glancing back at him, trying to keep the raw lust from her voice, she whispered, "But you'd better make sure they're as good as the last twenty minutes."

Judging by the grin on his face, Lisa guessed the next twenty minutes were likely to be even more exciting. And she figured, if he still had her wanting more, she could always break the twenty minute rule once again this evening. It would certainly give her something exciting to tell Larry on the journey home.

The Gerswins
By Keeb Knight

Raising a mildly warm cup of coffee to her lips, she peered over to her husband who was skimming through the Sunday newspaper. He sensed he was being watched and tilted his head to the side of the neatly folded newspaper, catching a stare from a beautiful pair of light-gray eyes. It was their little way of acknowledging the presence of one another. An unspoken dialogue, so to speak. But this only lasted for so long, until after the seventh sip of her dark roast coffee.

"So what do you want for your birthday, babe," she said interrupting the deafening silence.

"Hmm . . . I don't know," he said as he snapped the creases out of the paper. "I do need a new putter. Or maybe you can take me to that new seafood restaurant down on Fifteenth Street you've been begging me to go to for the last three months. What's the name of that place again?" He looked up to the ceiling in thought. "Oh, yeah! The Stripped Bass. Yeah, that's it."

She gave him a hard stare and a negative headshake as he peeped at her response from behind the business section.

"Oh, okay. I guess I should wait until your birthday for that one, huh," he said with subtle sarcasm.

She nodded her head in agreement.

"Okay, I got it. How about you get me the librarian down at the free library?"

She damn near spit her coffee as she put her mug down heavily onto the kitchen table.

"Come again, Mikel?" she said not believing her ears.

"You know. The tall, beautiful, young, mocha-skinned woman who wears those great looking colorful head dresses."

She gave him a blank stare for a moment. "Mikel, are you telling me you want to start swinging again?"

"Maybe," he said, confirming that sometimes their unspoken thoughts were actually in sync.

"We haven't swung in about four years. I thought you'd lost interest in swinging?"

"I think it's because we've been so busy over the last few years we just slowed down to a halt. Even in our own sexual relationship. Don't you think? But no, I've never lost interest."

"Well, I see that now. Now you've got your Amazon librarian girlfriend locked in your sights," she said, rolling her eyes at him and taking a sip from her mug.

"Oh, come on, Zuri. Don't be like that. You're the one who got us started in swinging in the first place."

"Now how did I know you were going to throw that back in my face? But you're right, honey. I can't be too hard on you. I've been thinking about it myself every now and again. And it's been a while."

"Yeah, it's been a while," he seconded.

"So, you think I'll like this girlfriend of yours?"

"Will you stop? There's no doubt in my mind."

"Hmmm. She sounds like she's young. About how old is she?"

"She's not that much younger than us. About twenty-seven to thirty I'd say."

"Is she married?"

"I'm pretty sure she is. Unless she's wearing a huge rock on her wedding finger to ward off the wolves. I haven't gotten into any big conversations with her other than a hello or asking if I owed any fines."

"Oh, I bet you couldn't wait to return your books on the due dates. Did you even read any of the books you borrowed, Mikel? Because, now that I think about it, I don't remember seeing you reading any of those books over the past few months."

"Yeah, I have," he said with a tone of guilt in his voice.

"Which book was that?"

"It was a book on how to choose the right stocks for retirement."

"I think you just picked up any book that would possibly impress your fantasy girlfriend. Just in case she happened to be the one checking out your books."

"Oh, you know me all too well don't you," he said, smiling as he shook his newspaper, bringing his attention back to it.

"Anyway, Mikel, it just so happens that last month I came across our membership card to the Hedo Den Swing Club. And guess what?"

"What, dear?"

"Our membership doesn't expire until next month. Three weeks after your birthday, actually."

"So you withheld this important information from me, why?"

"Well, like I said. I didn't think either of us would be entertaining the thought to even do this anymore."

"Okay. Enough said. Let's go for it. I want us to go swinging on my birthday next week," he said with assurance.

Zuri looked at his childish behavior, shook her head and smiled. "Mikel, what do you think the chances are of your librarian friend buying into this lifestyle? You know it's not for everyone. And how do you suggest we approach her?"

"I haven't thought that deep about it since we're just now discussing it. But I think we might have a chance."

"What do you mean?"

"She's been checking me out."

"That's her job, Mikel. To check you out."

"Don't be funny. You know what I mean."

"Big deal. I'm always checking men out."

"Exactly."

"And this makes her a swinger?"

"No, it makes her at the very least a potential swinger. She doesn't just give me a passing glance. I can feel her eyes."

"You can feel her eyes ripping your clothes as she checks out your books that you're not reading? This gives her swing potential?" She laughed.

"Ha! Funny. You're not a man, so you wouldn't know."

"Oh, thank the heavens I'm not a man. You have it so rough getting eye-fucked by a pretty librarian."

"Yeah, it's just one of the perks that come with my library card."

"Well, it seems like you're serious, and this conversation is starting to turn me on. She seems like a confident woman. My kind of woman. Have you seen her checking out women?"

"Is it my birthday or yours?" he said with a wink.

She stared at him for a quick moment. "It's our birthday. Marriage makes us one. So, you're supposed to share."

"Hey, I like to share," he said.

"Share my foot, mister. You like to watch."

"Okay, you caught me. Handcuff me and throw away the key why don't you."

"You'd like that," she said, rolling her eyes and caressing the rim of her coffee mug with her fingertip.

There was a brief moment of silence.

"So, do you have any books to return?"

"Of course I do," he said without hesitation. "Why?"

"Yes, of course you do. Why did I even bother to ask? How about we take a trip to the library this afternoon and see if we can have a chat with this fantasy woman of yours."

Mikel looked at his watch. "They open in about an hour. We should wait a couple hours before we swarm in on her. We don't want her to think we're just this dirty couple who couldn't wait to talk to her about swinging with us."

"Good point, sweetheart," she said, raising her cup.

* * *

Zuri stood in the foyer near the bottom of the staircase with her arms crossed and car keys in hand. She jingled them every few seconds just loud enough that he could hear them from upstairs.

"I'm coming. Stop with the keys already," he shouted from the bathroom.

"What are you doing up there?"

"I'm getting ready."

"You've been getting ready for the last hour and a half. We're just going to the library not a banquet. Normally, I'm the one who takes this long. What're you trying to do, make yourself handsome for your girlfriend?"

"Yes," he shouted. "We have to sell ourselves if we want her to bite, right?"

"How do you know she won't be only attracted to me when we get there?"

He came down stairs in a fluid, but methodically timed fashion. It was almost as though he rehearsed every downward strut. When she looked up her jaw nearly hit the floor when she saw her husband looking like the dark prince that swept her off her feet six years ago. His six-foot-four frame was adorning long-sleeved, superfine soft cotton, slim-fit pale pink shirt with a pair of black straight-leg denim jeans, and a pair of nicely polished black Italian loafers. Long loafers.

She couldn't help but to be speechless seeing how this beautiful man easily got away with wearing a pink shirt, untucked and all. And to top it off, he wore neither a t-shirt nor a vest underneath. She was in awe of this lean, Nubian man as he approached her with his firm, well-muscled chest making itself known through the semi-sheer pink linen wall that came between them.

"What was that you were saying, dear?" He smirked.

"Shit no, uh-uh!" she muttered.

"What's the matter?" he asked as though he didn't look damn good as hell. "I'm just making sure all the bases are covered."

She just looked at him and rolled her big eyes as she started up the staircase.

"Oh, no you don't," he said as he grabbed her by the wrist, making her turn back around, guiding her back down the steps. "You had your chance. Let's go! Boy, you're so competitive."

"Shit!" she said in a loud whisper under her breath.

"Or is someone jealous," he said mockingly.

"Be quiet. Here, you drive," she said while handing him the car keys. But not before thumping them against his chest.

* * *

It was just a ten-minute drive. They pulled up to a metered parking space in front of the library.

"Aren't we lucky? Got a spot right at the entrance. This is working out great already," Mikel said proudly.

"Yeah, well if it doesn't work out we'll at least be able to make a quick getaway," Zuri replied sarcastically.

"So, are you ready to do this? Have you calmed down a little?"

"Yes and yes, baby. Let's go met her." She leaned toward him for kiss and her probing hand managed to slip its way under his shirt and down into his pants. "Oh, my. No underwear. Allowing junior to hang free today are we? You really are serious about this," she said in between kisses on his soft full lips, at the same time single handedly stroking his alter ego.

"Zuri, what are you doing? We're right in front of a public library."

"I'm sorry, baby. You just look so fucking hot it's making me horny."

"Yeah, thanks. Now I'll walk in saluting her with a fresh hard-on."

"That's funny, Mikel," she said while removing her hand. "Okay, you ready to do this?"

"Yep."

The couple climbed out of the car and headed toward the entrance of the library. Mikel opened the door for his wife. She proceeded to walk through the door, but then stopped suddenly. Mikel bumped into her from behind.

"What's the matter?" he asked.

"That's her isn't it?"

He looked ahead and saw her standing behind the counter checking in a stack of books. She was wearing an earth tone African head wrap and adorned a pair of large gold hoop earrings. Her features were distinctive. High cheekbones, almond-shaped eyes, arching eyebrows, and a pointed chin accented her mocha oval face.

"That's her," he confirmed.

"She's absolutely gorgeous," Zuri said almost in awe of the woman. "Now I see why it took you for-goddamn-ever to get ready. I'm going to remember this for when you want to have a fem dom night."

"Sounds like I'm in trouble."

"Oh, yeah. You are."

The woman sensed she was being watched and looked over into the couple's direction.

"Can I help you?" she said.

Mikel placed the palm of his hand at the small of Zuri's back to nudge her forward.

"Yes, maybe you can," he said.

She smiled at the deep voice but appeared not to recognize him at first from the distance between the dimly lit entrance and the counter.

"Oh, hi!" She said with full awareness and captivating smile. Her eyes seemed to take in his polished look. "How are you today?"

"Fine thanks," he replied.

"This must be your lovely wife."

"Yes. This is Zuri."

"A pleasure to meet you, Zuri. That's a pretty name."

"That's exactly what it means – pretty," Zuri emphasized.

"I'm sorry. I come through here all the time and I've never got your name," Mikel said.

"It's Ayanna. Yours is Mikel with a K, right?"

"Wow! You know my name."

"Oh, I'm sorry. I hope that's all right. I'm pretty good at remembering names."

Zuri pursed her lips together to keep from saying anything and made a pointed look down at Ayanna's left hand at what appeared to be an engagement ring and a wedding band.

"You're married, too, I see," she injected.

Ayanna turned to her then glanced at her hand. "Yes. It will be a year come next Wednesday."

"Really? Next Wednesday?" Zuri said with a surprise tone in her voice.

"Yes . . . why?"

"That's Mikel's birthday."

"Oh, wonderful! What do you have planned for your birthday," she asked as she turned her attention back to Mikel.

"Well, that's why we're here," Zuri said.

"I don't understand," Ayanna said with a perplexed look on her face.

"Ayanna, we came here to see you."

"To see me? About your birthday?"

"We can explain if you have a moment. Is there a place in here where we all can talk in private?" Mikel asked.

"Well, sure. It's not that busy yet. How long is this going to take? And should I be concerned?"

"Not long and you need not be concerned," Mikel assured.

"We're harmless, Ayanna. At least while the sun is up anyway," Zuri said jokingly.

"Oh so you've come for blood have you," she said, catching on to Zuri's witty humor.

Zuri turned to Mikel. "I'm beginning to like her."

"We can go into one of the study group rooms upstairs," Ayanna said.

She asked one of her nearby associates if they could mind the front desk while she was with the couple. She then led them to the second floor. Ayanna was a slender woman with subtle curves to her hips that had a pendulous sway with every step she took. She was wearing a tan blouse; a brownie-colored slim skirt complete with a pair of four-inch bitter-chocolate, strappy platforms. Both Mikel and Zuri were transfixed by the movement of Ayanna's body as she walked up the stairs ahead of them. Zuri nudged her husband with her elbow and tossed him a wink letting him know her approval of the sexy librarian.

She led them past a bank of twenty or so computers to where there were four vacant study group rooms. She unlocked the door to one of them, held the door open, and gestured with her hand for them to enter.

"Have a seat," she offered while closing the door behind her.

The couple sat next to each other and Ayanna sat down in the chair across the table from them.

"Okay, so what's so private that we couldn't stay downstairs?"

They both looked at each other as to who was going to speak first. Mikel nodded to Zuri to go ahead.

"I guess the only way I can start off is to tell you bluntly that we've never done this before with anyone and so far you're being a very good sport about talking to us. Quite brave I might add. Anyway, we have a proposition for you."

Ayanna looked over at Mikel then back to Zuri. "I'm listening."

"Let me just come out and tell you. My husband and I are swingers."

"Swingers?"

"Yes."

"Okay," she said with curiosity.

"I haven't frightened you yet, have I?" Zuri said.

"Oh, no, no! But if I start to see fangs this conversation is over," Ayanna said with a smile. "Go on."

"Well, my husband really admires you and we talked about it and we were wondering if you and your husband ever swung. And if so, would you be interested in swinging with us?"

"On his birthday. My wedding anniversary," Ayanna finished.

"Yes, that's right," Zuri said.

There was a long moment of silence. Ayanna looked at Mikel. Studied him and how he looked in his crisp, clean, pink shirt. She turned to Zuri and her alluring gray eyes. Given her distinctive slanted eyes, Ayanna deduced when they first met downstairs that Zuri was biracial—of Amerasian decent. She was a natural beauty. Her fair, flawless face was smooth and supple and eloquently framed by her long black hair. She liked how she wore almost no make-up with the exception of scarlet lipstick. Her lips were almost as full, but just as delectable, as her husband's.

"To answer your question: yes. My husband and I do swing. That's how we met actually."

"I would've never suspected," Zuri said.

"Your husband must have very good instincts or he was a bloodhound in a former life." Ayanna smiled.

They all laughed.

"So, is that a yes?" Zuri asked.

"It's yes," Ayanna said.

"Looks like we struck gold," Mikel said. "Are you familiar with The Hedo Den Swing Club?"

"Yes, I've heard of it. But we've never been there."

Zuri reached in her purse. "Here's a guest pass for two," she said while handing the pass to her. "I look forward to meeting your husband."

"Great!" She said. "Party of The Gerswins," she read aloud off the card. "The Gerswins? I thought your last name was Morgan?"

"It is," Mikel confirmed. "That's the name we use when we're there. It's a play on letters of another name if you look closely enough.

She paused for a moment to study the letters. "Oh, my God! How cute."

"I think she's got it," Zuri said.

"Well, I am a librarian you know."

Zuri, smiled. "Well, I can't wait to meet your husband. Do you think he'll be fine with this?"

"He'll be surprised as to how this got initiated, but I'm pretty sure he'll be more than okay with it. I must warn you though, he likes to watch. So he may need a little coaxing."

"I'll make a note of that. Here's my cell phone number and the time that we'll meet there," Zuri said as she wrote on a piece torn out from her daily planner.

"Thanks. Well, I better get back to work. It was very nice meeting you Zuri. And Mikel. Make sure your candle is ready, too, birthday boy," Ayanna said as she stood up to leave, giving Mikel a seductive look and a wink.

Mikel dared not reply to Ayanna's remark the way he wanted to while his wife was present—at least not until next week. "I'm sure it's going to be a birthday I won't forget," he said, choosing his words carefully.

"Bye. Bring the key back down when you're done," Ayanna said as she left the room closing the door behind her.

"That didn't go too bad at all, honey," Zuri said.

"It went pretty well. I'm excited. You excited?"

"Yeah, I am. I'm eager to meet her husband."

"If Ayanna is any reflection I'm sure they're a great swing couple for us."

"I think you're right."

They both looked at the key left on the table by Ayanna.

"You, know. This room is sound proof," Mikel said.

"So when I make you scream no one can hear it," Zuri said. "Come on, big boy. Let's save our energy for next week's hump night."

* * *

It was 8:05 p.m. Wednesday night a week later when Mikel and Zuri arrived at The Hedo Den. When they entered, they saw Ayanna standing over at one of the open bars with a tall, handsome man with long, dark hair neatly combed back behind his ears down to his shoulders. His chiseled features went perfect with his intentional five o'clock shadow. He was casual, but sharply dressed in an all white collared-shirt tucked perfectly in his black designer trousers. He had a hand wrapped around Ayanna and the other wrapped around a drink.

"Hi," Zuri said as she and Mikel approached the couple.

"Hi and happy birthday, Mikel," Ayanna said.

"Thank you," Mikel replied.

"This is my husband, Tristan."

"Nice to finally meet you," he said with a strong French accent, shaking both their hands.

"Happy anniversary," said Zuri.

"Thank you," Tristan said, taking in an eyeful of Zuri.

"So what are we drinking there, Tristan?" Mikel asked.

"A Slippery Nipple," he said.

"Of course. Bartender! I'll have a Slippery Nipple as well. Ladies?"

"No, thank you, babe. I'll wait until later," Zuri said while ogling at Ayanna's Wonder Bra enhanced breasts as they oozed out of her turquoise baby doll dress."

"I'm still working on mine," Ayanna said showing her glass and adjusting her girls at the same time.

Moments later a man approached the group. "Gerswins Party, your private room is ready. Please follow me."

"Thank you," Mikel said, accepting a key from the man.

The group followed the man to a wall of elevators. "Take this elevator to the second floor. Your room is to the left when you step out. Room 269."

"Thanks."

The group got onto the elevator. "So what do you have planned, Mikel?" Ayanna asked.

"My plan is quite simple. It's to have my way with you while my wife watches. But based on the way she hasn't taken her eyes off your husband since we got here, I have a feeling she won't be watching for too long—if at all."

"Then it looks like my fantasy will be fulfilled at the same time then. I've dreamed of this moment—daydreamed it actually."

"What?" Mikel said with a confused look on his face.

"I told Tristan all about you. As my fantasy man that is. Tristan and I openly discuss who our fantasy lovers would be. And you've been mine for a good while now, Mikel, so I hope you're ready.

"I knew it," said Zuri under her breath before adding with a smile, "I'm beginning to think that she willed this entire event."

They entered the room. Off to the left was large red bowl with an assortment of brand name condoms. Ayanna walked over to bowl.

"What size?" she asked.

"Take a guess," Mikel replied.

"I'm not good at guessing, Mikel." She walked over to him and slipped her hand down the front of his pants. "Oh! Okay. How far down does it go, Mikel? My God. Glad I checked. Let's me know what I'm in for."

They all continued further into the room. Ayanna was ahead of them, making appreciative sounds at the intimacy of the room: two king-sized beds with lots of pillows, two Cleopatra love sofas, and a mirrored ceiling.

Mikel sat down on the edge of one of the beds. Ayanna saw this and made her move.

"Perfect. That's right where I want you," she said.

She walked over to him, stood in between his legs, and leaned forward, pulling the straps of her dress off her shoulders. She unhooked the front of her bra and her heavy breasts tumbled out onto his eager face. He instinctively took her left breast in his mouth and began to suck and circle her nipple with his tongue as he clinched it gently between his teeth. He did this for long moments, making her gasp. She grabbed the back of his head and pulled him in tighter against her bosom.

"Yes, Mikel," she moaned. "Nibble a little bit harder for me, baby. Leave your mark."

He obliged. Engulfing a majority of her breast in his mouth, he sucked and chewed her swelling nipple like a newborn baby starving for his mama's milk. He could feel the dampness between her legs as he cupped her panty-free buttocks from underneath her baby doll dress. He briefly guided her up off his lap so he could unbuckle his belt to save his full-blooded cock from asphyxiation. He, too, wore no underwear. He kicked off his shoes and slid off his trousers while she stood up, compromising her straddle. He sat back down and lowered her wet pussy against the underbelly of his thick stiff cock. Clutching the cheeks of her buttocks he pressed her closer, guiding her pussy lips up and down against his thick-veined shaft. Teasing her. Letting her know what was to come.

He picked her up with ease and stood and turned her around until she sat on the edge of the bed. In the same motion, he kissed her long, deep and wet, making her tongue chase his. He pulled away slowly and tactfully slid his tongue down the length of her swan-like neck, then into her cleavage, and down toward her naval where he paused long enough to send a pleasurable shiver up her spine. She spread her legs apart as he trailed his tongue to the dampness of her treasure of pleasure.

She slowly fell backwards on top of a couple of small pillows, which aided in arching her back. She spread her legs farther apart.

He wasted no time as he slowly licked his way up from her inner thigh, circling her fleshy mound all in one long wet stroke with the tip of his tongue. He deliberately avoided her clit and she knew this.

"Don't fuck with me, Mikel. Suck my fucking pussy," she demanded.

This was the first time he'd heard the librarian swear. He loved it. She was letting loose. He obeyed and wasted no time in using his lengthy tongue, slipping it in her as deep as he could, stroking his tongue meticulously along the inner walls of her vagina.

"Oh fucking God, yes!" she moaned.

With his tongue buried in her pussy he began to suck her clit. He sucked at it for what seemed like an eternity. Her flowing juices, mixed with his saliva, drooled from the sides of his mouth, trickling down her crotch and between her buttocks. The harder he sucked the wetter she got. He was literally gulping her girl-juice down as her body went in to minor spasms.

"Shit, Mikel! You really know how to lick a girl's pussy. "Oooo! That's it, baby—right there. Don't hold back, baby," she said as she lay in total bliss, eyes half-lidded, looking in the direction of her husband who was leaning against the wall near the other bed still sipping on his Slippery Nipple watching them—and watching Zuri.

Zuri was sitting on a red Cleopatra love chair just across from Mikel and Ayanna and was having lustful thoughts of ravishing Tristan. In all her glory and her smiling femininity, she sat there alluringly caressing her clitoris.

And sure enough, Tristan could not resist as long as his wife thought he would. He put down his drink and started over toward Zuri. He stood directly in front of her where she sat. He ran his firm fingers through her long, silky black hair with both hands from front to back, and then grabbed two fistfuls of hair.

With her head tilted back and her big, round, gray eyes affixed to his, she began to unbuckle and unzip him. It didn't take long to release his girthy cock from its confines as his pants puddled around his ankles. She began to do what her husband was doing to Ayanna. The Gerswins were very adept when it came to oral sex and their new young swing friends didn't know what they were in for.

Zuri liked what she saw. She immediately licked him from behind his heavy balls and up the length of his shaft, stopping at the slit of his bulbous head, French kissing it with hard flicks and deep darts of her tongue as she gripped and squeezed his cock tightly at the base.

Tristan decided to participate and slowly moved his hips back and forth, groaning on every stroke as he looked up into the mirrored ceiling. Methodically pacing his movements as Zuri grabbed his butt cheeks every so often in effort to deep throat his huge organ.

To prolong her pleasure, their pleasure, Mikel continued licking, teasing, and deliberately avoiding Ayanna's clit on every long lick of her slit.

"Oh, God! Take me there, Mikel," she moaned as she ground her pussy further into his mouth. Ayanna blindly reached for one of the contraceptives above her head, ripped it open, brought it down between her legs, and waved a chocolate-colored condom in front of Mikel. He saw this while he was nose-deep into her muff. He wasted no time, got up, and walked around to the side of the bed sporting his huge erection.

Ayanna leaned to her side, reached up, and expertly rolled the chocolate condom over the length of his virtuous cock. Her shapely legs were still up and spread apart. Mikel's large warm hands moved over her thighs as he rotated her body on the bed to the side where he was standing so he could see what Zuri and Tristan were doing while he filled Ayanna with his chocolate covered cock. He cupped his palms behind her knees, pushing them back onto the bed at the sides of her breasts, then slowly penetrated the wet folds of her labia, clinching his buttocks as he eased his way high up inside her, before he began to undulate his hips into a rhythmic crescendo of deep long strokes that sent him and her to new heights.

Ayanna moaned with delight at the way his cock felt inside her. It felt wickedly longer and harder with each thrust, sending her floating on a wave of pleasure she could never describe.

"I want you to really fuck me, Mikel! I want to feel your balls inside me. You do whatever you want, baby, but I want you to fuck me like you never fucked any other woman."

Zuri heard this. She raised her head and frowned before turning her attention elsewhere.

Tristan and Zuri were already well settled into a sixty-nine. Zuri was on top lying comfortably across his hard chest and cobblestone abs, with a rock-hard French cock in her mouth as he licked the wet folds of her pussy and sucked her clitoris with a fury. Her pelvis convulsed as she felt the powerful orgasm grip her, then exploding, sending shock waves of pleasure throughout her body.

His cock began to throb and his body started to quiver as she continued to slurp, squeeze, and stroke his succulent manhood. Soon Zuri's mouth was filled with his life-giving juice, gushing as she sucked every last drop out of him.

The Gerswins   Keeb Knight

Mikel and Ayanna were lost in a world of untamed passion. There was only his cock splitting her, lifting her, and driving her remorselessly to a silent yet deafening explosion of pleasure. As she arched her back, she crossed her legs tightly around his hips. Her breasts bounced up and down, while his big strong hands clutched her buttocks, controlling the rhythm of thrusting that filled her ravenous wet pussy on every stroke, her mouth filled with his generous tongue.

"Yes! Yes," she screamed as she wound her hips to the pleasure of the dogged thrusts of his unyielding cock that pressed against her spot just right, causing a mind-numbing orgasmic wave of pleasure and ecstasy. She bucked uncontrollably, gasping repeatedly and then melted underneath him, and he into her arms.

"Mikel?"

"Yes?"

"I need to tell you something."

"What is it?"

"Your library card expired today. Can you stop by the library sometime to renew it when you have chance?"

"Yes, of course."

"Bitch!" Zuri muttered.

Costume Party
By Sage Vivant

A large man in a *bauta cappello* mask held out a white-gloved hand. "Invitation, please," he said from behind the golden mask. His voice was controlled and refined but decidedly baritone. Celeste thought she detected a European accent but couldn't be certain.

Benjamin handed the man the parchment card with their names inscribed on it. After a cursory inspection, *bauta cappello* pushed some magic button in an invisible place, and the impressive wooden door of the mansion slowly opened.

"Welcome," the man said warmly. "Enjoy yourselves."

Benjamin knew Celeste's trepidations exceeded his own, so he took her hand and led the way inside. In his dark-skinned Pantalone mask, he felt the confidence that anonymity provided. Behind him in her exquisitely painted civette mask, Celeste felt her fears subside a little. Nevertheless, she shook her head when Benjamin asked if she wanted to check her cloak. He decided to keep his, as well. If they needed to make a speedy exit, he didn't want to have to stop to retrieve them.

Lighting consisted of several hundred candles and a few gaslights mounted on the walls. Although the ceilings were high, the subdued illumination cast ominous shadows and gave the illusion of smaller spaces. Corners disappeared almost entirely. Dark wood reigned and most of it was carved and polished to perfection. The atmosphere was as spooky as it was majestic.

Several long tables were lined up in the middle of the enormous room. An abundance of food graced all of them. Grapes, bananas, caviar, cheese, chocolate, and assorted breads and crackers were arranged in artful piles, and wine bottles dotted every available space on the tabletops. Despite the decadence they implied, the noise level in the great room was surprisingly low. Over a steady din of murmurs were strains of Mozart's *Eine Kleine Nachtmusik*.

Very little at this mysterious party suggested that its guests were anywhere other than the 18th century.

Benjamin and Celeste meandered past the luscious offerings at the tables but neither of them could eat. As their eyes adjusted to the light, they began to notice that most of the fifty or so guests gravitated to the perimeters of the room. Benjamin tried to read Celeste's expression but couldn't because of her mask.

"Would you like to explore a bit?" he asked quietly. Her hand was still in his, and he'd noticed that it was still as chilled as when they'd been outside.

She nodded, a small smile twitching at the corners of her mouth.

Her strawberry blonde hair was piled high on her head in beautifully fashioned cascades of curls. When her hair stylist had asked what the occasion was for her sophisticated up-do, Celeste had been pleasant but evasive. "A costume party," had been all she'd divulged. Anything more was nobody's business. But the hairstyle added a good four inches to her 5'8" stature, and combined with her high heels, she was now taller than Benjamin.

Two days earlier, the couple had visited a costume shop that specialized in outfits for the annual Renaissance Fair, because she fancied a corset that would cinch her waist and accentuate her breasts—she had always secretly desired to dress like a bawdy maid and she viewed this party as her opportunity. Benjamin encouraged her to buy whatever she wanted, but the truth was that he was eager to see her dressed as a bawdy maid, as well. Together, they selected a forest green satin corset trimmed in braided gold filigree. When the store clerk paired it with a velvet skirt in a rich violet color, Celeste knew she had her ensemble. She handpicked the civette mask from the case because it was not only gold but contained accents of both the green and purple in her outfit.

For his own tastes, Benjamin chose the Pantalone mask because he enjoyed knowing that it represented a rich merchant of Venice. A burgundy-colored chamois tunic and trousers completed his outfit.

Just as they turned away from the table to begin their exploration, a man appeared in a black, unadorned civette mask and a regal, royal blue cape that ended at his knees to reveal black leggings. He plucked a grape and held it before Celeste's mouth. The act was so unexpected, her lips parted automatically to taste the morsel of fruit he offered. As she chewed, he spoke.

"I understand why skin as fair as yours might need shielding from sunlight, but I assure you, milady, it is protected here in this most special of sanctuaries."

His voice was educated and cultured. His manner was courteous. Benjamin felt that if they walked away from the man at this moment, there'd be no ugly scene.

"On behalf of many curious men who ardently appreciate feminine beauty, I implore you to remove your cloak," the man continued. "I would be honored to assist you, in fact." He held out a black-gloved hand and his full mouth widened into a warm smile.

"And please allow me to introduce myself," he continued. "I am Agostino, a frequent guest." He bowed with a flourish of a hand gesture and one leg extended.

"I'm Benjamin and this is my wife, Celeste," Benjamin said, extending his hand. The bow may have been appropriate for Agostino, but he'd be damned if he was going to do it and possibly make a fool of himself.

"Hello," Celeste said softly, grateful that Benjamin had interjected himself in the exchange.

"Enchanted," Agostino said. "Please, Celeste, allow me to take your cloak."

She looked from Benjamin to the stranger, and decided she was indeed growing overheated. She untied the strings at her neck and allowed Agostino to take possession of the garment.

"Ah!" he gasped, sweeping the cloak across his arm. "As exquisite as I suspected. Your skin is a creamy revelation!"

With that pronouncement, he fed her another grape, this time more slowly, deliberating controlling the speed at which she accepted and chewed it. He watched, licking his lips.

"You have unearthed yet another unearthly creature, my pet," purred a brunette in a cat's head mask of pink and white. She wore a black catsuit with pink slashes at her ribs. "Please excuse my husband's enthusiasm for beautiful women," she told Celeste. "It is his only weakness."

Agostino laughed heartily but not audibly. "I fear that Alice is right," he admitted, turning from Benjamin and Celeste to Alice. As swiftly as he'd selected a grape, he now tucked his fingers into the slit crotch of Alice's

Costume Party

Sage Vivant

catsuit. The slit ran from her navel, between her legs, and up to the small of her back. It would not have been apparent had Agostino not deliberately parted it to show Benjamin and Celeste her pale skin beneath it. "And my wife's only weakness is her insistence on easy access."

Agostino plunged deep into the slit to finger Alice's crotch, but the woman was not the least bit fazed. She smiled and extended her hands to Benjamin and Celeste. "Won't you come with us for a little while?"

Celeste's pulse pounded in her ears. Benjamin's mouth went dry. They exchanged quick glances that determined nothing because they couldn't discern each other's expressions. Benjamin tried to read Celeste's thoughts by interpreting her posture, or the way she held her mouth. He did not sense fear from her.

Celeste wanted him to say yes. She fervently hoped he would understand what she wanted, even though she was too shy to say it herself.

Benjamin took one of Alice's hands. Relieved, Celeste took the other. Together, they followed the shapely cat woman to a dark corner of the room. As they passed by the shadowy recesses between wall and floor along the way, Celeste caught glimpses of contorted bodies in intimate contact. Benjamin heard moans punctuated by heavy sighs. Celeste tried to remind herself that her mask gave her more freedom to steal a glance or two, and that everyone else's masks liberated them from accusation and fear. Still, she didn't want to gawk—it seemed unsophisticated.

Benjamin's cock had been undergoing a slow, stiffening process since he and Celeste had arrived at the mansion. Something about the way Agostino fed Celeste the grapes . . . Even the way he addressed her felt erotically charged. And when he had helped himself to Alice's pussy without any embarrassment, Benjamin moved from stirred to shaken.

Agostino parted the taupe-colored velvet curtains that hid their corner hideaway from onlookers. Celeste wondered to herself how people claimed their various spots—did they purchase them like church pews or theater seats?

Their corner was the size of an average American bedroom. It was lined with a three-foot tall banquette upholstered in an understated taupe and red paisley pattern. Red pillows of varying sizes and thickness were strewn about. The little corner looked quite a lot like a miniature harem.

Agostino gestured to one of the benches and nodded his masked face at Celeste. He placed her cloak on the same bench. "Please have a seat, my luscious beauty," he said, keeping his voice low, despite the added privacy.

Costume Party   Sage Vivant

Benjamin noted how soothing the man's demeanor was and how Celeste was probably responding positively to it. As if to prove him right, Celeste moved to the spot Agostino indicated.

Agostino knelt before her. Alice curled up—catlike—on the opposite banquette, grinning behind her kitty mask. She patted the space next to her in a silent instruction for Benjamin to sit there.

"Beautiful, beautiful breasts," whispered Agostino, running his palms over the swell of Celeste's tits over the corset. He caressed them and let them awe him into silence. Celeste waited, breathless, for his next move. Benjamin was on alert, ready to pounce if the man mishandled her.

But with every circular motion of the man's hand, Celeste felt her body lean in closer to him. His breath warmed her cleavage, enveloping her in his invisible web. Mozart's music swirled in her head as Agostino put his lips to the spot where her breasts parted.

"Will you reveal them to me, lovely Celeste?" he asked, with his fingertips poised to peel away her corset from her body.

"Yes," she whispered.

With one highly adept movement, he pulled the fabric forward and lifted her breasts up, holding them like succulent fruit whose juice he craved. His tongue circled one areola, then the other. Benjamin watched as her nipples blossomed and darkened.

"How very responsive she is," Alice murmured to no one in particular. "Surely this is having an effect on you, Benjamin?"

He hadn't expected to be addressed and so he paused, staring at Alice's mask while he collected his thoughts.

"Why don't you remove your cloak? I can keep it here, next to your wife's," Alice continued. Her tone was honey, oozing over his subconscious until his thoughts were sticky and immobile.

He fumbled with the ties of his cloak, so she helped him. She stood to take the cloak, placed it on top of Celeste's then knelt before him. How she extracted his dick so efficiently, he would never be sure, but the heat of her mouth surrounded it before he could analyze the situation.

Agostino delivered gentle nibbles to Celeste's hardening nipples. Her eyelids fluttered as her eyes rolled to the back of her head. Her panties worked overtime to absorb the tremendous rush of moisture between her legs. She was vaguely aware of Alice's attentions to Benjamin's cock and yet seeing it made her decidedly wetter.

Costume Party   Sage Vivant

Alice's oral skills were potent. When combined with the visuals of Agostino's teething at Celeste's tits, Benjamin's balls unleashed a torrent of come into Alice's mouth. Clearly, even she had not expected such a quick eruption, for she squeaked as it passed over her tongue.

The moment Alice believed Benjamin had given her all he had, she removed him from her mouth and touched her husband's arm. Agostino released Celeste's deep pink nipple and leaned toward his wife. With her mouth still full of Benjamin's ejaculate, she gave her husband a long, deep kiss. Benjamin and Celeste watched, transfixed, as the couple savored another man's come.

The kiss lasted a while. So long, in fact, that Benjamin and Celeste silently agreed that their presence was redundant. They unobtrusively left the couple's sexy sanctum santorum, remembering to grab their cloaks. Agostino and Alice were oblivious to their departure, which made the escape all the easier.

When they were in the middle of the room once again, where the murmurs of party guests combined with moans for an eerie, consistent din, Benjamin noticed that Celeste's breasts were still exposed. Celeste saw him notice and grinned sheepishly, but she made no attempt to cover herself.

Just as Benjamin was about to inquire further into this uncharacteristic behavior, a vampirish couple lounging against a banquette gestured for them to approach. Their party space was smaller than Agostino and Alice's—it was not a "corner lot"—but it was ample enough to hold a small round mattress covered in velvet pillows. Sapphire blue curtains were pulled back with violet tassels, giving either the space or the center of the room the appearance of a stage, depending on one's perspective. The gothic makeup on the inhabitants did not give them a ghoulish look but rather a delicate, intriguing one, especially as they sat there, smiling in their black attire. As the woman's finger curled to invite Benjamin and Celeste into their lair, they saw that it was very long and very red.

"Do you want to?" Benjamin whispered under his breath.

But Celeste didn't hear him. She was already halfway to the blue curtains. Benjamin stared in disbelief. Was this his reserved, shy wife of thirteen years?

Celeste paused at the curtains and turned to look for Benjamin, whose face betrayed his surprise. She almost giggled at how disconcerted

Costume Party   Sage Vivant

he looked, but then realized how strange her curiosity must seem to him. It baffled her, as well, and yet the compulsion to squelch it eluded her.

"Please come in, you beautifully-nippled child," the man said. "Those morsels look far more tasty than what's on the buffet tables." His brown hair was slicked back and his eyebrows accentuated. He parted his black robe to reveal a hairless, naked body sporting an advanced erection. His brilliant red mouth smiled to reveal modest fangs.

"And do bring in your handsome escort," the woman added. She was a less endowed version of cinema star Elvira, complete with long black dress and chopped black hair. Her large, kohl-rimmed eyes glittered. Her lips matched those of her partner's but when she smiled, no fangs were in evidence.

Celeste reached her hand out to Benjamin, who clasped it instantly. He was still on the alert for signs that she might want to make a quick and painless exit. Instead, she tugged him into the vampire couple's space.

"I am Fitzroy and this is Ernestine," the man said, not extending his hand.

"I'm Benjamin and this is Celeste," Benjamin replied, nodding.

"Well, Benjamin and Celeste, Fitzroy and I are not ones for words. We prefer action. And the moment we saw the two of you, we wanted to see you in action."

Benjamin and Celeste exchanged glances, uncertain of what these vampires were trying to say.

"Benjamin, we'd be simply delighted if you took the lovely Celeste doggy style right here in our quarters," Fitzroy explained, stroking himself.

Celeste stared, fascinated by the man's ease as much as by his impressive cock size. Although she'd never received such a proposition before, she couldn't say she objected to it. If someone wanted to watch Benjamin fuck her, she rather liked the idea of obliging them.

Benjamin, whose exhibitionist streak was no secret to Celeste, welcomed the request. He looked at Celeste to confirm her interest, and seconds later, Celeste was on her knees on the round mattress, with Benjamin stuffing his dick inside her.

"Ohhhh, yes," Fitzroy commented as Benjamin drove in and out of Celeste. "Ernestine, aren't they a charming couple?"

Benjamin and Celeste kept one eye on the vampires to see what they were doing. Both were masturbating, but Fitzroy was much further along than Ernestine, who rubbed herself through the fabric of her dress.

"They are indeed," Ernestine replied. "They make my blood run hot."

A moment later, Fitzroy slumped forward and landed on his knees before Celeste. He masturbated a little more and then offered his prodigious erection to her. Its size and shape attracted her so much, she needed no more of an invitation to open her mouth and accept it.

For the first time in her life, Celeste enjoyed two cocks simultaneously. Benjamin's pumped harder at her pussy as Benjamin watched her suck off Fitzroy. As she thought about how she must look to anyone who passed by, she felt her cunt get tighter and warmer.

And juicier.

She saw movement from the corner of her eye and realized that Ernestine had risen and was heading for Benjamin. She couldn't see what the lady vampire had in mind but she hoped that Benjamin would like it at least as much as she was enjoying eating Fitzroy's dick.

Ernestine's long red fingernails danced between Benjamin's cheeks, tickling his balls and threatening to advance on his asshole. Her touch fueled his thrusts into Celeste, who began to moan into Fitzroy's knob.

"What a divine asshole you have, Benjamin," Ernestine said slowly and distinctly, as if to be sure that all participants heard her. "I simply must lick it."

She wasted no time spreading his clenched cheeks and helping herself to his sphincter. Although the position was not ideal for her, surely, she gave him a glorious rim job, circling him with sensual precision for several minutes.

"Would you ride me, Beautiful Celeste?" Fitzroy rasped. "Ride my fat cock so I can suck your titties?"

Celeste stopped sucking and smiled up at the vampire. As she moved to accommodate his request, Benjamin was forced to withdraw from her. His balls were near the bursting point, and he turned to Ernestine for relief.

"Don't you worry, Benjamin. I'm going to ride *your* fat cock," the lady vampire assured him.

Fitzroy returned to his seat at the upholstered banquette. Celeste dropped her skirt to the floor, placed her knees on either side of the man's thighs, and mounted him as if she did it all the time. The sight of her straddling the mysterious fanged man hardened Benjamin further, especially when he saw the heavy balls and thick rod that awaited her.

Costume Party — Sage Vivant

Celeste felt herself cream as Fitzroy eyed her breasts and passed his fingers over her glistening cunt. As his girth filled her, light-headedness threatened to upset her balance. He stuffed her so thoroughly, she wanted to cry out.

Ernestine smiled indulgently as Benjamin watched Fitzroy and Celeste. "Sit down next to them," she said softly.

Soon they were copycats to Fitzroy and Celeste, with Ernestine riding Benjamin in a rhythm syncopated with Celeste's. Ernestine had hiked her dress up to her waist to expose a pantyless cunt. She rode Benjamin with the agility of a gymnast, using his neck as her anchor as she slammed down on him hard. Her pussy juices smeared across her thighs as well as his.

As Celeste bobbed up and down on Fitzroy's cock, she let out a small yelp when Ernestine's fingernail began to play at her ass. She looked Benjamin in the eye to see if he knew what the woman was doing while she rode him, and it was at that moment that he noticed it. Fitzroy lapped at Celeste's nipples with his eyes closed, missing the exchange entirely.

Ernestine's skillful fingering was the icing on the cake. The sensations pushed Celeste toward a staggering climax, and the sight of her in the throes of such passion triggered Benjamin's orgasm. Ernestine felt it coming and disengaged from him. Fitzroy lifted Celeste off his cock before he, too, joined the *petite mort* club. Both men shot powerful loads that spurt high and fast into the darkness.

The men then positioned the women to replace them on the banquette, leaning them to rest against the mahogany walls to aid in their recovery. Celeste and Ernestine looked at one another and smiled, with Celeste unable to stifle a contented giggle. Ernestine reached between her own legs to wipe at her wetness, and then spread it over one of Celeste's nipples.

"Would you like some wine, darling?" Ernestine asked her as she rubbed her pussy juice into Celeste's skin.

"Yes," Celeste cooed. "I'd love some." She winked at Benjamin, who winked right back. It appeared that they would be there a while.

Plato's Retreat
By Karmen Red

My pace quickens as I think of jumping Jenny when she arrives. I crave just a little taste, to tide me over, to start our trip out with a bang, to enjoy Jenny as long as she lasts. Karl and I have taken a few small excursions with her, our girlfriend for the last three years, but this trip we're particularly excited about. We anticipate completing Jenny's first time to New York City with our latest find in Manhattan's nightlife, Plato's Retreat. Now that it's the 80's, swinging is exploding with clubs catering to almost every desire and fantasy. What a bisexual gal's delight—infinite possibility from an abundant buffet, alluring and promising. Plato's stands alone as the pinnacle of a swing club, famous in its own time, a hotbed of disco dancing, captivating people, swinging, surprises, and amazements.

Jenny's due soon to scheme sexy dance outfits with us, then we depart in the morning. The three of us leave a scorching path wherever we go, but Jenny and I blend our heat so uniquely we leave no one untouched. My nipples stiffen under my tank top as I reflect on our many matching outfits, how we dress to themes at our favorite local clubs, winning contest after contest, exposing our erotic harmony. A twitch, then another, between my legs and I am utterly distracted. I change the 8-track to blues, as we'll be dancing to disco this weekend. The beat rouses my eroticism as I lose myself in a zealous illusion, cares drawn out of my body with multiple tongues, fingers, and . . .

Karl walks in, holding a few pairs of slacks in one hand and a jacket and shirts in the other. He fusses about clothes more than any man I've known who isn't gay. That's okay, he always looks handsome.

"Suki, should I bring the navy or white slacks for dancing?"

"The white shows up better on a dark dance floor, especially with some black lighting and strobe," I say, as I pick a red silk shirt with its wide, pointed collar to go with the slacks. We make such a stunning couple, threesome, foursome, or whatever. A tender kiss warms and comforts me, aided with a tickle from his full sandy-haired mustache, curving all the way to the jaw line. Always sporting something unique, I remind him to bring his gold neck charms; a nude woman riding a half moon, another a flasher figure with a cock that pops out at the push of a lever, with a hot, red ruby on the tip. We love to creatively indulge our exhibitionist sides, at clubs and at our home parties, but the clubs satisfy our voyeuristic natures as well.

Jenny bounces in with all her smiles and innocent good nature. Her tall, willowy dancer's body is perfectly suited for the halter catsuit she brought with her, unlike my petite Japanese frame. Her tit-length blonde hair barely needs curling tongs to form "Farrah hair", the big wispy flicks away from her face. My normally straight black hair is too heavy to keep flicks for long, so I've got massive volume with a perm, curls cascading just below my shoulders. Overall I'm pleased with my exotic looks, even with a bit too much nose from the Cherokee side. It finds itself useful against a throbbing clit, like when I'm buried in Jenny's fine, delicate powder puff of pussy hair. The softest Karl has felt as well, we nuzzle our faces often, the smell of her salacious sweetness urging us deeper.

"Jenny, we have a surprise for you," Karl says, as I pull out a little black box. She opens it and removes a pair of gold nipple rings, with sapphire blue drops.

"You have to try them on," I say, pulling off her midriff top and fastening them on, pinching a little tighter with the adjustable tension.

"Okay, that's it, we have to finish packing," I say, just producing the nipple rings for a tease. Our aches for each other will only grow more intense as we wait. We try on outfits, prancing about for Karl's opinion. Our transformational exercise grows hotter with each change of costume. Jenny's beside me wearing gold spandex pants, which serve as a second skin, magnifying her rump with every shimmer of light. I'm wearing a matching silver pair. Before long we're slow dancing, crotches grinding. I strip off Jenny's remaining clothes, caressing her skin of fresh cream. Now we're in matching thigh high boots, one pair white, the other pair red. Karl leisurely undresses as well, getting in the spirit of things by grabbing pieces of our outfits to assist us, occasionally seeing how they work for him.

"Not your color, babe, and a bit small. What's that lump sticking out?"

"I sucki Suki," Karl says in his animated Japanese play on my name.

"No, *we* sucki Suki," Jenny corrected, and they do. I grab Karl in and the three of us fervently romp until at last we snuggle and fall asleep. Respecting that Karl and I need our own space, especially if she doesn't return to her apartment for a while, Jenny retreats to the guest bedroom, where she has two dresser drawers and half a closet. The three of us are inseparable, seeming more like a couple than a threesome. I credit our longevity in part to Karl and me, secure and stable as a couple, knowing we must communicate, be excited about, and gel with, whoever shares our innovative sexual play, and often our friendship and love as well. About five years ago we had to let someone go who we loved being with, which was difficult for both of us. We couldn't jeopardize our relationship, which is primary, or our established terms.

We wake to smells of bacon and fresh coffee and follow them to Jenny making breakfast for us. We devour it, then devour a bit of each other, just a quickie, then head to the airport. Discussions and dares about Jenny's initiation into the Mile High Club, and our gluttony, ensue until all of the sudden we're in New York. Damn. Perhaps we'll give it a go on the return.

After a short business meeting, Karl joins Jenny and me as we explore Village shops, where we pick up a leather garter belt and bra set with chains and a Barbie dipped in latex. Then we head to the Metropolitan Museum to see their extensive collection of Japanese prints. We love showing Jenny another city besides our own. We're not much older than her, but enough that we feel protective. She hasn't been away from rural life for long, and is still a bit naïve. We don't want to lose her to the vulture-like seductions of "professional swingers", who smell a virgin to the lifestyle and pounce on them. She's comfortable at our regular off-premise club, at a hotel ballroom with open bars, wild themes and contests, and a floor of rooms for further exploration. Sometimes a smaller, more intimate club relaxes a novice swinger. We took Jenny to a club in a rural area once, which started the weekend with nude volleyball, swimming and a barbeque. She was clearly in her element, and the voyeurs feasted as well.

I don't know if we'll have time, but another club we like in NYC is Le Trapeze, in Midtown. It's small and intimate, with soft lighting and classic décor. A friend of Karl's from Long Island brought his wife there for her first time when we were in town. Being with friends enhances many journeys of discovery. Here, the single hot tub is almost in its own little room, just off the locker area. A spiral staircase leads up to the swing

Plato's Retreat   Karmen Red

rooms, divided off a narrow hallway. But Plato's is in a class by itself, world famous already as a hot, hot swing club and disco. We heard Madonna was there last week. I want to see the drag queen who wears a white wedding dress and roller skates to Studio 54.

We hope Plato's isn't too overwhelming for Jenny. Her sensuality absolutely melts us, as does her dancing. Lessening her inhibitions involves a little cocaine, and Quaaludes relax in a delicious, glorious way. The start of the 80s has presented a new generation of mood altering substances. Many initially uncertain lovers have succumbed to their inner desires with such chemical assistance. Jenny's close connection to us assures her trust in this, and she's naturally curious and open to sexual experimentation. Lucky us. The innate exhilaration of genuine, giving, heartfelt sex is unmatched. Blissful moments, already existing, become magnified, elevating the soul.

Chilling indeed is recent news of a potentially fatal new virus called AIDS. Herpes has been all the talk, and now doesn't seem so bad in comparison. Some clubs have started putting condoms in little baskets in the swing areas, along with the lube, towels, occasional eye mask, handcuffs, and other sexual accessories.

Some come just for the adult excitement. Often a couple or group coming together will stick together, getting an added kick from having sex in front of everyone in the semi-private rooms. The three of us sometimes do this. I envision the opulence of the classiest, most beautiful club we attended, in a huge city loft. The mood was set with classical music done with modern sound, nude ice sculptures at the buffet, canopied and curtained beds, and a classy crowd. A local friend joined us there one time, with a girlfriend he begged to go there with. His wife isn't interested in the lifestyle. If men could attend clubs alone, they would be overrun with horny dicks looking for something to stick them in. Those of us who occasionally have a house party make our own rules, as they aren't public. Women are lucky, but we generally behave. I enjoyed the scene before I committed to Karl. For a bisexual gal like me, dating a couple was the ideal situation, especially when not seeking a commitment.

We just have to show Jenny. After a great dinner, we arrive at Plato's. Inside, near the middle of this awesome place accommodating a thousand people or so, is a growing frenzy of disco dancing on a huge dance floor, with semi-nudity and sexy, flirty, and outrageous costumes. To the right is the Olympic sized pool, with waterfalls, surrounded by tables with umbrellas, a food bar against one wall. We catch sight of two couples

Plato's Retreat   Karmen Red

wasting no time, arms and legs flailing about in impossible contortions on an angled bench. Other props and varied pieces of apparatus for creative sex positions dot the pool area, allowing people to display their sexual prowess and acrobatics. Karl and I choose a prop that spreads the legs wide, and we show Jenny what can be done on such a thing. We fool around with some possible positions and play a bit, but not for long—there's so much to see. We take Jenny to the far end of the pool.

"This is the orgy room, where anything goes. When you step in here you surrender yourself to the masses," I explain. Jenny looks through the window, viewing a huge floor covered with mattresses.

"I can't believe it—you can't tell who the arms and legs belong to, you'd never know whose mouth or hand or cock or pussy or fingers are. . ."

"Yes, it's like the orgy room at the club back home, just bigger. The largest one I've ever seen," I say.

Karl adds that in the orgy room, even UFO's (Uglies, Fatties, and Oldies) are guaranteed to get laid. I tease him about being such a snob, but then again, we can afford to be choosy. The orgy room seems just plain animalistic. People here enjoy the natural, yet hedonistic pleasures of lust. I wonder if the orgies and feasts of ancient Rome were any different. The only thing new is the reemergence of a public venue, and group sex for all classes, not just for the amusement of bored aristocrats. The prominent and wealthy do show up here, however, and Jenny hopes Elton John comes tonight.

We put our bag in a locker on the other end, where the showers and the private and semi-private rooms are also. At least two-thirds of the people on the dance floor are semi-nude now, and cocaine flows. We're cautious and don't accept any drugs from strangers, they could be cut with something dangerous. We've been warned that cops often pose as cab drivers out these doors, asking for drugs. It's apparent they're plentiful.

Jenny and I are dynamite dancing together, with our matching gold and silver spandex pants. We create a sensation almost everywhere we go. We're HOT! High on the little bit of coke with us, high on the sexual energy, mesmerized by the mirror balls, strobe lights, and the beat of the disco music, it feels like we're in a mirage of a hypnotic fantasy. Every turn promises a glimpse of an outlandish outfit or costume, and various stages of nudity. The DJ mentions something about us I can't make out, then spotlights us, elevating and energizing our dancing. I take the lead and spin

Jenny around a few times, pulling her in close as we intertwine and hump and grind our crotches together, completing the dance. We're divas celebrating ourselves, loving our power to command attention, to seduce.

Karl joins us for a three-way slow dance. He points out a man in a red velvet smoking jacket who holds a chain attached to a woman's collar and cuffs. She's nude, except for a brown velvet hooded cape and feather mask, dressed as the bird of prey like O in *Story of O*. What an enchanting, mysterious creature, provoking me to explore what's behind not only the mask, but the choice of O. I stare at her in fascination. Sensory overload illuminates an intense sexual promise, which hangs in the air with the music, each breath and beat awakening my desires.

At one or two a.m. people dressed in tuxedos and black tie dresses wander in, settling to eat at the tables by the pool and watch the action. One striking couple arrives, the woman of dark velvet skin, enormous, alluring eyes, and an immaculate Afro adorned with red and gold jewels. Large gold hoop earrings swing with every movement of her head.

"Look at that woman's dress! And her hair!" Jenny says, spotting the woman I'm staring at, especially the red satin full length halter dress, and red patent heels. The man with her sports a white cutaway tuxedo with a black mask. I'm mesmerized. By 2:30a.m. the tables fill with the Who's Who of New York's disco scene, socialites, celebrities, and voyeurs, who are either swingers themselves, or simply wish to be entertained by horny nude people running around. Elton John and Mick and Bianca Jagger had appeared recently, but no one of note was here now...

"Jenny, let's give them something to look at," I say, pulling her closer and kissing her long and hard, caressing her ass, slowly moving toward her crotch, rubbing sensually up and down deep between her cheeks. She responds, and we quickly forgot about our audience. Karl watches from a table, smiling.

We talk later about getting together with that couple. Karl said to dance and have some fun, but otherwise he thought we should stay away from them. Shit. I don't argue or try to persuade him otherwise—if either of us is uncomfortable with someone, for whatever reason, they are a NO. He says he thinks they're too smooth, and his instincts are usually right. They probably were too much for Jenny. Sometimes one of us will make a case for a person or people, and iron out a compromise. This isn't the time or place for that, as we have to consider Jenny as well.

Plato's Retreat

Karmen Red

We lose ourselves on the dance floor. Already high and heady, and intoxicated with this festive matrix, a fog sneaks onto the dance floor, expanding the surreal. It changes from dusty blue, to green, then blood red, and creeps upward, blending with the smell of hot, moving bodies. I feel as if I'm outside my body, observing from somewhere else. Images of brilliant costume flash before me. There's a petite, beautifully full-figured woman with a peacock feather headdress worthy of a Vegas showgirl. She wears nothing else but black platforms and a few feathers over her crotch.

Yet the grand masquerade is later when the cloak of nudity and raw sexuality is worn. Feathers are shown with bodies and sexual technique. Individuality blends into the masses. Threesomes, foursomes, whatever, form their own identity, morphing as they go along, webs of interacting desires. The three of us are tight, a unit, with Karl and I, as a couple, the strong core.

I notice another stunning couple. He's a bit older than us, sophisticated in a nicely tailored jacket, carrying a cane with an ivory nude handle. She's tall, slender, wearing a sexy batwing sleeve dress in a gold satin that glistens in the light, with matching gold platform heels. She carries herself as if an aristocrat, befitting her fine facial features and full lips. Some of the women wear their sexy outfits in the Early Slut fashion, but this woman captivates me with her enticing elegance. I point this couple out to Karl and Jenny, and soon we're talking with Bill and Diane. She's bisexual, as Jenny and I, and Bill's straight, as Karl is, but has strayed on rare occasions.

The Ladies Only dance is announced—Diane and the gorgeous lady with the red dress and fro join us (she saw me staring at her), as others form their own little groups. Nipple sucking, crotch grabbing, and kissing strengthen with each song. The disco beat seems to be louder. Careful not to block the DJ in front, the men form a horseshoe about ten deep around the dance floor, cheering the best shows.

When the men are allowed back on the dance floor, they quickly find their places in the groups of gyrating women, forming longer chains, with no shortage of groping and grinding. Occasionally a man dances behind his lady and steers her, front facing out, into a girl or couple of their interest. The three of us dance with Diane and Bill, kissing, petting, familiarizing ourselves. Arousal ignited, we all agree to continue in a semi-private room, our usual preference. We head toward our respective lockers—the three of us ready now for some mellowing Quaaludes, our supply reserved for times like these.

We change to only shower tongs, take a quick group shower, slowed down only by Jenny and I fussing with the Lily of the Valley scented soap and perfuming ourselves. We show Jenny the row of bidets. She'd never seen one, and once the pulsating water was hitting right on her clit, we didn't think we'd get her off of it.

We head for the semi-private rooms, where we meet up with Diane and Bill. Some of the rooms are out in the open facing each other, but the one we choose has a thin half-wall, cubbyhole-like divider with another room. No one is obligated to do anything, but interested persons will talk to you as if you will, because you're at a swing club after all. Most people are respectful of choices, but we've encountered pushy proposals.

We begin our sexual play with great enthusiasm. Diane's just as stunning naked as she is dressed—beautiful proportions to her hips and full breasts, which aren't too big; but perfect for her. Karl loves that body type also. I find Bill to be amazingly fit, stocky and solid, a commanding figure. He has an enticing crop of curly hair on his chest, black with flecks of grey, like the hair on his head. I can't resist running my fingers through this mass, finding his nipples as I circle about. Karl has fine, light hair, sporting a great head of hair, but not much on his body, with skin softer than mine. I love to stroke the silky hair on his balls and all around his crotch. The contrast of Bill's chest hair helps enliven the whole experience for me.

Soon Karl eats Diane while she sucks Bill, and I kiss and finger Jenny. Before long Karl is fucking Diane, as I sit on her face and kiss him. Bill is with Jenny, and occasionally my hand wanders over to stroke Bill and play with Jenny's perky boobies. No one knows what the next entanglement is—we succumb to the sensual, savoring the flavor. We hear sporadic groans of pleasure from other groups, literally right next to us.

We fall into various contortions, caressing, stimulating, sucking, and fucking. Resisting nothing, we ravish each other with overwhelming zeal. Sensing something, I glance over at Karl, beads of sweat shimmering on his face and chest, perhaps a bit out of frustration, in addition to the drug supplementation. He looks at me deeply, with love and trust in his eyes, wide with a plea to help him out. A new situation or girl sometimes unnerves him, delaying the necessary mechanics. He depends on me in these rare situations. He's come to my rescue at times when the reality of

Plato's Retreat   *Karmen Red*

someone isn't as exciting as the thought or pursuit of them. Karl and I can rouse each other at any time.

Holding Bill's cock with one hand, I reach over and suck Karl's nipple as if a hungry kitten, deeply taking the area in my mouth, then move out to the nipple's edge with increasing suction, focusing on milking it in and out, then flicking it with my tongue. Next I suck his cock, holding the base firmly with my hand. He grows in my mouth, as I open up my throat with impassioned longing, allowing him to fuck all the way down, unimpeded. I stop and quickly steer him into Diane's wet pussy—he barely misses a beat. With an appreciative little grin, he takes it from there, fucking with eager intensity. I ponder with a bit of self-satisfaction the talent I've developed in swing situations—the creative ability to manage multiple mouths, dicks, and pussies to everyone's satisfaction. I often feel it my responsibility to set the tone, and initiate things so no one is unfairly singled out or left out. This adds to my yearning for the three of us to share our spicy eroticism, usually creating an exhilarating time.

The guys take a break and the three of us gals indulge each other, feeding our hunger for female sex. Karl and I sometimes talk about what we both like in a woman, like eating pussy. We also share an appreciation of a woman's unique beauty, as a work of fine art, physically as well as personally. But women with each other often share a personal, empathetic element. I give sex to a woman of my enchantment as I want it given to myself, and find great joy bringing her to ecstasy.

We aren't left alone for long. Diane sits on my face, sucking on someone's cock above my head. Jenny laps at my pussy, losing herself. I hold her head, stroking her hair and tickling her scalp. She's a giving soul, yearning to please, and we're happy to let her do so, returning the favor eventually. I worry that someday she may get hurt, with such a trusting, innocent nature, untarnished as yet. We watch out for her, admittedly with some selfishness—she could be snatched away.

Karl suggests one of my favorite positions with two men. I'm comfortable with everyone here, and my passion, kindled with the Quaalude, has reached a feverish pitch. I suck at Karl a bit, although he's already hard. He puts a fresh condom on, as does Bill, with some lube. I sit on Karl, facing toward his feet, and slide his hard cock into my ass. Then I lean back and Bill gets on top, straddling Karl's legs as his cock finds my pussy.

Plato's Retreat   *Karmen Red*

Now, I'm utterly consumed, my ass and pussy getting fucked simultaneously by two dicks. I rub my clit in hard, circular motions. Jenny twists my nipples and Diane moves about fondling everyone, kissing Bill, kissing Jenny, kissing Karl and me. This is her playground and her choice. I hear the music in the background, as our intensity escalates along with our moaning, and faster thrusts by the men. Jenny is licking Bill's cock and my clit together as he continues to fuck me. He cries out when he comes, and Karl follows. My ardor reaches a hot-blooded burn; I tremble with sensation. Don't stop, please. I want to capture the feeling, but they're done and I didn't cum. So, so close.

Diane heads to the bidets, then joins Bill for a splash in the pool. We're starting to get hungry. We've had enough foreplay *and* play with Diane and Bill to last a long while. Karl and I look at each other with desire for some passionate lovemaking, not the impersonal sex of swinging, which doesn't go beyond an emotional fondness. Swinging reminds us of what we have, and creates a deeper appreciation for each other. Sure, I've fallen in love with some women, and even had some feelings for a man or two, and so has Karl, but we never lose sight of our commitment to each other primarily, and keep communication open. Swinging and having a girlfriend adds diversity and enhances our sex, as well as our relationship. As great as the fucking was with Diane and Bill, I didn't allow myself to cum. My mind and emotions contribute to a passionate surrender, drawing it into lovemaking.

The three of us lay comfortably holding each other, relaxing. We love our time together, just the three of us. We usually have the best sex with our private home parties; we know each other well and are uninhibited. Jenny's in the middle, I'm on the outside in spoon position, snuggled against her soft little rump, my top leg between hers. Karl faces her, his outer leg competing with mine, but I win out. We hold hands across Jenny, look into each other in gratitude for this moment and each other and to have Jenny to share between us. I can stay in this serene moment for eternity, loving Karl and holding Jenny's boobie with my other hand. At home we might take a break, all of us standing naked in the kitchen around the butcher block, eating, laughing. My hunger returns, but I am distracted once again.

"Let's finish where Diane and Bill left off," Karl eventually said to Jenny.

"Sucki Suki?"

Plato's Retreat — Karmen Red

With the love of my life, Karl, and with Jenny, whom I trust absolutely, I divulge every amorous passion and desire. We have the best sex of the night, the osmosis of our sexual energy acting as if a natural evolution. It thrills me to rouse both of them, culminating in their exhilarating climaxes. Now I cum, a full, encompassing, profound cum, resonating deep throughout my whole body, and with my whole being.

Epilogue

Plato's Retreat, an on-premise swing club and disco, gained world fame when it moved in 1977 to the Ansonia Hotel building at 230 West 74th Street, in New York City (it later moved to 509 W. 34th Street). The basement location formerly held Continental Baths, and an upscale gay bathhouse. *Plato's* retained the pool, saunas, and dance floor in its conversion, and instantly became legendary, riding the wave of the disco and sexual frenzy of the late 70s and early 80s, along with *Studio 54* and others in Manhattan. With more than "dirty dancing" happening at *Plato's*, the city closed it in 1985, along with gay bathhouses, in response to the AIDS epidemic. Smaller clubs, less in the public spotlight, remained open. Reopening as *Plato's Retreat 2* in Fort Lauderdale, Florida, it never achieved the fame and reputation as the original. In 2006, it changed to a sex club for men only.

John Updike Made Me Do It
By Donna George Storey

Roots of an Obsession

John Updike made me do it.

He definitely deserves a lot of credit anyway.

Because when I think back on that night in Tahoe, it's almost as if he were right there in the hot tub with us, his lips stretched in a patrician smile as he guided my hand over to caress the rock-hard cock of a man who was not my husband.

Of course said husband was too busy sucking the rosy nipples of the German woman, Katharina, to notice or care. And Jürgen and Jill were already kissing as if they'd done it dozens of times, which they hinted they had when Jill spent her junior year in Bonn. None of them seemed to need John Updike's help, although no doubt they had his blessing.

Updike had been softening me up for this night for years. Sitting in the effervescent spa water with five other horny married people, the Sierras soaring around us into the star-flecked sky, it was just like stepping into the pages of a steamy novel. In fact, it was the same surreal excitement I felt as I devoured *Rabbit is Rich* or *Couples* under the blankets as a teenager. Sneaking them from the bookshelves in my parents' room, I instinctively knew I could only read them when I heard the soft click of their bedroom lock at night.

While my parents "did it" the customary way—with each other in their marriage bed, their lust invisible to the world—the couples in John Updike's stories were fearlessly experimental, so they ended up all jumbled together like Halloween candy in a plastic pumpkin. They'd jet off to the Caribbean where the wives would confer to redistribute sex partners for the night. Or they'd fall into affairs and then confess to their spouses who would graciously consent to sleep with their cuckolded counterparts to

John Updike Made Me Do It   Donna George Storey

even the score. Even Updike's memoirs glittered with shocking transgression. I can't tell you how many times I masturbated to the scene of Updike fingering a neighbor's wife through her ski pants as they drove back from Vermont through a starry winter night.

I knew these were just stories, maybe even pure fantasy, but I sensed, too, that John Updike was giving me a glimpse of the hunger and restlessness of the adult world. What were these people looking for in their swaps and affairs? Did they ever find it?

Would I?

The Games Begin

We'd just passed Auburn on our drive up to Tahoe to spend the weekend with Nick's old friend Jill when the snow started falling hard. Before long, Nick had to pull over and put on the chains. I suppose I started playing the "swinging" game because the poor guy was half-frozen when he got back in the car. With the traffic inching along I-80, we were sure to miss dinner at the cabin. He'd need more than Power Bars and trail mix to warm him up.

I explained the rules to him: we'd take turns naming a couple we knew and then describe what we thought it would be like to swap for the evening. I opened with the most obvious couple in our lives. "How about switching with Grace and Jack?"

Nick's eyebrows shot up. Grace was one of the most talented programmers he worked with and he once mentioned casually that he found her attractive. With her porcelain skin and hourglass curves, I doubt he was alone in that opinion.

"I could see that as a possibility," he said cautiously.

"A possibility? Come on, you'd love it. Grace straddling you, cowgirl style. Those melon breasts jiggling as she rides you. Her pale skin all flushed with arousal. You could grab her nice round butt and knead it while she creamed all over you. Then you'd tickle her ass crack—you're good at that—and when she came she'd probably give that sweet little laugh, like she did when she was drunk at the Christmas party." I giggled in what I thought was a decent imitation of his favorite colleague.

"Jeez, you don't have to get so graphic." It was already dark, but in the glow of the surrounding headlights, I could see he was blushing.

John Updike Made Me Do It Donna George Storey

"What's the matter? Am I giving you a boner?"

Nick shifted in his seat. "So what about you and Jack?"

"I don't know. He's not the worst candidate. But, to be honest he's too good-looking for me."

"*Too* good-looking?"

"Yeah, blond muscle boys like him are used to being worshiped by women. They don't try hard enough. If I'm fucking someone just for the sex, I want a guy who has something to prove."

"You're hard to please." Nick narrowed his eyes at me, but I suspect he liked me that way. "How about Michael and Heather? He strikes me as the ambitious type."

I shook my head. "He's so hairy. And he is ambitious, but not in a good way. He's bound to be selfish in bed. But Heather? With that limber little body of hers you could do it in all kinds of kinky positions. Maybe push her legs to her shoulders until she was practically bent in half? Her vagina would be all stretched and tight like a warm, wet glove, gripping you with every stroke. She's so light; you could do it standing up, too. You could take her up against the wall, her ass banging against it like you were spanking her. I'd bet you'd make a lot of noise, you two."

Nick laughed, discomfort mixed with definite arousal. "Well, I've always thought Heather was nice. So, that makes it two to nothing. Can't think of anyone you'd like to be with?"

I paused. To be honest, I was having so much fun turning him on with my dirty words, I hadn't even thought about it.

"Maybe Jill's German friend will be right for me. If you believe John Updike, vacations are a good time to do a little swinging. The rules of ordinary life don't apply. How about you and Jill?"

Nick grimaced. "Don't even mention Jill, okay? She's practically my sister." He turned and studied my face. "I know you like Ben, though."

"For his mind, darling. He' a little . . . soft . . . for me."

"True. He's not particularly athletic," Nick agreed. "Hey, what's with all of this swinging talk anyway?"

"I was just rereading Updike's *Couples* and everyone's screwing around and swapping like crazy." I closed up the bag of trail mix and leaned back in my seat. "I always wondered how often it happens in real life, though."

Nick glanced over at me again. "Is this something you'd like to try?"

John Updike Made Me Do It   Donna George Storey

"No, I'm just curious," I replied rather too quickly. "How about you?"

"I guess if the right opportunity arises, for both of us, I'd be okay with it. Not that there's much of a chance, being married to Ms. Choosy."

"How can I top perfection?" I said, reaching over to pat his crotch. He was still hard from the fantasy romps with Grace and Heather no doubt. I was pretty damp myself. I knew at least one couple would be having sex at the cabin tonight.

The truth was that the idea of trying a swap with another couple did turn me on, but I never thought in a million years it could ever be more than a game.

Aural Orgy

We finally got to the cabin in King's Beach around eleven. Good old Jill was waiting up for us in the kitchen with a pot of cinnamon tea.

"Sorry about the bad luck with the weather, you guys."

"No problem," Nick said, giving Jill a peck on the cheek. "Maria and I had a nice long talk in the car."

"Actually there's another little complication tonight," she continued. "I thought this place had three bedrooms, but the third queen bed is the sleeper sofa in the living room. Katharina and Jürgen took the bedroom on the other side of the house, and they'll be walking through your room to get to the bathroom."

Nick and I exchanged glances. That could put a dampener on the sex part of our holiday weekend—unless we decided to live dangerously.

"And . . . um," Jill began with an apologetic smile.

"What is it now, Jilly-bean?" Nick said, in not-quite-mock annoyance. In fact, they did act a lot like brother and sister.

"So, you know how Germans are more comfortable with their bodies than Americans?"

Nick shot me a what-the-fuck grin. We were both a bit punchy from the drive.

"Just so you're prepared, sometimes Katharina and Jürgen walk around the house in the nude."

We held our laughter until we were snuggled together on the sofa bed, snowflakes still battering the windows.

John Updike Made Me Do It   Donna George Storey

"Beware the naked Germans," Nick whispered as I muffled my giggles in his shoulder. His hands slipped under my nightshirt and he slowly, teasingly, inched it up over my breasts.

"Hey, are you sure you want to do this? A naked German might walk in on us any minute."

"We can pull them into bed with us. That's what you want, isn't it?" Without waiting for my answer, Nick scooted under the blankets and eased open my thighs. He knew once he got to work with his mouth *down there*, I'd stop arguing.

Sure enough, the instant his tongue met my clit, jolts of familiar pleasure shot through me. I arched back on the bed, but remembered where we were just in time to swallow down a moan. However, to be honest, the thought of fucking in a semi-public place where a stranger might see us turned me on in a big way. Besides, keeping quiet seemed to increase the sensation, sounds of my pleasure trapped and throbbing in my belly. My mind was teeming with images, too, fragments from the evening all tumbled together like trail mix. Nick fucking Grace, while Heather rode his face, their sweat-slick breasts swaying as they writhed in ecstasy. I watched the lewd scene before me while Jill's faceless German friend groped my nude body, pinching my nipple, twisting it, just as Nick was doing in real life now.

I bit the corner of the pillow to keep from crying out. Every moist click of his tongue, every creak of the cheap mattress as I rocked my ass up for more, seemed to roar in my ears like a jet engine.

They could hear everything. They all knew exactly what we were doing.

Suddenly, I heard a soft knocking filtering down from Jill and Ben's room in the loft. *Tap, tap, squeak.* It took a moment before I realized what it was: a headboard nudging the wall, another mattress protesting under the thrusts of joined bodies.

Ben must have been waiting up for Jill. He had to watch the German woman parade around naked all evening and he was desperate for release. Jill was now paying for her friend's provocation as she lay beneath her husband's big body, his dick sliding in and out of her swollen, pink pussy. *Tap, tap, squeak.*

My thighs began to shake. I was close. Nick pulled away and rose to his knees, guiding his cock into my very wet cunt.

He bent forward and his lips closed over mine. We began to move together in our familiar rhythm, making love as we always did. Except tonight we had company.

Tap, tap, squeak.

Now another voice joined the chorus, a low feminine moan, with a hint of Bach. Jill's friends from Bonn were fucking, too. On top of the blankets, of course, their nude bodies fully exposed. The heady mix of sex sounds swirled through my head in an aural orgy, dancing down my spine to gather in my cunt.

We're all fucking. Together. Friends, strangers, fucking, coming. It was too much.

I climaxed, my teeth biting into the pillow. Nick was right behind me, his face twisted in a mute grimace of pleasure.

A few moments later the knocking above and the moans from the front room subsided. I heard six pairs of lips exhale in a collective sigh of carnal contentment.

John Updike couldn't have planned it better.

On My Ass in the Snow

"The Winter Olympians have descended from the slopes," Ben announced, taking the last swallow of his third Irish coffee.

I was still on my second drink, but was definitely feeling the effect. I aimed a jaunty salute at Nick, Jill, Jürgen and Katharina from my perch by the fireplace in the lodge.

Nick swaggered over to me, with that cool-yet-clumsy gait of a man in ski boots. "Don't you look comfy?"

From his tone, he didn't exactly approve. Okay, so I did have my stocking feet resting in Ben's lap, but that was only because my legs were sore from doing the snowplow all morning and Ben kindly offered a massage. At that point it was all completely innocent.

Katharina strolled up and stood close to Nick—too close. They made quite the dashing couple in their ski togs, frosty goggles pushed up on their foreheads. "Your husband is a very good skier."

Her feline eyes twinkled like a German Christmas tree.

John Updike Made Me Do It Donna George Storey

"She's being kind," Nick said, giving her a fond smile. "It took me all morning to get back up to speed. I haven't skied in about six years. You were very patient with me."

"On the contrary, I had trouble keeping up with you. You were very daring."

Maybe it was the whiskey, but I watched all of this with a detached interest, as if I were observing someone else's handsome husband flirting with another woman. It occurred to me, too, that Nick had stopped skiing when we met. Had he stopped being daring, too?

Jill and Jürgen joined the circle. Amusingly, they made a good couple, too. Jürgen was tall with a close-trimmed blond beard and ponytail and looked every inch the Olympic skier. Jill wore her golden hair in a ponytail, too and the stylish red outfit showed her long legs to advantage.

Ben and I were definitely the low-rent pair of our happy group in our rented gear. But I strongly suspected we had just as much fun off the slopes critiquing the elitism of winter sports and redefining our sorry performance in the snow as a protest against the tyranny of consumer capitalism.

"How was your day, sweetie?" Jill gave Ben a quick hug.

"Well, I spent most of the morning on my ass in the snow but things improved considerably when Maria and I decided to hit the bar instead."

"Don't listen to him, Jill. He was the king of the bunny slope. I, on the other hand, spent the *whole* morning on my ass in the snow," I added.

Katharina laughed. "'Bunny slope?' That is very adorable. In German, we call it the 'idiot's hill'."

Nick grinned at her, as if he found *her* adorable.

Ben lips shifted into a crooked smile. "I definitely feel like an idiot with those skinny sticks on my feet. Give me food, wine and the hot tub. Those are my gold medal events."

I giggled conspiratorially and drained my Irish coffee, tipping my head back like a floozy in a beer ad. When I rocked back up again, licking the last bits of whipped cream from my lips, Nick was staring at me, eyes glittering, as if he saw the stranger in me, too.

Updike's Hand

John Updike Made Me Do It   Donna George Storey

Since Ben and I had the easiest day on the slopes, we offered to make the fondue dinner, which also meant the two of us got to loll around in the hot tub in our swimsuits while the others did the dishes.

Fortified by the Riesling, I was telling Ben about John Updike and how I couldn't seem to get him out of my mind. That led to a discussion of Updike as the chronicler of a particular moment in American cultural history—the generation who came of age in the 1950s and experienced the allure and angst of the Sexual Revolution after they were married. It was exactly the sort of mildly provocative intellectual bullshit Ben and I had indulged in all afternoon, but when Nick joined us in his swim trunks, he seemed to feel the need to explain.

"Sorry, Ben, my wife has this fixation on John Updike stories. She likes the spouse-swapping."

Ben arched an eyebrow at me. "I didn't know you were a fan of 'the lifestyle'."

Before I could reply, the sliding doors swished open behind us and Jürgen and Katharina appeared. As Jill promised, they climbed into the hot tub totally nude.

I felt Nick's body stiffen beside me. No doubt he was stiffening in his swim trunks as well. I myself snuck a look at Jürgen: dark blond pubic hair, an uncut dick, and gorgeous thigh muscles. No wonder Jill lingered on the deck in her robe, enthralled at this vision of Nordic male beauty.

"Get in, babe," Ben called, gesturing to the empty place between him and Jürgen.

"I'm not sure I have the nerve to do this," Jill said with a small laugh.

"You've lived in Europe, liebchen. I remember when you were not so shy," Jürgen teased.

Jaw set bravely, Jill took a deep breath and shrugged out of the robe. She practically sprinted the five steps to the hot tub, one arm over her full breasts, the other shielding her crotch.

"The sky did not fall down upon you, did it?" Jürgen said with an indulgent smile. He smiled at the rest of the bathing suit brigade, eyebrows lifted in a dare.

Nick shot back with a "no thanks" and Ben shook his head.

I'm not sure why I rose to the bait. Maybe I wanted to shatter their image of me as a coward and a prude. Or maybe on a subconscious level, I wanted to nudge things along. "Oh, I'm going to get naked. I just thought I'd wait until we all start having sex."

John Updike Made Me Do It   Donna George Storey

Five heads turned to me, mouths gaping.

Jürgen's eyes flickered with approval. "I have no argument with that. Or is this an example of the famous American sense of humor?"

"Don't underestimate Maria," Ben said with his usual I'm-just-joking grin. "She acts innocent, but I'm told she has a wild side. She's into swinging."

"So are we," Jürgen replied matter-of-factly. *He* obviously wasn't kidding.

Katharina's serene smile left no doubt it was true. "It is very refreshing to meet another daring couple," she said, turning to Nick. "I see you agree sex is a healthy adult pleasure also. Like skiing."

Nick and I exchanged a glance. *Be careful what you wish for...*

But I saw something else in his eyes, too, a reflection of my own dark urges. The barriers of ordinary life had indeed softened in the thin mountain air. It was as if I were floating, beyond the rules of time and space. This could be Europe or 1968. We could be our parents or grandparents, taking that first sweet taste of sexual possibility, or characters from a novel whose very existence depended on doing something shocking to keep the pages turning.

I'm not exactly sure who actually made the first move, but things moved quickly from there. Before I knew it, Jürgen bent to kiss Jill, murmuring something softly in German. Katharina took Nick's hand and guided it to her breast, her eyes hooded in lust. This time my husband did not resist the dare. He circled the large nipple with his fingertip then bent to kiss it.

I turned to Ben. We'd been talking all day. This time we spoke with our eyes alone.

Do you want this, Maria?

Do you?

Why wouldn't I? I've had a crush on you forever.

That's funny, just last night I was imagining what you'd be like in bed.

Back when I was dating, I rarely made the first move with a man, but now I curled my fingers around Ben's hard-on. His thick, meaty cock twitched in my grasp and a jolt of forbidden excitement shot through me. At the same time, the odd floating sensation grew stronger, as if part of me were gazing at the scene from far away.

As if the hand reaching out to seal the deal were Updike's, not mine.

John Updike Made Me Do It   Donna George Storey

Compare and Contrast

John Updike didn't write orgies. His couples retired to separate rooms to explore their new partners and pleasures. So did we. The last to touch, Ben and I retired first, claiming his bedroom after stopping in Jürgen and Katharina's room for a condom.

Stripping off our swimsuits, we crawled onto the bed, again without words, as if we were playing out a script we both knew by heart. When Ben kissed me, it wasn't like I thought it would be; sex for the sake of sex. I always imagined unbridled passion, a desperate, animal coupling. But Ben's lips were surprisingly soft and tender. The strange taste of him took me back to high school, when I made out with many different boys, reminding me that kisses are like ice cream, the same creamy treat, but each with a different flavor or spice.

I liked Ben's kisses and his satiny skin, and the heat of his broad body. He was different from Nick who was sinewy and hard. My palm tingled at the new sensation.

Is this what the swingers in the stories were looking for?

"This doesn't seem real," Ben confessed. From the deck below, I heard Katharina laugh, a throaty, sexual sound.

"It isn't real," I said. "We're in a John Updike story."

"I'll have to read his stuff." He smiled and cupped my breast, brushing the nipple with his thumb.

I sighed to show him he got it right.

"You're beautiful, you know," he said, repeating that pleasurable motion until I squirmed and my breath came faster.

I laughed. "Are you trying to seduce me?"

Ben's expression was serious. "I want to make you happy tonight, Maria." He took my hand and guided it between my legs. "Teach me how you like to be touched."

Under the circumstances, a little hands-on tutoring wasn't a bad idea, but in truth it had taken me a while to feel comfortable touching my own pussy in front of Nick.

So I closed my eyes, touched my sweet spot and started to strum. My clit swelled beneath my fingers into a hard, aching diamond. It was just like masturbating in my bedroom as a teenager, biting back my moans while I imagined John Updike rubbing me through my ski pants in the backseat of

John Updike Made Me Do It   Donna George Storey

the car on a wintry night. That is, until Ben's large hand closed over mine, and his very real finger carried on with the task.

I spread my legs wider. Ben was a fast learner. He slipped his left arm around my shoulder to rub one nipple, while he suckled the other. It felt good, very good, but still it seemed more like a fantasy, my old naughty dreams made flesh: a cold winter's night, a ski weekend, another man with his hand between my legs, working my clit patiently, and I had to come soon and oh-so-quietly; or my husband would be pulling the car into the driveway, stopping the engine then turning to catch us doing that naughty, forbidden thing.

Before long, I was indeed shuddering and thrashing in Ben's arms.

He kissed my cheek afterwards. "Thank you for that. Tell me what you want next."

"I feel greedy," I confessed.

"Don't. I like pleasing you.

"Okay, I want you on top now. I want to feel you all around me."

Tap, tap, squeak.

I almost laughed at his bed's encore performance as we rocked together, my legs clasping him, feet hooked behind his thighs. I didn't come again with him—I actually pushed his hand away when he tried to finger my clit again. Instead I floated somewhere outside my body, drinking in the sounds of his ragged breath, the way he suddenly tensed, then bucked rhythmically, his quivering moan of release.

These are the things I would remember best, my small, shiny souvenirs from the land of Updike.

Answers

"Did you have a good time?" Nick asked when we were back in bed together again. I'd guess it was sometime after midnight.

"Yes. And you?"

"It was nice."

We both seemed to sense detailed descriptions weren't in order now. As if on cue, we rolled toward each other and embraced. I stroked his back and shoulders, filled my lungs with his scent, seeking some change in him, some mark to prove it was real.

John Updike Made Me Do It   Donna George Storey

"I should be tired, but I want you." His voice was hot in my ear. "I want you naked inside and out."

What happened next was the real surprise of the evening.

Because those words broke something in me, like a balloon blown to the bursting point. A sigh, more like a sob really, forced its way through my lips and I clutched him, squeezing until my muscles burned.

He groaned, too, his lean body pressing against me as if he would crush me to pulp.

When we kissed, it was more like a bite, our lips banging together, stinging from the pressure. Our hands roamed over each other's bodies, grasping, reclaiming what was ours. I wanted him, too, his naked cock buried in my wetness. And I wanted him now.

I rose and shoved him over onto his back—I never knew I had such strength in me. When I yanked down his sweat pants, his cock sprang up like a jack-in-the-box, bobbing against his belly. I struggled out of my own pajama pants and straddled him. Our genitals met like a head-on collision with my pubic bone jamming onto his belly over and over. There were no questions. We knew just what to do. Nick grasped my nipple and rolled it between his fingers. His other hand circled around to my ass, the territory on which he still had sole claim.

I started to fuck him, angling my hips so I could feel his cock pressing against my front wall the way I liked best.

"Come for me, baby. Come for *me*," Nick growled.

Which is just what I wanted, too. And with his finger invading my ass and his lips tugging my tit, I did, roaring as my orgasm tore through me, not caring who heard.

Only afterwards, when I lay in my husband's arms, my pussy raw and slick with his jism, did it finally make sense. The story had two acts: a wandering off to glimpse the familiar in the foreign and to watch the stranger in the man I knew best. And now the rush of bittersweet pleasure you can only know when you come home to real life from a fantastic journey.

I never felt closer to Nick than I did that night.

I suppose I have John Updike to thank for that, too.

Initiation
By Rick R. Reed

> **F*CK CLUB**. For gay men with insatiable appetites.
> To join, e-mail pics and stats to f*ckclub@sexmail.org.
> All responses private; all responses answered.

1.

The first thing they had me do was simple, but humiliating. "For your first task, we want you to go into the restroom at the New Life Theater, stand next to someone at the urinals, and look down at the guy's cock and say, "That's a really nice piece you got there. I'd love to suck it." It didn't matter who the guy was, what he looked like, what his age was, I had to say the words, and then I had to take whatever came after that, whether it was to be ignored, get a fist to my jaw, or an invitation to step into a stall and do what I had just offered to do.

It was my entrée, if you will, into the world of swinging. See, my boyfriend and I had been together for going on nine years and, while our love had grown and grown during that period, becoming what the right wingers would hate to call a *family*, the sex life had diminished to almost nothing. Alan was like a comfortable pair of old slippers: cuddly, warm, always there. But the fireworks had long ago launched, burned bright, and faded to ashes.

So we agreed to do what so many other gay couples like us in terms of longevity had agreed to do: open up our relationship. Some guys did three-ways, but Alan and I opted for a "don't ask, don't tell policy" in

Initiation   **Rick R. Reed**

which we could have outside sex, but nothing that would intrude on our real and abiding love for one another. We would see how it went. If it didn't work out, we could always go back to the fraternal way things were. No harm done. Right?

I found the F*ck Club online and thought it would offer the perfect outlet for the kind of no strings attached sex that posed no threat to Alan's and my relationship.

And so I now found myself ducking into the theater, with all sorts of things going through my head. Every scenario had a bad ending, the badness of varying degrees. First, the guy could take offense and take a swig at me, or loudly call out to anyone within earshot what I had just done. Or, he could grab my arm and force me to find a security guard with him and make sure I was arrested. Or the guy could smile and nod down at his cock. If we were alone, I would be expected to kneel and take it in my mouth without question. If not, we would have to go wherever he wanted, whether it was as close by as one of the stalls, or his house across town. But in my imaginings, the only guy who would do with this would be someone hideous: an old, old man with rheumy eyes and bulbous nose, his body shaking with palsy, his breath smelling of onions, body reeking of perspiration. His dick would be covered with sores.

So, I was scared: scared of being arrested, scared of being beaten up, scared of having to suck a troll off, and scared, too, that going down this road was traveling a route that led to a parting of the ways. "And when the guy comes, you better take it all," they had said. And I didn't know this for sure, but I figured they would have some way of knowing that I followed their instructions to the letter or not and, if I didn't, well, I didn't want to think about that. If I didn't, what would happen to me was far worse than any of the things I just described above. But I plunged forward, thinking that I needed a release, needed to find a way to shore up my loving and comfortable, albeit boring, relationship with my other half.

When I opened the door, my heart was pounding. I didn't expect there to be anyone in the men's room, because Act I of *King Lear* was in progress and intermission was a good hour away. This wasn't the Cineplex, where teenage boys ran in and out of the movies as if the theater was their living room, but a legitimate performing arts venue that did a lot of Shakespeare. It was under penalty of death (or at least re-admission) that you left your seat.

Initiation   Rick R. Reed

So I was surprised to see someone already at one of the urinals when I pushed open the heavy oak door and stepped into the men's room. The fluorescent light was bright and unforgiving on the stark white marble walls and the tiny black and white patterned tile floor. The squeak of the door opening and closing echoed in the cavernous space, with its high ceilings and unforgiving acoustics. I paused for only a second, sizing him up.

It was hard to tell anything about my "prospect" from behind. He wore a voluminous black wool coat that hung down to the lower part of his calves. His shoes were black, with a high gloss; he wore charcoal slacks in a good fabric, gabardine perhaps. There was a small cuff. His hair was black and wavy and dusted the collar of his coat. I moved in closer and peered into the bank of mirrors over the sinks, trying to see what his profile was like, but his head was turned toward the stall and all I could see was the back of his head.

Although his face could have been akin to Frankenstein's monster or, worse, George W. Bush on a bad hair day, I had to admit to myself he looked like he had potential. His shoulders were broad. He was tall, well over six feet; his body had a presence that radiated strength. Those were all good things, I told myself, if he decided to take me up on my offer. Bad things, I told myself, if he decided to beat me to a bloody pulp and leave me whimpering on the cold tile floor. I also thought both scenarios could be carried out with relative ease because, as I said earlier, it was unlikely anyone would be in the men's room at this point in the play.

"No hesitation. Just do what you're told," I could remember them saying and thought I had lingered long enough. I took a breath and strode over to the bank of urinals and stood right next to my target.

He looked over at me and my knees went weak. His face was as strong, handsome, and solid as his broad back tapering down to his thin hips promised. He had a Roman nose, full lips and grey eyes that stood out from his olive-toned skin; the ledge of thick black eyebrows above them made his eyes even more startling. A tuft of curly black hair peeked out of the top of his starched white button-down shirt. He returned his gaze to the business at hand.

And so did I. His cock was thick and probably close to six inches long (even though there wasn't a hint of tumescence). A big vein snaked up one side of the shaft and he had pulled back the foreskin to reveal a perfect helmet head. Piss gushed out in a forceful stream.

Initiation — Rick R. Reed

Even if I weren't doing this as part of a test, I would have had trouble tearing my gaze away. Hell, I would have had trouble keeping the drool in my mouth.

Yet, my heart pounded so hard against my chest, I wondered if the flesh above it was actually moving outward with each pump of blood. A line of sweat formed along my hairline and another trickled down my back. My mouth was dry, and I tried to gather up some spit. I closed my eyes, unzipped, pulled out my own cock, then turned my head slightly.

Now or never.

"That's a really nice piece you got there. I'd love to suck it."

It seemed like all sound in the room stopped: no more traffic going by outside, no hum of the fluorescent lights.

He turned, looking me up and down. A grin played about his full lips and I wasn't sure if it was a smile of mockery and derision, or one of interest. I began to tremble. They had said I could say nothing further, so I wasn't able to apologize or explain why I had said what I did. I simply had to wait, mute, and let him be in control.

He said nothing for a while, but I could sense him shaking off his cock (I didn't dare look down), and then he leaned close and whispered, "That's cool, but let's step into one of the stalls. I don't want to get interrupted." He had a foreign accent, Greek maybe.

I followed him. He leaned against the marble of the stall wall to let me go in after him and I immediately sat on the toilet, leaving my pants up ("Under no circumstances," they had said, "are you to touch yourself."). I looked up and watched as he grinned down at me, one of the most gorgeous men I had ever seen, as he undid his belt and pushed his fine pants down to his ankles. He was no longer soft; in fact he was rock hard and his cock jutted out proudly from a matte of black pubic hair. A drop of precum glistened on its tip. He stroked it lightly, that same enigmatic smile (or was it better called a smirk?) playing about his lips. Then he thrust his hips forward.

And there was no hesitation. I opened my mouth and took him all the way to the root without gagging (although my eyes did tear up) and before I resigned myself to my work, I thought that if the other two parts of my initiation were as easy (or as wonderful) as this, I could be initiated for the rest of my life.

Initiation   Rick R. Reed

I placed my hands on his muscular thighs, thick with coarse black hair, then moved up to his ass, the cheeks clenching as he pounded himself into my open, and very receptive, mouth.

2.

I left the theatre, casting nervous glances around me, almost expecting to see Alan leaning against the concession stand, arms folded across his chest, grinning at me, as if this was all something he'd made up for me, a test of sorts. Was the guy in the corner in the dark blue suit security? Was the old woman near the exit a friend of my mother's? I couldn't believe what I had just done. The memories were still playing in my head: a lurid porno loop. I could see nothing but a flat stomach crowned with coarse black hair moving toward my face, then away. I could still smell the musk of his crotch. I could still hear his sighs and breathing increase as he quickened the thrusting in and out of my mouth, his ass muscles clenching as he forced his cock all the way down my throat.

I could still taste him.

I didn't know how long this initiation would continue. Would the next two parts arrive immediately? Or would it take days . . . or weeks? I was soon to find out.

When I emerged onto the sidewalk, crisp autumn air hit me. There was a guy emptying the trash: gray hoodie, faded jeans, construction worker boots, a dark blue bandana wrapped around his head, emphasizing dark Latin features. He lifted the trash can into a bigger plastic bin on wheels. He was good at it and got everything in with the first fluid throw.

Everything, that is, save for a piece of fluorescent yellow paper. He glanced down at it, then back at me, and moved on.

I watched him head on down the busy street, wondering if it was a sign. I hurried over and picked up the piece of yellow paper before it had a chance to flutter away on the October breeze.

I opened the folded paper. "Walk three blocks. In each block, go up to one man of your choice and grab his ass. When he reacts, your only response should be: 'Oh God! I'm sorry. I thought you were someone else.' Move on to the next . . . if you're able."

I stood staring at the piece of paper and my anxiety, so recently abated, returned full force. I began to wonder if I shouldn't abandon this

Initiation   Rick R. Reed

whole idea and head home. Clubs were for high school . . . and one like this was something I could hardly get my head around. It seemed like they were setting me up to be bashed . . . or worse.

And yet something inside urged me on. I was like an addict, even though I had done very little to even get hooked, or in fact, to even know what the ultimate thrill of my high might be.

I thought again about my experience in the theater and tried to use what happened there as motivation to move me onward (that, and the mystery of it all). After all, the guy in the men's room could have been a plant and all of this could be very benignly watched over. How could anything bad happen?

Even I knew the answer to that question.

Up ahead was a man waiting for the bus. He looked pretty harmless: slight frame, wearing a brown suit and tassel loafers, a *Wall Street Journal* tucked under his arm. He was slightly balding and, when he glanced down the street to see if the bus was in his field of vision, revealed a clean-shaven face made slightly more distinctive by small gold wire rimmed oval glasses. He looked to be about forty; not like the kind of guy who would punch someone out, no matter how outraged he might be. He wouldn't have been my first choice for ass grabbing but, lust briefly abated by my earlier encounter, I took a deep breath, strode up behind him and grabbed his ass, squeezing the surprisingly muscular cheeks hard.

He turned immediately (no surprise), mouth ajar and eyebrows raised. "Wha—?"

"Oh God! I'm sorry; I thought you were someone else." I let a giggle loose, embarrassed by how high-pitched it was.

The guy's eyebrows came together and for the moment, the briefest flicker of outrage moved across his features. Then, he softened, even smiled a little. He shook his head, looking me up and down.

"You want to watch that, fella. You could get yourself in big trouble."

He turned back to watching the street for a bus, or cab, or whatever he was waiting for. He snapped open his newspaper, dismissing me. But I could see his hands were trembling slightly.

I moved on.

The next guy I went up to was someone I wanted to touch. There were no rules against that, was there? And, not to stereotype, but I was pretty sure he was gay, just because of the fact that he was so aggressively masculine. He was standing looking in the window of a bookstore at a display of the latest outpouring from David Sedaris (clue one) and a small grin played about his lips (I could see his reflection in the glass). He was broad-shouldered and looked even more so because he was only about 5'8". He didn't wear a jacket, so I could see the tense muscles bunched beneath the fabric of his form-fitting, long-sleeved white T-shirt. His hair was salt and pepper, buzzed, and his face had a strong jaw line and was enhanced, rather than marred, by a light covering of acne scars. He looked tough . . . and mean. But the tight Levis and engineer boots said "leatherman" in a loud voice.

I grinned, strode up to him and gave his ass a squeeze, trying to ignore the fact that my mouth was dry and my heart was doing an irregular thump.

He turned to look at me and his hardened features lit up with a 100-kilowatt smile.

I almost forgot what I was supposed to say. Anxiety and lust warred within me. Guess which one was winning. I might as well have been winking when I said, "Oh God. I'm sorry; I thought you were someone else." I made it apparent from my delivery I didn't think he was anyone else, just the gorgeous hard-bodied stud standing before me. I looked down at his crotch, where a sizable basket presented itself.

He cocked his head. I felt no fear and, in fact, was hoping for a proposition. The hell with this initiation thing—I was up for an encounter. No one said the third man's ass I had to grab had to be *right away*.

"Did you really?"

I grinned stupidly, the perfect Rose Nylund. "Really what?" The deep timbre of his voice made my dick hard.

He slowly shook his head and then spoke slowly, looking me right in the eye (his were green, flecked with amber). "Did you really think I was someone else? Or is that just your standard come-on?"

I shrugged. "I guess I'm busted," I said in a soft voice, meant to be charming.

He jerked his head toward a quiet alcove: the entrance to an office building. He smiled at me. My dick was straining against my jeans, begging for release . . . of any sort.

"Listen, I don't have any bad feelings about what you did, other than the fact I think it was pretty stupid. What if I wasn't gay?" He snorted, realizing the fact that he was homosexual was pretty damn obvious. "Or

Initiation   Rick R. Reed

even though I am, what if I didn't take kindly to be groped by a stranger? Which, by the way, I really don't." The smile disappeared and he leaned his face close to mine. "You gotta watch it, buddy. People's bodies belong to them. They're not around for you to sample when you feel like it and then try to get away with it by using some lame-ass excuse."

My face flushed crimson with heat. And this was no longer the heat of lust, but of humiliation.

"I oughtta punch your fuckin' lights out, you little twink." His features softened a bit, but not enough to quell the unease in my gut or the sweat pouring down from my pits. "You need to take a good hard look at yourself and your life. You can't be proud of who you are. No one could. It's not so much the gay thing; it's the out-of-control crap that's messing *you* up." He fumbled in the leather bag slung over his shoulder and pulled out a small magazine and handed it to me face down. "Read this. And *think*. Think for once in your little faggot world."

And he strode away. I was dizzy with shame and embarrassment. I turned the pamphlet over: it was familiar. It was an issue of *The Watchtower*, the propaganda put out by the Jehovah's Witnesses. The cover asked if the devil was real.

I started to laugh, never mind I was in the middle of a busy city street. I laughed. I roared. The tears streamed down my face. The guy was a Jehovah's Witness? Oh God!

And I started laughing all over again.

Finally, I leaned against a lamppost and let my breath return to normal. "Is the Devil Real?" the cover almost accused me.

I shook my head, the last few laughs sputtering out. I whispered, "He sure is. And he has a sense of humor."

I took a deep breath, tossed the pamphlet in a trash can and hitched up my jeans. I had one more ass to grab.

I'd had enough. I wasn't even sure I wanted to continue. What was the F*ck Club anyway? Ahead, there was a fat guy waiting to cross the street. His bulbous frame stretched out a sweatshirt with the AF logo emblazoned across the back. Jordache jeans sagged across his wide ass. I rushed up behind him, grabbed it, squeezed, and hurried on, calling over my shoulder, "Oh God! I'm sorry. I thought you were someone else."

He gave me the finger.

Initiation   Rick R. Reed

I almost ran straight into a black man dressed impeccably in a navy blue pin striped suit. "Watch where you're going," he growled and thrust a manila envelope in my hand.

I debated whether I should just toss the thing in the nearest trash receptacle. Instead I paused at the other side of the street, staring after the black man, who strode briskly away, not looking back.

Inside was a card and on the card was written: "The old millworks down by the river. Find the entrance with the broken chain. Go inside and wait. Eight p.m."

I looked down at my Swatch. Four more hours.

3.

I debated whether I should go to the abandoned millworks down by the river. Maybe I should just go home to Alan, where I could curl up next to him on the couch and pop an old, 1940s tear-jerker into the DVD player. I debated for about five minutes. I mean, come on, the idea was hot: imagining any kind of sexual encounter in the confines of an empty steel mill where men used to manipulate hot slag in hard hats, old jeans, steel-toed boots, and dirty wifebeaters made me hot. I though the F*ck Club must be worth the initiation if this was the kind of imagination the group possessed. It could be a porno movie come to real flesh and blood life. I could hardly wait for the appointed hour to arrive.

Alan was not at home and part of me hoped he was out getting the same; taken a dive into the deep end, so to speak. I took a shower and cleaned myself carefully (you know what I mean). This third part was to be the last part of my initiation, and I wanted to make sure everything was perfect. I stood before my open bedroom closet wondering: what does one wear to an abandoned industrial site for a sexual initiation? Shows like *Project Runway* and *America's Next Top Model* had given me no clues. In the end, I opted for the practical: the place would be dirty and cold. I pulled out a long-sleeved T-shirt, a heavy plaid flannel shirt, a pair of my favorite Levis, hiking boots, and a University of South Carolina baseball cap that bore the provocative slogan, "Go cocks!" Over these, I wore a black leather jacket.

It was about a half hour drive by car from our apartment to the millworks. Once I neared the river, I nosed my Civic over a rusting piece of

Initiation Rick R. Reed

chain link that lay across a cinder drive. The millworks stretched before me, blocking my view of the river. Running over half a mile, the dirty brick buildings topped with smokestacks rising up into the night like spires exuded an air of either menace or provocation. Since I was horned up and ready for some hard-hat type rough trade, I was down for being provoked. The car bounced up and down on its suspension as it meandered down the gravelly road. I glanced over at the card the black guy had given me earlier and tried to peer through the darkness each time I came to an entrance to one of the buildings, looking for one with a broken chain across it. So far, there was no luck, but I was confident that soon enough, some industrial-sized metal doors would emerge out of the darkness, inviting me in with a broken chain and the promise of unspeakable sexual delights.

And soon enough, that image emerged on my right. The last building of the series of industrial housing making up the millworks had exactly the entrance described on the card. I pulled the Civic over and sat for a moment in the darkness, listening to the ticking sound of the engine as it died down.

Suddenly, I wasn't so eager to get inside. The half hard-on I had driven around with for the last fifteen minutes shrunk and relaxed. My heart rate accelerated.

The place was foreboding. The windows were opaque with a film of grime. It was so dark you could barely see your own hand in front or your face. When I stepped out of the car, it was as though the temperature had dropped about fifteen degrees since I set off from my house. It was *cold*. Good excuse, I thought, to shiver.

I looked up at the building, which suddenly seemed impossibly large and imposing against the starless slate blue sky. Deep gray clouds raced across, pushed by the wind.

I shivered, plunging my hands deep into my jeans' pockets and hurried toward the entrance.

I pressed on the door, and it opened easily at my touch. It didn't squeak. *These guys think of everything. Someone must have gotten here early and oiled the hinges.* I moved inside; the air smelled of metal filings, and I swore there was the echo of machinery: wheels turning, generators humming, stuff like that. Something scurried across the floor in front of me. I took a deep breath and continued moving forward, keeping my hand out in front of me for protection in the pitch.

Initiation   Rick R. Reed

As I moved further ahead, the quality of light changed, becoming more grayish, paler. I wasn't sure if it was my own eyes adjusting to the darkness or if there was actually a light source up ahead.

I rounded a corner and came into a large open space. Now, I could see. Someone had placed several of those oil Coleman lamps in a circular formation on the floor. The light they cast was weird, shining upward. It all looked menacing, like something out of a horror movie directed by Quentin Tarantino, or something of the modern extreme horror genre, like *Saw* or *Hostel*. I wanted to laugh. These guys were good.

I found myself growing excited again, especially with what else awaited me in this open space.

In the center of the lights stood a metal frame upon which was suspended a leather sling. That wasn't the best part. The best part was the half dozen men that stood waiting around the sling. All of them were naked. All of them had nearly identical bodies: packed with solid muscle, ripped and defined. Each sported what looked like an almost painfully hard erection (Viagra anyone?). Each stood perfectly still. The only difference in the men was that some were white, some were black, and others bore the olive complexion that spoke of a Latin heritage. Some were hairy, some smooth, others cut, still others in possession of foreskins. They were all Adonises, and representative of the beauty of the male form in all its different guises.

I could make no comment on the faces, though. Each man had donned a black ski mask. This part of things both excited and frightened me. My heart was thumping for very different reasons in my chest. And I had a peculiar thought: what if one of these guys was my Alan? Again, I considered the fact that somehow he was behind all of this.

I didn't need anyone to tell me what to do. I mean, come on, the set up was pretty clear, my initiation would climax (if you'll allow the term) with a gang fuck, something I'd fantasized about but never had the nerve or good fortune to have happen to me before.

No one moved forward. No one said anything. They all stood waiting. And I was amazed that not one of the guy's erections so much as wavered. I looked at the cocks pointing at me, sending out their own form of mute instruction. All were huge (which left out my poor, diminutive in every sense of the word, lover). This really was like a porno movie!

I smiled and began taking off my clothes. The cold air bit at my skin as I exposed more and more of it. I wondered again how these men

Initiation   Rick R. Reed

managed to keep their erections; the air was downright biting. As I dropped the last sock to the floor, I strode slowly over to the sling and hopped up in it, struggling just a bit to put my legs in the leather straps made to hold my ankles and spread my legs wide. I grinned. In spite of the chill and the rather grim, stalwart atmosphere, this was going to be fun.

I lay back, letting the leather sling embrace me, and waited. After what seemed like fifteen minutes or more had passed, two of the men from the circle moved forward. *Finally.* I wriggled down a little further in the sling, making my asshole even more available and, I hoped, inviting.

The first man positioned himself near my head. He had a purplish looking dick with a long foreskin that actually drooped down a bit over the head. I reached across my chest to grasp it; it was so thick I could barely encircle it with my hand. I pulled back the foreskin to expose the shaft. The head was shiny with precum. I took it into my mouth, savoring the salt taste, the thickness that pressed against the back of my throat, and the slight drip of viscous precum that I gulped down greedily. Suddenly, it wasn't so cold in here anymore. I matched my sucking and the swirling of my tongue to the thrust of his hips, which increased in tempo, building slowly, but gradually growing faster and faster, the head of his dick hitting the back of my throat, pounding into me. I knew what was coming and couldn't wait to taste him.

Suddenly, he pulled out (just as I could feel his balls tightening and was readying my throat for an explosion). I looked over at his rigid bone, now actually dripping pre-cum to the floor below, so hard the long foreskin was pushed back. He squeezed at the base of it.

Why stop now?

He leaned over me and it was then I saw the blindfold in his hand. He stretched it across my face and then lifted my head tenderly from the sling to knot it behind my head. I could hear other men in the room moving forward and oddly, the rustle of plastic. It sounded like they were laying out some kind of sheeting below me on the concrete floor. I squirmed: this was getting kinky. And so gay: who else but homosexuals would worry about keeping things neat in a filthy abandoned steel mill?

I then felt the warmth of a body between my spread thighs. *Now it's going to get good.* I swallowed hard and tried to relax. None of these guys looked like they had less than eight inches and I knew penetration would be a challenge. I hadn't seen any evidence of lube (or of condoms for that matter) but I had come too far to turn back now and to even say anything

Initiation   Rick R. Reed

under these circumstances just suddenly seemed so strange: it was simply too quiet, almost reverential. This part of the initiation had the feel of ritual. I hoped they would be gentle.

My hopes were quickly dashed as I first felt the delightful sensation of a turgid cock head at my waiting hole and then I tightened and let out a small cry as he pushed savagely into me, sending white hot needles of pain throughout my entire body and making me see red beneath the blindfold.

I felt nauseous and wanted to get up from the sling. In fact, I started to rise up. But immediately, there were hands holding my chest down, strong hands coiled, snake-like, around my wrists and ankles. I tried as best I could to relax and enjoy the feeling of being nearly cleaved in two by this insistent dick. It had to be the biggest of the group.

The thrusting went on, pounding, slamming into me, and I went somewhere else in my head for just a little while. By the time the third guy entered me, I was open. I could feel warmth dripping down my thighs even though I wasn't sure I wanted to analyze too closely what the liquid was. I even began to enjoy the experience somewhat. The queasiness ebbed and I found myself squirming to meet my mystery lover's thrusts.

I was sure I was passing the initiation. I was showing them I could take whatever they could give.

Even though I was blindfolded, I closed my eyes and surrendered myself completely to the experience. I was fucked six, seven times as the men lined up to take second, and third turns. It went on for what seemed like hours—and probably was.

And then it all stopped. I was left feeling open and empty. A sticky residue oozed across my chest and stomach.

When had I come?

It got so quiet I wondered if they had left me.

"Hello?"

No one responded, but I could hear the rustle of movement near me. And then I felt something cold and metallic at my throat. *Okay. Here comes the hard part of the initiation. Just let them run the knife over you and show them you're not a pussy.* The blade pressed against my skin and even then, I tried to relax, to think of it all as a game. When I felt the slight release of tension in my throat and then the quick heat of knowing they had broken through skin, I began to tremble. I started to scream and something acrid smelling and balled up was stuffed into my mouth before I could make any further

Initiation   **Rick R. Reed**

sound. I thought of Alan, praying he would enter stage right and would assure me this was all a perverse joke. Was this what I really wanted?

I winced as the blade went deeper. I winced as the world went red and then darker, in waves.

Someone was entering me again. Down there. Up here.

Again and again until it all went black.

The Best of Friends
By M. Millswan

This is one of those stories usually confessed to priests, shrinks and cops as, "This wasn't me . . . You see I have this friend, who told me . . ." Such is the case here, as, of course, this could have never happened to me.

* * *

While driving down a lonely highway one night, not long after a familiar old song on the radio had faded away, a friend I'll call "Ron" suddenly began to reminisce. After one deep sigh and then a few moments later another, he fell into a memory, describing a girl from his high school Biology class, whom, he said, had sat two desks up and one row over. He recalled that thinking about it now, he realized he'd noticed Eileen right off. Though he admitted that wasn't really anything out of the ordinary, even today he rarely missed noticing any attractive girl who came his way.

With that touch of wistfulness we all get when we recall meaningful events from the past, Ron delved deeper into his recollection saying when they'd first met, Eileen had been a senior, while he'd been only a lowly sophomore.

Keeping his eyes fixed out on the road as the power of long-lost emotion took hold over his voice, he described her vividly, from the way she wore her brown hair long and in tresses, to the way her smile seemed always so bright and sincere.

He added, Eileen wasn't one of those girls who could ever be described as thin; but the way she carried herself, it wasn't possible for any over-eager teenage boy to be in the same room with her and not be aware of how entirely feminine she was.

As a member of the drill team for pep rallies on Friday's he described her wearing a blue and gold spangled outfit, which accentuated how busty

The Best of Friends   M. Millswan

she was and the fullness of her hips. Yet, for a member of the drill team she wasn't one of those popular girls who were aloof or arrogant. But for a guy like him, Eileen remained entirely unapproachable, untouchable. And Ron confessed that had it not been for the fortune of later events, he most surely would have forgotten all about Eileen, as the closest they had interacted throughout that entire semester was once being at the same table while dissecting a frog.

As the miles ticked away, Ron grew philosophical. He said that the fact that high school is not a permanent condition is proof positive that there is a God and he loves you. Life moves on, friends drift away, new opportunities come and go; and once free of the social constraints brought on by the teenage caste system, it can become entirely possible to become friends with a person who was once entirely outside your social reach.

As proof, he said that by a strange quirk of fate a couple of years after graduation, he'd become friends with a guy named Paul who had graduated two years ahead of him. Coincidentally, they shared the same passion for cars, and an acquaintance who worked at a local hot rod shop introduced them to each other.

When Ron first visited Paul's small upstairs apartment and met Paul's wife it didn't dawn on him who she was. Ron was single and still in college, whereas his new friend and his wife already had a child, real jobs, and their own apartment. Ron didn't recall exactly when it happened, but sometime afterwards he and Eileen realized they knew each other from that Biology class years ago. Curious how life moves sometimes, isn't it?

Paul and Eileen were fun and friendly people, and they all hit it off. Little by little Ron grew into the role of "friend of the family." They would go cruising in the evening, they played poker together, went to movies, and Ron was a regular at all their parties.

When Paul and Eileen bought a house, they moved to a new neighborhood way out on the outskirts of town. By then Ron was busier with work and school. And though he wasn't able to hang out with his friends as much as they had before, whenever possible they still tried to find time to get together.

Time flies, and before Ron knew it, his five-year high school reunion was behind him, and they were all now well into their twenties. Paul began to travel frequently as part of a new job, and Eileen was busy with her own career and raising their son. But as a friend of the family, Ron still came around whenever they could find the time.

The Best of Friends   *M. Millswan*

With Paul traveling so often, it really didn't come as too much of a surprise when one evening he called and asked if Ron would take Eileen and their son to the beach on Saturday. An unexpected trip had come up, Paul explained, and he had promised their son he could go before it got cold. Though Ron and Eileen had never interacted without Paul rounding out the threesome, their friendship was such that it didn't seem strange at all when Paul asked Ron to do him a favor and step in.

After all, Ron and Eileen had become great friends on their own. She was so much fun, especially with that infectious, hilarious, giggling laugh of hers. Playing cards, and with more than a few drinks under their belts, sometimes they would hit on something funny and just laugh and laugh. And of course, by now they both knew full well about having been in that Biology class together. And it was during one of these late night card sessions that Ron learned an interesting revelation. Eileen confessed that she had indeed noticed him, after all . . . but in a negative way.

She'd been on the drill team and involved in other mainstream campus activities. But Ron had been a hippie, with long hair and a wild reputation . . . even if it was mostly undeserved . . . mostly. And so it was testament that life truly can move in mysterious ways that these two past classmates found themselves now spending a day at the beach together.

For Ron, that day was a milestone in his life; one of those unplanned for twists and turns that changes one's perspective as much as one's path. On more than one occasion it had been the lyrics of a song which spoke to him, drawing him towards a different horizon. But in this case it was that trip to the beach. Though he had been close with Paul's family for years, Ron had never before actually envisioned having a family of his own. But that day with Eileen and her son the entire experience was all so easy and entirely cool.

Unlike being on a date, being with Eileen was so comfortable, as they were already such good friends. They'd taken Paul's car and driven down to the coast. It was a gorgeous day. The summer's heat was gone, and the September sun was warm but not hot. Eileen had looked so full, and feminine, and sexy in the blue, one-piece swimsuit she'd chosen to wear. Time and again, Ron noticed he was noticing her, especially in one particular instance when she'd just returned from the water and was drying her hair.

With the sun behind her, Eileen had her arms up as she worked vigorously with the towel. Standing before him but a few feet away her legs

The Best of Friends   M. Millswan

were slightly spread and her head was thrown back, a truly alluring site. When she'd looked back down and caught him staring up at her she'd simply smiled. What a day. They'd all had so much fun; picnicking on the sand and playing in the surf. Driving back that evening, Ron truly felt contented and at ease.

Time, though, continues to fly. A couple of months had quickly passed since the trip to the beach when Ron was invited over for a party. That night the house was packed. There was so much booze, and it got so crazy they all even played Twister. But with people now having kids and responsibilities, around midnight the party began to wane.

With only the three of them left, they were sitting in the living room. Paul and Eileen were on the love seat, and Ron was sprawled out on the couch. They were pretty drunk, and this was definitely going to be another night when Ron would stay in the guest room. And so Ron didn't think anything about it when Paul suggested they play a little poker. After all, they'd played poker hundreds of time, penny ante, nickel limit. No big deal.

But Paul didn't break out the change. He just began dealing out the cards, with them playing only to see who had the better hand.

After a few rounds, out of the blue Paul asked, "You ever played strip poker, Ron?"

Ron stared back at Paul, who only grinned, waiting. Next, Ron glanced to Eileen, who made eye contact for a moment, then quickly looked away. Then came one of those pulse-pounding moments.

People love to blame things on alcohol. It's only human. But a famous man once countered with, "When people claim to be only human, it's usually because they've been making beasts out of themselves."

With Eileen not protesting, the call was entirely up to Ron. And though his mouth had gone dry, and his palms had begun to sweat, there was no way he was going to say no. Ron looked back to Paul, who was still grinning broadly. "Sure," he shrugged. "Okay. I'm game if everyone else is. Go ahead, Paul. Deal 'em."

In the background The Eagles were on the stereo as Paul shuffled the cards: "Life in the Fast Lane." While they waited, again, Ron looked to Eileen. And this time she didn't look away, giving him a "why not" shrug.

Sitting across from each other on the shag carpet, they were pretty much toe-to-toe as Paul dealt the cards. Betting wasn't necessary as the stakes were fixed; all you could do was draw once, then lay.

The Best of Friends   M. Millswan

Paul lost on the first hand, giving up his shirt. But it was Eileen who lost on the second.

With Ron looking on in intense anticipation, and after a brief hesitation, the events of the evening took a giant leap forward as quite matter-of-factly Eileen began to unbutton her blouse. Button by button, Ron watched in breathless anticipation as her fingers worked their way down.

With his eyes on her, Eileen didn't look up, instead keeping her own gaze fixed upon her fingers. And in peeling the blouse off her shoulders she appeared so entirely voluptuous and feminine in how she so amply filled out her bra. Of course, Ron had seen Eileen in her bathing suit. But this was something entirely different.

Amazingly, though obviously blushing, Eileen didn't seem the least put-off. For a moment, she appeared as if she was going to fold it up, but then she casually tossed her blouse over onto the couch. And if anything, now that the ice was broken, she appeared to have noticeably perked up.

With the next deal, Ron lost. And like Paul and Eileen before him, he removed his shirt. The next two hands Paul lost. And he had such bad luck, seemingly in no time he was reduced to only his briefs.

Of course, this wasn't what Ron was looking for. Having already experienced his first taste of forbidden fruit with Eileen having removed her blouse, Ron was eager for Eileen to lose. And strangely, it seemed as if she was, too.

On the next hand, Eileen dealt herself a loser. For Ron there was such a palpable thrill of anticipation; not just for what she'd decide to take off, but to be able to watch as she did it. And as Ron looked on, Eileen stood, and then tugged down her shorts. Tossing them with her blouse she then sat back down, now dressed in nothing more than her panties and bra.

As Ron shuffled, he couldn't help but keep stealing glances at Eileen. Being a mother now, she wasn't the same size she'd been in high school. But she was a real woman, voluptuous, invoking a mature feminine flavor, fully filled out, and appearing not the least bit uncomfortable about her lack of clothing.

The next hand Ron lost, so he, too, removed his pants. And as the clothes began to dwindle, the excitement kept building. Soon, the evening was going to change drastically for someone.

With Eileen's next deal, again she lost. This was another moment of truth. Having played strip poker before, Ron had seen people chicken out.

The Best of Friends   M. Millswan

But Eileen wasn't one of those. She reached behind her back, unhooked her bra, and slid it off her breasts. Then she tossed it atop her other clothes, her rosy flush matched only by her smile.

It was Ron's deal again, and he was finding it difficult to shuffle. It wasn't simply that Eileen was sitting across from him with her breasts exposed. It was that he was as nervous as he was excited. This was completely new territory. These were his best friends. As close to anything approaching intimacy he'd ever experienced with Eileen was a few friendly hugs. But everyone seemed cool with what was going on; and after all this was their house, their game.

With the next hand, Paul lost. And there wasn't even the slightest trace of bashfulness as he stood and stripped off his shorts to stand there naked.

With this, Ron thought the game was probably over; time to put back on their clothes and make his feverish way to the guest bedroom.

But, the game didn't end here. Paul announced he was going to the bar and asked if anyone wanted anything else to drink while they finished the game.

Ron was definitely ready for another drink as over the past twenty minutes he'd seemed to have sobered up entirely. And when Paul walked out of the den to the bar it was just the two of them, Eileen clad only in her panties and Ron in his briefs.

Eileen unabashedly gathered up the cards and began to shuffle. To Ron, watching closely, she was so sexy; one of those full-figured women, her breasts big and plump, yet her nipples were tight, rosy buttons. And after she dealt the cards, for a moment they peered across at each other, and all Ron could hope for was that his face and ears didn't appear as heated as they felt.

Ron looked at his cards. He had nothing, save for the stirrings of a royal erection. Drawing the maximum of three, he still had zilch. Just as Paul returned, they laid down their cards, proving that tonight lady luck was with Eileen. Ron didn't know what to do. Technically the game was over, and Eileen had won. He wasn't sure if he was going to be required to pay off the debt, but Paul made that clear. He handed Ron a drink, also offering his grin and an entirely amused, "I guess it's off with your underwear, Dude?"

Ron looked to Eileen who was unsuccessfully attempting to hide her smile. So, there was nothing else to do. Ron got to his feet and stripped off

The Best of Friends   **M. Millswan**

his briefs, standing entirely naked before Eileen. It was all such a rush, so unnerving, yet so exciting, too. He'd been in their living room hundreds of times. Yet, now, tonight, here he was naked.

What happened next was even more amazing. Paul asked, "Have you ever had a Vaseline job?"

Technically he'd never had a Vaseline job. KY? Yes. But not Vaseline. Ron's response was cautious, "No . . . I don't think so."

Immediately Paul came back. "Would you like one?"

Assuming Paul wasn't talking about administered by him, Ron offered a hesitant, "Yeah . . . Okay . . . Sure."

Paul reached down to Eileen, giving her his hand. And when she was on her feet, she slipped her panties down her legs.

From there everything began happening so fast, with Ron following them into their bedroom. All these years and he had never seen inside their bedroom before. They had a king-sized bed, and the only light in the room came from a red lava lamp on a corner table beside an overstuffed chair. Following Paul's lead, Ron lay down atop the comforter, and Eileen settled in between them. From somewhere she produced a jar of Vaseline, and pending her first touch, Ron was already as stiff as he could possibly remember.

It was all as unreal as any dream. He was so intensely aware of being naked, the feel of the air on his skin and the texture of the bedspread beneath him.

Ron was lying on his back, looking up in awed anticipation as Eileen dipped her fingers into the jar. Looking down, his erection was standing up rigidly, offering itself to her. Looking on in excitement, he watched as lightly, even teasingly, she dabbed him all about. Once properly lubricated, she wrapped her fingers about him, squeezing lightly and causing the Vaseline to ooze out. Gripping him firmly, she played her thumb over the tip, rubbing it around and around. Then slowly, she slid her hand down the entire length of his erection. She repeated this twice more, going ever so slowly and keeping her fingers tight, experiencing him, feeling every bit of his length, his thickness.

Reacting to her touch, Ron had become stiff, so achingly, bone-hard, hard-as-rock, stiff. And Eileen seemed ravenous, as though she was consuming him through her touch. Her eyes deep and intense, her mouth was slightly open as she looked down, watching her hand as she squeezed and kneaded and stroked. In a deliciously surprising move, she flipped her

The Best of Friends M. Millswan

hand over, changing her grip so that her thumb and forefinger were down, gripping him tightly at the base. Then very deliberately she drew her hand all the way up until with a smacking release of the vacuum that had built up she slid the top of her off over the tip.

Ron gasped, looking up, his eyes wide. Eileen smiled, giving him such a knowing, and pleased-with-herself grin. Then she placed the top of her fist down over him, and causing a sensation as if he was penetrating her, she kept her thumb and forefinger pressed tightly together and let the lubrication of the Vaseline do its job as she slid all the way back down. Each time as she repeated this, Ron began to lift his hips as it felt so exquisite when she would come to the end of the stroke and her thumb and forefinger would catch at the rim of his head and squeeze him just before sliding off.

Eileen had just completed another such pass, and with his hips up off the covers the squeeze she gave him at the end had sent shivers all the way down through his spine. She then reversed her hand, purposely re-gripped him firmly in her fingers, and looked up. They made eye contact, which was, in itself, so luscious. She had him. He was as hard and as excited as he'd ever been, and this was Eileen who had her fingers wrapped about him. There was such excitement in her eyes, and seeing how aroused she was really turned him on.

It was one of those supreme first moments. Sex in itself had always been so exciting, but by its nature first sex is thrilling on an entirely different scale. And, too, this wasn't just any woman who had her fingers wrapped around him. This was Eileen. Even if he hadn't just seen it in her eyes, he was intimately aware of it through the touch of her fingers. There was no escaping how much she was enjoying everything about what she was doing. From the moment they made eye contact, with every touch and caress, Ron lay back and soaked it in as her fingers felt entirely exquisite. She eagerly began to work him up and down.

The experience was thrilling on so many different levels. Their bedroom was dark with only the ruddy glow from the lava lamp supplying any illumination. Eileen was naked, and Ron could see her clearly as she stroked and played. It was all so supremely erotic.

As she concentrated on pleasuring herself through pleasuring him, sometimes Ron would close his eyes, but mostly he kept them open. Every now and then he would catch a glimpse of Eileen stroking on Paul's erection with her right hand as she kept at him with her left. Time and again he and Eileen made eye contact, and it was in those moments that his excitement grew that much stronger. There was such a fire to her; she wanted this; she did. Ron could feel it through her fingers as much as see it in her eyes. Touching him, having him lay out naked and offer his erection to her was every bit as exciting for her as it was for him.

Some of his thrill might have been because it all seemed to have happened spontaneously. But if he'd been inclined to think about it, Ron could have easily deduced that Paul and Eileen had most surely planned this. And later, afterwards, when he did spend time thinking about it all, the idea that they had planned this was as flattering as it was exciting, in that Ron surmised Eileen would have to have been thinking of him, possibly hoping for some time to have this night happen.

The only downside was that he didn't know what to do. This was so unlike any experience he'd ever had one-on-one with a girl. These were his best friends: husband and wife. He was a guest in their bedroom; the last thing he wanted was to do anything that might be considered out of bounds or inappropriate. And the truth was, he desperately wanted to touch Eileen, but didn't know if that was permissible. He had no idea what was allowed. But what was going on was extremely pleasurable. So Ron left well enough alone and just lay back and enjoyed.

The way in which her fingers were sliding up and down was so hypnotically erotic. And it wasn't simply her stroking; at times she would toy with him, playfully swirling a finger tip 'round and 'round anywhere she pleased. Then a few moments later she might slide her fingers deliciously all the way down to caress and fondle his balls, little by little pushing him towards ecstasy.

Ron had closed his eyes and was nearing the edge of losing control when Eileen's hand stopped. One or two more stokes, and that would have been it. But she stopped. Opening his eyes, Ron saw that Paul had sat up and pulled Eileen down to kiss him. Eileen let go of Ron, and moments later Paul rolled over on top of her. If Ron didn't know what to do before, now he was even more lost. But, obviously, Paul and Eileen knew exactly what they were up to. Eileen parted her legs and pulled up her knees while Paul settled in on top of her. And with Ron watching only inches away, Paul began to thrust into her.

Maybe it was that everyone was so close on the bed, but Ron felt extremely awkward. He didn't know if his part in the evening was now over, and from here on out he was to be a spectator only. They were really

The Best of Friends   M. Millswan

getting into each other; Paul and Eileen didn't seem even to be aware he was there. Eileen had latched her arms around Paul, and her initial gasps were now becoming moans. Paul was becoming more excited, too; beginning to arch with his back while thrusting into her with a deeper passion.

Seeing them fucking up close was a sight to behold. Ron had visited Boy's Town in Mexico and had seen live sex acts. There, it had been raunchy and raucous, with a woman on stage chained to a pole and getting her brains fucked out by a guy wearing a bull mask, yet he was hung like a horse. But this was something entirely different. This was Paul and Eileen, and seeing them was so immediate, so close, so real.

Feeling self-conscious, Ron got off the bed and sat down in the chair by the lamp. From there he watched in explicit detail as Paul and Eileen had sex on the bed.

Watching them was exciting. Eileen had her feet in the air, her knees at his shoulders, her fingers clutching the covers. Paul was now thrusting into her with wanton abandon, and she was eagerly pushing back.

Ron was as hard as ever he could remember, and his erection was still slippery and glistening with the Vaseline Eileen had applied. With the feel of her fingers still on him, he was tempted to touch himself, but with how worked up he'd become, he knew it would be best to give it a rest, lest he lose control right there in the chair.

There wasn't any subtlety to their sex. It was all wild, animal passion fucking, pure and simple; the mattress bouncing, and the bed squeaking beneath them. Eileen was beginning to moan in earnest as Paul rose up off her, locking his elbows and thrusting into her again and again.

Intent and excited, Ron was sitting forward. Like being on the set in a live porno shoot he could see everything with great detail in the ruddy cast of the red light from the lava lamp. With Paul above her, Eileen's breasts were bouncing up and down with each thrust. Her eyes were closed, and Ron could see her tongue each time she licked her lips in anticipation.

Suddenly, her eyes flickered opened, and amazingly she looked over to Ron. They made eye contact, and what he saw in her eyes was a revelation in what makes sex enjoyable to a woman. It was all there: her excitement, her abandon, her thrill. To Ron's wondrous eyes, Eileen appeared lost, carried away in the throes of willing addiction to the carnality of her passion. And he knew, absolutely knew that a portion of her excitement was that she liked Ron watching her. It wasn't just that Paul was fucking her. She was fucking him back, using her body for her own enjoyment even as much as his.

Then they came. Or, at least Paul came. Ron couldn't be entirely sure about Eileen. From what he'd seen in her eyes she'd been almost there. Even though she'd put up an awesome show of feigning an orgasm, Ron suspected it was more for everyone else's benefit than for hers. And it wasn't that Paul had not done a good job, as he'd been vigorous and virile. It was that there was something about Eileen Ron had never been privileged to witness before; a side to her personality which revealed her hidden sexuality. The heat and lustful carnality, the essence of a woman on fire she exuded was so voracious it bordered on insatiable.

Sitting where he was, maybe it was the excitement of what he'd just witnessed catching hold of him. But no, it was tangible. He could feel it. And it was then that it hit him: No wonder she wanted two men.

When Paul rolled off her, Ron was again at a loss of what to do. For a while as they caught their breath, neither one seemed to notice him in the chair. Then Paul sat up on the edge of the bed, sweated and flushed, and grinning broadly. While behind him, Eileen was still lying there naked, her legs still slightly spread and breathing heavily.

"What about you?" Paul was positively beaming. "You want a turn?"

Ron was hesitant. "It's okay?"

"Sure." Paul stood and stepped away from the bed. "Go on. Now it's my turn to watch."

Ron got up, and Paul took his place in the chair. Coming over to the bed, Ron was all eyes. Since she'd stripped naked in the den things had happened in a blur. But now Ron took his time, relishing the view of Eileen naked, lying there before him on the bed, eager, ready and waiting.

"Go on," Paul urged. "What're you waiting for?"

Still, this was Eileen. No matter his own excitement and Paul's urging Ron couldn't just jump on her.

And, too many times taking it slow enhances the fun. The view Eileen offered was a portrait in sensuality. Atop the rumpled covers in the dusky red light, Eileen's uninhibited nakedness was a thrill in itself. He could see all of her, feasting his eyes upon her breasts with her nipples drawn so tight and stiff. Then naturally, the inviting spread of her legs attracted his eyes to the dark curls between. There was such a heat there—

The Best of Friends — M. Millswan

sultry, steamy, wet—he could feel how hot she was inside, even if by only touching her with his eyes.

As if Eileen was experiencing what he was thinking, she stirred, shifting her hips. Sultry, inviting, she was pure feminine sensuality lying there ready and waiting. And Ron was hard, incredibly hard, still glistening and slick with the Vaseline.

Eileen reached up and touched him, lightly and gently drawing her fingers playfully down his entire length. Then she brought her arms back to stretch them out in back of her head, spreading herself out before him. It was in that next moment when Ron and Eileen again made real eye contact. And what she communicated left no doubt that it was truly Ron's turn.

Having gotten up on the bed and seeing Eileen close up in the flesh was as unnerving as it was thrilling. After the buildup of the strip poker game, the hand job, and then watching Paul and Eileen fuck, Ron was extremely worked up. Emblazoned in the ruddy light as if pointing the way, his erection was standing out at full attention. Crossing over, he got on his knees between the spread of her legs. Hazarding one quick glance to Paul, the way in which he was so eagerly sitting forward in the chair said that he was entirely okay with what was about to happen.

Turning his attention back to Eileen, Ron slowly lay down atop her, and immediately she wrapped him in her arms. The sensation of her naked body beneath his was incredible. Her breasts were so plump and full, her nipples tight little buds pressing up against his chest. There was so much he was aware of; most exciting being the sensation as she spread her legs wider, causing the tip of his erection to brush up into contact with the source of the steamy heat between her legs. Ron was poised, just the very tip, almost, but not quite yet in her.

On the verge of penetration, they again made eye contact. Seeing Eileen like this, being atop her and almost nose-to-nose, the both of them naked, he ached to kiss her. Never before had he been this intimately involved with a woman he hadn't yet kissed. Yet, somehow, even though they were on the verge of fucking, he sensed kissing might be deemed inappropriate, as a kiss could be interpreted as more affectionate than carnal. And this wasn't about romance. This was about sex; sex for its own sake, not for love or amorous affection.

Eileen solved the problem. She nudged her hips forward, and she was so wet Ron slipped inside. That was it. The bridge had been crossed. He was actually in her, and she truly was so incredibly hot and wet within.

The Best of Friends   M. Millswan

And amazingly, she was tight; it was as if she was clenching him, holding him closely within her.

Being all caught up in events and moving as if in a dreamy daze, Ron hadn't known what to expect. In fact, even only two seconds ago he hadn't consciously imagined this far. But now here he was in her. There was no escaping that heart-pounding reality. This was Eileen, the girl from two desks up and one row over in Biology class. This was the wife of his good friend. They'd all been to bar-b-ques and parties over the years. And now Ron's erection was in Eileen's vagina, touching her deeply, intimately, experiencing her as he'd never dreamt possible.

Ron was so excited, he pushed in further. In response, Eileen opened her legs, taking him all the way inside her, and that subtle communication of feminine acquiescence was as exciting as anything he'd experienced so far. Buried all the way in her, he was rock hard solid. She was steaming inside, soaking wet and feeling him just as eagerly as he was feeling her. The intensity was such they were both lost in the moment, yet Ron's attention wasn't focused solely on this most intimate contact. As he lay atop her, she had her arm around him, holding him to her. Pressed to his chest, her breasts were so plush, her nipples so taut. His heart was pounding and pounding. He could feel her heartbeat as well.

Ron brought his face close to hold his cheek pressed close up against hers, his lips next to her ear. Slowly, hesitantly, he moved his hips, inching back; the sensation they shared as he withdrew being equal parts of thrill and trepidation. But he didn't draw out, instead he stopped at the most exciting threshold of penetration. And as Ron again slid all the way back inside her, Eileen drew in a breath, holding it as he once more filled her as deeply as he could.

Only a few feet away, Paul was watching. Joined together so intimately, Ron knew Paul was there, but what he and Eileen were sharing was nonetheless something powerful and personal only they could know. At this point there could be no turning back. Slowly at first, then with more and more passion, Ron began to stroke her.

Their bodies were pressed together cheek-to-cheek and it was Eileen's breathing at his ear that communicated her passion to him almost as openly as her body. With each gasp it was evident her excitement was building. It was all so intense. Stroking her, the way her arms tightly clutched him to her, the slick sweat between them, the sensation of her nipples and breasts, it was all so erotic and intimate, even more so with Paul looking on.

Being this excited, Ron knew he might lose control quite quickly. Yet somehow, despite how tight, and willing, and wet Eileen was; despite how electrifying it was to know that this was Eileen he was fucking; despite that he was intensely aware her orgasm was almost there, he would maintain his control.

With her lips at his ear, she was making quick little gasps only he could hear. They were coming rapidly now, each pant right on the heels of the other. Aware she was at the brink, he plunged all the way in and held himself there, pressing into her and reveling in the sensation of experiencing her body as deeply as he could. That was it. Suddenly, her muscles contracted, and she clutched on to him as she didn't even try to stifle her cry. And for Ron, it was such a personal and private thrill to be aware of every nuance of her body as Eileen lost control and her orgasm coursed through her. There was such passion and uncontrolled abandon in how the throes of her orgasm swept her away. She was gasping and clinging to him as she quivered and shook. And Ron, still so hard within her, was biding his time, only too eager to wait until the moment was ripe to once again drive her over the edge.

Sitting on the very edge of the chair, Paul clapped his hands. Taking his cheek from Eileen's, Ron looked over and noticed Paul was again hard. Seeing this, Ron was hit by the thought that maybe because Eileen had reached an orgasm, Paul thought they were done. Yet, such was most definitely not the case.

Pressing with his arms and burying his palms into the mattress, Ron arched his back, rising up to look down upon her. Maybe it was the red light from the lamp, but she seemed to have gone crimson, her cheeks, her neck, her breasts, every inch of her appeared flushed and on fire. Perhaps partially as a demonstration to Paul that he wasn't yet finished, Ron again pushed himself fully back into her, wiggling his hips and nestling in as deeply as possible.

Seeing this, Paul must have been aware there was more to come. And in Eileen's expression as she looked up, and the way in which she gave Ron such a subtle, intimate little squeeze, there was no question that she, too, was still very eager to go on.

Paul must have sat back in the chair. But that was only a guess. Ron was concentrating on other things. Slowly, evenly, and with a great sense of erotic deliberateness, he began to stroke her anew. All the while she was looking up, obviously enjoying the sight of Ron as much as he was enjoying looking at her.

From the side, suddenly Paul spoke up as if cheering them on. "Yeah ... That's right. Do him, Eileen. Do him. Let me see."

With Paul looking on and even rooting for them, any lingering sense of Ron's earlier feelings of apprehension vanished. Yet, even though Paul was there watching, and Ron had his absolute approval to be fucking his wife, this now had nothing to do with Paul outside of him being a spectator. This was all between Ron and Eileen.

After a deliciously long moment of enjoying her, all the while looking down and appreciating her every reaction to each probe and thrust, Ron unlocked his elbows and again lay back down atop her. Instantly, Eileen's hands were once more clutched about his back. Both of their bodies were slick with sweat, and the aroma of her heat and sweat up close was as exciting as any aspect of what they were doing. Her secret aroma was so hot and salty, yet by her ear, he was aware there was also a trace of a feminine sweetness, perhaps a lingering aroma from a bath or perfume.

Now so close and intensely aware of each other's bodies, Ron was positive Eileen was as in tune with his excitement as he was aware of hers. And God, suddenly how he craved to kiss her. But still, he didn't dare. In a way, it seemed unnatural to fuck without kissing, but he just couldn't bring himself to put his lips to hers. He could lie atop her naked and fuck her as she fucked him back. But they couldn't kiss; as somehow, instinctually, Ron knew that such a thing was surely taboo. So he put all of himself, all of his passion, all of his hunger into stroking her. There was a new goal now. Now he was going to fill her. That was something new they could share. He had felt her shudder, quiver and lose all control more than once now. And now it was going to be her turn to feel him do the same.

It was give and take now. They were totally into it. Eileen's knees were up, and her feet were in the air. Ron was stroking her with abandon, feeling her body slide slick and sweaty beneath his with every thrust. She was so hot and wet inside. He was so hard and stiff. He was compelled to keep driving in deeper and deeper. With her legs rising further up, Eileen was moaning, each heated gasp for breath revealing how completely she had given herself over to her passion.

Paul was watching and Ron was still aware he was there. However, his friend's presence as he fucked his wife was only slightly on Ron's mind.

The Best of Friends

M. Millswan

This was Eileen beneath him. That was what he knew. She had her left arm wrapped around his back, holding him pressed tightly to her as they fucked. Her cheek was so smooth against his; her gasps and moans in reaction to each thrust and plunge were heard from between her lips brushing close at his ear. And Paul was watching. But they weren't making love; they were fucking, fucking each other right here in front of Paul on Paul's bed.

Eileen's nipples were so hard against his chest. To Ron she felt so entirely naked beneath him. Again, suddenly he ached to kiss her, to feel his lips touch hers, the sensation of her tongue tasting his, kissing him as he kissed her, kissing him back with just as much passion as at this very instant she was fucking him back. But he didn't. He didn't try. He just couldn't.

Somehow though, she must have sensed his desire as with her right hand, Eileen's fingers sought Ron's. Hidden from Paul's view as he was on the other side, her fingers found his and they wrapped together in a private communication of intimacy only they could know. And with this, Ron knew his time was coming. And he knew Eileen knew it, too.

It was all too much; physically, mentally she had him. He was hers, and she was absolutely caught up in the desire to make him erupt deep within. It was a subtle little tightening of her muscles that tossed him over the edge. Eileen knew exactly what she'd done as she did it, and with her fingers knotted even tighter within his, she clutched Ron to her with her other arm as he shuddered out of control. Again and again he jetted into her. He couldn't seem to stop. The way she held him to her, forcing him to pulse so deeply had him frantic and wild as he abandoned all awareness except for that of his pleasure. Yet, the best was still only moments away. Just as Ron quivered his last, Eileen gasped then came, too. And the sensation of her complete meltdown drew him down with her, causing him to experience a woman's passion as he'd never imagined possible.

"Damn!" Paul called out, suddenly breaking the silence. "That was wild! I mean— I mean—" At a loss for words he paused, then again blurted out, "Damn!"

Lying atop Eileen, their breathing began to slow. With Ron keeping his nose nuzzled to her ear, he felt the side of her lips upon his cheek. Now more than ever he so wanted to kiss her. Just bring his face over to hers and kiss her. One long, hot sealing of the deal. But it was now that she released her fingers from his. The moment was lost. Ron sighed softly with his lips to her ear as only she could hear, and then slipped out of her, rolling off onto the side of the bed.

The Best of Friends — M. Millswan

Lying there, catching his breath, Ron became aware that the covers were thrashed into a state of ruin. When he'd gotten on the bed the covers had seemed only slightly rumpled. Yet, now it looked as though a tornado had hit the room.

Watching his wife fuck another man must have lit a fire in Paul, as it seemed no sooner was Ron off Eileen than Paul was back. And this time Ron stayed on the bed watching as Paul quickly brought him and Eileen to another climax.

Ron, of course, didn't sleep with them. He spent the rest of the night in the guest room, at first finding it impossible to fall asleep, then drifting off deeply. In the morning Eileen made breakfast. Their son was there and happy to see that "Uncle Ron" had spent the night. Ron did his best to act as if nothing had changed.

It was right before Ron left that he and Eileen found themselves alone. In retrospect, maybe she had purposely set this up so they could talk. Up close her eyes were so intense, and she seemed flustered and maybe even a bit ill at ease.

"I just wanted to let you know," she whispered, "that I would never think of doing such a thing as . . . as . . . you know . . . if Paul wasn't here."

This was like the proverbial ton of bricks. Suddenly Ron realized she feared he might now come calling sometime when Paul was away. Taken aback, as cheating on his friend was the last thing he would have ever considered, in response, Ron could only nod, at a loss for anything to say.

And now, as we drove along, Ron told me he could still recall everything about that moment when Eileen confessed her love and fidelity to Paul. Ron said it defined his experience of that unforgettable night. She loved Paul, and Paul loved her. Yes, she had shared herself sexually. And naked atop her on their bed, Ron had experienced an intimacy with her as powerful as it was profound. After all, she was a woman, and he was a man. Even if they would never kiss, they had fucked; there could be no getting around that. But Eileen's kisses were for Paul, her husband, and not for Ron. After all, it was with Paul that she had experienced their first date, their first kiss, and they were still very much in love.

And for me, as exciting as Ron's story was sexually, it was all such a wonderful revelation. To this day I admire Eileen and Paul for what they were able to hold on to with each other, even as they so openly shared everything that there is to give. Eileen gave of herself, and Paul gave of himself just as deeply in that they both invited a friend into their bed. And

The Best of Friends *M. Millswan*

according to Ron, besides the passion, besides the intimacies shared, and the memories to be embraced for the rest of his life, the best of it was that they were still able to remain . . . the best of friends.

Premises
By Lara Zielinsky

Jan stepped from the car, careful not to snag her ebony fishnets, and adjusted the short skirt as she stood. After straightening, she had to pull her right heel from the soft sand of the parking field. Pushing a loose golden curl away from her face, she looked back out toward the roadway they had left. Her spine still vibrated a little from the washboard conditions of the unpaved road.

Chris walked around the back of the car toward her. She smiled into his darkly handsome face and accepted a kiss as he took her hand. "You still sure?" he asked. His green eyes searched hers by the light of a string of Japanese paper lanterns.

"I wanted to do this where no one would know us," she said. "This place seemed perfect since we were already vacationing nearby." She might have had her first time at an off-premises club closer to home, but she preferred the anonymity over meeting someone she might eventually see at the grocery store. Also, this being all on-premises, she wouldn't possibly kill the momentum if she met someone who might suit, so it was a chance to get a little wilder. She might eventually grow to love swinging, but she had had to be honest—Chris had wanted nothing less—and she was a little nervous.

She had confessed she had always fantasized tasting another woman's lips and skin, and was turned on by the idea of Chris watching her with another man or woman. They rented movies and talked over more of the realities. Chris had been swinging with a previous girlfriend, and he had stressed it took honesty.

Moving away from the car and finding the stepping stone path to the entrance, Jan's head turned at the sound of another car pulling to a stop. She held Chris back a moment with a slight squeeze on his arm, and they

Premises — Lara Zielinsky

stood silent, still mostly in shadows. Another couple got out of the car, and walked easily and familiarly along the stepping stones toward the fence.

Jan studied the couple avidly, her newly accepted sexual tastes sampling their appearance. He was broad shouldered, a little older from the evident retreat of his hairline, wearing a pair of khaki shorts and a Hawaiian print shirt open to the navel showing a furred chest glinting silvery in the lighting. Where Chris was dark, handsome and slim, this man by contrast was maybe a football or soccer player in his youth. She had a vision of both of them together, sandwiching her body, or rising over him while Chris plunged into her ass. Raw and primal heat surged through her veins.

As the couple reached the gate, Jan turned her attention to the woman as the introductions were made in voices too low to carry back to her. The lanterns' swaying light played with the petite woman's hair and features, revealing fiery highlights in the short styled dark brown curls. Jan's fingertips tingled with the desire to stroke through it. Her mouth went dry and she licked her lips at the sight of the woman's profile. She had a lean, mature face and was probably more than a few years older than Jan. Her bone structure cast her face vaguely heart shaped with rounded cheekbones drawing down to a prominent but roundly pointed chin. In contrast to Jan, the woman's lips were thin, a faint ribbon of dusky red against healthy tan skin.

The woman wore a sarong style emerald green dress, translucent in the light, gathered and pulled in vaguely Greek classic folds. The length curved around her legs, ending at mid-calf. One side of the fabric separated from the other showing shapely calves and thighs as she moved to step up into the house. Her male partner shook hands with the host at the door as they walked through and disappeared.

"Let's go," Jan said at last. Chris took her hand, and she caught his smile. He had seen her examination of the couple. His nod said he approved if she wanted to make a move.

He pulled out his wallet when they reached the door and handed over the cover charge. When asked for their names, he answered, "Chris and Jan from Las Ritas."

"You called from the resort." Their host smiled. He was unremarkably attired in a button down red shirt and jean shorts. "So you're new?"

"Here. Yes," Chris answered.

"Common areas are out front. Eats, music, dancing, a pool table. Sofa and chairs for conversation. The pool area with hot tubs separates the front from the back." He nodded toward a plump brunette currently exchanging kisses with the previously arrived couple. "I'm Buck. That's my wife, Lil. This is our club."

Jan had been watching and was pleased to see the other woman share a thoroughly intimate kiss with Buck's wife. There was going to be a possibility, she thought with a smile.

"Rules of course," Buck went on. "No means no, and anyone who doesn't get that gets lost. Sex is only in the back rooms, or the specialty sheds out back. Clothing is optional throughout the place beyond the foyer. You'll find lube and free condoms in all the rooms."

Jan felt a surge of confidence. Chris shook Buck's hand. "Gotcha."

"Questions?" She turned her gaze away from the couple as Buck spoke again, clearly reading her mind.

"Introductions?" she asked.

Despite the fact that the foyer space had probably a dozen other people mingling and the low murmur of several conversations, Buck apparently knew immediately who had caught Jan's attention. "Right this way." As he stepped from the doorway, he stroked the shoulder of a nearby male, his outfit just a few strategically covering strips of leather. "Len, catch the door for a few."

Jan, with Chris at her back, followed Buck to Lil and the other couple. The music was a mix of eighties and nineties rock, and there was a light haze of smoke in the air, and she inhaled a little, catching a flowering scent, maybe peach blossoms. On the dance space by small card tables a couple of women gyrated up and down each other's bodies and the body of a bare-chested man between them. Jan's groin clenched and she turned her gaze forward again just as they reached the trio.

The three were lifting disposable Champagne cups to their lips. Lil stepped back, opening the space in front of the other couple as Buck slipped an arm around her hips. Smiling, Jan watched Lil as she lifted her head to accept Buck's kiss. Her face was rounder, a little fleshy, but pleasant.

Her voice was very sexy when she spoke. "I'm Lil." She nodded to the couple and Jan accepted the permission to look again at the fascinating woman with the come-hither smile.

"I'm Jan," she said.

"Chris," her husband said.

"Tim," and Chris shook hands.

"I'm Kay." Jan met a direct gaze sizing her up as much as she was doing to the other woman.

"Come here often?"

Kay answered, "We've been swinging for about ten years. We're local. Where are you from?"

"Las Ritas. We're on vacation from tax season," Chris answered.

Tim asked, "Accountant?"

"Yes."

"Heck of an economy right?" Tim and Chris moved off.

"Champagne?" Kay's voice reached Jan's ear as her hand touched her arm.

Jan was disconcerted by the men moving off. "A little. Thanks."

"You're new to this," Kay said. She picked up a Champagne cup, and offered it with a couple squares of cheese. Jan started to take a cheese cube with her fingers. Kay brushed them aside gently. Jan clued in and took the cube between her teeth, closing her lips around it and tasting Kay's fingertips before they withdrew.

"I guess it shows." Jan reached for a fruit cube to offer herself.

"You have talked about it though?" Kay obligingly took it from her fingertips.

"Oh yes. Chris and I have talked a lot about it. Started with fantasies, but . . ." Jan tried to shrug, aroused by the feel of Kay's lips on her skin.

"You've got the control here," Kay said. The words and the voice sent a thrill through Jan's body. "So be sure to take it."

Jan sipped her champagne. "What do you do?" she asked.

"I sculpt."

"Really? Would I have seen any of your work?"

Kay shook her head. Jan reached for the hand sliding up her forearm and traced the fingers while she held Kay's gaze across their joined hands. Kay's fingers closed so the tips stroked the back of Jan's hand. "You haven't asked what I do."

"Let me guess."

"All right." Jan laughed.

"You are married to Chris?"

"Yes."

"So you married an accountant. You work outside the home. Do you have children?"

"My only son is spending these two weeks with his grandparents."

"You're not young enough to be a pre-schooler's mother," Kay said with a smile. "So you don't teach primary school."

Jan laughed. "Is that how that works?"

Lil brushed past Kay drawing both women's attention as she stepped onto the dance floor with Buck. Chris and Tim were watching them. "Let's get the men going," Kay suggested.

"How?"

"Dance?"

Jan nodded. "All right. You still haven't guessed what I do."

"I've got all evening to figure it out," Kay said. She called Tim to her. "Let's dance, honey."

So Jan and Chris followed Kay and Tim to the dance floor. The two couples gyrated, circulating around each other. Chris cupped Jan against his body and murmured in her ear, "Tim says Kay goes both ways."

Jan nodded, meeting his brown eyes. "I know."

"So you want to hook up with them?"

"I'd like to ask her to dance first."

Chris nodded. They watched Kay and Tim swirling in and around Lil and Buck. The two men took their wives in their arms, backs against their chests, gyrating and stroking up and down their figures, the couples facing each other. Lil reached for Kay and the women gradually became a couple, in the middle between their husbands' bodies, clothed curves sliding against each other as they kissed and danced.

Jan smiled. Oh yes, she wanted to dance with Kay. Chris kissed the back of her neck, his hands plying their magic trailing across her stomach and hips. Kay had advised Jan to take control if she wanted it. "May I cut in?" she asked, as they moved in close to the gyrating couples.

Kay looked over her shoulder at Tim with a smile. "Kiss her if she'll allow it, and I'll switch partners."

Jan lifted her face and Tim's hand fell from his wife's shoulder to Jan's hip as she met his lips for a kiss. He had a soft touch, and she found herself eager to watch him make love to his wife later.

Kay's mouth was on Jan's throat before she disengaged from Tim's lips. The music's rhythm matched her changing heart rate and Jan chuckled a little as Tim's mouth left hers.

Premises   Lara Zielinsky

"She's all yours," Tim said.

Jan opened her eyes and found Kay's eyes searching hers. "See?"

Kay's hands moved from her hips at the same time Jan's moved to Kay's hips and they swayed into a rhythm together, stroking up each other's sides and back. Jan dipped her head finding Kay's coming up. Their lips met and she hummed with pleasure. Kay chuckled against Jan's mouth, and the sound was almost lost in the roar of blood in her ears. She started to reach around Kay's hips, to pull the woman in more closely, and found Tim's hip there. Jan opened her eyes, and he made a slight move of separation.

Sliding against the other woman's front, Jan tightened her embrace. Kay's figure meshed erotically with her own, and Jan knew she had been right. She did want a woman's touch, a woman's body. She dipped her head and murmured against Kay's ear, "Can we move someplace else?"

"Yes."

Jan gestured to the pool area. She slipped a hand inside the side of Kay's dress, outlining the side of a breast with her palm. "Hot tub?"

Kay smiled. Tim smiled. Chris smiled. Jan stepped out of her shoes first when they reached the pool deck. Several couples in the pool played a version of Marco Polo. Jan realized the game would be a perfect ice breaker, blindfolded or not, as it granted permission to touch. She spied a small sign as they walked to one of the hot tubs: *No coming or going*. She chuckled.

Kay went to Chris to help him unbutton his shirt. They kissed as she did so, and Jan enjoyed the view for several seconds. Tim touched her back. "May I?" he asked her.

She assented, and his hands and lips roused her skin to a rosy flush as he slipped her free of her skirt. The fishnets were crotchless and his fingers, broader and flatter than Chris's, brushing there caused a pleasant shiver. When she turned around, Chris and Kay were settling into the heated water, the steam coating their unsubmerged skin in a sheen of perspiration.

Tim held her hand as she stepped in, with the other low on her back. They both watched Kay nuzzling against Chris, obviously stroking him as his hips lifted rhythmically. Jan slid her fingertips over Tim's furred chest, enjoying the different sensation, and she brushed her hip against his thickening member, recognizing it as thicker than Chris's. She kissed him.

"Later?" he asked.

"Definitely," she acknowledged.

Premises *Lara Zielinsky*

Kay leaned back, resting her head against the side of the hot tub, and Chris, Jan knew from the flush on his face he was hard, moved to caress the woman. Jan looked to see Tim reach out and catch Kay's right hand as Chris's touch set her hips in motion. Kay's responses were wonderful, and Jan acknowledged again she would be enthralled when she could see this woman orgasming later, and if she could cause one.

"Jan," Kay called softly, her eyes closed to enjoy Chris's contact.

Jan complied with the call, straddling Kay as she crossed the hot tub. Kay circled Jan's neck with her arms, and as her pelvis ground against Jan's thigh, they kissed. Jan tasted the salts of perspiration and the warm chlorinated water as she trailed her lips down from Kay's mouth, reaching for her breasts and lifting the pert mounds just above the water line, flicking the nipples with her modest nails. Kay's throaty voice ebbed and flowed with Jan's strokes. Jan moved one hand under the water, caressing Kay's stomach, not sure if she should go lower yet or not. When her fingertips found the wet hair and combed through it lightly, Kay's hand came down over hers, and she pressed firmly and rhythmically over her pubic bone with their joined hands. Jan returned her mouth to Kay's, and they lingered in small kisses, tasting each other's mouth, outlining the shapes with the tips of their tongues, and tasting lipstick remnants.

When Jan eased back, Kay looked at her seriously through lowered lids, arms spread across the back of the hot tub. "We'd like to share," she said with a nod toward Tim. "You?"

Chris looked to Jan who nodded. "Clean?"

Tim nodded. "But condoms. Always."

"Of course."

"Would you want my husband?" Kay asked Jan.

"Yes." Jan asked, "You want me?"

"Oh yes, sweetheart, I want you." Jan chuckled at the deep sincerity in Kay's throaty voice.

"Then yes."

They moved from the pool, nudity easy now, as hands stroked visible flesh wherever it was to be found. Jan had Chris's and Tim's cocks in her hands as Kay led the way to the rooms. They checked several and Jan spied writhing and sinuous bodies making orgiastic noises. As they paused in one doorway, Tim positioned himself with his hardening cock between Jan's thighs, the bulbous head compressed in the slight gap between her thigh muscles as he moved.

Premises *Lara Zielinsky*

    Chris, taller than Kay, had his cock hard against her mid-back as they watched. With her arm around Kay's shoulders, Jan stroked Kay's breast. Kay curled her arm around Jan's lower back and stroked Jan's hip.

    Within the room, a black man lay blindfolded on his back, his mouth open and tongue straining to lick at the naked white pussy gyrating above his head. Another woman, hunched over and stroking his balls, repeatedly lowered herself onto his condom-covered cock that was thick like a deli salami. The threesomes' sounds were pleasurable, adding to Jan's eagerness to be making her own version of these sounds. Kay took her hand.

    "This room." Kay moved to the next door and put her panty on the doorknob, signaling it would be for their private use only. Jan stroked the green silk strip of cloth imagining the heat and scent still lingering in the crotch.

    A king size mattress and box spring dominated the middle of the room. Faint moonlight beamed in through the curtained window. Kay pulled herself backward on one side of the bed, and Chris took Jan to the other side of the bed where she lay down. By mutual accord, the women lay side by side, while Tim and Chris knelt on the floor between their legs.

    Jan enjoyed Chris's ability with his tongue, and while she was enjoying the occasional view of Kay's pleasure and Tim's face between Kay's thighs, she also was caught up in her husband's thumb as it stroked her clit and his fingers curving inside thrusting toward her g-spot.

    Kay's hand found Jan and their fingers intertwined as they lay together, each woman experiencing the pleasure of her own husband. Jan enjoyed the sounds Kay made beside her, but she missed the other woman's first orgasm as her own washed over her. She felt Kay's soft hands soothed over her face and throat as she lay there a moment with her eyes closed. Chris still licked between her thighs. She turned her head and found Kay's lips and opened her eyes as Kay's mouth left hers to trail down her throat and onto her chest, where lips and teeth latched onto a breast. Jan found Kay's breast dangling above her. She reached up, stroking the skin, and kissed around the pert mound before licking her way to Kay's nipple and latching on. The tugging at her own breast paused as Kay gasped in pleasure. Then they resumed mutually sucking on nipples.

    Jan's hands moved over Kay's back, stroking the muscles as she switched from the right to the left breast. Kay moved as well, inching forward, until her knees met Jan's shoulders. Up through Kate's thighs, Jan saw Tim fingering his wife's slit. While he continued, Jan nuzzled into the dark pubic hairs with her nose, enjoying the scent, and finally sought out Kay's clit.

Chris's fingers withdrew from her own slit, and Jan's lower region convulsed, wanting the contact to resume. Soon other, narrower, more delicate fingers spread her labia apart, swirling the moisture. Thin, silky, ribbon-soft lips and a narrower nose were between her legs, and a new tongue lapped at her center, kitten delicate. Jan's hips surged and she moaned with pleasure.

Tim's cock was hard again, and after he passed one of two condoms to Chris, he moved behind Kay. Jan helped Tim unroll the condom over his thick length then she watched him feed his cock gradually into Kay. Jan stroked the thickness, played with his balls, and tasted Kay's fluids each time he partially withdrew.

Chris pushed forward between Jan's thighs, and then she felt the slight rocking as Kay obviously took him in her mouth while Tim thrust into her from behind. But Kay's fingers never stopped within Jan's center. Jan rearranged herself, grasping the round swells of Kay's rear, as she kissed the woman's clenching stomach muscles. She was there for Kay's second orgasm, watching the way her labia fluttered, brushing her own thumb rigidly against Kay's clit and tasting the juices actively dripping from the warm slit. The woman's cries were grunts and moans and at last a completed sigh. Kay collapsed slightly, her body slick against Jan who looked up between Kay's thighs to see Chris unrolling a condom onto his cock.

"Over," she said. It was the first word she'd spoken in a while and she wasn't surprised to hear her voice a little raspy and her throat dry. Kay moved away. Up on her hands and knees now, Jan lifted her hips, asking wordlessly for Chris's cock. With Kay's and Tim's hands stroking her upper body, and Chris thrusting at this deeper angle, Jan was soon skyrocketing toward her own second orgasm of the night.

Kay turned around under Jan, until their legs were both around Chris and with Jan's mound rubbing Kay's pussy every time Chris pushed her forward, and their breasts sliding against one another. Kay kissed her, sliding her tongue deep in Jan's mouth allowing Jan to taste her own juices which Kay had been lapping up, as she came at Chris's own orgasmic twitching within her channel.

Premises *Lara Zielinsky*

Gasping as Kay stroked her hair, Jan felt Chris pull out of her, and the women were in the middle as the men laid down; Tim a furry pillow for Jan's back, and Chris against Kay's back.

Stroking Kay's skin under her fingertips, Jan arched under Tim's thick fingers stirring in her quivering slit juices. She closed her eyes and just felt Kay's lips moving across her exposed throat as she writhed to Tim's ministrations. His fingers seemed almost as thick together as Chris's cock and she began to grow hungry to feel Tim thrusting between her thighs remembering how he was stretching Kay.

"Tim's ready," Kay murmured near her ear. "You want the top?"

Jan knew she could control the depth and timing, and nodded. Kay kissed her again.

Everyone separated. Tim laid back against the pillows, propped up a little. Jan and Kay, with Chris stroking Jan's lower back, shared kisses around Tim's turgid cock. It grew harder under Jan's hand as Kay guided her to grasp it.

Kay fingered Jan as Jan unrolled a fresh condom over Tim's cock. Then as Jan lowered herself, using her knees for balance, Kay straddled Tim's legs behind Jan's back. Stroking Jan's upper body and kissing her throat and shoulder, Kay tweaked Jan's nipples. Chris walked around and sat next to Tim, both men appreciating the show as Jan first felt the mushroom tip. She planted her hands on Tim's chest, leaning forward.

Kay held her up, her skin soft and warm and damp against Jan's back. Tim's hands moved to Jan's thighs, and he tipped his hips up. She pushed down another inch. Kay tweaked Jan's nipples again. Jan rocked, pulling Tim in another inch and bearing down as her muscles quivered.

This is fantastic, Jan thought, pleasure coursing through her veins. She lifted her right arm, caught Kay behind the head and pulled their mouths together for a deep kiss as she rocked down and felt her cunt spasm around Tim's throbbing cock. He groaned. Jan caught Chris's smile as he watched alternately where Kay played with his wife's breasts and where Tim's cock appeared and disappeared as Jan rose and fell rhythmically, caught in the sexual tide between the couple.

Jan heard Tim murmur something and saw Chris rise to his knees, stroking his cock as he leaned across her shoulder to kiss Kay's mouth.

"Oh!" Jan gasped at the sight as a particularly acute bolt of arousal shot from her center to her chest.

Premises *Lara Zielinsky*

Tim's fingers met Kay's and Chris's on Jan's hips then moved inside her thighs. She experienced spasmodic shocks as each in turn flicked the top of her swollen and very ready clit.

"Oh. Ah. Uh. Ohhh." She rocked her hips into the circular strokes of Kay's fingertip, and rose up and down on Tim's cock.

Kay pressed her forward, her fingertip still working Jan's clit but now her arm was between Tim's and Jan's bellies. "I want to lick you as you come around his cock," Kay whispered.

Jan was unsure how it might work until Kay demonstrated. Kay pulled back from Jan and Chris stroked her warm skin before it could cool in the room's air. With Tim deep within her, her thighs spread wide over his, her backside was probably very visible. She remembered this position in a few of the DP films she and Chris had watched, but she hadn't thought about how easily a woman's mouth would go there as well.

Kay's tongue swiped Jan's tightly stretched skin and she felt herself throbbing and loosening. A soft, warm, but dry caress, obviously a fingertip stroked the perineal skin between her stretched hole and her anus and Jan almost felt as if she orgasmed again. Tim's grunt suggested she had at the very least massaged him very pleasantly with her internal muscles.

Aware Chris was watching the whole thing, Jan spasmed again. Tim groaned. He was absolutely massive. She adjusted herself and waited for Kay's strokes again on her intimate flesh.

This time it was Kay's tongue that lapped around the point where her husband's cock disappeared into Jan's grasping cunt and he moved minutely.

Jan lifted her head and smiled at Tim as his wife licked them both below. "Love it," she murmured.

"She does too," Tim said. Jan quivered at the connotation. She had done something similar for Kay earlier when she was being plowed by Tim. She was glad she hadn't been mistaken or misguided in her eagerness to touch. No wonder Kay had come so hard.

Her mind, distracted by the image, gave her own orgasm the unusual chance to sneak up on her. A delicate fingertip pushed inside her loosened anus with surprising ease and Jan's throbbing set off Tim, who pushed down on her hips, impaling her more firmly. His throat muscles strained as he groaned and drained spasmodically.

Kay kissed Jan's shoulder, accepting a languid stroke to her cheek. "May I have Chris?" she asked Jan.

"Yes."

Jan rested against Tim's furred chest, surprising herself only a little now as the evening had worn on with the contented stroking from another man as she watched Kay push Chris down to the bed. As Jan and Tim watched, Kay stroked Chris's cock, making it glisten with lubricant. With it hard between their bellies, she spread her body over his and they kissed. She kissed down his chest, pausing to teethe his nipples. Jan smiled as she knew this drove him crazy with lust.

With Chris's hands urging a bit at her shoulders and stroking through her hair, Kay moved further down to the cock springing from its bush of hair. After rolling down the fresh condom, Kay sucked at Chris's balls, still moving her fist in short, piston-like jerks over his cock.

Jan stroked Kay's thigh as the woman finally straightened up and lifted herself over, then down, in one single motion, to impale herself on Chris until their pubic mounds slapped together.

Kay didn't move up and down much, but it was apparent from the pleasure screwing up Chris's features that her inner muscles were working magic on his cock.

"You wanna stroke her," Tim said.

"All right." Jan got up next to Kay and began stroking her breasts. Between her thighs, she felt Tim's fingers find her own slit again. She smiled and kissed Kay's mouth as it sought hers.

They played with one another's breasts as Kay's stealth massage had Chris writhing and moaning. And, finally, coming.

Chris's groans were sharp, and he grasped Kay's hips, forcing her up and down slightly on him as he continued to come. Then Kay was wrapped up in his arms, and he was kissing her as he slowed his hips.

Kay however turned almost immediately back to Jan. She remained straddling Chris and urged Jan around in front of her.

As Jan lifted her leg to straddle Chris's chest, two of Tim's fingers slipped fully into her channel. She gasped and caught Kay's mouth. Chris's hands moved to the back of Jan's thighs, holding her up for Tim's thrusts. Jan's center convulsed as she realized that Chris was enjoying the show of another man's fingers spreading her open. She felt her fluids slipping out and heard the sloppy sounds with Tim's continuing thrusts. She looked deep into Kay's gray-blue eyes while stroking through her fine auburn hair, her hairline moist with sweat.

Inhaling the commingled scents of sweat, sweet womanly sex, and spent male semen, Jan couldn't believe the sensation when it rumbled up, spreading out first from languorous throbs in her groin to quivering in her thighs that went back to make her clit twitch. Her nipples were as tight as she had ever imagined they could be. Kay twisted the right one before lowering her mouth to the left one. The edges of Jan's vision darkened slightly before she closed her eyes and, clasping Kay's head to her breast, she came once more.

Kay chuckled a bit as she lay down with Jan, snuggling between the two men. "I think I finally figured out what you do," she whispered to Jan.

"What?"

"You're a writer."

"I am?"

"You were cataloging this place with your eyes all night."

"What do you think I write?"

Kay stroked Jan's breast. "I don't know what you wrote before, but I bet it's erotica from here on out." She nibbled Jan's ear causing delicious shivers and Jan turned on her side, feeling Chris's arm over her hip, and meeting Tim's arm as it slipped over Kay's hip.

Jan chuckled. "I write romance."

"So will I be in your next book?"

"I'll have to do more research." Jan turned her head slightly and lifted her chin to bring her mouth to Kay's. "At least the rest of the night."

Kay laughed. "I'll be happy to teach you all I know."

Just Desserts
By Tawanna Sullivan

"Don't worry," Peri said. "In a few hours we will be back in our own bed and this disaster will be a fading memory."

Cru closed her eyes while her girlfriend massaged her temples. "Whose idea was it to have a family reunion? Your relatives would put a Tyler Perry movie to shame."

"I thought that staying in a hotel instead of with my parents would shield us from the drama."

"Ha!"

Grandma Rose had insisted that both Uncle Mason's ex-wife and his current, estranged wife be invited to the reunion "so that all of the kids can meet each other and the rest of the family." No one told Mason, and the fool showed up with his pregnant mistress. That was the touchstone that set off a week of drama. Peri had spent most of the time playing peacemaker. As soon as one situation calmed down, someone else would get their feathers ruffled.

When she wasn't handing out tissue, Cru tried to stay as far away from the group therapy sessions which meant she spent a lot of time outside . . . with the men. Except for a lecherous cousin who had to be put in his place, the guys were okay. However, she never wanted to talk about barbeque or sports ever again.

Peri leaned over and her breast threatened to spill out of the tank top. "Don't worry," she whispered. "I'll make it up to you."

Though they weren't closeted, Cru had struggled all week to keep her hands to herself—lest the less accepting family members be freaked out by a kiss. Even now, she fought the desire to reach out and stroke Peri's luscious brown curves. "I'm fine," she said. "You are the one who needs to relax."

Just then, the airport shuttle pulled up. It was empty, so they took the prime seat up front. Cru thought she would have time for a quick catnap, but the driver had other ideas.

"My name is Rebecca and you girls are my first pick up this afternoon. Did y'all enjoy your stay?" She was an older lady who almost disappeared into her uniform. In an ideal world, she would be in some retirement village sipping mint juleps while a hunky attendant rubbed Ben Gay into her ankles

"Yes, ma'am," Peri said, her southern accent front and center.

"Down here for business or pleasure?"

"Family reunion."

"It's nice that you girls come back to see your family. My sister and I can barely stay in the same room."

Cru looked at Peri and rolled her eyes, but Rebecca didn't notice. "Hope you come back soon. We really do need the tourists to keep coming in."

Not one to favor silence, the driver continued. "Times are hard for us down here. Jobs are disappearing, there's that foreclosure mess—it's getting so that people will do almost anything for a dollar. Take the Westin Diplomat. It used to be one of our nicest hotels. Guess who had a convention there this week? Swingers!" She waited a bit. "You know, those people who swap wives and have orgies."

Peri perked up. "Oh, really?"

Rebecca nodded. "When something like that becomes acceptable down here, you know we are really living in the last times. After the swingers it's some porn people. Now, tell me who's going to stay at the hotel after that? I wouldn't feel comfortable there."

"It wouldn't make a difference to me. People have sex in hotels. That's not unusual." The conversation had suddenly turned boring and Peri slipped on her earphones.

"You don't understand. Those people ran around stark naked and . . . and left nastiness everywhere. Those poor maids have to clean everything."

Cru finally decided to chime in. "The swingers probably haven't done anything that others haven't done first." She put an arm around Peri. "We've had sex on the sofa, in the shower, on the counter of the kitchenette. That's just regular hotel behavior."

From time to time, Rebecca stared at them in the rear view mirror but didn't say another word for the rest of the ride. As they were getting off the bus, Cru tossed a five dollar bill into the tip bucket.

Peri shook her head and laughed. "You ought to be ashamed of yourself. Were you trying to give the lady a heart attack on the freeway?"

"What? Rebecca may have been disgusted, but she didn't refuse the tip." Cru flagged down a skycap. "Besides with a mind like hers, she still probably thinks we're sisters."

"Eww!"

After doing the boarding pass-bag check-security shuffle, they were at Gate 28 waiting for permission to board the plane. The customer service rep announced bad weather in the Northeast was causing delays. Peri bought some magazines and Cru struggled to find a comfortable position for a nap.

Three hours after their scheduled take off, Cru had a stiff neck and the waiting area had started to resemble a refugee camp. She stood up and tried to stretch the kinks out.

"I'm glad you're awake." Peri pointed to her lifeless iPod. "My battery is dead and I've read the latest gossip on Brangelina twice."

"Fine, I'll keep you company. What's the latest news?"

"The weather is so bad that they aren't allowing any planes to travel in the Northeast."

"We're never getting back home."

"In other news, I spotted a couple with a Westin Diplomat shopping bag."

Cru surveyed the miserable crowd. "Where? Rebecca would be scandalized."

"Gate 27, second row, third seat from the left; the Halle Berry look-alike."

Cru's eyes settled on a beautiful, honey brown woman. "Hmm. Is she with the dude on the left or the gorgeous sister on the right?"

"You mean Iman? That's what I've nicknamed her. Yes, they are together."

Iman whispered something to Halle and they both smiled. Peri smiled back and nodded. "While you were scaring children with your snores, I've been making eye contact. You don't mind, do you honey?" She gently raked her fingernails across the back of Cru's hand.

"Of course not." The touch had sent a jolt through Cru that made her tingle from head to toe. Flirting came second nature to Peri, and it had led them into all sorts of adventures.

A familiar voice rang through the loudspeakers. "Ladies and

gentleman, we want you to know that we do appreciate your patience. In a bit we will be distributing a snack and bottled water."

"This doesn't look good." Peri got up. "I'm going to speak to one of the reps. An airline giving away anything is not a good sign." She returned about ten minutes later clutching her cell phone. "The plane sitting at the gate isn't ours. Our plane hasn't left Newark yet—and it's not going to."

"Our flight has been cancelled?"

Peri nodded. "Word came down while I was at the counter. They'll be announcing it soon. I've already called the travel agent. We're booked on a seven a.m. flight to Baltimore. I figure there are hundreds of people trying to get to Newark, so we'd be better off renting a car and driving the rest of the way."

"That's fine. I'll drive, but you have to make sure something decent is on the radio."

A few people noticed that the word "Cancelled" had replaced "Delayed" on the flight monitors and the crowd became agitated. The counters were swarming with angry customers.

Cru's stomach flip flopped. "Now that they've mentioned food, I'm starving. A bag of chips isn't going to be enough. I'll treat for dinner."

They got to Chili's Too in time to get the last free table. The waitress took their drink order and disappeared into the crowd. Peri took a cursory glance of the menu before tossing it aside. "We should have gone over and introduced ourselves."

"We don't know that they were actually at the convention." Cru shrugged. "We're not even sure they are a couple. They could be sisters or something."

"Now you sound like Rebecca."

"What was your plan? Stroll over there, point to the bag and say, 'So ya have a good week?'" Cru leaned forward and was winking and gesturing wildly.

"We had a fabulous time, but it would have been even better if you were there."

There they were—Iman and Halle in the flesh. It was the dark chocolate Amazon that spoke.

"I'm Mona and this is my partner, Erica. We decided to swing by and say hello." It was corny, but it broke the ice.

Peri didn't miss a beat. "I'm Peri and this is my partner, Cru. Please join us for dinner."

Just Desserts   *Tawanna Sullivan*

Erica was the one with the suspicious shopping bag. "Are you sure? We don't want to impose."

Cru found her tongue again. "It's no problem. We're stuck here for a while, might as well make friends."

"We like making new friends." Mona sat next to Peri. "I take it you ladies are trying to get back North. We're from Albany. Where do you call home?"

"Jersey City. We're practically neighbors—give or take a couple of hours." When Peri passed a menu to Mona, her fingers lightly grazed the woman's forearm.

The waitress came back and was very perplexed by the new faces at the table. "Do you two want something to drink, too? Let me get you a couple of menus."

"No need," Cru said before the woman vanished again. "Everyone is ready to order now."

They chatted and flirted through salads and light appetizers. Peri loved being the center of attention. Mona and Erica were clearly under her spell.

Cru sat back and watched the three interact. Away from the not-quite-in-laws, she was finally free to look at women and see sensuality bubbling just underneath the surface. Erica's nipples had hardened, and every time she breathed, part of a tattoo peeked from under her satin shirt. Mona liked talking with her fingertips. She could hardly get out a sentence without touching a forearm or caressing the back of a hand. Peri's eyes always sparkled with mischief, as if she knew your most secret kinky, fantasies and wanted to help fulfill them.

It was Erica who asked the question that had been lingering in the air. "So, do you two like to play?"

No one had actually asked outright before and Cru found herself fumbling with the answer. "Yes, but not in any kind of formal way. We don't go to parties or anything like that."

"But," Peri added, "if we are at a club and the mood is right, we may not go home alone."

After exchanging a glance with Erica, Mona licked her lips and smiled. "We've booked a room at the airport Holiday Inn, and you're welcome to join us. We can order dessert, watch a little television, relax, and you won't be more than ten minutes away from the terminal."

A wicked smile spread across Peri's lips. "What do you think, Cru?"

Just Desserts

Tawanna Sullivan

"I think you deserve a sweet treat."

* * *

It was a nice room with a queen sized bed, a sitting area, and a kitchenette. Mona kept her word about dessert, and it was not long before room service appeared with hot fudge sundaes draped with extra whipped cream.

Peri had slipped off her shoes and got comfortable in the recliner. She winked at Cru and then looked at Mona. "I want your cherry."

"Watch this," Cru whispered to Erica.

Mona took a cherry, made sure it was drenched in cream, and dangled it just above the goddess's lips. Peri's tongue wrapped around the fruit and took the entire piece into her mouth. In less than a minute, the stem re-emerged tied around the pit. There was applause all around.

Cru felt Erica's nose nuzzle against her ear. "That was impressive, but what kind of tricks can you do?"

Goosebumps shot up her arm and the sundae Cru was holding tilted too far to the left spilling warm sticky sauce on her pants. "Fuck!" Rubbing it with a napkin didn't help. "I'll take care of this and be right back." She went to the bathroom, stripped off her jeans, and tried tackling the stain with a washcloth and soap.

"You aren't supposed to rub a stain." Erica sat the lopsided sundae on the sink, took the cloth and began blotting the stain. "Rubbing only makes it spread and pushes it deeper into the fiber." Then, she pulled a stain removal pen from her pocket and the dark spot all but disappeared.

Cru was suitably impressed. "Now, that is a neat trick."

"I have two kids. There's not a stain around that I haven't mastered by now." Erica took a step back and admired the shapely form before her. "I didn't figure you to be the type to wear boxers."

Looking down, Cru realized that she'd thrown on the pair that had a gigantic smiling face over the slit. "They just feel good, you know. Give the illusion of not wearing any underwear at all." Maybe it was the bathroom light or the awkward silence, but Cru began to sweat. "Look. Peri usually plays and I like to watch. Seeing her cum is so amazing, she's so beautiful—"

"What?" Erica's voice was thick with disappointment. "Well, if that's what you want to do, let's see what they are up to."

"No, wait. I'm just saying that's what we usually do." She sighed. "I feel like a teenager again—and that's not a good feeling."

"I make you nervous? I'm not going to bite. Just tell me what you like."

Cru let her fingers drift to the hem of Erica's shirt. "What I'd like is to see the rest of that tattoo."

"You noticed it, huh? I knew you were checking me out at the restaurant." Erica took off her top and leaned against the door frame. On her abdomen were two dragons that formed a heart. Their intertwined tails disappeared under the skirt.

"This is amazing." Cru got on her knees to take a closer look. Twisting her hips, Erica let her skirt and panties fall to reveal it all. The tails melding into a crisp arrow pointed to the top of her bush. "Did it hurt?"

"One person's pain is another person's pleasure. Besides, it's a great incentive to stay away from carbs."

Cru pointed at the ice cream. "What are we going to do with all of this ice cream?"

"Just because I'm through, doesn't mean you can't enjoy it." Erica took a spoonful and let it dribble down her stomach.

Cru met the river of chocolate as it rolled past the dragons' tails. As she rose to lick and suck the trail of sweetness, she caressed Erica's calves and cupped her firm ass. The bra hooks were released and a few seconds later the breasts were completely free. "That's my trick."

Erica braced herself as Cru gently dipped her breasts into the bowl but the shock of cold made her shout. Then, Cru's mouth set to cleaning up the new mess and paid extra attention to the cream covered nipples. Erica gently pushed her away. "You better be careful or you'll get chocolate all over you."

"That's exactly what I want." Cru nearly tore off her shirt and shorts. "You all over me."

Scooping the last of the cream on her fingertips, Erica let Cru suck them dry. "Now, give me a taste." They wrapped their arms around each other and began kissing. Tentative at first, their tongues and limbs intertwined.

Cru reached back and turned on the shower. "Let's clean up, so we can get really dirty." The bathroom was filled with giggles and laughter as they lathered each other up.

"Assume the position," Erica turned Cru toward the tiled wall and made her spread her legs. Reaching around, she palmed and squeezed her nipples while nibbling the back of her neck. "Are you still shy, baby?"

"No," Cru managed to whisper between moans.

"Good." Erica backed up under the water and put her leg on the side of the tub. "I hope you're thirsty."

Cru crouched down and watched the droplets of water slide against her glistening clit. Her tongue gently explored the delicious folds. She curved her tongue around the clit and sipped at the rivet of water cascading from it.

Erica gripped Cru's shoulders, holding her in position, while she rode her face to the pentacle of pleasure. She wasn't prepared to feel the tip of a tongue darting into her opening and lost her balance when the force of the orgasm pushed her back. Cru had wrapped her strong arms around Erica's torso and wouldn't let her fall.

After drying off, they tumbled out of the bathroom and fell across the bed. Erica pulled Cru on top of her. "You're going to have to take another shower. You can't get on a plane smelling like hot cream."

"I said I wanted you all over me and I meant it." The unmistakable sound of a hand smacking against flesh reverberated throughout the room. "It sounds like someone out there is getting a good spanking."

"Want to watch?"

"How?"

Erica dimmed the lights and opened the closet door. When she got the angle just right, the mirror inside gave them a perfect view of the sofa. Peri was bent over the arm while Mona alternated between spanking and fucking her.

Peri was radiant. Her breasts were free and bobbing to the rhythm. Her eyes were partially closed and Cru knew that she was in her space. Anything could set her off now—a feather stroking her arm, a gentle breeze blowing against her back, hot breath against her ear . . . anything.

"Get on your knees," Erica whispered. "Not all the way up. On all fours. Yes, like that." Lying down next to her, she reached up to play with Cru's clit. "Don't look down at me or I'll stop. You don't want me to stop, do you?"

"No." Cru wanted to clamp down on the fingers inside of her, but she stayed perfectly still.

"You watch her. I want to watch you."

Just Desserts   *Tawanna Sullivan*

Erica matched Mona's tempo and Cru felt herself losing control. She tried focusing on Peri but, when their eyes met, Cru gave in to the joy spreading through her body like a wildfire. She collapsed and Erica pulled her close. "You are beautiful when you cum, too."

Bob & Carol & Ted (But Not Alice)
By M. Christian

"What are you afraid of?" Not spoken with scorn; with challenge though. This was Carol, after all. His Carol. The question was sweet, sincere, one lover to another: Really, honestly, what are you frightened of?

Robert fiddled with his glass of ice tea, gathering his thoughts. He trusted Carol—hell, he'd been happily married to her for five years so he'd better—but even so, it was a door he hadn't opened in a long time.

They were sitting in their living room, a gentle rain tapping at the big glass doors to the patio and dancing on the pale blue surface of the pool beyond. In the big stone fireplace, a gentle fire licked at the glowing embers of a log.

Carol smiled and, as always, when she did Bob felt himself sort of melt, deep inside. Carol . . . it shocked him sometimes how much he loved her, trusted her, loved to simply be with her. He counted himself so fortunate to have found the other half of himself in the tall, slim, brown-haired woman. They laughed at the same jokes, they appreciated the same ear of jazz, they both could eat endless platters of sashimi, and—in the bedroom, the garage, the kitchen, in the pool, in the car, and everywhere else the mood struck them—their love-making was always delightful, often spectacular.

"I don't know," Bob finally said, taking a long sip of his drink. Needs more sugar, he thought absently. "I mean I think about it sometimes. Not like I don't like what we do, but sometimes it crops up. A lot of the time it's hot, but other times it's kinda . . . fuck, disconcerting, you know? Like I should be thinking of what we're doing, what I want to do with you—" A sly smile, a hand on her thigh, kneading gently, "—instead of thinking about, well, another guy."

Bob & Carol & Ted (But Not Alice)   M. Christian

Carol leaned forward, grazing her silken lips across his. As always, just that simple act—one sweeping kiss—made his body, especially his cock, stiff with desire. "Sweet," she said, whispering hoarsely into his ear, "I don't mind. I think it's hot. I really do."

Bob smiled, flexing his jean-clad thighs to relish in his spontaneous stiffness. "I know. It just feels weird sometimes. I can't explain it."

"What do you think about? Talk to me about it. Maybe that'll help a little bit." Her hand landed in his lap, curled around his shaft. "Pretend I'm not here," she added, with a low laugh.

He responded with a matching chuckle. "Oh, yeah, right," he said, leaning forward to meet her lips. They stayed together, lips on lips, tongues dancing in hot mouths. Bob didn't know how to respond, so he just followed his instincts. His hand drifted up to cup Carol's firm, large breasts. Five years and she still had the power to reach down into his sexual self, to get to him at a cock and balls level. But there was something else.

"I think it's hot," Carol said, breaking the kiss with a soft smack of moisture. "I think about it a lot, really. The thought of you with—what was his name again?"

Bob doubted Carol had really forgotten, but he smiled and played along. "Charley. College friend."

Charley: brown curls, blue eyes, broad shoulders, football, basketball, geology, math, made a wicked margarita. Charley: late one night in their dorm room, both drunk on those wicked margaritas, Charley's hand on Bob's knee, then on his hard cock. "We fooled around for most of the semester, and then his father died. Left him the business. We stayed in touch for a year or so, then, well, drifted away. You know?"

"I think it's wonderful," Carol said, smiling, laughing, but also tender, caring, knowing there was a Charley-shaped hole somewhere deep inside Bob. Carefully, slowly, she inched down the zipper on his shorts until the tent of his underwear was clearly visible, a small dot of pre-come marking the so-hard tip of his cock. "I think about it when we play. When we fuck."

Bob suspected, but hearing Carol say it added extra iron to his already throbbing hard-on. Carol normally wasn't one to talk during sex. This new, rough, voice was even more of a turn on.

Bob felt a glow start, deep down. Even to Carol, Charley was something private—but hearing Carol's voice, he felt like he could, really, finally share it. "He was something else, Charley was. Big guy. Never would have thought it to look at him. That sounds stupid, doesn't it?"

Bob & Carol & Ted (But Not Alice)   M. Christian

"No, it doesn't. You're speaking from the heart, sexy. Since when is anyone's heart logical or fair?" Carol had gotten his shorts down, quickly followed by his underwear. Bob's cock had never seemed so big or so hard in his life. It was like two parts of his life had met with the force of both working to make him hard . . . so damned hard. Carol kissed the tip, carefully savoring the bead of come just starting to form again at the tip.

He smiled down at her, taking a moment to playfully ruffle her hair before allowing himself to melt down into the sofa. "I wouldn't call him 'sweet' or 'nice', but he could be sometimes. He just liked . . . fuck . . ." The words slipped from his mind as Carol opened her mouth and, at first— slowly, carefully—started to suck on his cock. "Fuck . . . yeah. He liked life, I guess. I don't even think he thought of himself as gay or anything. He just liked to fuck, to suck, to get laid, you know. But it was special. I can't really explain it."

"You loved him, didn't you? At least a little bit?" Carol said, taking her lips off his cock for a moment to speak. As she did, she stroked him, each word a downward or upward stroke.

Bob didn't say anything. He just leaned back and closed his eyes. He knew she was right but that was one thing he wasn't quite willing to say— not yet. He'd come a long way, but that was still in the distance.

Carol smiled, sweetly, hotly, and dropped her mouth onto his cock again. This time her sucking, licking, stroking of his cock was faster, more earnest, and Bob could tell that she was aching to fuck, to climb on top of him and ride herself to a shattering, glorious orgasm. But she didn't. Instead, she kept sucking, kept stroking his cock, occasionally breaking to whisper, then say in a raw, hungry voice: "I think it's hot . . . not him just sucking your cock . . . but that you have had that. Bet sometimes . . . we look at the same guy . . . and want to know what he'd be like . . . to suck . . . to fuck."

Even though Bob was somewhere else, damned near where Carol wanted to be, he knew she was right. It was hot, it was special, and he recognized that. He wanted to haul her off her knees, get dressed, and bolt out the door to do just that. The kid who bagged their groceries sometimes at the Piggly Wiggly, that one linebacker, Russell Crowe—he wanted to take them home, take off their shirts, lick their nipples, suck their cocks, suck their cocks, suck their cocks . . .

Then something went wrong. Just on the edge of orgasm, Carol stopped. Bob felt slapped, like ice water had been dumped into his lap. He

Bob & Carol & Ted (But Not Alice) — M. Christian

opened his eyes and looked, goggle-eyed as Carol got up off the floor, straightening her t-shirt over very hard nipples. "Didn't you hear that? Of all times for someone to ring the fucking doorbell."

* * *

Tugging up his pants, Bob rehearsed what he'd say: Mormons? Slam the door in their faces. Door-to-door salesman? The same. Someone needing directions? "Sorry, but you're way off," then do the same.

Just as Bob got to the living room door, he heard Carol, who'd been a lot more dressed to start with, saying. "Ted! How's it hanging?"

Bob rounded the corner, a smile already spreading across his face. Of all the people to have knocked on their front door, Ted was probably the only one who would have understood.

Ted and his charming wife Alice lived just across town. Normally, Bob and Carol would never in a million years have crossed paths with them, but it so happened that Ted worked in the coffee place right across the street from where Bob worked. After six months of going back and forth, Bob finally struck up a conversation with Ted and found out, much to his delight, that the tall, sandy-haired young man and he had a lot in common: the Denver Broncos, weekend sailing, and Russell Crowe movies. Bob and Carol felt very relaxed and even sometimes sexually playful around Ted and Alice—even going so far as to having a kind of sex party one night, when they all got way too wasted on tequila and some primo greenbud that Ted had scored the night before. All they'd done was watch each other fuck, but it had been more than enough to blast Bob and Carol into happy voyeuristic bliss and fuel their erotic fantasies for weeks afterward.

"Low and to the right," Ted answered, smiling wide and broad and planting a quick kiss on Carol's cheek. Bob gave Ted his own quick greeting—a full body hug—that, only until he finished did Bob realize had probably given Ted more than he expected with regard to Bob's still rock-hard dick.

Bob and Carol smiled at each other, feeling relaxed and still playful in the presence of their friend. "Where's Alice at, Teddy? Somewhere in the depths of Columbia?" Bob asked.

Bob & Carol & Ted (But Not Alice) M. Christian

Alice was the other half of Bean Seeing You, their little coffee house, and was often away trying to wrangle up all kinds of stimulating delicacies, not all of them coffee-related.

"Worse than that," Ted said, playfully ruffling his friend's brown locks. "Deepest, darkest Bakersfield. I'm kinda worried about her. The last expedition down there vanished without a trace."

Everyone laughing, more out of released tension than Ted's weird brand of humor, they retreated back to the living room and the couch. As Bob and Ted sprawled out on the couch while Carol got some drinks, Bob couldn't help but wonder if their friend had figured out that they'd been almost screwing their brains out a few minutes before. The thought of it made Bob grin wildly.

"Come on, bro," Ted said, picking up on the smile. "Out with it."

Suddenly tongue-tied, Bob was glad when Carol walked in with three tall, cool drinks. "One for the man of the house. Bob. One for the handsome stranger . . . Ted . . . And one for the horny housewife . . . Carol. Cheers!" she concluded, taking a hefty swallow of her own drink.

Bob and Ted toasted her, Bob almost coughing as he drank. The drinks were stiff and then some. He smiled to himself again as he sank back into the sofa. Talking about Charley made him feel like a secret had been released from some dark, compressed part of his mind. He felt light, airy, almost like he was hovering over his body, looking down at Ted—tall, curly-haired, quick and bright Ted—and Carol. Carol, who even just thinking of her made his body and mind recall their wonderful love-making.

Sneaking a furtive glance at Ted, Bob looked his friend over more carefully. In his new, unburdened vision, Ted looked . . . well, he wasn't like Charley, but there was still something about Ted that made Bob think of his college friend—no, his college lover. Something about their height, their insatiable appetite for life, their humor.

"Is it hot in here or is it just me?" Carol piped up, laughing at her own cliché. Bob and Ted laughed, too, but then the sound dropped away to a compressed silence as Carol lifted off her t-shirt and theatrically mopped her brow.

Bob's mind bounced from Carol's beautiful breasts, and her obviously very erect nipples, to Ted's rapt attention on them. He was proud of Carol; proud that she was so lovely, so sexy. He wanted to reach out and grab her, pull her to him. He wanted to kiss her nipples as Ted

Bob & Carol & Ted (But Not Alice)   M. Christian

watched. He wanted to sit her down on the couch, spread her strong thighs and lick her cunt until she screamed, moaned and held onto Bob's hair as orgasm after orgasm rocketed through her as Ted watched. He wanted to bend her over, slide his painfully hard cock into her, and then fuck her still she moaned and bucked against him as Ted watched. He wanted Ted . . .

Carol's shorts came off next. Naked, she stood in front of them. Like a goddess, she rocked, back and forth, showing off her voluptuous form. But even though he loved her, and thought she was probably the most beautiful women he'd ever seen, Bob turned to look at Ted.

Ted, with the beautiful Carol standing right there in the room with him was, instead, looking at Bob.

Bob felt his face grow flushed with . . . no, not with what he expected. It wasn't embarrassment. Dimly, he was aware of Carol walking towards him, getting down on her hands and knees again, and in a direct repeat of only minutes before, playfully tugging his cock out of her shorts and starting to suck on it.

Still watching Ted watching him, and Carol sucking his cock, Bob smiled at him. In Carol's mouth, his cock jumped with a sudden influx of pure lust.

Carol, breaking her hungry relishing of his dick, said. "Bob, I really think Ted would like you to suck his cock."

Now Bob was embarrassed, but not enough to keep him from silently nodding agreement.

"I'd love that," Ted said, his voice low and rumbling. "I really would."

"Take your pants off, Ted." Carol said, stroking Bob's cock. "I want to watch."

Ted did, quickly shucking his shirt as well as his threadbare jeans. He stood for a moment, letting Carol and Bob look at him. Bob had seen his friend's cock before, but for the first time he really looked at it. Ted was tall and thin, his chest bare and smooth. His cock was big—though maybe not as big as Bob's (a secret little smirk at that)—but handsome. It wasn't soft, but it also wasn't completely hard.

As Carol and Bob watched, Ted's cock grew firmer, harder, larger, until it stuck out from his lean frame at an urgent 45 degree angle.

"Bob . . ." Carol said, her voice purring with lust, "suck Ted's cock. Please, suck it."

Bob & Carol & Ted (But Not Alice)   M. Christian

Ted crawled up on the sofa, lying down so that his head was on one armrest, his cock sticking straight up. His eyes were half-closed, and a sweet, sexy, smile played on his lips.

Bob reached down, turning just enough to reach his friend and not dislodge Carol from her earnest sucking of his own dick, and gently took hold of Ted's cock. It was warm, almost hot, and slightly slick with a fine sheen of sweat. He could have looked at it for hours, days, but with Carol working hard on his own dick, he felt his pulse racing, his own hunger beating hard in his heart.

At first he just kissed it, tasting salty pre-come. With a flash of worry that he wouldn't be good, first he licked the tip, exploring the shape of the head with his lips and then his tongue. As his heart hammered heavier and his own cock pulsed with sensation, he finally took the head into his mouth and gently sucked and licked. Ted, bless him, gave wonderful feedback, gently moaning and bucking his slims hips just enough to let Bob know that he was doing a good job.

As Carol worked him, he worked Ted. They were a long train of pleasure, a circuit of moans and sighs. Time seemed to stretch, and distance compress until the whole world was just Ted's dick in Bob's mouth, Bob's dick in Carol's mouth — all on that wonderful afternoon.

Then, before he was even aware it was happening, Bob felt his orgasm pushing, heavy and wonderfully leaden, down through his body, down through his balls, down through his cock, and, in a spasming orgasm that made him break his earnest sucking of Ted's cock to moan, sigh, almost scream with pleasure. Smiling at his friend, Ted followed quickly behind, with only a few quick jerks of his cock as Bob rested his head on Ted's knee.

Bob felt . . . good, like something important, magical and special had happened. The world had grown, by just a little bit, but in a very special way. Resting on his friend's knee, Carol kissing his belly, he smiled. Everything's all right with the world.

* * *

Later, the sun set, and everyone very much exhausted by many more hours of play, Ted stumbled to the front door, with Carol helping him navigate through the dim house.

Bob & Carol & Ted (But Not Alice)   *M. Christian*

"Thanks for coming," she said with a sweet coo, almost a whisper, so as not to wake the heavily slumbering Bob in the next room. She kissed him, soft and sweet, smiling to herself at the variety of tastes on his lips.

"I was happy to. Very. Thanks for asking me to—come," Ted said, smiling, as he opened the front door.

Carol smiled. "Thank you for giving him such a wonderful gift. Next weekend then?"

"Definitely. Next time I'll bring Alice."

Another gentle kiss, a mutual "Goodnight" and the door was closed.

Quick-Fix
By Jolene Hui

I opened the door to see Kevin standing there one afternoon. I was home and not working that day, suffering from a bout of depression again and just wanted to be alone. But Kevin's dimples made me smile. I couldn't deny he was gorgeous.

"I have a weird question," he said.

"Um, ok . . ." I answered, standing in my bathrobe at two in the afternoon. The flesh across my chest flushed when I spoke.

"Do you happen to have any Kool-Aid? Or something of the sort?" He ran his fingers through his brown, slightly mussed hair.

A small giggle escaped my lips. "Let me take a look. It might be ancient. I don't know if I'd trust it if I do." I stepped out of the way. "Come in while I investigate."

He stepped in and I latched the door carefully. A small stream of panic shot through me; like I was concerned someone might have seen Kevin come inside while I was in my bathrobe. I tried to push my nonsensical thoughts out of my head. It was really no one's business anyway.

"Have a seat," I said, motioning to the couch. Some of Luke's textbooks and papers were scattered all over the coffee table. Kevin didn't seem to notice and just sat down.

My kitchen was in good shape. I'd had a mother who slaved in her kitchen every night. Nothing there was ever out of place. At least I'd inherited one good trait from her. The cupboards were well organized, and I knew exactly where the powdered drink mix would be if I had it. I stood on my tippy toes at the tallest cupboard, trying to reach the second to top shelf. The belt on my robe loosened, but I paid no attention. A packet of cherry Kool-Aid stared back at me, daring me to reach it. I stretched my arm out, thinking of how amazingly I'd stretched in yoga class the night

Quick-Fix   *Jolene Hui*

before. When my fingers finally managed to knock the package down, the belt on my robe decided to fall down with it.

"Fuck," I said, dropping the packet and pulling my robe closed. I peered around the corner to see Kevin looking at me, a *People* magazine in his hands.

"You ok?" he asked.

"Yup," I said, my hand on my robe to keep it from gaping open. My face flushed when I realized there was a part of me that wished Kevin would have been standing by the cupboard when my belt had fallen off.

I walked toward him after picking up the packet.

"Here ya go. It might not be drinkable, but it'll probably do," I said.

"Thanks," he said. "I'm surprised you didn't ask me why I wanted it."

"I didn't think it was any of my business, I guess." Now my mind was focused on those dimples and red lips. A neatly trimmed goatee framed them.

Kevin set down the magazine and stood up, tapping the packet on his thigh. "That's a way to look at it, I suppose," he said.

I started to walk toward the door so that I could lead him out as quickly as possible. I didn't particularly like the fact that I was having these sexual thoughts about him. He followed me, still tapping the packet on his thigh.

"If you feel like it later," he said, stepping over the threshold, "come on over for a glass. I like to drink it when I paint."

I had nearly forgotten he was an artist. "Sounds good," I said, flashing him a genuine smile. I wanted to drink more than that. "Have a good one."

"You too," he said, walking into his apartment across the hall. I was suddenly thirsty for some Kool-Aid when I closed the door.

Things were easier when Luke wasn't in school. We'd been together ten years, four of which we had been married. And three of those four he'd been in law school. We'd moved across the country so that he could go to the law school of his dreams.

In a new city, I spent nights alone, wandering the streets, sitting in coffee shops, writing in my journal, and wondering if I had ever really wanted to be a wife. Life had been different before Luke started school. Now I hardly saw him; we never had sex; I missed my family and friends, and I wasn't sure what I wanted to do with my life. Our relationship was solid, and I always felt like I could talk to him about anything. I'd never felt such love for a person or like I was more suited to someone. But I needed something else. I was never satisfied with the ordinary and I wouldn't start being satisfied with it now. Sometimes, though, I had the feeling that if I could just get intimate with Luke again, everything else would fall into place. That part of my life was necessary for me to function correctly.

"Whoa, tiger," a voice said to me as I was rapidly trekking up the staircase the night after the Kool-Aid incident. When I looked up, I saw Kevin, carrying a large cake that I could have easily smashed had I been going just slightly quicker.

"Oh God, I'm sorry," I said, instinctively stepping aside and putting my back to the railing.

He laughed at the twisted and silly look on my face. "Don't worry about it. We averted disaster this time." His blue eyes glowed in the semi darkness of the lit staircase. I didn't get to stare at them long, though, as he jetted down the stairs tossing "Bye. Have a great night" out to me.

I looked after him, wondering where he was taking a chocolate cake and wondering what it, and he, tasted like. I also wondered if I'd just constantly be watching him walk away from me.

When I got inside, Luke was at his computer with his headphones on. He didn't even look up. I sighed and stood in the entryway for a second knowing it was probably a lost cause even trying to talk to him tonight. I was a freelance journalist so I understood the whole getting busy thing and didn't take it personally. Having some down time, however, was making me a little antsy.

I walked over and hugged him from behind, kissing him on his ear. He turned around, smiled and grazed my arm with his fingers as a way of saying hello.

"Did you eat?" I asked, always concerned with his stomach.

"Yup." He had already turned back to his computer. The lines in his forehead scrunched together.

I dropped my backpack into the study and took my clothes off in the bedroom. I didn't like feeling alone, especially since we were married and both young. There had to be something to do to spice up our relationship. I had to get Luke's mind off of his books every once in a while. I knew I was far from boring in bed, but maybe introducing another woman might give him a jolt to his parts?

Quick-Fix   *Jolene Hui*

Had we ever had an open relationship? No. But as I masturbated in the steamy shower, the folds of my pussy welcoming my fingers, I started to feel a little angry that I wasn't getting sex from my husband. I leaned my head against the wall after I came, somewhat disappointed that it was going to be a cock free night.

I dressed, brushed my teeth, and got into bed, all the while thinking of ways to make our sex live better. I knew he wouldn't be up for another man, but perhaps another woman. I wondered if he'd ever done that before. Strange that we'd never talked about it before. I fell asleep picturing me with Luke's cock in my mouth and another man's cock in my pussy. In the sexy but muddled dream, I thought it was Kevin behind me. And Luke tasted like chocolate cake.

I was jolted awake when Luke crawled into bed. I looked at the clock: 2:10 a.m. I put my pillow over my head and went back to sleep.

"Kevin called this morning," said Luke the next day. "He wanted to know if we want to come over for dinner tomorrow. He and his girlfriend Missi are cooking."

"He has a girlfriend?" I hadn't ever seen a woman with him, but then again, I hardly knew him and had only been in his apartment a couple of times.

"Apparently he does and they're making prime rib."

Nerves built in my stomach. "Aren't you studying tomorrow night?"

"I can take a break," he answered, shrugging. "I wouldn't mind a little social interaction." He leaned in and kissed me before he ran out the door.

For two days I stared at my computer, nerves wracking my stomach. My hand kept moving to my crotch when thoughts of Kevin's messy hair and dimples floated into my brain.

"Hey Lara, hurry up!" Luke stood impatiently by the door with a bottle of merlot and a bottle of cabernet.

"Just finishing up my hair," I hollered back.

I had taken extra special care in doing my hair. I wondered what Missi looked like. I'd had fantasies all afternoon of us all playing footsie under the dinner table.

Luke let out a long whistle when I met him at the door. "Whoa, babe, you look hot!"

"Are you surprised?" I winked.

He gave me a deep kiss before we exited our apartment. His kisses still sent my heart into a panic. I looked into his eyes and was reminded that he was the sexiest man I'd ever met in my life.

"I love you, Luke," I said.

"I love you, too." He knocked on Kevin's door.

Missi was beautiful. She had dark hair, freckles across her nose, a cute little body and a serious laugh.

She walked around in an apron when we got there, setting the table, tossing the salad, serving us cheese and crackers. I saw Luke's jaw drop slightly. I walked over to Kevin and gave him a hug, boldly rubbing my chest on his.

"You have any Kool-Aid?" I asked, giggling.

"As a matter of fact," he opened the refrigerator behind him and pulled out a pitcher.

I laughed and turned my head toward the table. Missi laughed loudly while Luke gestured.

"Did the Kool-Aid help you out?" I asked.

"I finished a painting, if that's what you want to know. Do you want to see it?"

He led me through the hallway to his bedroom. It was obvious an artist lived here as about twenty canvases hung on the walls. Kevin pointed to one on the wall opposite the door. It was a woman, her back exposed, a hand placed on the pale curve of her back.

I walked closer. Her hair was the exact dark brown shade of mine. The rest of the colors were vivid, yet calming.

"Do you like it?" He asked. I felt him standing right behind me, his breath almost on my neck.

"It's beautiful. It really is." I turned around slowly. With my heels on we were almost eye-to-eye. His hand reached around to touch the small of my back, his eyes locked on mine. The right side of his mouth turned up in a smile, the dimple a delectable indentation on his face. I held my breath, trying not to smell his aftershave. I could hear Luke and Missi still laughing in the other room. They sounded so far away.

I felt like there was a magnet in me, tipping me off my heels into him. His fingers seared a hole in my back. I almost moaned. His lips brushed mine delicately, barely gripping my top lip before he released it. The fingers on my back pushed me forward to lead him out of the

Quick-Fix   *Jolene Hui*

bedroom. My breath started to slow when I saw Luke pouring Missi a glass of wine.

I joined them at the table. Luke leaned over and kissed my cheek. I smiled, wondering what the rest of the night had in store for us.

"This beef is delicious," said Luke.

"An old family recipe," replied Kevin, pouring everyone more wine. We'd polished off the second bottle.

"Dinner is really scrumptious," I said. "Thanks so much for having us over."

Missi giggled and Luke blushed. I looked over at Luke puzzled, and he just rested his hand on my knee. I wondered what was going on between them, but at the same time I wasn't sure I wanted to know. When Luke set his hand on my knee, I looked at Kevin who gently placed his foot on mine. My pussy moistened thinking about the possibilities.

I helped Missi clear the table after dinner while the guys sat in the living room and talked.

I felt my husband approach me. "Can I talk to you for a second?" He led me out of the kitchen into the hallway.

"Hey," I whispered, slightly annoyed. "What's wrong?"

"I have a weird question."

I thought of Kevin asking me for the Kool-Aid and figured this was probably a little stranger.

"What?" I tried to keep it down so the other two wouldn't hear.

"This may sound odd, but I was just talking to Kevin, and he mentioned something about me entertaining Missi for a little while," he paused to gauge my reaction. "What do you think about that?"

Luke, my husband, whom I had been monogamous with for ten years, was asking me this. And the words tumbled out a lot easier than I thought they ever would. "Go for it. I'll stay here. Just don't use our bed."

He looked stunned.

"Use a condom and don't use the bed. Those are my rules. How about you? Are you ok with me staying here?"

He pushed me against the hallway wall and put his lips on my neck, kissing a path to my ear. "Think of me at least once when you're fucking. I'll see you in a bit."

Breaking free from me, he went back into the living room to resume his conversation with Kevin. Stunned, I went into the bathroom for a breather and to piece it all together in my mind.

They were gone when I got out. Kevin was sitting alone at the dining room table, a piece of chocolate cake in front of him and at the seat across from him.

"Thought you might want dessert," he said.

Although I was extremely found of chocolate and definitely had wanted to taste the cake, I confessed, "That's not exactly what I had in mind."

I approached him with more courage than I knew I had. "I liked your hand on my back earlier," I said.

"Did you?" He asked, standing up to meet me eye to eye again.

"And I liked your lips on mine," I stepped closer into him so that our lips were almost touching. He finished off the act, stepping toward me and putting his lips on mine. They felt almost electric. He was an expert kisser, his tongue weaving in and out of where it was supposed to, not too quickly and not too slowly. His hand went to the small of my back again and this time I moaned aloud.

Our kissing took a bit of a turn when he put his hand up my dress. I hadn't felt a man's hand other than my husband's in that area for a very long time. Without thinking I spread my thighs and welcomed his hand.

"You feel warm." His words were hot on my mouth. I opened my eyes and looked into his.

"I'm warm and cozy," I replied, pushing my pelvis toward his hand and edging my cunt toward his fingers.

The fingers responded to my thrust by pushing my thong aside and rubbing my wet folds. I put my hands on his chest and then under his shirt, feeling his hot skin. Seconds later, I unbuttoned his pants and slid down his black silk boxers. I quickly took off his shirt and let him fuck me with his fingers. I slid my fingernails down his arms and to his back. I wanted his cock inside me. I had almost forgotten we were still in the dining area until he put his hands around my ass and propped me up on the table. He tugged my skirt up around my waist and tucked it into my waistband. My juices dripped onto the table. His cock was thick and straight. It stood hard, urging me to shove it inside me.

He slipped my shirt over my head. My breasts were heaving in the pushup bra I wore. When he ran his lips over them, I leaned back and put my hands flat on the table.

"Put on a condom and fuck me," I moaned, as if I was in pain.

I closed my eyes and when I opened them, he already had one unwrapped and slid on.

"That was qui—"

His cock inside my pussy cut off the rest of my words. He fucked me hard and steady. My clit was already hard, my orgasm ready to burst after only a few seconds.

When I came, I thought not of Kevin standing right in front of me and inside me, but of Luke. I opened my mouth and closed my eyes, my cunt contracting around Kevin's cock.

The next morning I woke up in my own bed. I stared at the ceiling until I felt Luke stir next to me. I almost felt guilty until I felt his arm around me while his lips enjoyed my neck.

"Good morning," he said.

I felt his morning hardness through his pajama pants.

"Good morning," I said, smiling.

I figured he was going to get up after that, but he crawled to the end of the bed, positioning his head between my thighs.

Luke licked my pussy better than anyone I'd ever met. He always took special care to make me cum before he slid his cock inside me.

My pajama bottoms came off neatly. Luke ate expertly then pushed his bare cock inside me, fucking me almost artfully. I couldn't remember the last time we'd fucked. He seemed hungry. I grabbed his face with my hands as I came hard against him. He moaned when I did, blowing inside me.

We sat entwined and looking at each other.

"I'm going to start taking more study breaks," he said.

I laughed, kissed him on the nose and hugged him.

Careful What You Wish For
By D. L. King

"I've been thinking about sharing you with another woman; does that idea make your cock stand up and take notice? Oh, I see that it has definite possibilities."

Greg lay restrained by his wrists and ankles to the head and footboard. He was also blindfolded and gagged, but he could hear just fine. His wife's words created a zing from his ears, straight to his balls, making his cock shudder. He'd found, aside from moans and groans when he was in this state, he could communicate his thoughts and emotions quite clearly through his cock, and Eagle-Eyed Audrey always caught them.

Greg had been telling Audrey for months how he'd love to submit to her while her girlfriends watched, or maybe even joined in. It seemed she'd finally taken the bait, and he was going to get his fantasy.

"I have a friend, Moira, who thinks you're just adorable."

Greg smiled around the gag and a little more drool ran down the side of his face.

Audrey slowly inserted a well-lubed, gloved finger into his ass to the accompaniment of his sigh and moan. "And her boy is really quite special. He's about ten years younger than you and works as a personal trainer. I've been thinking that I wouldn't mind a bit handing you over to her and swinging with Ian. That would be fun, wouldn't it?"

Greg's eyes flew open inside his blindfold. No, no, no, this was supposed to be about him and other women. Audrey wasn't supposed to be with another guy. He made some appropriate noises and, even though the anal attention he was receiving was certainly arousing, he felt his cock start to wilt.

"Oh, what's the matter, baby? Not what you had in mind?" She continued with her gentle massage until he was nice and hard again before applying a cock ring to keep him that way. "You know, my darling, Moira's also ten years younger than me, and very attractive. You could do worse. They have an open relationship and go to various swinging functions and play parties. Anyway, I've invited Moira over to meet you and get to know you a little better before making up her mind. She should be here any minute."

Audrey unbuckled Greg's gag to a quiet whine. After he licked his lips and worked his mouth, the first words out of his mouth were, "Today? Right now? Both of them?"

"Yes—and no, just Moira. She wanted to get a sense of what you're like to play with before committing. She saw you when you came to pick me up after the book club meeting last week and thought you were sexy, but she wanted to watch you in action, or at least, *in flagrante*, before making a decision."

"But . . ."

"Oh, there's the door. I'll just go and get that, shall I?"

Audrey stood up at the sound of the doorbell, and as she started to leave the bedroom, Greg turned his head to the sound of her footsteps and again said, "But . . ."

He heard the door open and the sound of Audrey and another woman talking and laughing and couldn't help but squirm in his restraints. He'd been fantasizing about submitting to another, severe woman, while Audrey stood by—or by submitting to Audrey while another dominant woman—or women—watched, but now it would be for real. He was getting more and more agitated and nervous. What if she didn't like him? What if she was too extreme? What if she wasn't extreme enough? What if she thought he wasn't worth her time? What if *he* didn't like *her*?

He heard footsteps coming towards the bedroom and decided fantasy and reality colliding, while he lay naked and bound, was a bit on the anxiety-producing side.

"Oh, this is very nice. I like what you've done with him. But that's kind of a sad little cock, isn't it?"

"No, actually, he has quite a nice cock. I think he's just nervous."

Audrey's words washed over him like a calming balm, and he began to swell with pride.

"Ah, that's better. Yes, I see what you mean."

Greg felt a hand wrap around his growing member as his blindfold was removed. It took a minute for his eyes to adjust to the light, but as soon as he could see again, he saw her. She was pretty, but not beautiful—

not the way Audrey was beautiful. She looked like an Irish stereotype: red hair, green eyes, white skin, freckles, but it was the black leather dress she was wearing that got his attention.

She stroked his erection and stared him in the eye. "You're a pretty little boy, aren't you?" she asked. She picked up a black leather bag from the floor and set it on the bed, between his spread legs. Opening the bag without breaking eye contact with him, she reached in and brought out a red riding crop. "Would you like to play with me, Greg?"

Audrey drifted to the head of the bed. She sat down next to him and began a light caress of his nipples. As they reacted to her touch, he turned his head to look at her and smile before feeling an intense stinging on the inside of his right thigh. His head immediately snapped back to watching Moira. Even though he was no longer gagged, he had grown used to not speaking unless required to do so.

"I asked you a question, boy."

He sucked in air and gasped. "Yes, Ma'am."

"Boys are so easily distracted, aren't they?"

Audrey pinched one of his nipples hard, and he gasped, turning again to look at her before he felt the rhythmic stroke of Moira's crop on the inside of his thighs. She alternated sides, and he was sure there wasn't a square millimeter of flesh that wasn't cherry red by the time she stopped. Audrey played sensuously with the top of his body, caressing his nipples, playing with his ears and kissing him, while his lower body was being punished. It was almost complete sensory overload.

As if with a silent agreement, they both stopped touching him at the same time. His cock bobbed and twitched as he panted and gasped.

"Oh yes, he'll do. You've seen Ian. What do you think? Want to swing?"

"Totally," Audrey replied. "How about Saturday night at Franco's? About seven o'clock?"

"That place on Elm? Great. We'll be there." Moira made her way to the head of the bed and kissed Greg on the cheek. "I'm looking forward to it," she said, winking at him then turned and, with a no-nonsense motion, sent the crop into the depths of her bag, snapped it shut and walked out the door, followed by Audrey. Greg couldn't help wondering just what else she had hidden in there.

His wife came back, after showing Moira out, and set to unfastening him from his restraints. "Well, that's enough excitement for you today! You should save some of that energy for Saturday. It's only three days away, you know."

"Are you sure this is right? You sure you really want to do this? I was only talking about a little scene with one of your girlfriends watching or something."

"Yes, baby, I'm sure."

"So, you're talking about sex and everything?"

"Well, yes, of course. I mean, I guess we could just switch off and play, but I thought it would be fun to really swing. Why? You're not attracted to Moira?"

Greg just stared at her for a moment, not sure of the proper response. How do you tell your wife you're hot for someone else? It's not like he wasn't still hot for Audrey—he adored Audrey and was turned on by just thinking about her at least ten times a day. But Moira was exciting. And actually, the thought of Audrey playing with and fucking another man was also kind of exciting. Hoping he wasn't digging his own grave, he said, "Well, yeah, I guess I am. Is that OK?"

"Of course it's OK. That's the whole point."

"So you're not mad or anything?"

"Don't be silly. That's why I arranged this."

* * *

After three days of almost constant arousal, Greg found himself handing the car keys to the valet at Franco's. Audrey had picked out his clothes—a royal blue silk shirt and black wool pleated trousers, a black sport jacket and no tie. The shirt contrasted beautifully with his dark hair and set off his blue eyes to their best advantage. Audrey looked amazing in a black raw silk pencil skirt and a white silk blouse with silver cuff links. The skirt fell just below her knees and the blouse fell open almost to the middle of her chest. Her honey-colored hair had been slicked back in a tight chignon at the nape of her neck. She was devastating.

She patted his ass and gave it a little squeeze when he met her at the front door to the restaurant. "Ready?"

Butterflies were swept into a hurricane in his stomach and bees buzzed in his balls as he nodded his head and opened the door for her. As they walked in, he glanced towards the bar but didn't see Moira. The fluttering subsided a bit until Audrey gave their name to the maître d', who

Careful What You Wish For   D. L. King

nodded and said, "Yes, madame, your party is waiting for you at the table. This way please."

Just as Greg recognized Moira, seated at a three-quarter banquette, her blond and suntanned companion stood for Audrey as they approached. Ian looked like a kid, but a pretty impressive kid. He had tousled hair that looked like he'd just gotten out of bed and a trimly muscled chest, tapering to a small waist, all shown off by the fitted green sweater he was wearing. Audrey'd said ten years younger, which put him at about twenty-nine. God, had he ever looked that good? His wife's eyes were sparkling.

"Why don't you sit here, by me," Moira said, patting the booth next to her. Her hair fell in waves, past her shoulders. Greg couldn't see past her waist, but she was wearing a softly gathered black halter-top, which appeared to be silk. As she turned to him and smiled, he caught a glimpse of her nipples poking against the fabric and his butterflies woke up again.

The two couples shared a light dinner, accompanied by a nice Champagne. Audrey ordered for them both, as did Moira for Ian. They ate lightly, so as not to be too full for the activities ahead, and Audrey plied Greg with enough wine to help loosen him up.

Throughout dinner, Moira touched or caressed Greg's thigh for emphasis or attention and as the evening wore on, he began to feel more and more comfortable with the whole idea. The butterflies were still there, but they seemed more like excited butterflies, rather than nervous butterflies.

Greg wondered if Audrey was touching Ian in the same way. Ian didn't seem the least bit nervous, but then he and Moira did this all the time. Well, maybe not *all* the time, but often enough. He wondered whose idea it had been. Had Ian said the same thing about wanting other women to watch Moira dominate him? But, evidently, it worked to both their satisfaction. He was beginning to feel more and more comfortable with the idea and more aroused at the prospect of not only playing with another woman, but having sex with her as well.

When the check came, he reached for it, but Moira placed her hand over his. "No, let's let tonight be my treat." As she placed her credit card on the tray, she leaned over to him and spoke directly into his ear. "I'll exact payment from you later." As they got up to leave, it was quite obvious that her words had produced the desired effect. Sheepishly glancing at Ian, Greg noticed that he was in the same state.

Careful What You Wish For — D. L. King

Realizing he was slightly light-headed, Greg asked Audrey to drive. Moira and Ian arrived shortly after they did. Moira brought the same black leather bag from three days ago in with her. Once inside the house, Audrey ordered Greg to strip. Moira followed suit telling Ian to take everything off and leave his clothes neatly folded by the couch.

Being naked in front of another woman gave Greg an immediate hard on. This was a completely new situation for him, and he looked over at Ian. The man was essentially hairless. Greg couldn't tell whether his chest was naturally bare or had been waxed, but he knew Ian's genitals had been shaved—or possibly waxed—as he was completely bare. He was so exposed that Greg felt embarrassed to look. He felt a hand on his chest and turned to see Moira studying him. She put her arm around his neck and licked, then kissed, one of his nipples. As it crinkled from the attention, she reached up and placed a gentle kiss on his mouth. He turned to see what Audrey was doing, but Moira brought his face back to her and kissed him much more deeply. The arm around his neck moved down to the middle of his back, and she lightly ran her free hand down his side, causing goosebumps to form and his nipples to stiffen even more.

"Pick up my bag and show me to the guest room, Greg."

As he picked up the bag, he looked to Audrey, but she was already ushering a naked Ian towards their bedroom. Unsure of what to do with himself, Greg picked up the bag and looked to Moira before heading off after Audrey and Ian. Halfway down the hall, he stopped at a door. "This is the guest room, Ma'am."

"You can call me Moira, after all, we're all friends here, aren't we? I think you're a little nervous, but there's nothing to be afraid of. Audrey and I have had several discussions, and I know your limits. And, well, you know how to have sex, so I'm sure we'll have a fine time."

"You and Audrey have had several discussions?"

"Yes."

"About me?"

"Yes."

"And swinging?"

"Yes, of course. What's the matter? Don't you think your wife listens to you? Now, I want you bent over the side of the bed, face down, that's right."

"But she didn't say *anything* to me about this. Nothing."

"Well, that's fine. Now put your head back down on the bed. You have such a lovely ass." She stroked his bottom gently. "Are you saying you don't want to do this?"

"No. I'm just saying . . . She never said anything to me. That's all." Greg felt a hard smack to his bottom and jumped just a bit.

"Ah, that's nice. Your skin colors right away." She peppered his bottom with hard spanks until her hand became almost as tender as his red behind, before pulling a few lengths of rope from her bag. "Now, let's see, how had Audrey fixed you to the bed before? Oh yes, of course. Turn over on your back now, Greg, in the middle of the bed, and spread your legs for me. That's right."

She fastened his ankles and wrists to the bedposts and stepped back to survey her handiwork. She unzipped her black leather pants and slipped them off, then her halter top. Leaving only her black thong on, she stood otherwise nude before Greg. He couldn't take his eyes from her creamy breasts and their small pink nipples. Noticing where his attention was centered, she cupped her breasts and kneaded them, pushing them up and offering them to him. Although his ass was on fire, his cock stood proudly.

"Is this what you want?" she asked, showing him her breasts. "Well, maybe as a reward—later." Reaching into her bag, she pulled out several items, showed them to him and laid them down on the bed. Among them was the same red crop she'd used on him days before, as well as a pair of gloves, some condoms and a bottle of lube. When she'd finished laying everything out, they heard a loud yelp from the master bedroom.

"There now, that's what I like to hear. Audrey says you like anal penetration. That's good. Maybe next time I can really fuck you. Today I'll just explore you with my fingers. But first, let's see about getting your front to match your rear."

Greg was still back at the yelp. He wondered what his wife had done to Ian to make him yelp like that. He'd sort of forgotten where he was, and it wasn't until the crop hit his nipple that his own yelp brought him back to the present.

Moira rained smacks on his chest and both nipples until he was completely tenderized, then she went to work on his thighs again. Once his body was tingling and vibrating with sensation, she began to gently explore his anus, first just teasing the outside of his sphincter, then letting her gloved finger dip in and out while she played with his balls.

Greg had been hard for quite a while and the deeper Moira explored inside him, the tighter his balls became. When Greg pleaded with her to finally let him fuck her, she was ready for him. Kneeling between his legs, she'd been keeping close tabs on his arousal and already had the condom out when he begged. She rolled the condom down his cock, and while he was fastened, spread wide for her, she removed her thong and settled herself on top of him, slowly impaling herself on his length.

He groaned his appreciation and began to rock his pelvis with the little mobility afforded him. Moira leaned forward and lay across his chest, stopping his motion. "Now Greg, you stay still; I'll do the work." She bit one of his nipples and gripped his cock tightly inside her until he squeaked. Easing up on him, she sat back and let her body rhythmically milk him until she felt him begin to shake.

"Don't you dare come. I'm not finished with you," she said.

"Please Moira, I don't think I can last much longer."

Moira leaned forward enough to allow the base of his cock to rub against her clit as she bounced up and down on him to the music of his groans. "You just wait 'till I tell you. I know you know better than to come before me."

Her motion became more and more frantic until finally, in the middle of a stroke, she froze with his cock half in and half out of her. Greg could feel the vibration start in her body and transfer itself to his cock. Her orgasm broke over them both like a storm and somewhere in the middle of it, Greg came with a roar.

Once Moira relaxed, she rolled away from Greg and said, "I don't remember telling you to come."

"Sorry Moira, I couldn't help it."

"I guess next time I'll have to deal with that."

Put back together and dressed, they made their way into the living room to find Audrey and Ian already there, sitting on the couch, talking.

"This is one sexy husband you have here," Moira said.

"Yours too," Audrey replied.

"We have this little club of couples into more than just swinging," Moira said. "We get together at each other's houses about once a month. I thought you and Greg might like to join us. I think you'd fit in perfectly, and I know you'd like the other couples in our kinky swing club."

Audrey looked at Greg and he grinned.

"Well you think about it and let me know. I'll call you tomorrow, but now I think I need to get Ian home. Boys! They just come and go, don't they? I think yours needs to be put to bed too."

Greg could feel his eyes wanting to close, but got up to walk the other couple to the door, with Audrey. After they said their goodbyes and Greg closed the door, he put his arms around Audrey's waist and said, "Well, what did you think?"

"I think I'd like to see *your* privates shaved," she said, giving him a playful swat on the ass. "I'm exhausted! Let's go to bed."

Caught in the Act
By Beth Wylde

I crept out of bed as gently as possible, doing my best not to wake my husband as I slipped on my robe and snuck into the study. The computer was already on and humming as I paused to debate whether or not to shut the door. The thought that it might accidentally slam and wake my hubby forced me to leave it open.

I slid into the well-worn leather desk chair and touched the keyboard reverently. I almost felt like I was welcoming home a long lost lover. One quick tap of the space bar lit up the screen, and I opened up my favorites folder, zeroing in on what I wanted most.

After I entered my username and password, the adult website welcomed me back fondly, opening up another view box full of new video suggestions based on what I'd downloaded in the past. I picked the one that seemed the least cheesy when compared to the others and sat back to enjoy myself.

One hand flitted anxiously to my lap while the other stayed glued to my mouse. The one on my thigh tapped impatiently against my leg as my ancient machine took forever to scan the movie into the hard drive. After several minutes of waiting, the real time player popped open, announcing that my entertainment was ready for my viewing pleasure. I wasted no time in clicking play and divesting myself of my panties. Anticipation often made for powerful foreplay so it was no surprise to find myself already wet and eager.

As I started to explore my own body three girls popped to life on the screen, each one holding a different sex toy and using them on one another. I bit my lip to stifle a groan as I slid one finger over my clit, pressing slightly harder with each pass until my hand was coated in wetness.

Caught in the Act   Beth Wylde

My husband and I have a wonderful sex life, but I'd always felt like something was missing. I hadn't known exactly what that something was until six months ago when I discovered lesbian porn for the first time. The idea of making love to another woman set something deep inside my body and soul on fire. I wanted desperately to experience it firsthand, but since I was married and refused to cheat on my husband, I did the only thing I could think of; I snuck out of bed night after night to watch gay porn and masturbate until I was so tired I could barely make it back to our room. It was a truly pitiful situation, but there was no other foreseeable way around my nightly trysts.

I couldn't just up and tell my husband that I loved him, but I needed something more and I thought that something extra might be a woman. I was positive he'd either have me locked up in a loony bin for depraved housewives or divorce me on the spot. Neither one was a choice I relished, so I stuck to getting my kicks in private when I could. I'd been brought up to believe that sex was something a woman could only indulge in with her husband after they were properly married. If my mom knew some of the fantasies I'd been having lately, she'd have me committed long before Daniel could even set the process into motion.

I was right on the verge of an explosive orgasm when the sound of someone clearing their throat rang out right behind me. I froze, two fingers buried deep inside my pussy as I clicked on the little red "x" in the upper right hand corner to close down the site. I knew I'd already been busted, but I couldn't bear the thought of facing my husband while the three women continued to fuck each other in the background. It just seemed worse somehow.

I stayed put, waiting for my husband to explode. Instead of the explosive outburst I expected, he bent down next to my ear and whispered a question so softly I had to strain to hear him. "Did that turn you on?"

How was I supposed to respond to that? Wasn't the answer rather obvious? I kept my gaze focused straight ahead, on the now blank screen, and prayed for the floor to open up and swallow me whole.

"Do you do this a lot? Sneak off and masturbate to porn online?"

I could only nod in response, wondering why he seemed so calm about the whole thing. I wanted him to rant and rave, almost craved it. The relaxed tone of his voice seemed totally out of place with what he'd just walked in on. If our roles had been reversed, I wasn't sure I could down play it the way he was.

Caught in the Act   Beth Wylde

"Is it just girls or do you watch guys too?"

Oh God, each question seemed more degrading than the previous one. It was just more than my fragile self-esteem could take. I whipped around in the chair, coming face to face with my hubby in the dimly lit study. Our faces were only inches apart, but where I expected to find disgust and anger, I only found interest. He looked truly curious about what I was doing and why. Confronted with that attitude I couldn't help but answer. "Just women. The other stuff doesn't interest me."

He reached out and stroked my cheek, holding my face tenderly in his palm. I kissed the center of his hand and sighed. "I'm so sorry. I don't do this to hurt you."

He cocked his head to the side. "I believe you. Why don't you tell me why you do it, though?"

There were no words to express how I felt when I watched the women together. I didn't even try. In absence of a response, he threw out another question.

"Do you just like to watch or do you imagine yourself in their place? Do you think you'd like to have another woman go down on you? Would you want to go down on her too?"

I gasped as he spoke aloud what I'd been dreaming about for months. I felt like my mind was wide open and he was pulling out my every fantasy to examine. I pulled away and glanced downward, staring at the carpet beneath my feet. There was no way I was going to answer such a loaded question.

He took my chin in his hand and forced me to look him in the eyes. "I've seen the way you look at other women when we go out together. You try to be sneaky about it, but sometimes you get this dreamy look on your face when you see a female you're attracted to."

I pulled away, collapsing back against the chair in surprise. I couldn't believe he'd noticed what I'd tried so hard to hide.

"You study them, stare at them. I can see you undressing them with your eyes. Are you wondering what they look like naked or what they taste like? Does the thought of being with another woman excite you?" He hesitated just a moment before asking his next question. "Are you tired of me already?"

I jumped, shocked that he had come to such a conclusion even as I understood why he would ask. "No, I love you. You're my husband. I took our wedding vows very seriously. I still do. Till death do us part and all that."

"Then why sneak in here every night?"

I shook my head. "What else am I supposed to do? I pointed to the computer. "I couldn't exactly tell you about this could I?"

His eyes widened in surprise. "And why not?"

My reply was immediate. "What do you mean why not?"

"I mean exactly that. Why couldn't you tell me about this fantasy of yours?"

"What kind of wife would that make me if I woke you up in the middle of the night and told you that I've always wondered what it would be like to be intimate with another woman? That I want to be with another female so bad it haunts my thoughts all day and night? Is that what I was supposed to do? How would you have reacted to that?"

He smiled softly. "Am I reacting badly now?"

"No and that's what scares me. You should be throwing a fit. Ranting to the heavens and threatening me with a divorce. You shouldn't be so damn calm and understanding."

He nodded emphatically. "Yes I should be. I'm your husband and you're my wife. We're supposed to handle things together. You shouldn't have to keep secrets from me, especially where sex is involved."

I laughed harshly. "Well it isn't a secret anymore."

I started to get up, and he took hold of my shoulder gently. "Where are you going?"

I shook my head dejectedly. "I don't really know. I guess I'll just pack a few things and go stay with my mom for a while until we figure out a more permanent arrangement."

"What are you talking about? Why are you running away from this?"

The first stirrings of anger sounded in my voice. "I don't even know what *this* is! I love you. I love having sex with you. This attraction I have to women isn't normal! How can you possibly want me around after what you saw tonight?"

"How could I not want you?" He opened his arms to me, and I rushed into them, desperate to feel his body against mine for what might be the last time. He pulled me in tight against him, and I could hear the steady rhythm of his heart where my ear lay pressed against his chest. The tears I'd been holding back broke loose like water from a dam that had just collapsed. He stroked my back lovingly while I shook and sobbed in his arms.

His upper body was still warm from where he'd been snuggled under the covers and the only clothing he had on was his favorite pair of black silk boxers that he liked to sleep in. The thin covering did nothing to hide the sight or feel of his erection now that we were pressed so close together. With all the drama it took me a moment to register the fact that he was hard. I sucked back my tears and ran a hand curiously down his stomach until I reached the loose, elastic waistband, dipping beneath it to confirm my suspicion. I wrapped one hand around his shaft, and he pushed himself harder into my palm. I couldn't hold back several questions of my own.

I released him and he let me go. Instantly, I retreated to the other side of the room for some much needed space. "You're aroused."

He reached down and adjusted himself, drawing my gaze to the part of his body I'd just been fondling. "I am."

"You're not mad?"

"No, I'm not. Do you want the truth?"

I wasn't sure I could handle anymore deep revelations but I asked for some anyway. "Yes, I do."

"Not long after we started dating I realized you were attracted to women as well as men."

I felt my eyes pop wide. "You did?"

"Yes I did, but you never mentioned the attraction and there was never any reason for me to ask you about it. We fell in love and got married and that was the end of it. I always thought you were bi and that you'd just decided to settle down with a man instead of a woman. I considered myself a very lucky man to marry you."

Sarcasm dripped from my reply. "I bet you don't feel like that now."

He took himself in hand as he walked across the floor towards me. "Actually I do. Do you know how many men fantasize about seeing their wives make love to another woman?"

My eyes stayed glued to his cock as he released it from the confines of his boxers and began to stroke off in earnest. "What the hell are you talking about?" I forced myself to look at his face.

He stopped right in front of me, taking one of my hands and wrapping it over the top of his own as he kept pumping. "You like having sex with me, right?"

Considering what we were doing I didn't think an answer was really needed.

"Have you ever had sex with another woman?"

I shook my head as he increased our pace.

"But you want to?"

The gush of wetness that flowed out from between my thighs encouraged me to be honest. "Yes!"

He grunted at my answer and jerked in our combined grip, shooting his load all over our hands and his stomach. We'd just reached some pivotal point in our lives—I just had no idea what it was. Thankfully, Daniel knew exactly what I needed and what to do to make my dreams come true.

We cleaned up quickly and quietly, each of us absorbed in our own thoughts. My head was spinning with the implication that my husband was okay with the fact that I wanted to sleep with another woman—that I might actually get to live out my fantasy. I was both excited and scared. I had no clue what he had in mind though. Was he planning on bringing some random female home for me to fuck? Was he going to fuck her too? I wasn't sure I could handle seeing Daniel with another woman. I also wondered how he was going to feel about seeing me with one. Jealousy was a big issue we needed to discuss. The entire situation was all so confusing.

I was lost deep in my own disturbing thoughts when Daniel appeared out of the bathroom, dressed in a clean pair of pajama pants and carrying a small black folder in his left hand. He laid it on the table and across the front, in flowing silver script, was the word, "Celebrations." I pointed to the envelope and looked at him quizzically. "What this?"

He shrugged. "Open it up and see."

I did just that, popping open the clip that held the fancy folder shut. Inside I found a booklet with the headline, "Celebrations: where life is always a party!" And just below that a subheading; "Everything you need to know about living the Lifestyle!"

"I don't understand. What's the Lifestyle?"

He pulled out a chair and sat down at the table across from me, reaching out to take my free hand in his. His demeanor was totally serious, and I knew he was about to divulge something that would impact our lives forever.

"Have you ever heard of swinging or swingers?"

"Holy shit!" I jerked my hand out of his and jumped out of my seat. "You mean like swapping? No fucking way!"

Caught in the Act   Beth Wylde

"Now calm down, let me finish. I think you owe me at least that much."

I couldn't really argue with his logic, so I sat back down and zipped my lips. He ignored my outburst and started to explain.

"Swinging is not swapping. It's not cheating either. Swinging is for couples that have a healthy relationship. It doesn't fix a bad relationship; it just helps to enhance things. In fact, Celebrations doesn't even allow single males into the club because usually the guys are just looking for sex. Single women are allowed, however. In fact, the women are the ones that usually run the show."

"How do you know so much about this subject?"

Daniel sighed. "I have a bit of a confession to make. I found your porn collection about four months ago. Do you remember when I crashed the hard drive on my laptop?"

I was too stunned to do little more than nod my understanding.

"I was waiting on an important email from a client about the slogan for their new ad campaign, so I used your desktop. I was doing a little surfing while I waited and found all the recent websites you'd been visiting saved in the favorites folder."

"But . . ." I stuttered, "You never said anything. Didn't it freak you out? Why didn't you confront me about it?"

"I'll admit I was a bit shocked at first. Even though I kind of knew you liked women it was somewhat different to have the proof actually thrown in my face like that. I went through all of the movies you have on your hard drive. Not a one of them featured any guys. They were strictly lesbian themed. That's when I realized something had to be done." He reached across the table for my hand again, and I gave it to him, the need to hold on to something or someone almost overwhelming. "I want you to be happy. That's my main focus in life as your husband. I can't be a woman for you. I would if I could, but I can't, so the least I can do is help arrange the experience in an atmosphere where you will be safe and feel comfortable. Provided that's what you want."

"What about us?"

"What about us? We're still married and we still love each other. Do you think sleeping with a woman will make you want to leave me?"

My answer to that question was an easy one. "No. Definitely not. What I feel when I see a woman I'm attracted to is lust, pure and simple, not love. I know that sex involves some emotions, it has to if any attraction is involved, but no one could make me fall out of love with you."

He smiled a big shit-eating grin that lit up his entire face as he picked up the discarded folder and the information it contained. "That's exactly what I wanted to hear, and if that's really the case, I have a proposal for you."

* * *

It was nearly two a.m. by the time I finished looking over all the material Daniel had compiled for me. A lot of my previous misconceptions had been blown out of the water. It turned out that Celebrations was an on-site lifestyle facility. That meant that along with the main dance floor and other amenities you'd expect to find at a typical night club, they also had special areas and rooms set aside for intimate play among members. I had a totally different view on what swinging actually meant as well. At first, I'd believed it was just a fancy term for condoned adultery. Now I knew differently. Cheaters were actually abhorred in the lifestyle, considered outcasts and degenerates of the worst kind.

Swinging was more like a social preference. It wasn't just about the sex; it was about finding people you related to that shared some of your same interests and goals. It was like friendship with added benefits.

There was supposedly no pressure to perform either. No meant no! Rejections were as commonplace as acceptances. If a couple approached you and asked you to play you could decline the offer and they'd accept your decision gracefully and go on their merry way. It sounded absolutely fabulous on paper, but I worried that the actual atmosphere at the club would be nothing like the description. My concern must have shown plainly on my face.

Daniel got up and came around to my side of the table where I was still seated. "Celebrations is really as laid back as it sounds."

I arched one eyebrow. "Am I really that easy to read?"

He nodded and stroked one hand down my left cheek. "Only to someone who knows you as well as I do." He patted the back of my chair. "Why don't we take this discussion into the bedroom where we can get more comfortable? These hard wooden chairs make your ass hurt if you sit in them too long." He chuckled as I stood up, and he patted my nearly numb rear. "You can ask me some more questions, and I'll do my best to answer them."

As I followed him down the hall I asked the first thing that sprang to mind. "Okay then. How do you know so much about all of this?"

He hopped into our bed, laughing good naturedly at my initial inquisition as he shed his pants in the process. By the time he laid back he was completely nude, his dark tan in complete contrast against our white silk sheets as he patted the empty space by his side. "Lay down and I'll tell you all about it."

With his playful attitude and his cock lying half hard against his thigh it was an invitation I just couldn't resist.

For hours we fucked and talked and fucked some more until we finally reached the point of exhaustion sometime right before dawn. It turned out my husband had done some seriously thorough research on the Lifestyle, even up and to the point of touring and purchasing us a temporary membership at Celebrations. He had all the answers and everything arranged. He'd given me the key to fulfill a lifelong dream. The only question that remained was discovering if I had the courage to go through with it. I was still pondering his offer as the sun rose and Daniel drifted off to sleep beside me, his softened cock nestled happily against my ass. The thought that I might actually get to fulfill my fantasy was still foremost in my mind as I fell asleep as well.

* * *

The soft sound of the shower running close by woke me to find our bedroom bathed in the warm glow of sunset. I was appalled at the fact that I'd obviously slept all day even though I had a valid excuse for being so tired. Daniel's excitement at the prospect of seeing me with another woman had definitely shown through in the various and vigorous ways he'd made love to me throughout the night. My body was still pleasantly sore from all the attention. It was a wonderful way to start the evening.

I was just about to join my hubby in the shower when I noticed a garment bag hanging on the front of the closet door that hadn't been there earlier. It had a big red bow tied across it with a tag that read "Samantha" below it in big bold letters. It was obviously meant for me, and I couldn't help but investigate.

I had just unzipped the bag when Daniel came out of the bathroom. "I see you found your present already."

I turned and eyed him with suspicion. "You've been planning this for quite a while haven't you? How did you know I'd agree?"

He shrugged as he dropped his towel to the floor and started getting dressed. "For about two or three months." He chuckled at my shocked expression. "I wasn't completely sure you'd agree to it but I thought you might."

My heart melted in my chest. "You're absolutely perfect, do you know that? How'd I get so lucky to find a man like you?"

He grinned. "I think we both got pretty lucky." He pointed to the bag as he pulled on a pair of tan slacks. "Now go on and open your present. Time's a wasting."

I did as I was told, shocked to find not one but three outfits nestled inside. "What the . . .?"

Daniel finished dressing, slipping into his brown loafers before joining me by the closet door. "You have your choice of what you can wear to the club. The women can be as casual or dressy as they want to be."

I pulled the clothes out of the bag, laying out each outfit individually on the bed to get a good look at them. The first was a pair of casual black dress pants with a nice, yet slightly plain red top to go with it. The second was a very classy black dress, with a short, above the knee length hemline and a halter type strap that left my entire back exposed. The third was beyond a doubt the flashiest and the most risqué. It left very little, if anything, to the imagination. The bottom was a plaid pleated mini skirt that definitely wouldn't come to my thighs, if it even covered my ass. Since quite a lot of my rear was going to be on view Daniel had been thoughtful enough to include a little pair of lacy white panties to go underneath. The top looked like a standard white button down except for the fact that it stopped just below my breasts. It was more of a costume than an actual outfit, and I wondered if the naughty school girl look was one of Daniel's fantasies. I lifted the mini skirt and held it up to my waist. "Are you trying to tell me something?"

His eyes sparkled with mischief. "Maybe."

"Have you been fantasizing about making it with a school girl?"

"Nope." He moved closer. "I've been fantasizing about making it with you while you're dressed up like a school girl. Maybe you've been bad and you need a bit of discipline."

Caught in the Act   **Beth Wylde**

I put my hand out to hold him off. "Slow down honey. One thing at a time is all I can handle. Let's see how tonight goes before we start thinking about spankings and tying each other up."

Daniel sucked in a deep breath as he took a step back. "Alright. Sorry. The idea of you dressed like that and bent over with your ass in the air is just fucking hot."

It was my turn to grin. "The idea of you lifting up my skirt, ripping off those little panties and fucking me from behind is hot to me too." I put the skirt back down on the bed and reached for the black dress. "I'm going to go with this. Let's save the other one for next Saturday, okay?"

I left him unable to form a coherent statement as I headed into the bathroom to get ready for the evening ahead.

* * *

By the time we pulled into the parking lot next door to Celebrations my nerves were tied into knots. I was alternating between excited and terrified and Daniel knew it. He turned off the car and put one hand on my bare knee. "If you don't want to do this, we don't have to. Just say the word and we can go back home and pretend none of this ever happened."

I thought over his offer and knew refusing would be the coward's way out. I didn't want to be a coward anymore.

"No we're going in." I undid my seatbelt and got out of the car, making my way towards the entrance before I could change my mind. Daniel was next to me in a flash, putting his arm around my shoulders as we approached the front door. I'm not sure what I expected to happen, but I knew if I didn't at least give myself a chance I'd always regret my actions.

Daniel handed the guy inside the door a small black card with the Celebrations name and logo on it. The guy verified our membership and waved us inside. I was about to go in when Daniel took my hand and pulled me back. "My wife hasn't had a tour yet. This is her first time."

Several heads swiveled towards us in interest as my husband made his announcement. The guy at the desk smiled kindly and pulled a small phone out of his pocket. "Terry, we have a new client who needs a tour. Can you do it?"

He hung up and pointed towards a side door I hadn't noticed before. "Go on through and Terry will meet you in a minute." He looked directly at me. "Nice to have you join us. I hope you enjoy yourself. Please don't feel like you have to do anything you don't want to. It's perfectly fine just to watch. Although, if you want to accept an invitation to play, that's fine too." He winked at me as Daniel led me into the little waiting area for our guide.

Terry turned out to be a six foot tall blonde bombshell with a figure like an hourglass. Her skin tight red dress showed off a set of tits and an ass that were pure perfection. Her figure was so fine that even a gay man would have taken a second glance.

The look she gave me as we shook hands started a raging fire between my thighs that instantly told me I'd made the right choice. Judging by the way my heart was hammering and my cunt was throbbing I thought I might do more during the evening than just watch but I'd take things one step at a time and see where they led.

The tour was relatively uneventful. Whatever preconceived notions I'd had were tossed out immediately. On the surface the main room looked like any other club. Clothing ranged from dress casual to over the top extravagant and the bar and dance floor were packed. The DJ's booth watched over it all, where the mix of music was loud, decadent and designed to dance to. I only saw two real things that were different. There was a roped off staircase near the rear of the building that obviously led to the private rooms and more intimate play areas. Two security guards were stationed at the bottom checking membership cards and ID's before anyone was allowed up. The second difference was the attitude of the members. No one was overly loud or drunk and everyone I met was so friendly. They nodded or shook my hand and quite a few introduced themselves and welcomed me to the club. No one was pushy or grabby, they were perfectly gracious. It was a pleasant change of pace and put me at ease instantly.

Terry finally excused herself and Daniel and I settled in at a small table near the bar, close enough to keep an eye on everything but far enough away from the main floor that we could talk to one another without screaming.

"So what do you think?"

I took another sip of my rum and coke. "It's really nice. You were right. I do feel safe and comfortable." I caught sight of a slim brunette standing by the bar who kept looking over at me every now and then. A minute later a waitress walked by and handed me a fresh drink. I shook my head. "I didn't order another one."

Caught in the Act   Beth Wylde

The waitress set it down in front of me and tilted her head toward the woman at the bar. "Courtesy of Ms. Thompson."

As she walked off the brunette saluted me with her glass and took a long sip, smiling at me over the rim in a way that made my blood pressure rise. I mouthed a thank you and leaned toward Daniel. "Would you think I was a complete slut if I decided to do something tonight?"

Daniel choked a bit on his beer before he regained his composure. "Lord no. Did you have someone in mind?"

My throat felt suddenly dry. "There's a woman that keeps looking at me. She's over by the bar." Daniel turned slightly in his seat so he could see who I was talking about. "The one with the long brown hair and the stiletto heels. She's the one that sent me the drink."

"Wow. Um . . ." Daniel turned back to face me with a deep flush of arousal plain on his cheeks. "You do whatever makes you feel good. No pressure. Can I let you in on a little secret though?"

"Sure."

"The thought of her kissing you, on both sets of lips, has me hard as a rock right now."

I moaned. I couldn't help myself. "What should I do?"

Before I could decide my next move she approached our table, towing a thickly built, yet handsome older gentleman behind her.

"Hi there." She stuck out a well-manicured hand with short, unpolished nails. "I'm Greta Thompson and this is my husband James. I couldn't help but notice you from across the room." She sat down in the empty chair right beside me. "I've never seen you here before and my husband and I come to Celebrations quite often. Are you both new members?"

"Yes we are. My name is Samantha and this is my husband Daniel. This is my first time anywhere like this." I looked down into my drink. "I'm a bit nervous."

James sat down and started talking to Daniel while Greta kept all her attention focused on me. It was a heady feeling to have such a gorgeous female flirting with me.

She patted my knee but didn't withdraw her hand. "No need to be nervous. We're all friends here." She stroked lightly over my skin, inching her hand up just a bit under my dress. "You're so beautiful. Such soft creamy skin." She halted just shy of the crease where my leg met more intimate flesh. "Would you like to play?" She leaned forward until our mouths were just a hairsbreadth apart. "It can be just the two of us if you like. James doesn't mind. He likes to watch and truth be told, I'd like to have you all to myself. Of course if you'd rather swap or make it a group thing we can do that too."

I wanted to kiss her so bad, but I was afraid to initiate it. Her offer had me almost dizzy with need but I knew I needed to be honest about my wants up front first. "I'm not looking to be with another man."

She nodded her understanding. "I totally understand. I'm quite partial to the women as well." One slim finger slid beneath the edge of my black bikinis, stroking the smooth skin I'd just recently shaved. "Have you ever been with another woman?"

I shook my head and her sudden smile lit up the room.

"You don't know how much I was hoping you'd say that. I just love virgins. Why don't we go upstairs? James and I have a private room already booked. We can get a bit more comfortable and see if we can't make your first time something you'll always remember."

By the time we reached the private room upstairs I was contemplating calling the whole thing off. I was so worried I actually felt lightheaded. Greta shut the door and I opened my mouth to decline. Before I could say anything she pulled me into her arms and the rest of the world drifted away. Her mouth descended on mine, and I felt the liplock all the way to my toes. My every objection died then and there.

Something soft and wet slid across the seam of my lips and I responded automatically, opening my mouth to admit Greta's searching tongue. My knees felt so weak I almost fell, but Daniel was suddenly there, helping to guide us over to the bed.

We fell back, still kissing, as her body assumed the dominant position on top. I pulled back for a much needed breather and found Daniel and James seated near the door, their eyes glued on Greta and me. Judging by the visible erections they were both sporting they were enjoying things as much as we were.

Greta straddled my waist, her hands reaching behind my neck to undo the strap holding the top of my dress together. As it came loose she pulled the front down, completely exposing my breasts to the cool room air and her hungry gaze. She grasped one breast in each hand, squeezing ever so gently as she ran her thumbs over my rapidly hardening nipples.

"So gorgeous. You fit perfectly in my palm." She leaned down and gave each tip a bit of extended attention with her mouth and tongue. The sensation shot straight to my clit. I could only groan my approval as she moved further down my body, inching my dress and panties off over my feet until I was clad in just my high heels. Her mouth followed the exact same path her hands had taken, nipping and licking until her face hovered right over the spot where I needed her the most. I wanted her to feel as good as I was but I was so on edge I wasn't sure I could move. Forming a coherent sentence took almost all my effort.

"Wait!"

Greta lifted her head and looked up at me. "Is something wrong?"

I shook my head. "Yes, no, I mean . . . I want you to feel good too."

In response she slid one finger through my slit, pulling back to show me the wetness I already knew she'd find.

"Don't worry so much about me right now. This first time is all about you." She looked over at her husband fondly. "No one will go without tonight. That's one of the best parts about the Lifestyle. You get to go home and relive the experiences all over again with your partner." She kissed me right above my pubic bone, blowing on the area afterward until chill bumps covered my arms and legs. "You and Daniel will go home tonight and fuck like bunnies, but before you do that, I want you to come all over my face."

She thrust two fingers deep inside my sopping wet cunt and used her lips to zero in on my aching clit.

"Holy Fuck!" I screamed, pushing my pelvis up into her face as I rode her fingers and her tongue. Within moments I was on the verge of a powerful climax, my thighs shaking as she pushed me higher and higher. In the edge of my vision, I saw both Daniel and James with their cocks in their hands openly masturbating. James threw back his head and groaned as he shot halfway across the room, my husband following closely behind. The sight of him coming combined with the third finger Greta pushed up inside my pussy was all the stimulation I need. I came on a wail, thrashing and flailing as my body split apart and put itself back together again.

When Greta finally came up for air her face was slick with my juices. As she licked away the remnants, I felt a goofy satiated grin spread its way across my face. I couldn't work up enough energy to worry about it. The entire experience had been better than I'd ever dared to dream.

Greta gave me a quick kiss, sharing my taste with me before she got up and crossed over to her husband. Once there she cleaned him up with her mouth, tucking him gently back inside his pants and sharing a kiss with him afterwards as well. Daniel looked completely drained. I could totally sympathize. Greta smiled and patted him on the cheek, pointing towards my lax form on the bed.

"She's all yours. You're a very lucky man." She turned back towards me as she led her husband to the door. "I'm honored to have been your first. James and I come here every Saturday. If you'd like, maybe we can meet up again real soon. Next time I'll even let you be on top."

I could only stare as they walked out and secured the door behind them. Small, orgasmic aftershocks deep inside my womb still flowed through me and silently, I took Greta up on her offer. Daniel plopped down next to me on the bed after rearranging his clothes, looking me over to be sure I was okay. "Was it as good as you thought it would be?"

"Yes it was." I gave him a moment to let the information sink in before asking, "Same time next week? Maybe you could help me get dressed beforehand. I might need some help getting into that school girl uniform."

The silence in the room was deafening but the expectant look on my husband's face told me we'd be visiting Celebrations quite a lot in the near future.

I was looking forward to every trip.

Check and Mate
By Jeremy Edwards

"Nervous?"

Gail nodded.

"I understand." Dawson patted her hand. "Just remember, you'll be with people you trust, and no one's going to pressure you to do anything you're not comfortable with."

"You're sweet. But I'm not nervous about the *fucking*. I'm nervous about the chess."

"Oh," said Daw, looking a bit crestfallen over the fact that his solicitousness had been misdirected. "Well, I'm afraid I can't help you there. Livia's going to make short work of both of us, as far as I can foretell. Your only consolation will be in winning your game with Clement. And there's not much challenge to *that*. I mean, Clement's a genius . . . but he's a right-brain genius."

"Yeah. Damn, I almost wish I could just compete against you. We're so well matched."

Dawson chortled suggestively, and stroked his wife's thigh. "But, darling, it's a swingers' night."

It had been a glorious coincidence that Gail and Daw had found out that their friends were chess players right around the time the swinging experiment had been discussed. Conversation had revealed that Livia was a chess wizard, even by Gail and Dawson's standards, and that Clement, not to be outdone, had some swinging experience dating back to a previous marriage. "It was a number of years ago," he had explained, "but I think I still remember how to do it." He'd smirked charismatically at Gail as he said that, and the idea of having his body between her legs had immediately shifted from a speculative folly to a compelling contingency.

Predictably, Livia had been the one to insist that the inaugural sessions of chess and swinging be mixed. "I don't know how good I'll be at

Check and Mate   Jeremy Edwards

fucking an auxiliary man, so I want to make sure we also do something that I have a proven talent for." Dawson's face had turned adorably red at this remark.

Livia's chess set pitted an unapologetically vivid shade of purple, luscious like a silk negligee, against a sky blue that reminded Gail of cotton panties. "Chess, to me, is not a black and white game," Livia stated as she carried the magnificent board toward a glass coffee table. "It is as rich with ambiguity and possibility as human endeavor."

"Easy there, girlfriend," Gail teased. "I said I'd screw your husband, but I never said I'd listen to your aphorisms."

Livia, having situated the chessboard where it belonged, rebutted Gail's point by throwing a sofa cushion at her.

"It's good that you two are drinkers," said Clement, bearing tumblers. "Livia has suggested we play vodka chess tonight."

His wife cackled mischievously. "But it's only fair if all four of us are drinking the martinis."

"Fine with me," said Daw. "Just don't laugh if I accidentally capture your king's rook's olive with my queen's knight's onion."

This was going to be fun, thought Gail. Dawson would make certain of that.

They'd considered using two boards for side-by-side play, but Clement had recommended that they do one round at a time. "We want an intimate vibe, not a convention atmosphere." No one could argue with this. "I think we all need to be focused in the same place. That goes for the whole evening."

Gail squirmed on the sofa as she recalled those words. The ideal of two couples collectively "focused in the same place," making the most of an "intimate vibe," piqued her pussy, as the first sip of martini piqued her tongue. She was a wine connoisseur, and not much of a hard-liquor fan; but vodka seemed like exactly the right thing tonight. Maybe she was more nervous than she'd realized about the fucking. If so, it wasn't a negative kind of nervousness. She was pleasantly excited.

She studied the two men as they settled into position at the coffee table, cross-legged on the floor. Clement's pale eyes had always attracted her, and this evening they were set off extra-handsomely against a silver oxford shirt. She noticed how comfortable Dawson appeared, his black-denim ass on the carpet and his drink to his side. This made her feel comfortable as well.

Check and Mate — Jeremy Edwards

"Nuts?"

Livia, assuming correctly that Gail would take her up on the offer, was handing her the dish without waiting for an answer. Livia smiled at her over the polished-wood nut bowl. It was a rare conspiratorial grin from a friend who was close to Gail, in a way, but usually too fascinated by her own mental trajectories to show signs of intimacy.

Gail noticed, not for the first time, what a finely detailed beauty Livia possessed—from her thin nose and curls of chestnut hair; to her petite breasts; to her sensuous hips, and beyond. Sitting next to Livia on the couch, Gail could smell a delicious cocktail of subtle perfume and sweet skin. She was so glad that Daw was going to sample this refined flower of flesh and intellect.

An image of Dawson's sturdy cock splitting Livia open on his lap shot through Gail's head and moistened her panties. But she forced herself to concentrate on the chess game, so as not to slide into a sexual heat too early in the proceedings. It was only 5:30, and four cross-couple matchups—and dinner—lay between this moment and the extracurricular portion of the gathering.

Clement expressed a preference for music while they played, and Daw didn't object. "It won't improve my game," Clement admitted. "Even Mozart can't do that. But I'll relish the chess more."

"His pawns look so suave when they topple to the strains of violins," kidded Livia, leaning forward to massage her husband's shoulders. He turned his head, and they kissed with enthusiasm.

While Clement darted to the stereo, Gail admired his tight, lean legs, and the lock of hair at the nape of his neck. She licked her vodka-suffused lips and made eye contact with Dawson who was beaming at her.

As everyone knew, Clement, the right-brained painter, was out of his league. By twenty minutes in, his now-sparsely-populated half of the stage was a smorgasbord of threats to his king. His queen had long since been retired from the board, and it tickled Gail to fantasize that Clement's queen was happily ensconced with one of his equally obsolete purple bishops, who looked like they would make good vibrators for someone restlessly awaiting her king.

Within another few moves, Clement and Mozart had capitulated.

"Time for the next round of drinks?" asked Clement, moving swiftly from capitulation mode to host mode.

Check and Mate   Jeremy Edwards

Daw was still working on his first, but Livia and Clement had empty glasses, and Gail's was getting there. She gulped what was left, enjoying the burn, and got in line for her refill.

She and Livia settled in for their matchup. The vodka was already taking a toll on Gail's concentration, but she'd agreed to the four-way inebriation pact, so she couldn't complain. Besides, she knew that even soap-bar sober, she couldn't hope to triumph over Livia's formidable chess circuitry.

Their hosts had let the stereo go idle—per Livia's preference—when she was playing. Gail had liked the violin concertos, but she now appreciated the friendly quiet of the room. The anticipation in the air, the slow-cooking essence of sexual chemistry building among them all, made the silence feel anything but empty. Clement sat on the floor at Livia's side, nursing his drink, and Gail noticed how sensitive his lips looked.

Moisture trickled lazily into Gail's fuchsia thong, making her short black hairs damp and aromatic. It excited her to think that her underwear was exposed to the vacant space under the table. She smoothed her miniskirt in her lap—an excuse to grant herself an instantaneous touch—and Livia's eyes met hers.

"Blue moves first, sweet."

"Go on, sweet," Daw echoed playfully from the sofa. "Or do you need a pat on the ass to get you going?"

Gail laughed immoderately. No, she didn't need anything to get her going. Not that she would have objected to a pat on the ass.

She went with her safest opening, but all too soon it was clear as vodka that her first-move advantage was history and her peeps were drifting into uncertainty and, inevitably, trouble.

But the beauty of it was that she didn't really care. Her competitive streak was submerged in the warm, pulsing waves of her libido. As they played on, she imagined being undressed by Clement, with Dawson watching intently.

Despite this umbrella of eros and serenity, it came as a shock when Livia actuated a ploy whereby Gail had to sacrifice her queen to protect her king. Gail swallowed her pride along with the next gulp of vodka. Then she sought comfort.

"Guess I could use that pat on the ass now," she told Dawson.

Her husband set his drink down, and began to get up. But Clement raised a polite hand. "Please, Daw. This one's on me." He spoke softly, enchantingly, his smooth voice slightly hairy around its edges. He approached Gail and, with great gracefulness, squatted beside her. Smiling self-consciously, she leaned forward on her knees to elevate her skirted behind for him. He gave her a flirty, gentle swat, and she felt her clit twitch.

There was a moment of precious silence.

Then all four of them cracked up. The ice had been broken.

Even Livia's attention no longer appeared to be entirely on the game, as she quickly destroyed Gail's remaining defenses and claimed her victory. As for Gail, what little there was left of the contest passed by her in a blur, with the hopeless moves that were forced upon her happening as if automatically.

Over dinner—a simple sandwich spread, as chess and sex *and* cooking would have been a bit much—Clement suggested they take turns describing each other's attractive features.

"I'll start," he said between mouthfuls of Swiss on rye. "Gail has a beautiful chin. It's rounded but confident, like she's up for anything."

"My husband has fine nipples," Livia proceeded to say, with a matter-of-factness that Gail found touching.

Gail cleared her throat; and, when she began speaking, it took her by surprise that she was choosing to talk about the only other woman in the room. "Livia, lady . . . your bottom, my dear. That day at the beach, in our bikinis—I wanted to eat you up." Suddenly, it felt natural to Gail to be lusting after a round, feminine ass.

Daw chipped in. "I'll second that, Liv. Gail can vouch for a few rhapsodizing comments I made last night regarding your tush."

Livia's eyes grew large. "You're kidding."

Daw shrugged. "Well, you know, there was nothing good on television . . ."

"Okay then, Dawson," Livia purred, "Let me say that *you* have a very handsome bulge in your pants."

"You probably tell that to all the fellas you're about to cream in chess."

About to cream. Gail was on martini number three and wondering idly what it would feel like to stick her finger into Livia's cushiony derriere. But this didn't stop her from savoring the thoughtful strength of Dawson's back as he crouched over the chessboard, setting the pieces back to their starting configuration.

"Your guy's got muscles," Livia breathed with a slight slur, making the last word a wet, molluscular *mussssels*.

Gail noted the implied comparison with Clement's stick-figure elegance, even before Livia rendered it explicit: "Clemmy's my pretty boy, but sometimes I crave some meat to sink my teeth into."

Gail wagered that Daw could hear their conversation, at least on a subconscious level. The back of his neck seemed to glow a little pink as Livia's remarks diffused into Gail's ear like a hot vodka mist. Livia wriggled, and her narrow shoulder bumped Gail's arm.

Dawson turned their way. "Liv, I'm as ready for you as I'll ever be."

Gail did an arena-style "Whoo!" at the double entendre, and Daw winked at her affectionately.

With a few drinks in her, Livia took more time over each move; but the moves were as good as ever, once they emerged. And although there was still no music playing, Livia hummed to herself each time she scrutinized the board.

Gail was digging the mellowness that had slowly displaced Livia's characteristic angularity of attitude. She wondered if Livia's pussy lips were warm and wet. No—she wondered *how* warm and wet they were. Gail tittered at her own train of thought, and everyone looked up at her for a second.

No two chess games, Gail reflected, were ever the same. What had Livia said? "It is as rich with ambiguity and possibility as human endeavor." Gail had teased her for sounding pretentious, but the observation returned now, with more weight. Sitting here in a room with the familiar man she fucked every night, and a half-strange man she was scheduled to fuck tonight . . . and an increasingly alluring woman who . . . well, Gail felt as if she were joyfully afloat on a sea of ambiguity. And possibility. And, yeah, vodka.

She sucked on her olive.

"Fuck!" Dawson said, softening the expletive with laughter. He was a gracious loser, even a jolly one.

Livia reached across the board and touched his hand. "Don't despair. I haven't finished you off yet."

"Ha—*yet* is right. I think we both know where this game is headed. Anyway, I'm not despairing. I'm admiring."

"Thank you," said Livia.

Check and Mate   Jeremy Edwards

Daw took a swig of his drink. "You're a top-notch player. Too pro for these 'burbs."

"Thank you again, Dawson."

"And, in a little while, I'm going to lick your pussy till you scream."

"Thank you, um . . . in advance?"

"I love having friends over," Clement said to Gail.

She petted his chest, tentatively but purposefully. "You're a good host."

He had a clean, minty kiss. Gail remembered hearing him brush his teeth after they'd eaten.

"You're a good guest," Clement answered, mouth to mouth.

A luscious giggle from the vicinity of the chess game distracted them. Beneath the intellectual contest on the coffee table, Dawson and Livia were evidently playing a parallel game of footsie.

"Checkmate," said the giggly voice.

"Um-hmm," Dawson growled agreeably.

Clement's deft fingers were caressing Gail's right breast now, through the delicate interface of her silk top. She fumbled with her own buttons to clear the way for him.

"Do you wanna play chess with me?" he asked.

"Not if it means losing that hand from inside my blouse."

He kissed her again, more passionately this time, burning through the toothpaste. Out of the corner of one languidly open eye, Gail saw Livia brush the remaining chess pieces to one side. She sat at the edge of the board for Daw, holding her peasant skirt up at the knees as if she were about to go wading or stomp some grapes. Daw unzipped his jeans, then grasped Liv by her feet. He began kissing her cherry-painted toenails.

Gail moved a hand into her own crotch. An instant later, Clement's hand met hers there.

That hand felt good. The man had finesse; and, in order to take full advantage of his light touch, Gail removed her own hand and just let herself go, grinding against Clement's palm.

Clement moved his face down to the level of Gail's nipples, and while he suckled her, she turned her head to get a better view of the other couple. She saw that Livia's feet were trembling as Dawson fondled her ankles.

Need had been building in Gail's miniskirt all evening. As Clement made a furrow in her panties and titillated the periphery of her clit, crimson sparks were already beginning to flash in her head.

"You're going to make me come," she panted, and Clement chuckled seductively.

"I know."

These two words—and his direct pressure on her button as he spoke them—put her over the edge. She reeled with wetness and pleasure and electricity. From far, far away, she heard the succulent smacks of her husband kissing his way up Livia's naked legs.

"Let's focus, everybody," said Clement in a voice that was, for him, a loud one. "Gail's having our first orgasm of the night."

Our first orgasm. The pronoun, bold like Livia's nearly-bare ass on that beach, transformed Gail's climax into a double-decker, and she cried out as the renewed euphoria rippled through her. She was coming for four, and, damn it, she was going to do them all justice. Her heels kicked into the front of the sofa as another generous flood of nectar stained her silk.

Sinking into the couch with post-release heaviness, she seemed to hear her own moans continuing on in a disembodied voice. She realized that these were Livia's moans she was listening to. "Your wife and I moan in the same key," Gail remarked to Clement, who responded by nuzzling one of her orgasm-warm ears.

Livia's moans were the result of whatever Daw's mouth was now doing under her skirt. Her head was thrown back in a textbook posture of acute ecstasy. Gail watched Dawson's shoulder muscles tense and relax with the precision of his wonderful task; and yet her gaze was repeatedly drawn to Livia's exquisite face.

She had an impulse, and she acted on it.

"Mind if I cut in?"

Dawson had to pull out to see who was tapping him on the shoulder, and Gail inferred that he hadn't heard her question over his hungry lapping. Livia opened her eyes, and Gail had a moment of fear that she'd be pissed at her for interrupting, or freaked out by Gail's display of Sapphic desire. But Livia's pupils glowed with fierce anticipation when she took in the scene.

"Plunge in, babe," said Daw, who had registered what Livia wanted. "I recommend it."

Check and Mate Jeremy Edwards

The world beneath the peasant-skirt tent was a moist, spicy, palace for the senses. Livia's pussy—slightly trimmed, but ninety-percent natural—was a tropical garden of feminine fragrance and pooling love-oils. Livia's thigh muscles pumped against Gail's ears, while her cunt beckoned to Gail, spasmodically clenching and unclenching. *Come to me, my dear, come taste me and fulfill me,* it seemed to chant. Gail was virtually paralyzed by the feast—then paralysis melted into frenzy, and she angled her head right and left and right to lick, kiss, and nibble the flesh of upper thigh and outer pussy. The cunt gaped and quivered in utter heat, and Gail rushed in to satisfy it. Livia's long, throaty sigh reverberated off every wall of the suburban living room.

What really got Gail was the release of control that Livia acceded to as pleasure consumed her. Here was a masterful chessboard schemer, dripping, cooing, giggling, squirming . . . completely and ecstatically undone by sensation, dissolving six ways from Sunday around the tongue of a friend. It thrilled Gail beyond belief to be steadily licking Livia into an incoherent soup of gratification. At that moment, she almost felt as if she never wanted to come out from under Livia's skirt. Almost.

Caught in a delightful squeeze between Livia's legs, with a rose-petal pussy orgasming in her face, Gail suddenly felt fingers yanking down her thong at the rear, and rubbing greedily along the crack of her bottom. Thick, male fingers. Dawson's fingers. She wiggled her ass, luxuriating in the dual sensuality of being tickled behind while Livia's cunt lips tickled her mouth under the magic skirt.

Gail rejoined the larger party after Livia had finished coming, and she saw that both men had their cocks out: Dawson was standing at the corner of the coffee table, dick in the air, while Clement sat in a corner of the couch, cradling his martini in one hand and something hard and fleshy in the other.

"I saved a seat for you, Gail," said Clement.

She rose to her feet.

"Wait," said Dawson. She turned to him, and he ate her mouth lovingly, grabbing her ass for good measure. "Have a good time, sweet."

When Gail pulled her panties off and eased herself backward onto Clement's prick, she knew that she had the best seat in the house. Her liquid pussy was throbbing with solid satisfaction, and her eyes were feasting on the sight of Livia, now nude, climbing atop Daw, who sat on the table. Livia straddled Daw face to face, and Gail was in heaven watching the woman's lewdly spread ass as it started to bounce. Daw sculpted Liv's breasts, and the gorgeous ass flounced harder in sympathetic delight.

Gail moved her ass, too. She felt as if she were both women at once, fucking both men. The aroma of cunt filled the place, and the whole world was sex. Chess was sex. Vodka was sex. Gail was going to explode with sex, like an engorged, excited cock. She would have laughed at this incongruous, paradoxical image, but she was too immersed in arousal to find anything funny. Everything went straight to her pussy, where she wrung every sensation from the situation with tingling, slow-motion rapture, using her ass as both motor and navigator. She was sitting on pure pleasure, churning and wallowing.

Then Clement shifted his position slightly, and his beneficent dick scraped Gail's G-spot. Her vision honed in on a specific locus where the round of Livia's left ass cheek squished itself sensuously onto a crease in Daw's brand-new jeans. Gail wailed with abandon, clutching frantically at her own clit and dragging herself up and down, up and down along Clement's shaft. As her juices soaked his exposed boxers, Gail felt as if she were snogging with everyone in the room, pawing them all.

Beforehand, she'd imagined two male-female couples, classically naked in twin beds, fucking symmetrically. Formally matched up like chess opponents. But tonight had been a carnival of spontaneity that was so much richer than that. Couch and coffee table. People too aroused to get fully undressed. A chess game scratched from the schedule, in the heat of the moment.

And a woman up another woman's skirt.

Back in private, in the quiet of three a.m., Dawson and Gail kissed long and hard, hovering at the foot of their bed.

"Did it turn you on to see me fucking another woman?" he asked, as their pelvises got reacquainted.

"No," said Gail. "It turned me on to see you fucking *that* other woman." Yet again, she felt a delicious tickle of lubrication making itself known.

"Check," said Daw, with a twinkle.

"Mate," said Gail, pushing him onto the mattress. She slapped him lightly on the ass. Then she pounced on him. "*Pretend I'm Livia*," she whispered.

Ghost Swinger
By Amanda Earl

Did you know Betty and Bruce are swingers? Course that's not what we called it in our day, is it, Mattie? Back then it was "wife swapping." Oh, I know I wasn't legally your wife at that time. It's not like we were traditionalists. But you swapped me a number of times as I recall, and I swapped you too. We did some swinging as well. Back and forth from lover to lover. Oh, those were glorious times, weren't they, Mattie?

Remember that place? Tofino? That's where we landed our sorry American butts so you could avoid the Vietnam Conflict as our dumb ass government called it.

Tofino . . . what a wild and rugged landscape it was, right out of a painting. You couldn't call it calm though, could you? And it wasn't just those high winds and big waves, as glorious as they were. We'd watch the waves come rolling off the sea during storms. Wouldn't even wear raincoats, just let the water wash over us both while we watched the light play over the ocean, our own symphony.

But the main reason it wasn't calm was because the whole place was shimmering with unbridled sex. "Free love" we called it. We sure were rebels back then, weren't we, Mattie? Can't imagine how we'd fit in with this rule-abiding bunch.

I've watched them, these swingers. They go to these clubs where you have to be a member to get in. There are different rooms depending on whether you're a voyeur or an exhibitionist, or you want to have casual sex or chat first. It's all so complicated.

Betty seems very partial to some girl her age named Marjorie, and I can't blame her. I bet you'd give young Marjorie a run for her money, wouldn't you, Mattie? Just because we're not twenty anymore doesn't mean we can't dream now and again, does it?

They seem so organized now. You have to make reservations in

Ghost Swinger   Amanda Earl

advance. Some places don't let single guys in. Imagine that. And nobody's allowed to smoke. Yep, not even reefers. You have to show your membership card. Hell, we burnt up cards, didn't we, Mattie? Remember your draft card? We doused it in Jack Daniels and set the fucker on fire.

Ah the world's become so regimented, hasn't it, Mattie? Remember how we'd spread blankets out on the top of Radar Hill, eat a few 'shrooms and lie under the stars; David on his bongos while the lot of us fucked our brains out under a full moon? We didn't ask for a rule book then, did we? We just danced with somebody, and if they were hip to it, pulled them down onto a blanket.

At the end of the night, I'd wake up and crawl back into our tent, where I'd find you snoring away, some girlie nestled in the crook of your arm. I'd join you and go back to sleep. I still remember how you moaned in surprise when you woke up to not just me but also the other girl sucking your cock and playing with your balls as the rain fell heavy on the roof of the tent. By the time we were done, all sticky with sweat and cum, the only thing to do was to throw our exhausted bodies into the ocean, wash it all off and start over.

Some guy played guitar as good as Hendrix. Remember him, Mattie? Can't recall his name, but I sure remember his cock and those fine licks he played on his Stratocaster. Nothing like hearing "Red House" as the sun is setting and being sprawled out on the long grass getting my cunt eaten out by a girl who's an expert.

And how lucky was it that the guitar guy ended up being this chick's boyfriend. We all made beautiful music together. Brenda, that was her name, remember? Long black locks that kept getting tangled, sea green eyes. She looked like a witch or a gypsy. And the guy . . . oh yeah, I remember now, he went by the name of Raven. He had this wild afro and such gorgeous coffee-colored skin. I was as white as a piece of paper when I got to Tofino, but by the time I'd spent a week making love out in the open under the big Tofino sky, I was bronze and sunkissed. And kissed by a lot of lovers too.

Remember how we partied with Raven and Brenda? Oh, what times we had. Raven introduced us to acid. I still remember how your eyes got all wide, and you wrote the craziest rhymes, all about being in harmony with the universe. The sea looked to us like it was all the colors of a rainbow. You couldn't resist it, said it was luring you in with its colors and beautiful song.

Ghost Swinger — Amanda Earl

I was a bit worried when you and Brenda, both high as kites, jumped into the waves and pressed your bodies together while Raven and I watched from the shore. But it was such a turn on seeing the way Brenda dazzled you, watching her seduce you with those sparkling eyes. It was like the two of you became one with the sea. You dragged her with you far out into the ocean and then you both rolled back on the crest of a high wave, sputtering and laughing.

You looked over at me then, and I could see you were a little scared. Maybe the water grabbed at you a bit too forcefully, tried to pull you down. I smiled at you. I wanted to tell you that life was worth living to the full. The only thing to do was grab back at it and fuck the living daylights out of it.

Maybe you read my mind. I wasn't surprised when you pushed Brenda down onto the sand and entered her, and I laughed when the two of you howled as you fucked. Raven and I couldn't resist. We rolled over to where you were and joined in. I lay beside Brenda and parted my legs, looking over at you and laughing. You reached over and touched my naked breasts, making my nipples harden. Raven and you made jokes about our tits, saying we should have a contest to see whose nipples could get hardest.

Both Brenda and I stuck out our tongues and kissed each other while the two of you stroked yourself and watched us. I watched the two of you standing in the sand, your cocks hard as rocks as you looked down on us. It turned me on even more.

I took one of Brenda's nipples between my fingers. I seem to remember telling you that the better contest would be to see who could make Brenda's nipples hard. I leaned down and sucked and sucked, tasting the salt from the ocean, then reached over to the other one and tugged on it.

Her nipples glistened with the wetness from my mouth and the water. Her eyes shone as my hand reached down and caressed her beautiful stomach, all golden from the sun. I brushed the kelp from her body. Her hair lay splayed out in the sand, and she was as seductive as a mermaid. I let my hand rove further then tickled her inner thighs with the gentle motion of my fingers against her skin. She spread her legs for me. I moved lower until my face was hovering over her cunt like a humming bird over a flower. I gently parted her lower lips and began licking at the top until I reached her tiny clit. I sucked it into my mouth and Brenda moaned. I

Ghost Swinger   Amanda Earl

placed my finger inside Brenda's warm, welcoming cunt. She moved against it, begging for more. I put another finger in and another, and she cried out. I looked up at you and Raven, and you were rubbing your cocks hard at this point, the sight of me fucking Brenda driving you wild.

The waves were coming in faster now. The tide was going to come in soon. I moved my fingers in and out of Brenda's cunt. She writhed her hips to take them deeper inside. The two of you kneeled down to get a closer look. I felt a warm hand on my back.

It was Raven. You and he couldn't let us have all the fun. You moved up to kiss Brenda and Raven slid his fingers along the curve of my back and down to my ass. You straddled Brenda and she took your cock into her mouth while Raven slid his fingers between my ass cheeks. I opened for him while I spread Brenda's lower lips wide and slid my tongue inside her cunt, tasting her sweetness. I pressed my lips against her mound and curled my fingers inside her.

Her cries were muffled by your cock stuffed inside her mouth. You used your hand to guide your cock deeper down her throat. Raven danced a finger gently around the rim of my asshole. I wanted him to put it in there. I heard you telling him to stick his finger up my ass. You knew how much I loved ass play, how much I liked to be fucked in that tight, small hole.

Raven moved his finger in and out of me for a while. The beach was completely empty, one of those secluded spots so common in those days, but I doubt we would have cared if others were around. We would have just invited them to join us.

I could feel Raven's cool breath on my back as he leaned over me. He removed his finger and gave me a light slap on the ass. I remember hearing you laughing and thinking I would get you for that later. You knew I liked a little slap now and again, even sometimes a bit rougher, but that was something we hadn't shared with anyone else so far. I looked up at you and frowned, but you just winked and shrugged as if to remind me that anything was possible and that I should just go with the flow. I let my mouth return to Brenda's cunt and licked up all the juices flowing out of her. I changed my hand position so I could manoeuvre better. Then I pressed my thumb against her asshole and she moaned.

Behind me I felt the pressure of Raven's balls on my ass. I relaxed, waiting for him to enter me. I felt his cock nudge my asshole and then slowly, slowly slide in, waiting for me to relax enough so he could go

Ghost Swinger   Amanda Earl

deeper. I cried out then, told him to fuck me deep.

We were all moving in unison: I was licking Brenda's cunt; you were driving your cock in and out of Brenda's mouth, sometimes rubbing it over her eyes, her nose and her mouth, letting the precum drip onto her face; Raven's cock was plunging in and out of my ass. It felt like we were all one with each other, with the universe. My asshole tingled with the fullness of Raven's cock, so hard and full of come inside me. I moved my hips to pull his cock deep inside my ass. It felt so good, so tight. The pressure built. I ground my body into the sand, humping against it and moaning against Brenda's cunt. She screamed as she came, and then I joined her. Soon after I felt splashes of your cum on my neck. Raven kept pumping and pumping into me until he came hard inside my ass. The waves rolled in and soaked us, making us all break apart and sputter with laughter.

We had such a variety of lovers, didn't we? I wonder what happened to Raven and Brenda. I wonder if they stayed together like you and I did. Most of our friends got divorced long ago, but for you and me, it was till death do us part and even then . . . Being with others made it that much better, I think. It made us honest with one another, and it made us co-conspirators in a way, sharing our stories, our lovers.

It's not like we were looking for love with any of these people. We just wanted to have fun, to enjoy the moment of bodies merging together.

There's Betty and Bruce now, back from their adventuring. They're on cloud nine. I guess they had fun at the swingers' club. You remember these two don't you, Mattie? She worked summers at my office to earn money for college. We never saw him all that much. There was that one time we all ended up at the same play though, and it was cancelled.

Remember that dinner we had? Lots of wine. Us old folks telling them about the goings on back when we were their age. "Flower children" we were called. We told them about our arrival in Tofino, how we ran to the edge of the cliff and gathered up flowers: Indian Paintbrush, Yellow Monkey flowers, ferns and rolled in them together, feeling so young and free and lucky to be alive in that beautiful paradise.

They snickered at that. All sleek and slim they were, wearing black, both of them. Trying to look sophisticated, I guess. They seemed happy though, smiling like the cat that ate the canary. And you seemed quite taken with Betty, if I recall. Of course they didn't admit to us anything about their own adventures; although I sense they wanted to tell us something, just were a bit shy, I guess. Now we know their secret. About once a month,

Ghost Swinger   Amanda Earl

they get a babysitter for their young toddler, go off and get themselves good and screwed at that swingers' club.

I'm such a voyeur. I couldn't help peaking in on one of their visits to the club, just in time to see Betty kneeling in front of some silver-haired old gent, his cock down her throat. What a heartening thing to see. And that girl knew a trick or two. I got real close. At one point the old fellow asked her if she felt a draught, well that was me, lying on the floor, getting a close up view of the action. You'd have loved seeing how tenderly and languidly she licked at his balls. You always complained to me how bad some women were at giving head. Never spent enough time on your balls, you said. Betty has some definite possibilities, my dear.

Anyway, Betty gave that old codger a fine blow job. She licked the rim over and over, then slipped the head just a little into her mouth and let the wetness from her mouth run down his cock. When it was all nice and slick, she encircled the shaft and slid his cock in and out of her mouth, giving the old git a combination of hand and mouth. The guy had amazing stamina too and a cock very much like yours, very wide. I'm sure her mouth was tired but she was a real trooper, kept licking, sucking, stroking until he grunted out that he was about to come. Then the master stroke, she lifted her lithe young body and pressed her tits against his cock, rubbing and rubbing until he exploded all over her chest and cheeks. You could tell she was really turned on. I left at that point, but I wonder if the old guy is as good at tongue fucking as you are, my love. I doubt it. I wish Betty could experience your talented tongue on her clit.

Bruce was nowhere to be seen. Maybe Betty went home and told him all about her adventures while he jacked off for her. Remember how it was for us, Mattie? How we'd fuck like banshees after we were with other lovers? You only had to see me on my hands and knees, taking another man's cock from behind and you went wild with lust. Said it was the most intimate thing to be able to watch me with another lover.

Did I ever tell you how moved I was when you sat down beside me as I was straddling that guy, James? You reached up to my face and brushed the hair out of my eyes, touched my back and smiled and then headed over to your own little party at the other end of the beach. All the time James was fucking me, I felt that hand of yours, beautiful, warming my back. Maybe it's like that for Betty and Bruce.

I see you've got a bulge there, Mattie. Must be getting horny, listening to all these reminiscences. Or maybe it's the thought of Betty and

Ghost Swinger — Amanda Earl

Marjorie lying together at that club. Wonder if Betty and Bruce play games like we did? Maybe they like the sandwich game where the girls are standing up with their tits touching while the men fuck them from behind. Remember how we all tried to walk and ended up falling down? It's a wonder we didn't injure ourselves, isn't it, Mattie? Ah, but we had such fun.

You were so damn fine in your twenties, Mattie. I still remember all the Canadian girls going wild over those sky blue eyes and long blond hair of yours when we got off the bus from Seattle.

I guess it was brave of us to plan to set up our lives together in a different country, but we'd heard good things about British Columbia. I remember our long discussions together about Vancouver, where we initially thought we'd go. Lots of guys avoiding the draft ended up in Vancouver. You had contacts there. But remember how we got to talking to that young couple on the bus? They described this place, far out west on the coast in Clayquot Sound. Even the name Clayquot was exotic to us.

I still remember how happy we were to hear that people lived near the beach rent free. They were squatters. We were so broke. Tofino sounded like the perfect place for us. Gosh, how your dad yelled at you when you told him you wouldn't go to war. My parents weren't any better. They wanted me to stop seeing you. I don't know if I ever told you that my father called you a Benedict Arnold; said you were betraying your country.

Of course, we didn't see it that way. And you still don't. I've seen you getting all upset over this Afghanistan thing, rattling the newspaper. Not much changes in this world, eh Mattie? There will always be people fighting but luckily there will also always be people loving, and that's us. By the looks of things, that's Bruce and Betty too.

I wanted to tell you about these two for a reason, Mattie. I think it's time for you to make friends now. I've been gone such a long time, honey. And they're wild like we were, Mattie. I think you'd enjoy their company. And you could tell them about us, about all our escapades, about our lovers and all the different ways we fucked. All the different places. I'm sure they'd love it. I don't want you to be alone. It's time to stop coming here, Mattie. Time you took up your life again.

*　*　*

Once a month Matthew MacGregor visited his wife Alexa's grave, overlooking Radar Hill near Tofino. This time on a crisp autumn late afternoon he brought his friends, Bruce and Betty with him. They drank shots of Jack Daniels beneath the cypress and cedars and watched the sun set while he regaled them with stories about his adventures with Alexa. They helped him gather ferns and flowers to spread over her grave.

Betty and Bruce confessed to Matthew that his stories were turning them on. Betty unbuttoned her blouse. She wasn't wearing a bra. Matthew's dick stiffened at the sight of her upturned pink nipples.

Betty kneeled down on the ground and undid Matthew's zipper. He watched her pretty golden head lean forward. As she took his cock in her mouth, Bruce unzipped his pants and stroked his hard cock over the grave. Matthew played with Betty's firm young tits as she pressed her cunt into the soft hallowed ground. Matthew couldn't believe what a good cock sucker she was.

Somehow he wasn't really surprised. For the first time in years a woman had her hands on him. It felt so damn good. He reached down to touch his cock, glorying to find it so erect and hard. Bruce took his turn in her mouth while Matthew jacked himself off and watched the couple. Their passion for each other turned him on even more. Matthew's fingers entered her cunt while she sucked Bruce. She licked Bruce's cock for a while and then brought her lips back to Matthew's cock. She alternated between the two men. They both screamed out as her lips, tongue and hands brought them to orgasm. Their come spilled out onto Alexa's grave and mingled with Betty's come. The air was full of the scent of sex. Matthew hoped Alexa could smell it and hear their moans. He hoped wherever she was, that she was watching somewhere, pleasuring right along with them all.

The Swing Set
By Rowan Elizabeth

"What did you say when she ended it?"

"I asked her if she really thought she could live her life without a woman in it. She said she could. Broke my heart," I tell my lover of less than half a year. Don looks over from his place behind the steering wheel.

"Which begs the question: can you live your life without a woman?" he asks.

I've always known this moment would come, so I know what I want to say. "When I divorced, I decided I would be monogamous with the man I'm with."

"Mona, that doesn't answer the question."

I sigh and do the quickest soul-search on record. "I don't know. I really thought I could, but I don't know."

We drive along the scenic highway in silence for not even a mile before he says, "How would that work?"

"What do you mean?" I ask.

He keeps his eyes on the road. "What if you did have a girlfriend again?"

"I don't know."

"Well, until we know, why don't you tell me more about your bisexual experiences?"

I shift in my seat to face him, adjust my seatbelt, and tell him everything I can think of.

* * *

We are barely in the side door when his lips are on mine. We open our mouths and our tongues meet to skim over each other. I give in completely, as I always do. With his body pressing against mine, his hands on me, I melt to him. It's so easy.

He pulls back, looks at me and says, "We need to find you a girl. How do we do that?"

"Internet," I laugh.

He spins me around and starts me off with a little shove. "I'll meet you in the office."

"Don —"

"Mona. Scoot."

Once in our makeshift office, I turn on a low lamp and the computer. I don't know what on Earth I'm doing. I could be ruining the best thing that's ever happened to me.

Don comes in wearing a T-shirt and boxers. He pulls a chair up behind my office chair and sits. He pulls my long hair into a ponytail and gets it out of his way to kiss my neck. I shiver.

"Okay," he says. "Where do we start?"

I spin around in my chair and face Don. He's so handsome. His deeply lined face tells of experiences, but not of this type.

"Honey, how do you really feel about me having sex with another woman?"

He smiles. "Turned on." He moves my hand to his lap. He is indeed. He has me distracted.

I straighten up and shake my head. "No, really. I need you to know I couldn't stand to have you be with another person."

"Ok."

"I mean it! I'm a hypocrite. Completely. I want to be with you and with a woman, but I couldn't handle you messing with her."

"So, I won't. This is your thing, honey. I'm just along for the ride. You teach me."

I look at him long and hard. He means what he's saying. I just hope it holds up in action.

I turn back to the computer and type in a popular adult connection site. It's expensive. We check out a free adult site.

"I think this will work. We just need to make a profile," I say.

Don reaches around my chair and pulls my shirt over my head.

"This needs to go too." He unhooks my bra, slips it down my arms and drops it to the floor. "Go ahead."

"We need a tag line. Something catchy."

The Swing Set

Rowan Elizabeth

"Two looking for three," Don suggests as he caresses my breasts.

"Or four?"

"Four?"

I hesitate to bring up a possibility, but then run with it. "Four. Another couple. It's called a soft swing. The other woman and I have sex and then we each go be with our own partners. Then we all have sex in the same room."

He pinches my nipples, something I love. "Sounds entertaining. Two looking for three or four it is then."

I try to concentrate on a decent profile as Don happily plays with my breasts. I come up with a few good lines and set it loose. "Now we need a picture."

I turn around to Don and ask, "Are you sure you —?"

His hands are on my face and his lips on mine, quieting me. He leans back and smiles. "Let's get that camera of yours."

The bedroom is to be the setting. I slip off my pants, revealing black, lacy boy shorts and lie on the bed. Right off the bat we get a good shot with lots of cleavage and a big smile. But Don keeps going.

"These are for us."

I lay back, stretch, cover and uncover for the clicks of the camera and Don's devouring eyes.

"You look so hot, babe," he says. "So hot."

I get to my knees on the bed and crawl toward him. I look at his face and then at the significant bulge in his boxers. "Gimme that."

Don sets the camera on the floor and steps toward me. I run my hands up his strong legs, grasp the edge of his shorts and pull them down. I hum to myself and lean in to take him in my mouth.

The tip of his cock is wet with pre cum and is slick against my tongue. I use my mouth to stroke his dick, my hands digging into his ass cheeks. Don sweeps my hair back so he can watch me suck him.

"God, woman. You're going to make me blow. Between this and the pictures . . ."

I sit back on my heels and pull him to me. "Then fuck me."

I lie down and continue to pull on him until he's between my legs. His cock presses against my wet pussy and pushes into me. He brings his mouth down to mine and we kiss furiously.

Don works my pussy; works up into my G-spot. He sends me reeling. He keeps on like this until I think I may hyperventilate.

The Swing Set — Rowan Elizabeth

"Come for me, baby," I tell him. "Come with me."

"Yes!" He groans and his breath hitches through the sounds that take me over the edge.

He kisses my eyelids, my cheeks, lips and forehead. He brushes my sweaty hair from my face. "I'm so crazy about you."

I kiss him back. "I know."

* * *

"Anyone good?" Don asks.

"I've put out some feelers and have been looking around. We've had some folks contact us for full swings, and you can just tell they didn't read our profile at all."

We sit down and look through our responses and inquiries.

We do this every night for a week.

Monday, Don is taking a shower while I use the instant messenger to get in touch with some potential candidates. Nothing is tripping my trigger.

An instant message request pops up on my screen. *Couple4You* wants to talk to me.

Hi. This is Janet. Care to chat?

I go with it. We make our introductions and, as we talk, I look up Couple4You's profile.

The legs in the picture are beautiful and strong. Another photo reveals a divine female form. I read on and it seems like Janet and her spouse may just be on our track.

How about we pop into Yahoo? I ask.

By the time Don walks into the office after his shower, I'm giggling along with Janet's humor and seeming honesty.

All right, I tell her. *We'll try to talk again tomorrow night.*

Bi bi, she types.

"Who was that?" Don asks.

"That was Janet, with her husband, Al, on the side." I answer. "Look at these pictures!"

I show him long, strong legs stretched out on a bed. A smiling face framed in honey hair. A cute little girl skirt with knee highs and heels, standing on the shore. A tanned body with pale, full breasts.

"Wow!"

The Swing Set   Rowan Elizabeth

"I know!" I say. "But I'm worried I'm a bit too full-figured for her. She says she loves my pictures, but I'm worried."

"Honey, you're beautiful!"

"And bigger!" I cry. "She's tiny and petite and I'm so . . ."

"Curvy?"

"I guess."

"I love your curves and she's seen your picture. No surprises there."

I run my hand through my hair and sigh. "I think we need more pictures."

Don grins.

* * *

Janet and I instant message the next two nights. It's light and easy and we're looking for the same thing.

I don't want to have sex with another man, just Al, she says. *But I would love to play around with you.*

I want a full-on girlfriend. Kissing, touching, going down on each other. Are you up for that? I ask.

Oh, yeah!

We start a photo share, and she sends pictures of her fabulous little body. I get my courage up and send the latest shots—me in a corset and fishnets. My ample breasts are pushed up and my full thighs are separated to balance on the bed.

Wow! You are gorgeous, Janet says.

Awww . . .

Really. You've got a great body. Aren't I going to be too small for you to enjoy?

Are you crazy? Your body is perfect! Aren't I going to be too big for you?

Then it clicks. Just like every woman, we're both insecure about our bodies. I start laughing and type: *This is silly. We're both attracted to each other. Let's enjoy it.*

Janet comes back with a laughing smiley face and: *You're right. We just need to get over it. But what about our age difference?*

You mean the one where you are close to Don's age and not his younger woman?

Yes.

I'm not worried about it. At all.

As the conversation leads on, we start hinting at getting together. Finally, the hints become straight-on talk about a real life proposal.

The Swing Set   Rowan Elizabeth

Let's meet. Just the two of us first, I suggest. *It's our chemistry that really matters and then we can introduce the guys.*

But, I don't want to do anything without Al being involved.

I agree. I want Don to be part of everything. But I think you and I should really get to know each other first.

We decide on six-thirty, Friday and promise to talk to our men and confirm.

Can we talk tomorrow? I ask.

Anytime!

Bi bi.

Bi bi.

I sit back and tuck my hair behind my ear. "Don! Can you come here?"

"What's up, babe?"

"I want to meet Janet."

"Well then, meet her. I think that's important."

"We'd like just the two of us to meet the first time. No distractions."

"Is sex going to be involved?" Don asks.

"No, silly! Just drinks and food. And conversation. See each other in person, you know, to see if the chemistry is right. You, know? I'm sure it's going to be, but you know, we really—"

"Nervous?"

"Huh?"

"You're babbling a bit. You do that when you're nervous. It's cute."

I take a deep breath and say, "Yeah, I guess I am a little nervous."

"Then you should definitely go meet her. Cure those jitters." Don hugs me close. I relax into his arms.

"Friday it is then."

* * *

At the restaurant, I sit in a curved booth with a straight view of the front door. When Janet walks in, I watch her for a few moments before gesturing to her. We hug and nervously giggle.

"Have a seat," I say and scoot in next to her in the back of the big booth. I want to reach out to touch her hand, but give it a second thought and wait.

The Swing Set — Rowan Elizabeth

The waitress takes our drinks and appetizers order, and we sit in awkward silence for a moment.

I'd had a Pinot Grigio before Janet arrived, and I feel bold as I sip my second. "So what do you think?"

Her eyes dart to mine and then quickly away, the eye contact making her shy. "I think you're beautiful."

"Good. Because I think you're beautiful too."

She cocks her head in my direction but still is hesitant to keep my gaze. "I think I'm old enough to be your mother." She laughs lightly.

"Only if you were a child-bride," I tease.

"It doesn't bother you, my being older than you by so much?"

"No, it doesn't. We finally decided that our bodies weren't a hindrance. Let's put the age behind us too." I finally fix my eyes on hers.

"Yes. Let's try that." She smiles. A wonderful smile.

"Eventually, we'll actually be comfortable with each other," I tell her. I put my hand on hers. So soft.

Her fingers trip over mine and we feel each other's hands. As we talk, we subtly touch each other in punctuation. Janet crosses her legs and I take the opportunity to run my hand along her calf. She strokes my arm and, when I can't get her shyness to break, I brush back the honey hair from her face.

As we end the meeting, we promise to plan a cookout with Don and Al. A little something private at their house. We leave with kisses on cheeks and hugs. And smiles.

* * *

"Would you do her?" Don asks.

"Hell, yes I would." We laugh. "Seriously though, I would like to go up for the cook-out and see what happens. See if you guys get along too."

"Are you nervous?" He asks. "Because I'm so excited but so nervous all at once."

"Me too."

"Come here and let's calm our nerves."

We fall into bed and into each other. It makes everything all better.

* * *

The Swing Set

Rowan Elizabeth

"Should I wear panties with my skirt?" I call from the bathroom to the bedroom.

"No. You're not wearing a bra with that top. Keep it easy."

Easy, I think. *Whew!*

I look in the mirror to check my hair and make-up one more time. I sigh.

Don comes up behind me and lifts my skirt. He grinds his growing erection into my ass. "See how excited I am?"

I shut my eyes and reach back to caress him through his khaki shorts. "Maybe . . . ?"

"I would fuck you right now. But let's keep you fresh and pretty for Janet," Don says.

I turn around and prop myself up on the sink ledge, legs spread. "At least touch me," I beg.

Don's perfect fingers find my clit and assault it until I'm wiggling. He then slips two fingers into me and massages my inner walls. "I want you," I whisper.

Don withdraws his attentions and says, "And you will have me—directly after you have Janet."

"Poo!"

* * *

On the drive to Janet and Al's, we re-iterate our comfort zones.

"Janet said she likes to go slowly, usually." I laugh a little. "But she's not sure she can with me."

Don squeezes my knee. "That sounds good."

"We figure we'll flirt, touch and kiss and see what happens. But the only ones doing it will be her and me. And if we make it to the bedroom, it will still be just us with you and Al watching."

Don looks ornery. "You mean I can't talk dirty in your ear while she's going down on you. Tell you how hot it looks and—"

"Stop it. No. You don't get to play with us. Until you and I fuck after. You okay with that?"

"I'm very excited about it. And a little nervous."

"Me too. I just know how quickly two women can become intimate, and I don't want to freak you out."

The Swing Set   *Rowan Elizabeth*

"I know."

"I don't want to do anything to jeopardize us. It's you I love." I run my fingers down the side of his face.

Leaning into my hand he smiles. "I love you, too."

We pull into Janet and Al's curved drive, which takes us to a parking spot in the back. Sitting at a bar-style table are Janet and Al. Both wave energetically.

"Here we go." I smile at Don. He smiles back as we climb out of the car.

"Find the place alright?" asks Al as we come up the walkway.

"The directions were perfect." Don puts his hand on the small of my back to guide me on the cobblestones. My fuck-me heels are a bit precarious.

Janet slips down from her bar stool and walks toward me. "Looks like we're wearing the same type of shoes." She pushes forward one pretty leg and wiggles her foot to prove herself. "You look great!"

"Thanks. So do you." I look at her short skirt and wonder if she has indeed worn no panties as she had threatened days before. I breathe deeply and smile.

For a while we simply sit outside with appetizers and drinks and talk—nervously at first but gaining familiarity— until we decide to go in for dinner.

As I help Al with the drinks, Janet gives Don a tour of their lovely home. Light with many windows and fully redecorated, their home fits their lifestyle of empty-nesters.

"Mona," Al whispers conspiratorially, "Janet can be really shy. So, you'll probably have to take the lead."

I smile and find my confidence. "Alright."

Dinner is a fantastic mixture of nice wine, good food, and even better conversation. Don and Al seem to be getting along famously as we all begin to bond.

"Let's move to the family room, everyone," Al suggests.

Janet slips her hand into mine, and I feel warm with her touch and the wine coursing through me. I hear conflicting voices in my head: Janet's, telling me to move slowly. And Al's, telling me to take charge. I shake my head and decide to see what pace presents itself.

Janet, Don and I sit on the overstuffed sofa as Al puts in a DVD of the *Red Shoe Diaries*. Janet holds my left hand, running the backs of her nails

The Swing Set — Rowan Elizabeth

up my arm. I'd be scared of those nails if I didn't have some of my own and know they can be controlled.

Don holds my right hand until I squeeze it and let go to lean into Janet's space.

She is relaxed as I lean in to kiss her. Her lips part in a smile as I touch mine to hers. She is sweet to kiss and soon she is kissing back with as much fervor. I open my eyes as our lips part, and her smile is shy again.

I also see Al peeking around from his side chair, taking it all in. I reach back for Don to reassure myself he is still there and watching. He strokes my arm and sends me back to Janet.

She is soft under my hands as I unbutton her blouse to reveal her braless breasts. I kiss from her collarbone down to her nipple and pull it into my mouth. Hearing her moan gently into my hair makes me suck harder until she is wriggling against me. She is so responsive that I realize I must know how she reacts to other pleasures.

I run my hand up the outside of the smooth thigh of her gorgeous legs, and reach her hip without the hindrance of panties. I smile into her skin as I realize she indeed has not worn panties.

Reminding myself that I am the aggressor, I traipse my hand across her thigh to her lightly-downed mound. Her legs spread involuntarily to my touch, and I must find out how wet she is. I dip my fingers between her legs to find her moist and excited. She strains against my fingers and arches towards my hungry mouth, making delicious sounds.

I look up to see if Al is still staring and find myself almost face-to-face with him. I grin and he smiles in appreciation. I look over my shoulder at Don and find him to be entranced as well.

Al, or maybe Janet, suggests we go to the bedroom, but it's Janet who giggles something about the "love nest." The room is beautiful in blues and light greens, shaded with only the light from an open window to show it off.

Janet and I tumble into the middle of the large bed. Our mouths meet in expectant kisses. My hands are on her face, in her hair. I feel her hands on my arms, pulling me closer. Our bodies crush together.

Forever impatient, I lift up and peel off my shirt to reveal my bare breasts. I throw my discarded clothes to Don and cover Janet with more kisses. Her delicate hands are on my back, my shoulders, encouraging my ravenous appetite.

The Swing Set

Rowan Elizabeth

I pull away long enough for her to skim off her blouse. Janet throws it to Al with a strip-tease flourish and this starts the loss of all of our clothing—everything but our strapped-on shoes. There is no time to remove them.

The contrast between our bodies is evident, her tiny frame to my curvier form. I am aware of her pretty tan lines and perfectly pert breasts. My hands stretch down the slope of her waist to her slim hips, taking in the smoothness.

Our eagerness drives us on, blurring the fine details of lovemaking. We are nothing but hungry mouths, greedy hands and naked flesh. I suck on Janet's nipples and hear appreciative moans. She wriggles beneath me as I kiss my way down her belly. I am suddenly more aware of the men watching as I dip down to take her pussy in my mouth. The men make no sounds, but I hope that the show is as beautiful as it feels.

It's been so long since I've been with a woman, but the familiar tangy taste brings it all back. My tongue slips through Janet's wetness to her audible delight. I lie between her spread thighs and taste her as I suck on her clit. My fingers explore her folds and reach for her core. Janet comes with a suddenness that I have never known in a woman. I want to make her feel it again.

This time I press into her harder and suck deeper. I am rewarded with a new experience . . . Janet squirts.

I am surprised by it and am lost in the wetness and Janet's deep guttural moans. I sit up and smile at her. She smiles back as though she's been caught, questioning my reaction. I come up to kiss her, letting her taste herself on my lips, reassuring her of my joy.

"Do you think they've waited long enough?" Janet asks me.

I grin. "Yes. Long enough."

We sit up and stretch out our hands to our men. Al is quick to disrobe and join us on the bed. I curve my finger to beckon Don. Soon I feel the length of his naked body to my right and Janet to my left.

I wrap my arms around Don and feel his lips on mine. I think that he too tastes Janet on my mouth.

We stop kissing long enough for me to look to Janet and Al. She is sitting astride his hips and riding him. His hands cup and fondle her breasts.

With a laugh, he says, "Look at these! They're perfect." I had to agree that they are and Don responds with his mouth on my breast.

The Swing Set

Rowan Elizabeth

Don sucks my nipple, first lightly and then more urgently, biting it. The pleasure escalates as his mouth teases me and his hand finds my pussy. The feeling of Janet moving close to me and taking my other breast in her mouth excites me. Don's expert fingers press my clit and then reach inside to caress my favorite spot.

With my eyes shut, I feel nothing but hands and mouths covering my body. The feeling is surreal and utterly new.

I open my eyes when I feel Janet move down the bed. I look to Don who smiles at me in my delirium.

Janet's fingers spread the top of my pussy lips. She leans down to suck my clit into her mouth. I shut my eyes again to the overwhelming feeling of multiple hands and mouths, to the sounds of happy expression in the room. Janet's mouth teases me and Don's body presses against me. I tremble with my orgasm.

Janet lies next to me, and I look to her to also see Al leaning up on his elbow, a pleased grin on his face.

"How does it feel to be sucked on by both your lover and your girlfriend at the same time?"

My reaction is only to smile and return the favor to Janet.

* * *

Don and I lie wrapped together on the rumpled bed after Janet and Al leave the room to get drinks. We will meet them in the kitchen.

"That was amazing." We both say it. We are both overwhelmed.

"Is everything good?" I ask as we kiss.

"Very," Don says.

"Any regrets?"

"No."

"Then what are you thinking?"

Don grins and kisses me. "I'll make my famous pork chops when they come to our place for the next session."

The Party
By Neve Black

Tonight, I sink deeply into the over-stuffed, luxuriously soft, black leather chair. One arm lying on top of the armrest; my hand flung loosely over its side; exposing my recently manicured, light pink nails. My other hand holds onto a heavy leaded crystal glass; filled one-third full with 100 year-old scotch. I lift the glass to my moistened, ripe red lips and sip the liquid ambrosia. It feels warm as it trickles down my throat. I cross my legs and look down at my red patent leather, 6" stiletto, peep-toe pumps; lifting my pant leg and exposing the twenty-carat, diamond ankle bracelet; a past birthday gift from my ex-husband.

As I sit in the chair, basking in the ambiance, I think back on how I first became involved in swinging parties. Swinging was my ex-husband's idea. He wanted to spice up our sex life, and I really have him to thank for my inauguration into the world of non-monogamous sex.

I was very young when I met and married my ex-husband. I was a virgin and like any young, good wife, I was eager to please, oblige and obey him. The first time I attended a swinger's party was on a vacation with my ex. He told me he was planning an exotic trip in celebration of our fifth wedding anniversary. He told me to pack light for a week-long beach vacation in Mexico.

The minute we got to the resort, I was lulled into a nearly hypnotic trance. The resort was lushly gorgeous. Sun-drenched cottages lined the white sandy beaches all along the crystal blue water's edge and the staff that worked within the resort were stunningly beautiful with well-sculpted bodies, deeply tanned skin, and open, friendly smiles. I noticed how scantily the resort staff was dressed, and I remember feeling guiltily aroused at the visual feast.

The first night we were there, we had a wonderful, romantic dinner together on the beach and as the waves ebbed and flowed against the shore, he grinned sweetly at me, and pushed a square, black velvet box across the white linen table cloth. I opened the box to find a pearl and diamond necklace inside. "Happy Anniversary," he said, taking a sip of wine. Later that night, as we climbed into the cool, white sheets of our large bed, my husband made slow, passionate love to me. I felt wonderful and complete. I was very happy.

The next day my husband and I decided to swim and lounge by the resort pool, and I quickly noticed some of the other guests at the resort were walking around without any clothes on. The guests made open and suggestive sexual advances toward me and my husband. I was perplexed to say the least. My ex-husband never told me he had checked us into what I would soon discover to be a swinger's resort.

In the beginning years of our marriage, my ex-husband used to call me "babe," and I remember how much I loved the way he would say it: "Baaaabe." He'd draw out the letter "A", and his voice was incredibly tantalizing—sexy, deep and raspy. He would smile at me from across the kitchen table, his half-lidded bedroom eyes peering over his coffee mug and implore to me, "Baaaabe, would you do something for me?"

I realized later he would call me babe when he wanted me to do something for him, which he knew I wouldn't necessarily be open to. Sometimes, he would ask me to do things that he knew made me feel uncomfortable; disguising his requests with his good intentions, pushing me up against my boundaries. As I sat next to him by the pool that day, he looked over to me, raised his left eyebrow; grinning sheepishly as he sipped on his piña colada, and softly coaxed, "Baaaabe, having sex with strangers will help to make our marriage stronger."

Later, I came to detest it when he called me "Baaaabe." It's funny how the one thing you love about someone can be the single thing you come to despise.

I was stunned and my immediate response was outrage as I gathered my things and stormed back to our room. He followed me; pleading that he loved me, but he wanted to try new things sexually.

"Why didn't you talk to me about this before booking this trip to Hedonistic Island?" I asked crying, betrayed.

"Because I knew you'd react like this. I thought if we came down here in a peaceful setting and experienced non-monogamous sex together; it would help ease us into trying something new; something hotter and sexier." He said, still pleading.

The Party   Neve Black

"So, what you're saying is you want to cheat on me?" I asked, still crying.

"No. I want both of us to have the opportunity to experience heightened sexual encounters outside of our marriage bed. I love you Baaabe . . . won't you do this for me? For us?" He finished solicitously as he stood in our room, hands on his hips.

As I mentioned earlier, I wanted to please my husband, and what I came to realize later, was that somewhere buried inside me was the desire to experience sexual relations outside my marriage also. Maybe it was because I'd only ever known one man sexually, my husband, or maybe there was something that had always burned inside me, but I didn't realize it until my husband gave me permission to act on those lurid feelings.

After the third day of our trip, I finally conceded to my husband's desires and told him I would allow another woman to touch me, while he watched. He beamed with excitement and we both agreed the first experience would be a luxurious full body massage.

The masseuse, like all the people at this resort was very attractive. Her name was Heidi and she had olive-colored skin; red, pouty lips and well-defined, willowy arms and legs. Heidi wore a pair of khaki shorts. The nipples of her exquisite small, perky breasts pushed against her off-white tank top. Wearing the hotel's white terry cloth robe, I greeted Heidi; removed the robe and lay face down onto the massage table, my husband perched nearby.

I was completely naked.

It was late in the afternoon, and she opened the French doors to our balcony, letting in the warm, ocean breeze. The sensuous smell of warm spiced oranges and sandalwood whirled above my head as she poured the massage oil into her hands; sending sexual impulses deep inside my cunt.

Heidi began slowly massaging my shoulders, my neck, and my arms. I felt my body begin to relax as Heidi's expert fingers and hands penetrated deeply into my muscles. I took a deep breath in through my nose and exhaled as she manipulated my body. She worked me like wet clay, sculpting my body with every touch. I felt my pussy becoming juicy and slick. My husband sat quietly in his chair close to the massage table, watching me. Heidi's hands were strong as she worked the muscles in my lower back; moving down to the cheeks of my ass.

I let out a moan as her hands slid in between my legs. She spread my legs wider. She moved down to my legs, pushing her hands into my

The Party — Neve Black

hamstrings, my calves and feet. I moaned again and she moved her hand back up and in between my legs.

"I want you to turn over onto your back and when you do, I'm going to gently blindfold you," Heidi said softly.

I didn't speak. I lifted myself up and moved onto my back, keeping my eyes closed, and I felt the elastic from the eye mask slip around the back of my head. Heidi carefully lifted my arms above my head and began massaging my breasts with her fingers; my nipples hardening almost immediately. The touch of her fingers felt like shooting stars darting into my clit.

Standing above me, Heidi slid her hands down both sides of my torso. Her fingers slipped underneath my ass, squeezing, and I lifted my hips greedily to her touch. She moved to one side of me and glided her hands toward the glistening hair of my pubis mons. She dipped her fingers into the slippery cleft and rubbed my clit back and forth. Her strong fingers and the oils on her hands made me shiver in euphoric pleasure. She pushed her fingers deeper between my legs, slipping two fingers into my pulsating cunt, while the palm of her hand gently applied pressure against my clit. I came so fast and so strong that I'd forgotten that my husband was in the room, which in some ways was the first sign of the ultimate demise of our marriage.

As the years went by, we attended countless swinging parties. I surprised him and myself, because I grew to enjoy the excitement of sharing my body with different sexual partners—both men and women. I found myself craving the sex found at the parties more so than he did.

It's a little ironic that my ex-husband launched me into the alternative sexual world, and then later claimed not to understand my need and deep desire for multiple partners. He introduced me to the lifestyle, and then ultimately, filed for divorce, indicating irreconcilable differences, based upon my infidelity.

After being divorced for nearly five years, I never looked back with regret. I loved him, and I did what he asked in order to keep our marriage alive. I consider myself lucky, because I ended up finding a deeper aspect of my sexuality than I ever would've uncovered if I hadn't been married to him. I probably should send him a thank you note, but he probably wouldn't appreciate my sentiment.

Looking back, however, I can't recall when swinging evolved into a taste for the bizarre . . .

The Party   Neve Black

Jolted out of my reminiscence, I find myself back in the plush, overstuffed chair. I gaze down the contours of my body. The size twelve, blue and white, pin-striped suit clings to my medium-large frame nicely; accentuating my curvaceous hips and bust. My shoulder length, dark brown hair is pulled up and into a thick chignon and rests submissively below a black, wide-brimmed hat, tipped in black boa and pulled down and to one side. I want to look mysterious, beguiling, hinting at somewhat androgynous traits while at the party tonight.

My large, round, piercing blue eyes are lined in jet-black liquid liner, and I applied it thickly. I wear translucent powder across my small, straight nose, high cheek bones and forehead, pressing the powder into the cleft of my chin. I finished by dabbing just a hint of my red lipstick into the apples of my cheeks. The ruffles that donned the front of my white, cotton shirt whispered, "hello", and could be seen at the cuffs, around my neck and coming up from behind the pin-striped vest.

The man stands behind my big, leather chair, slightly to the right, engaged in a conversation with a man seated in the antique burgundy velvet settee nearby. They are speaking about Halliburton stock options. His hand gently touches the nape of my neck. I'm not paying much attention to their conversation. I close my eyes, feeling the soft pads of his fingertips touching me, sending goose bumps up and down my spine. He moves his hand around to the front of my neck, running his fingers back and forth across the indentation, and I swallow hard at his subtle reminder of casual violence; *he* is in control.

His cologne smells of woodsy spice; it's deeply masculine. I don't turn and look up at him; after all, what prey gazes into to the eyes of the predator? At any rate, I'm not allowed to make eye contact, party rules. So, instead I open my eyes and stare straight ahead, looking through a large picture window, trying to focus on the beauty of the pink blossoms that adorn a cherry tree across the street.

"Yes. I have a diversified portfolio," he says, still speaking to the man sitting on the settee.

His response claims my focus; my eyes shift to the man sitting on the settee. He wears a chic and expensive dark grey suit, with a robin's egg-tinted button down shirt and cumin spice-colored tie. He is a medium-sized man, and his eyes, nose and cheeks are covered, disguised behind a gold lame, ornate-looking mask, similar in appearance to masks people sometimes sport during Mardi Gras. He is wearing a long, blond wig, tied

The Party — Neve Black

into a pony tail, and it hangs down to the middle of his back. In some ways, he reminds me of pictures I've seen of the Chanel designer, Karl Lagerfeld. Only his tight, thin lips and big ears are exposed. Instead of finding the requisite Italian leather loafers on his feet, matching his expensive suit, he wears flip-flops; the juxtaposition strikes me as absurd.

Magic Fingers is moving again, moving down the front of my blouse, exploring my skin. The back of his hand pushes against the buttons, and the pin-striped vest I am wearing. I can feel my temperature start to rise; sweat forming behind my knees, my elbows, my armpits and between my legs. I wasn't wearing a bra or panties tonight, and my full-size breasts sway freely, my nipples rubbing up against the cotton, and I can tell they are hard; they ache. He reaches for my right breast and gently runs his fingers back and forth from where my cleavage begins to the outside, undulating curve, cupping it from the side and squeezing. The inside of his palm teases my now hard candy nipple.

Nervously, I uncross and re-cross my legs; my fingertips drumming against the arm rest; squirming at his touch as I place my drink on the table next to me; I am afraid I might drop the weighty crystal glass. He must have been pleased with what he felt because his hand moves toward my left breast and gingerly cups his hand around it, lifting my breast up from underneath and kneading. I feel his fingers brush back and forth across the nipple, stiffened and thrumming. I think I could have climaxed just from the way he touches my breasts, feeling the lips of my pussy moisten and heat. I close my eyes again.

"No. I'm not opposed to hearing about other investments. Why don't you contact my secretary on Monday and we can set-up an appointment to talk about this in more detail?" His words say one thing, but his hands clutching my breast speak another language.

I hear shuffling in front of me, and when I open my eyes, a man wearing black pants and a white button down shirt is seated Indian-style just in front of the man on the settee. He is dressed like one of the waiters working the party, serving food and drinks on silver trays to the other guests which now fill the room. He is also wearing a mask, and looks only at the man on the settee, saying nothing as he begins removing the flip-flops from his feet. He scoots himself back across the tightly woven, crème-colored carpet, giving himself enough room and lifts the man's foot. He begins massaging it: pointing, flexing, rotating and rubbing. The man

The Party Neve Black

on the settee presses his other foot into Waiter Man's lap, wriggling his toes against the waiter's groin.

Settee Man begins to moan as his toes are massaged. The waiter's erection rises elaborately as my breasts are being squeezed and plundered. It is all so highly erotic that my senses explode, sending tiny shock waves into my juicy, throbbing pussy. I, too, let out a low, guttural moan. Waiter Man is now sucking on Settee Man's toes, holding his foot steady with both hands, while he slowly sucks and licks each toe, in and out, in and out of his wet, insistent mouth. The man on the couch writhes in ecstasy, bucking his hips up from the settee, moaning and hissing, until he finally succumbs to the intense pleasure. He unzips the fly of his expensive grey suit, pulls out his quivering penis and starts to rub his cock, sliding his hand up and down, masturbating while his toes are being sucked by the masked Waiter Man seated in front of him. My head starts spinning and beads of sweat line my forehead. The depravity is euphoric, compelling!

Magic Fingers moves around the chair and stands in front of me now, but I don't look up. I'm not to know who he is. He wears black slacks and no belt. He moves his body in front of me, parting my legs with his knees and slipping his body between my open thighs until the tops of his shins bang up against the leather chair. He unbuttons and unzips his slacks, letting them fall to his ankles. He isn't wearing shorts, and his slightly stiffened cock looks up at me. It is very long and slender from the head to the base of his shaft, and it curves up. I think about how delicious a cock with a curve like that might feel when it hits my G-spot, fucking me hard, and I let out low moan of expectation and lust.

Magic Fingers wants me to suck his cock. I slide myself down from the chair, until my knees hit the floor, my back against the chair as I straddle his legs. I move my head closer to his erection. One hand grabs the cheeks of his ass, pulling his cock closer to my lips, while the other hand touches his smooth, honey-brown, well-developed thighs. I run my hand up and down the length of his hamstrings, massaging his muscles and then moving my hand around and kneading his quadriceps. He lets out a growl. I move my hand from his thighs, firmly grasping the base of his cock while I lightly graze my wet lips across the tip. I make painstakingly slow circles with my tongue around the head before tasting his pre-cum, and enveloping him into my mouth to suck on his cock. I move my mouth farther down, feeling his cock pulsate and grow bigger, sucking harder and licking his engorged dick. I push my other hand into the crack of his ass and move my hand up and down, pushing my pinky finger into the hole of his ass. His ass is sweating and his hips begin to thrust toward my mouth. My hat falls to the floor.

Somewhere in the background I can hear the sounds of sucking and moaning; I think I hear the man on the settee's voice say in a low, almost guttural tone, "Aaaah. That's it. That's it. Suck it hard. Suck it hard," but I can't be certain.

With Magic Finger's cock in my mouth, I squeeze his ass cheeks hard, pushing my finger deeper inside, as I pull him closer and deeper into my mouth, taking him all the way in. He moans as he thrusts in and out of my tight, wet mouth. I can feel his cock start to spasm at the base and I know he is going to shoot his load and cum in my mouth. So, I push my pinky finger into the hole of his ass as deep as I can and wriggle it back and forth until he screams in blissful agony and shoots his thick load of juice down my throat. I swallow his seed and slowly pull my mouth back and off his cock. He is still spasming and I lick his cock like an ice cream cone, still sensitive after the orgasm. Then he shudders, pulling away.

I keep my eyes closed while I hear Magic Fingers rustle with his clothes, putting on his pants. Minutes pass and I open them—he is gone. I sit up straight in the chair and smooth out my suit, find my hat and put it back on my head, cocking it to one side, casting an enigmatic shadow across my face again. I reach for my cocktail and look ahead, taking a long sip. The man on the settee is still there, but the masked waiter has gone. He is staring at me, smiling like the Cheshire cat.

"Great party, wouldn't ya say?" he asks me, still smiling.

"Oh, yes. It's one of the better parties I've attended all year," I respond, smiling slyly.

"Will you come again?" he inquired, lifting his right arm over the back of the settee.

"I fully intend to come as many times as possible." I respond, taking another sip and winking at him.

Our First Encounter   *Randall Lang*

> *He and his wife Pat are middle-aged swingers. They only swing occasionally and only with couples to whom they are attracted. He could never have imagined when your husband sent him and Pat a note that it would lead to a level of passion and desire that had escaped him for many years. He had forgotten that a woman could enflame his passion to this level. He found himself consumed by a lust for you that turned him into an eighteen year-old boy with raging hormones. It is YOU that he desires as he writes to you of "Our First Encounter."*

Our First Encounter
By Randall Lang

    My wife Pat and I have been married for over twenty years and have been swingers for the past eight. Although we deeply loved each other, the "sameness" of our daily life had greatly blunted the excitement and attraction that we felt for each other. It started as a joke about a male stripper that led to talk of a threesome. The flash in Pat's eyes instantly told me that she was serious. After some exploratory "What would you think . . .?" questions, honest feelings began to shape the conversation. I think we were both surprised with our own responses, but it was new and exciting. She stared over my shoulder as our computer searches yielded results. We had found the doorway, now we had to decide if we should enter. The decision came quickly. Basically, we agreed that the worst that could happen was that if we did not like swinging, we would not do it again.

    Our first couple lived over an hour away. We were both as nervous as high school kids as we drove to meet them. I kept telling Pat that she could say the word and we would go home. Honestly, I think I was so nervous that I hoped she would stop us, but she held firm.

Our First Encounter   Randall Lang

We met them at a restaurant. We had chatted a bit on the telephone, but we were still basically strangers. Just as our first impression had indicated, they turned out to be warm, friendly, and not the least bit intimidating. I suppose that, at that time, I expected swingers to have wild predatory eyes and attack us as food, but it was not like that at all. We discussed families, jobs, children, and all of the other commonalities of life, but as the evening wore on, the topic of swinging came up. They were open and honest with us; discussing their start and experiences. They also let us know that there was no pressure, and that we could leave at any time if we felt uncomfortable and there would be no hard feelings.

We traded spouses for the trip to their house. It was such a strange feeling to have a different woman in the car with me, but it was also new and very exciting. I kept stealing glances at her legs and her breasts as we drove. When I finally developed the courage to touch her hand, she turned to me and smiled warmly.

Their home was lovely and similar to ours in many ways. We sat in the kitchen and had drinks as we continued to talk. It was not long before our hostess took my hand an invited us to tour the house. As you might imagine, the tour ended on their king size bed with Pat and me side by side in someone else's arms.

The experience was life changing. All the way home and for days afterward Pat and I talked of the feelings we had experienced during our first outing. It had been comforting, relaxed, and thoroughly enjoyable. We never turned back.

* * *

After eight years we have settled down a lot. Once the newness wore off and we had a few negative experiences, we decided to slow down and to be more selective. We became less active, preferring instead to stay within our small cluster of friends for both swing and straight activities. We have been to swing clubs and to occasional parties, and we found both to be interesting, but lacking in that special element of mutual attraction. As with any "rich sweet", we knew that a small portion taken as an occasional treat was much better than over-indulging and spoiling the enjoyment. The bond between us remains as strong as it can be between a man and a woman, and our swing activities only enhance that.

Our First Encounter Randall Lang

We keep a profile on one of the swing web sites just to keep a toe in the water. We almost never write to others and turn down more offers than we accept. When your husband wrote to us, it was obvious that you were people like us: people who work hard and enjoy life's rewards. We could tell that you were people with an appreciation for that special magnetism between men and women and who revel in the mating dance.

Pat would sit next to me during our chats. I could sense the attraction that was building between her and your husband. And I am certain that she could also feel the fire that you have stirred within me. During our telephone chats, Pat took the phone into another room to talk privately with your husband. She rarely does that and it's a certain indicator that her attraction to him is strong. I could only wonder what she was thinking when you and I finally spoke. The very sound of your voice made me feel as nervous as a sixteen year-old boy talking to the prom queen. The pictures you sent were wonderful! Beautiful pictures of you in many settings. But for me there were only your eyes; those beautiful eyes that burned into my soul and lit a level of passion and desire that had eluded me for many years.

When our meeting was arranged I found myself counting the days and finally the hours until I would actually see you. The thought of holding you, of kissing you, of touching you, of making love to you filled my thoughts to the exception of all else. Then finally, mercifully, the day of our meeting approached.

* * *

The dinner had been pleasant enough. It was exciting to meet you and your husband at the restaurant. Pat and I instantly recognized both of you from the pictures and the small talk was spirited. Getting to know each other was genuinely fun as we sat at the table opposite each other. We really had a surprising amount in common. The years of experiences made for great conversation, but I found it increasingly difficult to concentrate upon talk. My eyes and my thoughts were drawn to you. I didn't want to stare, yet I found a fascination about you. The way your dark hair framed your face, the tiny wrinkles that match my own, the sparkle in your eyes, the brightness of your smile, all of these features attracted and held my attention.

Our First Encounter

Randall Lang

I could see a glimmer of passion in your eyes that teased and beckoned me, but at the same time a bit of nervous shyness. A spark would shoot down my spine each time our eyes would meet, but you would slowly turn away as if the intensity in my eyes were too strong for you. I would sneak glances at you enjoying the way your smooth white blouse followed the curves of your body. I wished that you had opened just one more button to expose a hint of cleavage. I remember how the black leather skirt softly wrapped about your hips accenting every curve, yet ever tasteful. When I extended my leg toward you under the table, you escaped my contact.

I talked with your husband of manly things; of jobs and home projects and personal accomplishments, but my heart wasn't in the chat. Instead I longed to feast my eyes upon the lovely lady across from me. I wanted to study every feature, but not to stare or make you uncomfortable. My eyes would not easily leave you.

Even as we left the restaurant, I watched the way your legs and your hips moved in a soft flow to your car. The elegance with which you carried yourself captivated me.

The drive to your house was short, but it seemed interminable without the sight of you. We followed you through streets and roads, through stop signs and turns until at last you turned into your driveway. The large garage door opened silently and your car slipped inside. We parked near the other door, got out, and followed you in through the garage.

Your house reflects you and your husband. Quietly tasteful, perfectly maintained and groomed; it projects the image of years of hard work and commitment. We followed you into the basement game room and over to the well-stocked bar. You and Pat put your purses down and chat like two old friends. Your husband begins to mix drinks while you show Pat around the house. He and I talk of home maintenance and gardening, but again my ears long for your voice.

Your feminine footsteps on the stairs are welcomed as you return, still talking and giggling like schoolgirls. I watch enamored as you gracefully descend the steps, your smooth, slim legs moving elegantly atop your high heels. You sit on a stool on one side of me while Pat sits on the other. Your husband slides a freshly made drink across the bar into each waiting hand. Mine is cool and refreshing but with the distinct bite of strong bourbon.

Our First Encounter   Randall Lang

    As the conversation resumes, I stare at your legs crossed at the knee and folded together in that uniquely female position that no man can achieve. Your legs are youthful, strong, and well toned, truly the legs of a much younger woman. It occurs to me that you appear to be that fantasy that all mature people wish for; the mind with years of experience and knowledge in a strong and energetic body. Your skirt slides up a bit higher as you twist on the stool.

    Your husband puts on some music and makes his way out from behind the bar to sit next to Pat. The tune is one of those oldies from the 70's that always bring back memories and start conversations that begin with "Do you remember?" or "Did you ever?" The talk is lively and filled with laughter. I try to catch your eyes with mine, seeking out that fire that I know is within you. You tease me with glances and smiles, holding me captive to your wiles.

    The song changes to a slow tune. I turn to you and ask, "Do you dance?"

    Without reply you put down your drink, stand up and take my outstretched hand. Your hand is small and soft. It is warm and inviting, and the mere contact sends a tingle through me. We walk three steps together before you turn to me and melt into my arms.

    At last! At last! Now I have you close to me. Your face is but inches from mine, your body presses against me. Your husband dims the lights as he and Pat move nearby. For a time I silently relish the feeling of you in my arms. My senses come alive with the sensation of your body against mine. My other hand touches the fabric of your blouse and presses it against the small of your back. We sway and take small steps in time with the music. You follow my lead flawlessly, inducing a silly thought into my mind.

    Suddenly, I spin us around, catching you off guard and causing you to laugh nervously as we almost stumble. But I hold you ever more tightly while we laugh and tease. You smile at me with that bright, perfect smile that takes my breath away. I can wait no longer.

    I pull you tightly against me and slowly press my lips to yours. Your lips are soft and moist. You hesitate at first then I feel your arms slide about my neck as mine wrap around your waist. This was the moment I have yearned for since our first meeting! Among a thousand other thoughts were my wonderings of your lips. Were they as soft as they looked? Would I ever get to kiss them? Would they be dry as mine became when I thought of you? Your lips were all I could have dreamed of and more.

Our First Encounter
Randall Lang

I kiss you softly, gently, to enjoy each contact. Your hand presses at the back of my head and I pull you more tightly against me. My body stirs and I start to stiffen; I know you can feel my excitement. Our lips part slightly and my tongue dances and teases against yours. Finally, our lips separate and we move back enough for me to see your face. Your eyes are different now. They don't turn down or look away. They shine now and lock onto mine to reveal the fire building within you. Your eyes entice me and challenge me to excite you. They cry out for me to give you what you long for. When I can no longer stand the separation, I again pull you to me. Our lips lock together while our bodies sway to the music.

The song ends and there is silence. Our lips part and once again I can see your magical eyes. I release you from my arms and we walk slowly to the couch across the room. For a moment, we sit face to face before wrapping up in each other's arms. My free hand begins to travel, starting in your hair. First my hand caresses the soft, black waves before my fingers slide through the silky strands. My fingernails tease your neck with glancing and slow dragging touches. I feel your body shudder at my touch. Your muffled sighs sound like purring. Your grip tightens around my neck as my tongue explores your mouth and dances with your tongue.

My hand moves to the front of your neck and my fingers gently brush at the front of your blouse. I touch you lightly, teasing you while enjoying the feel of your flesh. Finding the first button, I pull the fabric outward as my fingers release the button. I revel when it pops open. I open the next button, and the next, and the next, all the while struggling to control the urge to tear the blouse open to get to the treasures within. Finally, the blouse hangs open and I reach inside.

The smooth warmth of your belly greets my hand. I spread out my hand to touch all I can reach, rubbing lazy circles. You pull your lips away and place delicate, darting kisses upon my face. I listen to your breathing and the sounds that you make. I am caught up in the sensual world that is you. The scent of your hair, the sound of your breathing, the feel of your flesh; all combine to enchant me.

When I can contain myself no more, I slowly reach to touch that special soft smooth skin between your breasts. I linger to fully enjoy the feeling before tracing outward along the edge of your lacy bra. The swell of your breasts becomes higher and higher as I slowly move my flattened fingers over you. I tease back and forth at the edge of the lace, listening to your reaction. Finally I can wait no longer to touch you. My hand curls

Our First Encounter Randall Lang

under and around your breast, sliding easily over the silky material. Your breast fills my hand and invites my touch, its hardened nipple straining against the thin fabric. Our lips separate and I again look into your eyes and listen to your smothered gasp when I gently pinch and roll your hardened nipple.

My other arm comes free from behind you so that both of my hands may enjoy your offerings. As much as I enjoy touching you, it is the sounds that you make that truly excite me. I soak up each little catch in your breathing, every tiny gasp, every quiet moan.

I slide my face down to your chest and gently nibble at you through the fabric. I listen intently to your heavy breathing interspersed with whispered words of encouragement. You lean forward giving me the cue to reach around and release the binding bra. I fumble only momentarily before one hook opens, then the other. My hands slide around you, bunching the loose fabric and lifting upward. Your breasts spill into my hands in a flood of smooth, soft pleasure that sends jolts of excitement into my now-rigid cock. Your nipples are wonderful; large and full, jutting outward in their arousal, greeting my touch enthusiastically.

My mouth covers your breast, nursing heavily, and rolling your nipple between my lips and tongue. Your hands crush my face against you as sighs and pleas pour from your lips. With my mouth at your breasts, my hand slides down to your thigh. Your legs open to welcome my touch and invite me to move higher. I tickle and tease your sensitive inner thigh, dragging my fingernails backward along your smooth flesh. Your hands clutch at me, eager for more contact, but I move slowly, teasingly along your skin.

Finally I brush the silky triangle of your skimpy panties. Your body stiffens when two fingers find and slowly travel the length of your labia. I love the control that I have taken over you as again and again I run my fingers along your damp and puffy lips. I can feel the building dampness. You whimper in reaction and whisper encouragement. My light and feathery touch causes you to squirm, and gradually I increase the pressure.

Sliding my hand into the leg of your panties, I start to brush you, this time without obstruction. Your hands grab my shoulders and your fingers dig into my flesh. Your breathing is erratic and short. Cries and whimpers pour from you. I press a finger into you to find a flow of warm, wet fluid that lubricates everything it touches. Watching your eyes I work my finger deep within you, exploring for sensitive areas and stirring your increasing

Our First Encounter   Randall Lang

wetness. In a daring move, I remove my wet finger from you and move it up to my lips. Making sure that you can see what I am doing, I hold my finger horizontally in line with my lips and make darting licks along its length. Suddenly, you smile a wicked smile and press your lips to mine, trapping my finger between us. I can feel your tongue also licking my finger. My cock twinges at the thought of what is occurring.

My eyes find yours as you slowly pull away. Your hand guides mine back between your legs as your mouth whispers, "More." My hand finds you and my finger eagerly returns to its wet sanctuary. A second finger joins the first just before a third finger enters you. I twist my hand, pushing your lips apart and opening you as you grab my shoulders again. I feel the wet warm flesh yield to my touch. Even as my fingers open you, my thumb seeks an elusive target.

But suddenly, there it is; your hard little bud emerging from the folds of flesh. You stiffen and cry out as I touch it. My thumb rubs lazy circles while two fingers locate and massage your slightly rough G-spot. You squirm with pleasure making it difficult for me to stay on-target. By your reaction, I know it is time to move forward.

I slide from the couch to the floor and kneel between your legs. Pushing up the short leather skirt, I reach for the waistband of your panties. You raise your hips to help me slide them off. I move them slowly down your legs, enjoying the smoothness of your stockings and over your high heeled shoes. Once the way is cleared, I lower my face between your legs. The warm, wet scent of you is delightful. At first I just tease you with my tongue, licking slowly and lightly up and down your length. Then I part you and lick more tender areas. Your moans are my reward. Deeper and deeper I push my tongue. Your hands grab my head; your fingers tangle and pull at my hair. My fingers continue to massage your G-spot as my tongue touches your tender clit causing you body to stiffen. I have found my target and keep my tongue flicking and darting against it as you breathe faster and faster. Your words become slurred; your cries become louder and longer. Your body writhes and your hips twist.

Then you cry out and stiffen. My tongue moves even faster. Suddenly you grab my head as if trying to push me into you. Pulse after pulse shoots through you like jolts of electricity. I move with your pulses trying to maximize your pleasure. Gradually the pulses fade and you lay back exhausted and spent. I move up onto the couch to hold you. You smile and whisper into my ear,

Our First Encounter   Randall Lang

"My God that was good!"

I reply, "That's just the beginning."

Droplets of perspiration dot your forehead and dampen your hair. You cuddle against me.

Across the room your husband and Pat are naked and making love furiously on the love seat. Her cries fill the room. Even in the dim light perspiration glistens on your husband's back.

When you have recovered enough, I help you to remove your blouse, bra and skirt. Your shapely nude body is a tribute to years of careful diet and exercise. I help you to your feet and ask you to turn around and kneel on the couch, holding on to the back. I quickly remove my clothes and sit on the floor between your legs with my back against the front of the couch. I maneuver my head between your legs. You giggle at the awkward position and at my gyrations as I get into position, but you quickly stop when I pull your hips down onto my face. My tongue starts to explore you once more as you move yourself to find just the right position. Once found, your head falls back and I can tell by your moans that we've connected. Now your hips rock against my face pushing my head hard into the couch seeking more contact. Your moans transition into a steady series of gasps. Your hip movements become more intense. Your enthusiasm is obviously renewed. I lick you slow and steadily in rhythm with your hip movements. You move harder and faster, but after a while it becomes obvious that you require additional stimulation.

I put my hands on your hips and gently lift you up while I slide out from under you. As I stand up and look at you, a look of vulnerability and desire comes over your face. I silently answer with a smile as I position myself behind you. I see a sneaky smile as you turn your face away.

My cock is rock hard and eager for the comfort of your body. A couple of gentle brushes against your eager vagina and the head of my cock is wet and ready. With one gentle push I slide easily into you. The resulting pleasure is instantaneous and mutual. I hold myself deeply inside you and I bask in the euphoria. I begin to twist and grind my hips against you then slowly move in and out with tiny strokes.

Your wetness is extraordinary! Your muscles are tight and squeeze around me. I start with long, slow strokes, pulling almost entirely out of you then plunging deeply. You react by pushing back against me. I watch carefully for signs of what you seem to like best. You appear to like my long strokes, but you want them harder and faster. I hold your hips with my hands and move faster, driving deeply into you. The smacking sound of flesh meeting flesh echoes through the room. You seem to enjoy it faster so I speed up even more. Your low moans become gasps interspersed with the sound of flesh colliding. I can see your hands gripping tightly on the back of the couch as your head moves up and down. I would love to grab your hair and ride you like a wild horse, but I fear that I may hurt you.

I can tell from your sounds that your next orgasm is building. I feel my own creeping up and I fight for control. I want one last position change to make it as good as possible for you. You don't look happy when I withdraw from you and quickly sit beside you on the couch. When you look at me, I motion for you to straddle me.

It takes just an instant for you to position yourself and to settle down, taking me again deep within you. Your arms lock about my neck and your lips press against mine. The perspiration from our bodies smears together as you begin to rhythmically ride up and down on my rigid cock. Your hips rock slightly back and forth to rub your G-spot against the head of my cock. Our lips separate as you gasp for air. You clutch once again at the back of the couch while your hips move faster and faster.

My lips find a swollen nipple and lock onto it, sucking hard and flicking it with my tongue. Your breathing becomes panting and panting becomes rhythmic cries. I feel my climax building and my control crumbling. I know that I can't hold off much longer.

Then suddenly you stop bouncing and rock your hips hard and deliberately against me. You become driven. You rock methodically and your cries become louder. A long, low moan pours from you as your head tilts back and your hips frantically twist. The shock waves start through you, racking your body as I hold you tightly against me. Your muscles squeeze me tightly bringing on my orgasm. Even in my ecstasy I am grateful that I could hold off until we could share the experience. Blast after blast of my warm semen sprays into you as I thrust as deeply as I can. My cries join yours and I hold you tightly to me. Pulse follows pulse crashing through me, but finally they lessen and fade. As calm follows a storm, we stay wrapped together, soaked with perspiration, panting heavily, and completely spent. Neither us can or wants to move.

Eventually, as I recover, my lips kiss your neck, your cheek, your lips. No words are spoken. Your soft smile and the look in your eyes are nourishment for me. For it is that above all else that I have hoped for. Then a few kisses and a few whispered words break the silence. A low laugh, then a giggle brightens the room. When you move your body back from me, I am suddenly cold. When you lift yourself up off of me, I instantly feel both cold and empty. I'm a bit surprised when you gather up your clothes without a word to me. Then you turn with your clothes under your arm, smile at me, and extend your hand.

"I need a shower. Join me?"

"Then I'll massage you," I reply as I stand up and take your hand, pausing to gather up my clothes.

Your husband and Pat stand up and follow us as we walk toward the stairs. The evening has already been magical and it's only just started.

* * *

BUZZ-Z-Z-Z-Z-Z-Z-Z-Z-Z-Z-Z-Z-Z-Z-Z-Z-Z-Z-Z-Z!!!!

The screaming loud obscenity of the alarm has brutally shattered me from my sleep and a dream I shall never forget. Pat stirs next to me. Then she flings off the covers, stands up, and moves away from the bed. I fold back my covers and sit on the edge of the bed. My head is cloudy with sleep and my mind wallows in a sea of disappointment. Then as the clouds clear, reality begins to set in. This is Friday! It is this evening when we shall finally meet. It is the dawn of an interminably long day that will suddenly change to one of magic and burning desire when finally I see your face. There are thirteen hours remaining until we meet you and your husband at the restaurant. The countdown has begun.

One Weekend in Toronto
By Claudia Moss

Ever live for the next vacation the Monday you return from a holiday?

That's me, which is the number-one indicator I need to watch my frayed copy of *The Secret* until the DVD disintegrates. Yep, that's right. I have nothing to hide—outside of my personal cell while I'm at work. Other than that, most of my friends know I watch that film faithfully, so I'm reminded that whatever I focus on, if I can see it, and most importantly feel it, damn it, it's mine. And I see myself free of the academic plantation, with streams of income, and time to please my wife in every way. I know how.

Simple as that.

At work, my daydreams get blasted whenever Deni Epps, one of my professors, slinks into my office and leans in the doorway as though she fancies herself a starlet from an old Hollywood movie, her work wardrobe Victoria and Frederick's sexy. Suits painted-on and colorful, expensive pumps and wearable art jewelry. I don't give a precious halleluiah if she is one of Howard's best lecturers in my English Department. She never acknowledges the memo that nothing about her, aside from her taste in shoes and jewelry, is cute to me. Don't know what others see when she slithers up, but all I see is a country kitchen, her in an apron, smiling and waving, with that sexless mouth pouting, "Ya'll come on back, now, hear?"

"Good morning, Dr. Young. I trust you had a peaceful, yet exhilarating Spring Break?"

Her manicured fingertips twirl a gem clip inches above her small cleavage in a soft purple dress.

"I did, thank you, Ms. Epps. How was yours?" Like I cared.

"You always do that after a break."

Ugh! Lose that pout; it isn't cute.

One Weekend in Toronto   *Claudia Moss*

I lean back in my swivel chair and give her a baffled, somewhat annoyed expression. "What do you mean?"

"That 'Ms. Epps' business. It's Deni." Her lips smooch upward kinda sorta beckoningly, a close imitation of the young brothers in my neighborhood here in D.C.: chins lifted—cool and tough; a quick nod, lips bunched, wordlessly saying, "What up?"

"I see. So how did you spend your break, Deni? Performing?"

"How else? I performed in 'The Beauties of Burlesque Show' in Las Vegas. Fascinating. It had every cell in my body energized and charged from the moment I hit the stage to the second my flight ascended into the friendly skies."

Spare me the commentary. "Sounds fascinating. Well, listen, Deni, I—"

"I know you're a busy woman, Dr. Young. Only wanted to welcome you back."

I clock her look.

Note the googly eyes. And whenever did burlesque and academia mix?

"As much as I'd love to hear about the show and see the photos, I've got to pass."

Then my damn personal cell plays Diana Krall's sexy, jazzy "You Go To My Head" and I think about not answering it, but I'm coming off as entirely too conspicuous.

"Forgive me. Gotta take this." There is no avoiding opening my Racer, although she's posted in my direct range of vision, gazing at me soft eyed, heat brewing from her core and wafting towards me in wanton waves.

Wrong office, Barbie.

My cell's face illuminates with a picture of one of the most delectably dark pussies I've ever lapped. It's my girl, K.C.

"Hello, darlin'! Always a pleasure to hear your voice, love."

I shrug, my wrist flicking quickly towards the right window, left hand covering the mouth-watering view, and whisper more emphatically, "Deni, I'd like to take this in private please, if you don't mind."

Deni bows, a conspiracy in her tepid, turquoise gaze. Backing into the hall, her fingers flutter a sensual I'll-see-you-later and she disappears.

"One of my professors, girl," I whisper, looking at the empty doorway. "Sweats me worse than a student on probation a grade away from The Last Flight Home."

"Tell me about it. I was that student. Remember our junior year at Tuskegee?"

"K.C. shut up," I say, laughingly recalling her constant desperation. A blessing things change. No one would know that today. My girl runs Atlanta's CDC, with a reputed take-no-shit reputation.

"We're doing it again, Neco. Howard and I are organizing a weekend in Toronto. We know you and the wife are just back from a week in Cancun, but we figured you'd be good to go anyway."

That K.C. keeps a closet of golden carrots for times such as these. Besides, I miss her fine ass whenever she stays away too long. Howard knows she's the jam on my toast, the maple in my syrup.

"Our passports stay in order, woman."

"How about the French Connection? That bed and breakfast with six of the sweetest rooms you could ever wish to fall asleep in. Surrounding restaurants are on point, and I've got a few attractions lined up, although—" she growls low in her throat, "you know we ain't going for the attractions."

"No, lady, no. Can't take much more of this conversation. Am at work, Miss CDC." The papers on my desk start calling me names and threatening to multiply if I don't cut the conversation short. "Look, babe . . ."

"I know—me, too. We fly out on Friday morning. My travel agent worked the arrangements. Back Sunday evening."

"Who's all going?"

"Mimi and Kennedy, Fiona and Derek, and Di and Rusty."

"Girl, quit holding back. Who's the other couple? Newbies?"

We normally roll twelve deep.

"A *lagniappe*, as the French said in Old Louisiana. Wait and see, my love."

"You should've been the English Department Head, and I should be down there safeguarding the city from invading microorganisms."

K.C. laughs a professional laugh and disconnects the line.

* * *

One Weekend in Toronto   Claudia Moss

The day zips by.

I dive into my responsibilities with a renewed zeal, meetings taking place without a glitch; no hassles from students complaining about a professor not extending enough time to complete the semester's research paper, and no professors gripping about my stipulation to make their office hours more conducive for failing students and ambitious scholars. I'm a firm believer in going over and beyond the call of duty, so that when you get ready to handle up on your business, which might require special consideration, being you've given it to others, it flows back to you automatically.

That Layla works the hell out of this philosophy. For example, the girl adores my entire department. Why? I don't know. She caters a light breakfast for them, complete with a beverage selection on Wednesday, her "hoochie-coo hump day" as she likes to say, and it sets my group off. They love my angel. Probably why they abide me like they do.

The week evaporates after Wednesday.

On Thursday evening, I crawl in after working and volunteering at the local homeless shelter where I help cook and serve the folks, and am surprised. Layla has a tray of spicy Indian food, two goblets of plum wine, miniature vases of orange roses, a hyacinth-smelling candle, and my favorite Layla dessert: her savory sweet self served up exactly how I like her! On my face, around my fingers, under my strap, and above my head.

There's something about her fine proportions perched on the back of the sofa in our home's theatre room that drives me insane. And eating her out is damn near up there with breathing.

"Aaah, baby, what did I do to deserve you?"

"Just being you," Layla purrs, licking the sauce from her curry-chicken fingers. "That was good, huh?" She wipes her fingers on a cloth napkin and stretches out beside me, fingers drumming her slightly puffy tummy.

The fuchsia wrap she's wearing hugs her body in heavenly places. That short curly 'fro, sandy and spiky, looks so cute with the huge hoops in her earlobes. I can't help stroking her under the silky fabric.

"Look at you." She giggles, lashes fanning high cheekbones. "Want dessert early?" The wrap falls away, exposing supple jet thighs that float open, slowly, one leg hiking the sofa's back, the other seeking the seat of my pinstriped pants. She reclines languidly.

"When have you known me to pass up your dessert?"

One Weekend in Toronto   Claudia Moss

"Never actually."

She's thick, just the way I love her, and if she ever lost a pound, I wouldn't wait on her to pack my bags; I'd drive that midnight train to Georgia, on my way to another Georgia peach, 'cause you haven't been loved until you've had an intelligent, beautiful, thick, juicy Southern woman.

She's teasing my crotch with her big toe.

"It's ready. Been on simmer all day."

The minute I sniff her uncovered cobbler, my cell sings on the coffee table.

One look at the picture-ID tells me it's Fiona. "Hey, lady, how's Boston?" she says.

"Let me see, Fee." Layla pulls on my wrist, loving, as she does, my pussy phone.

Smiling, I show her the cell's ID. Pearly-white, the pussy is delicate, its inner lips glisten velvety and tantalizing, the inside a pink, pale sliver between fleshier outer petals, the mound is baby-bottom bald.

"Girl, you know we wouldn't miss it. Layla has us already packed. Derek got you set?"

"The next day."

"That's what I'm talkin' about."

"But who's the mystery couple? When K.C. plans the weekend getaway, she's gotta throw in a damn K.C. Kicker. I swear I could whip her ass sometimes."

"Something about that picture excites me. And since she probably won't volunteer for the ass-whipping, I suggest you take the initiative."

Layla listens quietly. So do I, while she fingers her clit, pulling the hood back on her sugary nubbin, and then massages it with a forefinger, circling and pressing, deftly causing the tiny lady to swell, redden and spit.

Fiona's laughter sweetens the silence. "Is she about to serve a sistah dessert?"

"Huuuh uh!"

"That's all you have to say, girlfriend. Catch ya'll tomorrow."

I close the cell and study Layla's ponany, all juicy, the spicy aroma intoxicating me. There's no other choice but to fall down in it, inhaling its mingling flavors with my eyes, then my tongue. The first mouthful always sends me. Mmmm. Brown sugar, cinnamon and nutmeg. I lap the wetness she's stirred. Deliriously delicious, she tastes divine. So I bury my nose right

One Weekend in Toronto Claudia Moss

there. Years ago, I learned from an older girlfriend not to be all over the place, calling myself pleasing a woman, learned just kissing her pleasure zone built my hot-ass reputation as Neco, the female Rico Suave.

"Babee, yeeessss," she moans, body flailing. "Give it to me, Neco, please!"

Her little butt is fucking my face and grinding, pumping my tongue. The moans grow loud and louder . . . then even louder, when I run my hands up and down her back, and bring her pussy closer to my mouth, cup her ass in my palms, before gently easing my thumbs up pass her sphincter muscle.

She goes into a fit, squirming and wiggling. I continue working magic on her little lady in the boat, until she leaps up and squirts another geyser of sugar water, soaking my face and neck with nectar.

A mesmerizing softness floods my senses when her hands touch my head, when she lowers herself, and electrifies me with kisses to my Netherland. The girl's got mad skills, too, and before long, we climax together, entwined in one another's arms.

* * *

Although Washington Dulles International Airport is hectic, our flight isn't. We touch down in Toronto, Canada, and the city feels like an old friend.

K.C. calls to say Howard loves The French Connection, and Mimi and Kennedy, who flew in earlier, were madly in love with the rooms. Perfect. Layla adores pretty rooms, too, as she and Fee and Mimi are good for giving the guys and me the slip, on most trips, so they can play in their rooms or bathrooms in girl bliss.

If we aren't golfing, the boys and I beg for front-row seats.

Once everyone is accounted for, we dine at a French restaurant, before boarding a one-hour, night cruise that showcases the city's breathtaking views from Lake Ontario. There is the gorgeous harbour front, the CN Tower, Niagara Falls and the unforgettable Toronto skyline. Hands down, K.C. is the shit, and Howard better recognize.

At evening's end, we all crash back at The French Connection, reflecting on the blessings of our safe arrivals and the shimmering beauty of Canadian nights.

Then Fiona gets beyond herself, a woman who stands by her word, a woman after my own heart, and saunters over to K.C.

"Sweetheart, you're awesome, but sometimes I wanna beat your ass."

She starts batting those long lashes like she does when she's hot and bothered. Starts sweeping that back-grazing hair, Asian straight and onyx black, and points a French-manicured forefinger inches from K.C.'s nose.

"If I'm that awesome, why you wanna do that? Jealousy?" K.C. banters in her characteristic sassiness, batting her lashes, too, and giving Fee challenging face, as the gay boys say.

"You're too good, that's why."

"At what?"

"Everything. Reason enough for your ass whipping?" Fee pivots and singles out Mimi and Layla accusatorily. "They'd love to do the same, except they're too ladylike to voice it."

"Uh huh." K.C.'s gaze sweeps the women, and a funky smile brightens her classic-pretty face.

"Let's save time here, Mama, and ask me, because you'll have more to envy when I tell you," K.C. pauses and puts her little cappuccino hands on those warrior hips, showing off her Ashanti thighs and legs in a sexy, short-ass skirt, "the ladies are cooking brunch in the morning in stilettos and ribbons. So ladies, be creative. That's why I wanted everybody to bring certain things."

"Darling, that should be fun, but K.C., may I whip your ass tonight?"

"A one-time deal, Miss Fee. Where do you want me?"

Determined, Fiona digs a flathead hairbrush from her handbag. And a fuchsia butt plug. Dainty purple paddle and coils of colorful yarn. Laying her toys on the sofa, she makes herself comfortable and motions for Howard, Mimi, and Rusty to find other seats and, face visibly softening, stares at K.C. and pats her lap.

"Strip," she orders. "Then ass up."

"My pleasure." K.C. obliges, and she and Fiona lock eyes as she strips.

Watching, I'm warming fast, a heatstroke flushing me, the room becoming unbearably hot. I look at Layla. She's glued to the scene before us, like everyone else, one hand in the waistband of her Capri pants, fingering her kitty.

The sheer sight of K.C.'s ass makes me shudder, just the way it's shaped, all fleshy yet sculpted and toned, just cocoa pounds of pure female

One Weekend in Toronto   *Claudia Moss*

delight. I always want to ride it and spank it and lick it and kiss it! The way her back flows into the tributary of her butt ought to be captured on screen, in photos, in print, on something! Goodness, I love women.

She does what Fiona asks, booty perfectly centered in the lighter woman's lap.

As Fiona strokes K.C.'s back, her face is an indication of how luxuriant the woman is. Then she strokes that ass, popping the cheeks, rapturously admiring the way the muscle jumps, and shakes. Childlike, she's oblivious to us now, the pleasure too enthralling.

One finger takes a leisurely stroll up and down the back of the toned thighs and suddenly darts to the crevice between her cheeks. My eyes follow. K.C. moans. Howard is chicken-choking himself with long, absorbing strokes.

"Spread them. Now," Fiona demands, voice dripping with desire and control.

Instantly, K.C. obeys, grabbing a handful of plump ass cheeks and gingerly pulling them apart. I nearly topple off my chair, looking, desiring.

Fiona brings the brush down hard on K.C.'s right cheek. It wiggles, K.C. releases a surprised whimper, and my breath catches in my throat. Oh, yes! The sound is intoxicating, the picture mind-blowing, the sound pussy clenching.

Whack! Whack!

Both cheeks jiggle now. Fiona gives it to her again. And again. We all lean forward, observing the slow purplish red burn under K.C.'s hot cocoa skin.

"Aaaw! Damn, Fee. God forbid I really piss you off!"

Pop! Pop! Smack!

"It's Miss Fiona to you, love." Then she reaches for the yarn and nods to Mimi to assist her. "Tie this mouthy wench's wrists to her ankles and leave a space in the middle so I can get back to the task at hand, please, darling."

"Howard, don't you agree this angel's a mess? Am I wrong?"

Howard bobs his head, bottom lip tremulous, dick bulging purple.

"Thank you." Fiona caresses K.C.'s succulent globes and whines, "See, baby, even your hubby thinks you deserve breakfast in bed tomorrow, on that luscious wooden breakfast tray, with flowers."

"Yes, Miss Fiona," K.C. moans, wrists softly bound with colorful yarn. "Whatever you say. Brunch in bed sounds delicious."

One Weekend in Toronto — Claudia Moss

"Perfect. Now, be quiet and moan prettily."

"Yes, ma'am."

Fiona can't seem to get enough of caressing K.C.'s tender plumpness, so she taps that ass now, lightly, before coming down with the flat end of the brush in a shower of stinging blows. K.C.'s sighs, moans, and pleas saturate the softly muted living room air.

"Come here, Neco," Fiona coos at me in a seductive whisper. She sucks the fuchsia butt plug into her bow-cup mouth, pushes it in and out slowly, until its silky wet.

"Here, put this in place, and make sure it doesn't shoot out, okay?"

A wicked smile on my lips, I say Ok. Just inhaling the salacious play between two polar opposite women, gorgeous in every way, turns me on.

I shove the pretty plug into K.C.'s puckered orifice and pause and pull it out and push it in again, and she lets go with a spicy moan that contributes to the gush of cum soaking my briefs. Damn! A beautiful, bound, willing woman is hot as hell! The plug stays in, and I return to the posh beige carpet, incinerated.

Next Fiona picks up the purple paddle. She examines it first, like she can't believe how cute it is, and when we least expect it, it rains licks on K.C.'s softness: pop, bam, slap, tap, whop, ouch, oooh!

The music of pleasure and pain, mingled, is sensational.

We draw in closer, falling deeper into the scene. "How do you feel, Boo?"

"Won . . . der . . . ful!" K.C. manages.

Down comes the paddle in a purple flash on both cheeks, softer, this time, but with equal swiftness and pressure. "They can't hear you, my love!"

"I said, 'Wonderful, Miss Fiona!'"

"Great! Now tell them what you want me to have someone do?"

"To me, Miss Fiona?"

Whack! "Of course to you, precious."

"Ooooh, yes, ma'am."

Fiona is eccentric. I've never seen this side of her, never knew she had it in her to exhibit dominatrix characteristics, and I've made love to her a thousand times.

"I . . . I . . . I."

Splat! Ping! Sting! "What?"

"I want someone to . . . to . . . eat me, please."

"Good, Beauty. Our thoughts run similar tracks. All your nectar is seeping onto my thighs, and we mustn't waste it." She cuts a passionate, half-mast gaze at Mimi, and the sepia-toned, pint-sized knockout with a single braided ponytail, thickly nappy, the pixie-sweet face smiling, crawls to Fiona and peers up through thick lashes, doll baby precious.

"Ma'am?"

Fiona pats the sofa, near K.C.'s bent knees, "Satisfy the sistah's request. Lick her pussy, before she soaks the sofa with this juicy stickiness. Hurry! Or I'll have your sweet tuna roll next."

Fiona strokes Mimi's head and allows her hand to float down to her jaw and neck and shoulders. Kisses fall on Mimi's ear. Fee pulls her into the gap between K.C.'s parted thighs and we all stare, consumed. Greedily, Mimi begins slurping K.C.'s streaming honey, but Fiona stops her abruptly and reddens K.C.'s ass to burnished claret. Then she double-checks the butt plug, and guides Mimi's lips to K.C.'s thighs, and pussy, and the slurping is a thrilling sound track to the tantalizing scene.

"Oh, goodness," K.C. moans, "oooh, mmm, I'm coming."

"No, not now." Fiona orders, the brush meaning business.

K.C. trembles and strains to stop the tide of emotion flooding her but can't.

"Stop!" More whacks jump both cheeks simultaneously.

"I . . . I . . . I'm tryin—"

I am drowning in wetness when K.C. releases. Everybody exhales. Breathing is the only sound. Flushed, I reach for the nearest woman. It's Mimi, who turns to pudding in my embrace, and I strip her hurriedly and devour her whole, gobbling her teeny-tiny breasts. She tastes salty, and citrusy. I leave a trail of kisses from her navel to her lips and smother her face and neck in soft kisses. I lick her up and down, then stay down, and position her spread-eagle across floor pillows piled high in one corner. When she climaxes four or five times, I let her up for air, cuddle her, stroke her joints, and gaze around the room.

Rusty, wide-shouldered with powerful thighs, is banging Fiona, who, while taking it doggy style, is draped across Howard's face. His eyes are closed, his moans coming around her pussy. Fiona deep breathes and grabs at the air. In the far corner of the living room, Derek has Layla up against the sofa back, in my favorite position for her, with her legs stretching east to west, him kissing and licking her enough for three men.

One Weekend in Toronto   Claudia Moss

It's well past one when we finally untangle ourselves and trudge upstairs to our beguilingly beautiful rooms.

* * *

True to her word, K.C. has organized a Saturday brunch for the stars. The ladies let their culinary talents do the talking while Rusty, Howard, Derek and I sleep late. Tempting aromas of sausages and pancakes and cheese eggs and cheese grits—forget the cholesterol for a moment—and diced fruit lure me to the shower. On the back porch, we're all starved after a night of delirious play, but the view rivals even the food.

The girls are dressed to the nines in pussy pumps and matching ribbons. Lady Layla showcases sunflower yellow, the satiny ribbon a pretty choker about her graceful neck and hanging like tails above her ass. Mimi sports a sexy look with her breasts outlined in orange ribbon matching burnt-orange, stunner stilettos. Fiona offers a lengthy white ribbon around her waist and tied in a bow above her ass, the white pussy pumps with a skinny silver heel, all class.

"Where's K.C.?" I ask.

Howard laughs. "In the bed. With an ice pack on her ass."

On cue, K.C. tips downstairs, in pink pumps and a tiny pink bowtie, pink cuff links, and, get this, one Velcro-ed to her bush, with coordinating ties around her ankles. Too cute.

After brunch and a sexy fashion show, K.C. announces we have a half hour to be dressed and standing on the porch, ready to hop the cab she'd called an hour ago.

"Folks, the evening's surprise promises to be better than Fiona's little charade that astonished even her."

K.C. laughs and kisses Fiona. And everybody bum-rushes the stairs.

Later, we are back at the Toronto Harbour, but this time, we board The Wayward Princess, a 92-foot cruiser with the capacity to accommodate 325 passengers. Fresh Canadian breezes kiss our faces and play in our hair as we congregate on the top, enclosed deck, admiring the shimmering water and amazing skyline. Then at Layla's suggestions, we boogie down on an open-air dance floor and ride the waves big time. Eventually, we settle down to a fully catered dinner, listening to a sexy female DJ spin one romantic cut after another.

One Weekend in Toronto *Claudia Moss*

"K.C., you've outdone yourself, lover! Shucks, this warrants you a play session with me tonight," Howard said from his 6'2" height back at the B&B. "I enjoyed that, though I'm dog tired."

"Getting old, Big Daddy?" K.C. snuggles under his arm. "The evening's young."

Then she spins around, addresses everyone, and begins spilling out of her clothes to topple onto a soft recliner. "Listen up! Get showered for the next part. I want you back here within the hour. And no peeking downstairs until I rap on each door."

I love her pirouettes. She does one and faces Howard. "Hell, no, sweetie. You and no one else will whip this gorgeous ass any time soon. If another ass gets whipped this weekend, I'll do it. Understand?"

"Yes, ma'am," Howard agrees. "Everybody, to your rooms!"

I break up laughing. That K.C. knows how to make him feel powerful.

* * *

K.C.'s soft rap comes about 7:15 p.m., and when I hear it, I grab Layla's hand and hurry her downstairs, or else we'll be another twenty minutes, easily.

In the living room, we stand in a wonderland of hanging stars, golden tinsel, bright boas, floral arrangements and varied mirrors. When did the woman have the time and inclination to organize this, and she's supposed to be on vacation like the rest of us?

There are trays of fruits and crackers and cheese and slivers of desserts. Silver wine canisters chill bottles of champagne and wine and wine coolers. Delicate goblets tinkle from hooks around the canisters.

Like Layla and me, as the others enter the enchanted space, laughter and conversation dry up instantly.

Music, a big-band number reminiscent of *Porgy and Bess*, vibrates the room, and confetti rides the air. Everything tinkles. Then, in slinks a sexy, masked vixen; arrayed in glitter from her russet gown to her fabulous blood-red feathery headdress. I am in awe and watch the tanned curves of the burlesque star's hips as she bends and bows and pouts, Mariah Carey sexy. Yeah, I can get with this!

One Weekend in Toronto — Claudia Moss

Her dance leaves me intoxicated and wanting more; especially when the Vixen begins a mesmerizing strip tease that reduces her to crimson pasties on her nipples and a dazzling scarlet g-string.

"Yeah, yeah!" Rusty shouts, sitting low in his seat and stroking Mimi's back.

"Bring it, baby! I said bring the damn thang!" This time Derek hollers. "Wow! Great show, baby girl!" Then to his wife, "Fiona Honey, where's my tip?"

K.C. rises, smoothing her gossamer gown. "No, Rusty Lusty, not now. Mommy's going to give everybody a small gift for being such an astonishing audience."

She gives us a beauty-queen smile and adds, "Starting with Dr. Neco Young. That okay, doctor?"

"Believe it," I say, grinning and unbuckling my belt.

In a flash, the burlesque star floats to me, slips to her knees, and makes short business of getting me out of my pants. I scoot down and widen my thighs, giving her full access. Blue eyes regale mine. Burgundy lips swallow my clit. Soft white hands flutter up my hips to my waist. A wet tongue trails moisture from my thighs to my fingertips.

At this point, the vixen lifts her mask, and I stare into a passion-drenched face. How could this be? I nearly snap my legs shut, but clutching me, she has me. And she's got skills. Damn it! My vision clouds. But I refuse to moan so I grunt, push her head backward, and sigh.

It's Deni Epps, and the heifer is phenomenal.

After an eternity of giving exquisite head, she gets up and walks Layla to me; has Layla to straddle my lap, her back to my chest, so she can devour us both. Savor a mixing of the nectar.

That woman might have eaten us all night if the others hadn't begun playfully complaining and threatening to snap pictures for our faculty meeting for the coming Wednesday. I grasp Layla's waist, her back to my chest, thighs atop mine, to keep me from losing my natural mind. That slut is good!

Later, I ask K.C. how the hell she knew Deni Epps. Of course she gives me that sultry "I'll never tell" K.C. smile. But the world is really rather small. Though she clocks me constantly, I never imagined Deni in the lifestyle.

One Weekend in Toronto   *Claudia Moss*

"It's Neco and Layla's turn to plan our next weekend!" K.C. announces at the end of the evening, as Layla and I trudge upstairs with Deni between us.

"Hope ya'll like our basement," I tease, and Howard tackles me from behind.

Upstairs in our boudoir, Deni is lying naked across our bed, showing off those long sexy legs, parting them spread-eagle wide, her pussy pumps prancing on air. The wife and I can hardly wait to have her to ourselves.

"I brought those pictures of Las Vegas, but I'll narrate them in the morning. Oh, and I want to share a business opportunity with unlimited, residual income when we get back to D.C., okay?" she asks. Layla and I look at one another and nod, agreeing simultaneously. "It involves wellness and referral marketing."

"Wait," Layla says, "I don't do that anymore."

"I guarantee you've never done this, sweetheart. Just give me two hours when we get back. Okay?"

"Okay," Layla agrees, reaching for our feathers and silver bullets.

"Okay," I concur. "This may just be the answer I'm seeking."

"Yes, my love, but right now I'd much rather we give Layla another stellar performance."

Deni straps on a double-headed strap-on. Laughing, I nestle in pillows and wait.

Then Deni goes to work . . . and the hair on Layla's kitty kat stands up stick straight.

Dez Moinez
By Alicia Night Orchid

There she was, my wife of four years, Mary Beth, on her hands and knees and naked. A man named Wayne hunkered over her, his cock plying the tight pucker of her sweet ass. Another man, Noah, stood beside her. She lifted her pretty face to his erection as he thrust between her lips. Beneath her, I could make out the long, lean legs of Noah's wife, Brianna. She fingered herself, squirmed, and busied her mouth on Mary Beth's clit. Wayne's wife, Katie, knelt behind Noah. She spread his cheeks and licked his drooping balls from behind.

Mary Beth glimpsed me out of the corner of her eye. She ceased sucking long enough to nod at Katie's glistening vulva. Her desire was clear.

She wanted me to fuck the other woman, while she serviced both men.

* * *

We met on the leafy campus of a sprawling Midwestern University. A journalism major, Mary Beth lived on the honors floor of the last remaining all-woman's dormitory. I lived off-campus in a run-down apartment and doggedly pursued a law degree. Mary Beth was seated at a table in the undergraduate library. She wore a neatly pressed blouse and jeans. Her blonde hair fell like a curtain on delicate shoulders. Her blue eyes shined with an intense curiosity. I wore chinos I should have tossed out a year earlier and a faded polo shirt with a stain. I could have used a shave and a haircut.

I spent an hour trying to figure out a masterpiece of an opening line. Finally, I shouldered my backpack and crossed the space between us. "Excuse me," I said.

She looked up, eyes wide, a smile playing on full lips that covered teeth so white they seemed to glow. It struck me that a thousand guys a day probably asked her out, and I forgot my line.

"Yes."

"Hi, I'm Billy Wisniewski."

"Billy, who?" That smile never left her lips.

"Wisniewski. Anyway, I'm a law student and I've been studying for like twenty-four hours straight and if I don't get a cup of coffee, I'm going to pass out. I thought maybe . . ."

"What's that stain on your shirt?"

"Ketchup. Or maybe pizza."

"Why do you want to buy me coffee?"

"Because you're beautiful and I'm too distracted to study, and if I can't get past this, I'll never graduate and pass the bar exam."

She closed her book. "I don't drink coffee, but a Chai Tea Latte will work."

* * *

We had no business being together. Her parents traced their heritage to the Pilgrims, while I was descended from a long line of hard-headed Poles. She grew up on Chicago's genteel north shore, her father a banking executive, her mother an English teacher at an elite private high school. I hailed from Bridgeport, a stone's throw from Comiskey Park. My old man ran a beer distributorship and a numbers racket. My mother consumed soap operas and romance novels at the same pace she demolished quarts of ice cream and bags of Cheetos.

Even so, for all her beauty and smarts, Mary Beth didn't get asked out as much as I'd thought. Pretty was one thing. Smart was another. But the combination of Mary Beth's pretty and smart scared off most guys

I was either too ignorant or arrogant to take the hint.

My plan was to bring her along slowly, convince her I was interested in her mind, her heart, her soul, before turning my attention to those firm breasts and what I imagined to be a moist, tight pussy.

Our first date, I took her to a movie then returned her to her dorm with no more than a polite peck on the cheek. Our second date, I pushed my credit card to the limit with dinner at a nice restaurant. Our lips briefly touched at the evening's end, and I thought I'd died and gone to heaven.

Our third date, we returned to the library, then went out for coffee and Chai Tea. Later, when we kissed, I ran my tongue over her lips.

To my surprise, her tongue greeted mine. Mouth to mouth, we dueled like pirates. She pressed her breasts into my chest and sharp nipples speared me. My hands slid down her back and grasped her round little butt. Her pelvis ground against my thigh and I went hard as a tire iron.

Someone walked past and growled, "Get a room."

Mary Beth giggled. When I tried to step away, she held on. "What do you want with me, Billy Wisniewski?"

Before I could put two thoughts together, I blurted out, "I think I want to marry you."

She giggled again. "We'll see about that."

* * *

We sat on the bed and talked all night. I told her about my dog, run over by a car when I was eight; Chooch Bartkowski, my best friend from high school who was doing time for grand theft auto; and my first girl friend, Debbie Lipschitz. That's right, Lipschitz.

Mary Beth didn't run away.

In fact, she told me about her mother's Valium addiction and her father's affairs. She told me about furtive hand jobs delivered in the back row of theatres and her friend Marnie who was having an affair with her English professor at Princeton.

Just before daylight, she removed her blouse and bra. She wriggled out of her jeans. "I'm a virgin," she confessed. "I guess I've been saving myself for you, Billy Wisniewski."

I'd like to say, I was tender and sure. I'd like to say, I was the restrained older man leading her to the Promised Land.

But I wasn't like that at all. I couldn't get it fast enough. I pushed my face into those breasts and suckled until she cried out. She unbuckled me with one hand, while clinging to my neck with the other.

She stroked, reached lower, and squeezed my balls. I pushed a hand into her panties. She was beyond moist, far into the wet zone. I pushed first one finger, then another inside. I finger fucked her long and slow and ground my palm against her clit. She bucked and spasmed, then pulled me over her.

"Do you have a . . ."

I reached for my jeans, dug into my wallet, and unwrapped the foil.

She took the condom and grabbed my cock. It throbbed like a toothache.

I rested between her creamy thighs. "You ready for this?"

"Do it, Billy."

I didn't have to be told twice. I thrust and she lifted her hips to receive me. We rocked and kissed and squished and slid. It took about three minutes. I'm surprised that condom survived the impact.

Six months later we were engaged.

Six months after that we graduated and married on her daddy's long, green lawn.

After a honeymoon in St. Lucia, reality settled in.

We moved to Des Moines. She took a job at the Register, and I went to work for a big insurance company. My office was the only skyscraper in town. Out on the prairie where we lived, safely ensconced in our affluent suburb, we were never out of sight of that building.

The lights of Midwestern Mutual burned all night long.

* * *

Charlie Whistler and I were eating cheeseburgers. Will Hennessey noisily finished his chocolate milk shake. Not far from where we were seated in the Uptown Food Court, workers moved to and fro, grabbing a mid-day bite before heading back to their cubicles. Our eyes glued on every woman who crossed before us. If one of them inadvertently gave us a flash of thigh or cleavage, we nudged one another and winked.

We'd all joined the company at the same time. We were all married, childless, and three years into life in Des Moines. We talked like sailors on leave, not lawyers charged with oversight of $200 million in assets.

"I'd fuck her right here, right now, in front of God and everyone," Charlie said.

He referred to a young woman in a tight sweater.

"No you wouldn't," I said. "First, you'd lose your job. Then you'd lose your wife."

"It might be worth it."

"No strange pussy is worth that."

"I'd give my left nut for a piece of strange," Will said, a faraway look in his eyes.

"How long's it been for you, Billy?" Charlie asked.

"Since I met Mary Beth. Four years or more."

"You can't tell me you wouldn't like a taste of another woman."

"You can get away with that here," I told him. "Not in good old Dez Moinez."

Des Moines wasn't a terrible place to live. The downtown offered a cozy accessibility. In an area south of Grand Avenue, large old homes and shady lawns sprawled as surely as on Lake Shore Drive. The suburbs had their share of malls and mini-marts, assuring the same unbridled consumerism that afflicted the rest of America.

But on the flip side, there was a sense of isolation. Cornfields gathered like natives at a feast, hundreds of miles in all directions. Right-wing nut job preachers, held forth against all manner of sin including adultery and fornication. And worst of all, for me, there was a loss of the anonymity you take for granted in a city like Chicago.

You couldn't fart on the street in Dez Moinez without someone commenting of the fragrance much less engage in an affair without your wife finding out. Anyway, I loved my wife. I didn't want to cheat on her.

"Maybe we could join a swingers' club," Will said.

Charlie and I stared at him. "Where would we find a swingers' club in Des Moines?" Charlie asked.

"I don't know. The Internet?"

"Mary Beth won't even go out in public without a bra," I said. "No way she's joining a club that features fucking with strangers."

"It was just a thought."

"Here's another thought," Charlie said. "Maybe we start our own club. Only three couples. All friends. No strangers."

"You want me fucking your wife?" Will asked.

"As long as I can fuck yours."

Will rubbed his chin. "I like it. Jen might be a hard sell, but . . ."

Charlie's eyes widened. "I think I could convince Chloe. She's got a kinky side to her."

I lost concentration as an image of Charlie's dark-haired, cheerleader-compact, dynamo of a wife, Chloe emerged. The idea of grabbing her hard, muscled ass, while fucking her from behind had considerable appeal.

"We could do an offsite weekend, the six of us," Will said. "You know, test the waters."

"Lots of wine and a hot tub," Charlie added, going with it.

"I know a place in Kansas City," Will said. "What do you think, Billy?"

I didn't think there was a snow ball's chance in hell, but I liked the fantasy of being with Chloe and Jennifer. "We've got nothing to lose," I said.

* * *

I made love to my wife that night.

In the four years since we'd married, our sex life had settled into a routine, as comfortable as my old chambray work shirt. Once a week we found each other in the early morning hours, before heading off to the trenches. We often reconvened on gray Sunday afternoons.

But that evening, I left work early, poached salmon filets, tossed a salad, and poured us each a glass of Chardonnay. After dinner, I led her upstairs.

Mary Beth still looked as good as ever. The only difference was she'd cut her hair and traded in jeans for business suits.

"What's got into you?" she asked, when I maneuvered her onto the bed.

"I'm still crazy for you, Mary Beth."

I pushed the skirt of her gray pin-striped suit over her hips and whisked off her pantyhose. I got that first whiff of her sex and dove in.

"I'm still crazy about you, too," she purred.

Oral sex between us had become a rare treat. Those weekday mornings when we got it on, I'd usually spoon behind her and squeeze her breasts a few times, before pushing her panties aside and plowing home. Sunday afternoons, she'd rub the head of my dick against her clit until she oozed nectar like an overripe fruit, then she'd squat over me, riding hard in front of the fireplace.

I couldn't remember the last time I'd had a blow job or given her a proper licking.

But tonight, I devoured Mary Beth's slit like a kid with an ice cream cone. I gazed up over her flat belly and the rise of her breasts. She bit a lower lip and thrashed. Then, suddenly, I was imagining Will's red-headed wife's pussy in my mouth. My already-hard dick nearly burst out of my jockey shorts.

A few moments later, Mary Beth/Jennifer grabbed the bed covers. Her thighs shuddered and clenched around my face. When she settled back to earth, I knelt beside her. I pushed my cock between her lips. She took the cue and swirled her tongue over the head.

She wet my shaft with her saliva and jacked and bobbed. All the while, her blue eyes looked up lovingly.

But I couldn't help myself. I started to think about Charlie's wife Chloe. I imagined cherry lips around me. I imagined her hand on my ass. I came like a freight train, spurting into Mary Beth/Chloe's mouth. She moaned and swallowed and stayed with it for the last few drops.

"Wow, baby," she said with a smile.

"Wow, yourself."

I leaned over and kissed her. "I love you, Mary Beth."

"I love you, too, Billy." She wiped her mouth with a Kleenex and cocked an eyebrow. "Is everything all right?"

"Sure, of course, absolutely. Why are you asking?"

She patted my thigh. "No reason, I guess."

She slid out from under me and headed into the shower. I collapsed on the bed and closed my eyes. It was Jennifer's pussy, Chloe's ass. We were fucking and sucking and fingering and eating. While Mary Beth rinsed off, I got hard again and jerked off, spraying a second load onto my belly and chest.

* * *

That weekend in Kansas City was nice, but it did little to get us down the road of Swingerdom. On Saturday, the girls visited a spa, while the guys drank beer, shot pool, and watched sports on TV. Sunday, the girls shopped, while Will, Charlie, and I trailed along, encouraging purchases we really could have cared less about.

We didn't get near a hot tub.

But a couple of weeks later, the six of us traveled to Omaha in Charlie's big-ass Escalade to visit Old Town and eat bloody steaks. After dinner, we managed to get the women into the hotel pool. Even my modest Mary Beth slid into the water in a black one piece. I got hard seeing Chloe's dark brown nipples through the wet fabric of her see-through white top. And I was sure Jennifer was looking at my boner when I stepped out of the pool.

Later on in our room, Mary Beth and I fucked like we had back in the day.

Then as winter approached and that steel-gray Midwestern sky settled over us, the wives announced that they'd formed the Gourmet Dinner Club of Greater Dez Moinez. Every other week, one of the couples opened their house to the other two couples. The host and hostess prepared the food, the guests brought the wine. Elaborate five course dinners were followed by movies in the family room, drinks in front of the fireplace, or just good conversation around the table. Sometimes one of us guys steered the conversation to sex.

One evening, Mary Beth piped up and said that she and I had tried anal sex twice with no success, but one of her favorite things was when I slid my dick between her ass cheeks like a hot dog in a bun while she ground against a pillow stuffed between her legs. I couldn't believe what I was hearing. Jennifer bit her lower lip and quaffed half a glass of wine. Chloe informed us that she and Charlie had anal sex about once a month. Will and I shared a glance.

Another evening, Chloe asked if anyone had ever tried swinging, and it was denied by all. Then Jennifer confessed that while in grad school she and her boyfriend had swapped mates once. Everyone at the table nodded and encouraged her to share the details, but she blushed and politely declined.

Then shortly after Christmas, on a night when the snow piled up, it was decided that after-dinner travel was too dangerous. Will and Jennifer had space for everyone as long as one couple was willing to sleep on the pull-out sofa. Mary Beth and I volunteered.

I was taking a leak in the middle of the night when Chloe walked in. She was there for the same reason and was dressed only in panties. Her bare nipples pointed like six shooters.

"I guess I should've locked the door," I said.

"Not on my account," she replied with a wink, her eyes on my water hose.

While I rinsed my hands, she dropped her panties and squatted. I glimpsed her dark bush and felt my heart skip a beat when I heard the soft sigh of her piss.

"Well," I said.

She reached out, her fingers playing along the inside of my thigh. "Nice boxers."

"Thanks."

She stood, tore off a wad of toilet paper with her free hand, and wiped between her legs. She wriggled into her panties and stepped between me and the sink on her way out, her pelvis pressed against mine.

Half way down the hall, I heard her whisper, "You're welcome."

Two weeks later came that fateful trip to Minneapolis and the Mall of America and the cat was out of the fucking bag.

* * *

A few days before our scheduled travel, I was seated at the table watching Mary Beth wash dishes. I loved the way her ass swayed beneath the tight-fitting navy blue dress she'd worn to work. I stood, positioned behind her, and nuzzled her hair.

"Hey," she said. "What's going on?"

I went hard and cupped her breasts through the fabric. "Couldn't help myself. You look so good."

She dried her hands, turned around, grabbed me by the tie, and pulled my lips to hers. She kissed me hard enough to bruise.

When the kiss was over, she continued to hold me tight by the tie. "I want to ask you something," she said.

"Ask away."

"Do you ever think about other women?"

I'm pretty sure the blood drained from my face. "Honey, you're the only woman for me."

She pulled tighter. "Don't give me that bullshit, Billy. I want an honest answer. Have you ever thought about fucking Chloe or Jennifer?"

I turned bright red. "I don't know, I mean, you know. I like them, but . . ."

"I've seen the way you looked at them. Chloe, especially."

"Well, it's natural to fantasize . . ."

"Look," she said, "if you want to fuck another woman, I'd rather it be Chloe and Jennifer than someone I don't know. I'd rather we agree that it's all right from the outset than have you cheating behind my back."

"I'd never . . ."

She released the tie. "But, just so you know, what's good for the goose is good for the gander."

"What does that mean?"

"It means I get to fuck Charlie and Will."

I stared at her for a long moment. It was the first time I'd seriously considered that possibility. It was as disturbing and exciting as anything I'd ever experienced.

* * *

We shopped the Mall of America Friday night after driving up from Dez Moinez in sleet and freezing rain. We settled on pizza in the Mall and retired early to Charlie and Chloe's suite at the Residence Inn. I plopped down on the sofa, Charlie reclined on the floor, and Will kicked back in an easy chair. Charlie worked the flipper, switching from Bear Grys and the Discovery Channel to Friday Night Fights.

I didn't even notice that the women had opened a second bottle of wine until they reappeared from the kitchenette.

But it wasn't Mary Beth who settled next to me and offered a glass. It was Chloe. My Mary Beth snuggled against Will in that easy chair, while Jennifer sat down beside Charlie. She took the flipper away and switched on the DVD player. Frank Sinatra's classic voice filled the room with "Strangers in the Night."

"What's going on?" I asked with what I'm pretty sure was a silly grin.

"I think you know." Chloe said, her face close to mine, her breath warm and rich with the scent of Cabernet.

Across the room, Mary Beth draped an arm around Will's shoulders and pressed her breasts against him. "This is what you wanted, isn't it?" she asked.

I sipped my wine and watched as Jennifer took Charlie's hand in her own. She was sitting cross-legged in a short skirt. I got a flash of white panty. "I know it's what I've been wanting," she said.

I felt Chloe's fingers on my thigh, just like that night in the bathroom. "It's what I've been wanting too," she said.

"How about you, Billy?" Mary Beth asked, her fingers playing with the buttons of Will's shirt. He had that deer in the headlights look.

"Well, I mean, we talked . . ."

Jennifer climbed on top of Charlie. He reached around and massaged her buttocks through her skirt. A moan escaped between bars of Sinatra.

"Then, I think you should go for it," Mary Beth said, just before she leaned in and kissed Will on the lips.

Chloe's hand encircled my cock through my khakis. I went hard in an instant. "Yeah, Billy," she whispered, "I think you should go for it."

I watched as Mary Beth stood and led Will into the upstairs bedroom. My eyes never left hers as she brushed past.

"Come on," Chloe said. "I need to be fucked."

She lifted her sweater over her head. Purple aureoles the size of silver dollars beckoned. A few minutes later, we were in the downstairs bedroom, no more than a screen separating us from Charlie and Jennifer in the front room.

I took her from behind, just like in my fantasies, that apple-hard ass twitching beneath me.

Just before I came, I heard my wife's familiar cries through the thin walls, "Yes, yes, oh God, yes."

* * *

It's one thing to fuck another man's woman. It's another thing to give your wife to another man. It's another thing altogether when your wife embraces fucking other men with the same surprising enthusiasm with which she'd fucked you when you first started out.

But that's what happened with Mary Beth.

Although there was a bit of awkwardness at the outset, as winter turned to spring, our every-other-week gourmet dinners became less about food and more about sexual experimentation.

The first few times, we paired off discreetly in different rooms. I alternated between Chloe and Jennifer, while Mary Beth took turns with Will and Charlie. I got my anal sex with Chloe, watching her smoldering pout in the mirror while I buried my hard-on in an orifice that gripped me like a vice. I got my porno sex with Jennifer, splattering her face while she did herself with a vibrator the size of a washing machine.

One night I heard Mary Beth call out, "Fuck me, Charlie. Fuck me in the ass."

She didn't say and I didn't ask, but apparently she got her anal sex, too.

Another time, I heard Will bellow. "Here it is, Mary Beth. On your tits. Yeah, yeah, yeah."

Those were my Mary Beth's breasts he was talking about, the breasts that had crushed against me that night outside her dorm before I took her virginity.

In the weeks between sessions with our friends, Mary Beth and I acted like nothing had changed. We didn't acknowledge our exploits. We kept up our weekday morning and Sunday afternoon routine.

Then one green Saturday evening, while tornadoes threatened the cornfields, things took an unexpected turn. I'd never fucked in front of a viewing audience, but as it turned out, I didn't have to worry about rising to the occasion. Jennifer walked in on Chloe and I, pushed me out of my sixty-nine position, and claimed the other woman for her own. While the two wives screamed and clawed the sheets, Charlie and I watched in awe. Afterwards, the women joined together, sucking Charlie first, then me.

The next morning things took another turn. After the four of us described our experience to Mary Beth and Will, Mary Beth announced that she'd sometimes fantasized about being licked by another woman. I couldn't believe what I was hearing from my prim and proper wife, but there was no denying the bulge beneath my robe. There was also no denying the faraway look on Jennifer's face as Mary Beth spoke.

"Do it, Jennifer," I heard myself say. "Eat her pussy."

While Chloe rubbed her clit, and Charlie, Will, and I tugged at our weenies, my wife came on Jennifer's tongue. I held her gaze through it all, our eyes locked together until she closed hers in that final earth-shattering moment of surrender. When Jennifer turned to face us, her lips wet with Mary Beth's nectar, I fell on her. Chloe, Charlie, and Will weren't far behind.

After that, no holds were barred.

A couple of weeks after Mary Beth came in Jennifer's mouth, I awoke deep in the night with my wife lying on her side, breathing softly in my arms. I pulled off the covers, propped myself up on an elbow, and studied the luscious curve of her body visible through silk pajamas.

I was suddenly seized by a fear that I'd lost her. Worse yet, I feared that I'd lost *us*—Billy and Mary Beth. We'd crossed a line and could never go back. I broke into a cold sweat and a sob escaped my lips.

Mary Beth roused and turned onto her back. In the pale light of Midwestern Mutual's distant pulse, she reached up and touched my cheek. "Are you all right, Billy Wisniewski?"

I brushed hair off her forehead. "I think so. I don't know."

After a long moment, she spoke, "You're the only person I could do this with. You know that, don't you?"

"I guess. If you say . . ."

"You're the only person I trust enough. You're the only person I love enough."

"I am?"

"Ever since that day in the library."

I slid over her, holding her, burying my face into the nape of her neck. "I love you, Mary Beth," I told her.

"And, I love you, Billy."

We held on until sunrise.

*   *   *

Over the next few months, our little group expanded. Who knew there were other couples in Dez Moinez just like us? Loving couples, who wanted to share their love and sexuality with others.

That's how we ended up with Wayne and Katie, Noah and Brianna.

Wayne owned fast-food restaurants all across the Midwest. Katie did charitable work for non-profits. They were empty nesters, their kids off at college, but if forty-five is the new thirty-five, they fit the mold. Noah was my stockbroker, while Brianna, lovely Brianna, taught middle school in West Des Moines, not far from where Mary Beth and I lived.

I'd been in another room, watching a porno video with a woman named Liz, who had tremendous tits and a clit the size of a baby's cock. We both masturbated ourselves to a frenzy, before she came in a gush and rush. I held back and went in search of bigger game. That's when I walked in on Mary Beth, Wayne, Brianna, and Katie.

Mary Beth was having a hard time sucking Noah. His cock slipped from her mouth every time Wayne rammed his whacker up her ass. Beneath her, Brianna was nearing orgasm. She rubbed herself frantically while slurping away at Mary Beth's pussy. Katie's tongue alternated between Noah's balls and his ass.

Mary Beth nodded to Brianna again. She knew I wanted the woman and had wanted her for a while. I wasn't about to turn down the opportunity.

I knelt between Brianna's thighs. The inner walls of her cunt grasped me like a fist. She continued to lick my wife while rubbing herself.

Mary Beth's face was only inches from mine. I could hear her gag and moan as she pleasured Noah while giving her ass to Wayne. Then Noah withdrew, and with Katie's tongue flicking at his sack, he shot white and hot across Mary Beth's lips and chin. Her eyes opened and caught mine. Then in the next instant, she was caught off guard by her own come. I recognized that look of surprise and ecstasy. I felt my own balls rise. I felt a quickening at the base of my cock.

I gushed deep inside Brianna, while Mary Beth crooned out her own climax. Below me, Brianna bucked. Wayne pulled out of Mary Beth's ass and launched a semen missile onto her lower back.

We all collapsed in a puddle. Somehow, I found Mary Beth's hand. When I squeezed, she squeezed back.

After a couple of failed attempts at anal sex, we'd given up, but I still loved her ass. I loved the curve and the cleavage, the darkness and the tantalizing glimpse of that orifice I'd so far been denied. A favorite thing for both of us was to rub my slick cock between her cheeks, while she ground against the bed.

She squeezed and tightened about me, my cock like a hotdog in a bun. Then that image of Charlie's wife Chloe I'd enjoyed earlier in the day resurfaced. Something about the way her olive skin, her earthiness, contrasted to Mary Beth's pale complexion and refined demeanor, caused my balls to rise. I buried my cock into Mary Beth/Chloe's dripping pussy. She cried out a second time, and I thrust like a piston in a sleeve. A moment later, I withdrew, spread her wide, revealing the darker colors around her rectum, and let go.

"Oh, oh, oh," she cried as I spewed spunk all over her crack and globes.

It was a beautiful sight. Her asshole, my cum.

She turned to look up at me over her shoulder, as I dribbled out the last few drops.

Before the Move
By Jolie du Pré

She's standing at the meat counter, talking to a woman. I can hear her all the way in produce.

"Everyone is in agreement. We've won!"

"Sodom and Gomorrah! The sooner we shut them down the better this town will be."

I grab the bag of oranges and hurry over to check-out. The last thing I need is to run into Shirley. She'd have no qualms about attacking me right in the middle of the grocery store.

* * *

Inside our house, my husband Dave is on his computer. Ever since we learned what the town is up to, he has put his focus on getting us out of here.

"It's all set! I'll be working with my brother when we move to Chicago. He's rented the space. All we have to do now is move in."

I grew up in a small town, where everyone knew everyone else. I'm used to that. Dave grew up in the city and only agreed to live in a small town due to the job offer here. He could deal with Chicago. As for me, I'm not so sure.

"I saw Shirley in the grocery store, talking to someone about us. She's all fired up that our club may close."

"Honey, the town has us by the balls. Not much we can do about it anymore. This is the wrong place for our club. We were crazy to think nobody in the town would find out about it. We'll start fresh in Chicago."

Dave had taken the stress of the situation and turned it into a positive. But it was a lot harder for me.

Before the Move
Jolie Du Pré

"I gotta go to work. I'll see you tonight." He gives me a kiss on the cheek. "Are you going to be okay?"

"Yeah. I'll be okay."

"Good." He grabs some keys. "I'll take the truck. See ya."

I put the oranges in the refrigerator and then walk into the bedroom. Why should I leave? We have every right to be here like everyone else. I fall on the bed, face down.

Shirley. Unfortunately, it wasn't just her. She's just the ring leader. And boy did she work hard. She must have spent six months gathering signatures, holding town meetings, sending us letters to let us know that what we do is not welcome.

Honest sex. That's what swinging is. Honest sex. What's so wrong with that? Our club is small—just the two rooms and the room with the hot tub. Our crowd is small. It's not like the entire town is swinging. We mind our own business. Yet, Shirley is determined for us to close.

I turn and lay on my back, looking up at the ceiling. I can see lots of dead bugs inside the ceiling light. Ever since this thing had gone down, cleaning has not been on the top of my list. I spend a lot of time wallowing in self pity. Just mustering enough motivation to get the basics done takes work. Like the post office. I really need to go to the post office.

I pull myself off the bed and gather the bills that I had been meaning to mail. This is my job, and Dave wouldn't be too happy with me for being so lazy lately.

* * *

I get back in my car and head to the post office. It's mid-January and very cold out. The grey skies don't help my mood one bit.

I walk into the building and wouldn't you know it? Once again, there's Shirley. I can't get away from her! She's standing at the counter, glaring at me.

"I'm sorry, Debra. But we just can't have your kind in this neighborhood." She says it loud, in front of everybody.

"Okay, but can I just mail this letter? I'm not bothering anybody here."

"You know I'm going to pray for you. You and Dave seemed like such nice people at first."

Before the Move
Jolie Du Pré

"Please leave me alone, Shirley! Dave and I are moving to Chicago soon." I look her in the face. "We're happy to get out of here."

Finally, Shirley leaves, and I'm seething inside, embarrassed. The sooner we move to Chicago, the better.

The cold wind turns my nose red as I rush to my car. Before I can get into my car, my keys slip out of my hand and fall down a shaft. I can't believe it. The tension inside me is so great I want to cry. I look for my cell phone, and then I remember that I left it at home. And now I do cry. I just stand there and cry.

There's a tap on my back. It's Shirley. I have no fear now. "Leave me alone!" I shout.

"Oh Debra, calm down! I'm sorry if I upset you."

"I dropped my fucking keys, so just leave me alone! Please just leave me alone!"

"You dropped your keys?"

"Yes! Down the fucking shaft. I can't get into my house or my car now! Dave went to work, and to make matters worse, I left my phone at home."

"I don't own a cell phone, but come with me. You can wait at my house until Dave can fetch you."

"No! Dave will come get me here. I don't need any help from you!"

"Are you sure? It's awful cold out."

"Yes!" I march back into the post office and then look in my purse for a quarter to use in their pay phone, but I don't have one. Shirley is still standing outside, staring at me through the window. Why won't she fucking leave? She motions for me to follow her to her car.

I have two choices: beg to use somebody's phone or get in Shirley's car. I choose Shirley's car. I don't know why. Maybe because it's so damned cold out.

* * *

The tips of my fingers are frozen, but they start to feel better in the warmth of Shirley's car. I look over at her; the woman who wants us to leave, the woman who has been stirring up the town. I look around. There's not a drop of dirt in her car. She's playing Christian music and there's a smile on her face. She looks like she's pleased with herself.

"Very nice and warm in the car, isn't it?" She says.

Before the Move   *Jolie Du Pré*

I don't want to talk. I don't want to give her a segue into what she's doing. Besides, there was no changing her mind, and it would just give her an excuse to rant.

We walk into her house. Just like in her car, everything is clean. No dust in the corners. No dead bugs in the lights.

"The phone is hanging on the kitchen wall." Shirley walks away. On the counter are a bunch of artificial flowers, the plastic kind. I call Dave; tell him how I lost my keys.

"Where are you?"

"I'm at Shirley's house."

"What?" He starts to laugh. I don't find it funny.

"I know, Dave, just come get me, please."

"Are you all right?"

"I'm fine."

"Okay, well, I sent a tow for the car. I'll be at Shirley's as soon as I can."

"I can't believe I dropped the fucking keys."

"We can replace them. Don't worry about it."

"Hurry, Dave."

"I will honey."

I hang up the phone and when I turn Shirley is staring at me. I almost jump.

"Won't you stay for dinner?"

"No. When Dave arrives we'll be on our way."

"I know we've had our differences, and I'm sorry about that."

"Differences? You're fucking trying to push us out of town, Shirley!"

"Must you use such language, Debra?"

I use the word "fucking" a lot, ironically, not in any sexual reference. I use it when I'm dealing with a bitch like Shirley. "You make me angry. So just lay off!"

"Okay, okay, calm down!"

Her husband John walks in. He's tall and thin with dark good looks. Very attractive. So is Shirley. I don't like to admit that they make a good looking couple. She used to be a beauty queen or something. He's known as this rugged hunk who likes to ride his snowmobile all over. He's won a bunch of contests. The town loves John and Shirley.

"Hello, dear! You remember Debra, don't you?"

Shirley's motive is to run us out of town. John is not as vocal, but he's right by her side. He knows damn well who I am.

"I've invited Debra and her husband for supper. Debra lost the keys to her house and car. She's staying here until her husband returns."

"We really can't stay. When he gets here, we have to go." The smell of the roast in the oven was pulling at me. Shirley can cook, but I've been too depressed to bother. I'm sure Dave and I will be ordering pizza again tonight.

The doorbell rang. I knew it had to be Dave. I run to him when he walks in. "I'm so glad you're here!" I give him a hug.

"Are you okay?"

"I'm fine. I just want to go now."

Dave looks over at John. "Hey there, John!"

"Hello, Dave."

"Mmmm... something smells good," Dave says.

He's being charming even though these people are evil. I can never understand why he does stuff like that.

"John, is that your snowmobile out back?" There he goes again.

"Yeah, let me show it to you."

Dave leaves the house with John to go gaze at the fucking snowmobile, leaving me with Shirley. I want to kill him. Dave has had an interest in snowmobile racing for the last couple of months. Last year he raced in a few with John.

"Let me just set the table, and we can eat!" Shirley beams.

Normally, I offer to help a host, but not this time. I go outside to find Dave. John is inside his garage, looking for something. Dave is standing outside, waiting for him.

"I want to go home," I say to him. "I can't believe you."

"Come on! Let's not let them think they got the best of us. We'll eat their food and then we'll go." He smiles. "You don't want pizza again, do you?"

I give him the meanest look possible, and then I walk away. Dave is so excited about Chicago that he could care less about sticking me with these evil people.

When we're all back in the house the table is set and the roast is out. We all take a seat. Shirley and John say a dinner prayer. I stare at Dave with another mean look. He just grins at me. After the dinner prayer, we eat our food in silence.

"So tell me about this swinging?" Shirley blurts out. When I hear that I just about drop my fork.

"What do you want to know?" Dave says.

John is looking at me in a way in which I find rather odd.

"You have sex with other women?" She continues.

"Yes, he does," I interrupt. "And I fuck other men"

Dave is laughing. Once again, I don't find it funny.

Shirley isn't fazed. "Do you have orgies over there or something?"

"Why are you asking, Shirley? You want us out of town? We'll leave."

She looks at me. "Now Debra, you mustn't get so upset."

I roll my eyes.

"Shirley and I have been married a long time. We've just never known anyone who does what you do."

I look at John. "What we do is none of your fucking business!"

Dave puts his hand on my knee. He does that when he wants me to quiet down. I don't want to quiet down.

"I saw a pie over there, Shirley. What do ya say?"

I can't believe Dave. He's just using them for their food, but still.

"Yes, I make a wonderful pie!" Shirley gets up to go get it. Dave is staring at her ass as she moves, and then he gives me a wink. He wants to make a big joke out of this whole thing. I just want to go home.

I look over at John, who is still looking at me funny. But he's got the most beautiful green eyes I've ever seen.

"So you like sleeping with other men?" John asks.

"Maybe she can teach you a few things, John," Shirley says.

What did Shirley just say? Where the fuck was I? Aren't these the people who are trying to run us out of town?

Dave laughs again. "Yeah, she's pretty good, that one."

I knock Dave in the ribs. "We should go, honey."

"You can't leave without tasting some of my pie," Shirley says. She hands him a piece, smiling at him, staring him in the face. This woman was coming on to my husband . . . after all her noise?

"Why don't we retire to the living room?" Shirley continues.

"Yeah, okay. Sure," Dave says. He gets up and follows Shirley to the living room, leaving me with John.

We hear music by Frank Sinatra. "Shall we join them?" John asks. His voice is gentle, unlike Shirley's screeching tone.

Before the Move   Jolie Du Pré

"Yes, we can do that."

We walk in and Dave and Shirley are dancing, close. John and I decide to follow suit.

Up close next to John I can feel how strong his body is. He holds me firm and then puts his head into my neck. I move in close to him, and I can feel that he has developed an erection.

I look over at Dave. He and Shirley are staring into each other's eyes. At about that same time, John begins to kiss my neck. Then Shirley looks over. John stops kissing my neck and says to her, "Go ahead."

That lets Dave know that it's okay to kiss Shirley, and he does.

I look at John and when I do he kisses me. I push into him some more. The feel of a man's hard cock against me is something that is hard for me to resist.

I look back over at Dave. Now his hand is on Shirley's generous breast. She's kissing him eagerly now and has wrapped one of her legs around him, as if she can't get enough of him.

Even though Dave is grabbing an evil witch, I'm still turned on whenever I see him with another woman. John's hands are on my ass now as he has returned to kissing my neck.

"Let's take this to the bedroom," Dave announces.

Shirley doesn't respond. She just grabs his hand and pulls him around the corner. John smiles at me as we follow.

Their bedroom is pink, the color of Pepto-Bismol. The bed is perfectly made and there's a thick black bible on the nightstand. Shirley snatches the covers back, without a care, and begins to remove her clothes. No hesitation at all. Her breasts are full and firm. Her waist is shapely, and she's shaved her pussy into a neat little strip.

Dave takes off his clothes. His cock is rock hard and sticking straight out. Shirley wastes no time descending on it, taking his swollen member into her mouth.

John and I have been watching, but as Shirley slurps up Dave's cock, I take my clothes off and so does John. When he is naked, his cock just as swollen as Dave's, I push him down on the bed and climb on top of him.

Shirley is lying down now, with Dave on top. The positioning is ironic. Here we are, Dave and I, on top of the two Christians who want us out of town.

Dave is kissing Shirley hard. I'm kissing John hard. Dave grabs my hand and places it on Shirley's breast. He enjoys it when I fondle a breast,

Before the Move

Jolie Du Pré

and I love the feel of a full breast. Shirley doesn't mind what I'm doing. She also doesn't complain when I reach over and put one of her breasts in my mouth.

As I do that, John moves behind me. His hard cock flaps against my ass and his fingers are stroking my clit from behind. I stop sucking Shirley's tit and lay on my back. Dave throws me a condom. He keeps them in his shirt pocket. "For emergencies," he says. I never would have guessed that this would be one of those emergencies.

"Good idea," John says. I slip the condom on John's cock.

"You have another one, don't you?" Shirley asks.

"Of course," Dave says. He hands her another condom. She eagerly slips it on my husband's penis.

I grab John's cock and shove it in my pussy. John moves hard into me. By now Dave is inside Shirley. She is moaning so loud that I can barely concentrate on my own pleasure. Her legs have fallen open, brushing up against me. Her head is back into the pillow, and she's practically screaming.

Dave pushes into her hard. He shows no mercy. John continues to ride me, but he's almost too distracted by the way his wife is reacting to Dave. Shirley's big breasts are bouncing all over. Her eyes are closed tight. John is sweating, pushing into me while he's staring at his wife getting fucked.

He makes a loud sound, and I know he has come. That seems to set his wife off as she lets out her own wail. Dave and I aren't there yet, so we just look at his other and smile.

Shirley moves out from under Dave and gets off the bed. She hurries into her clothes and smoothes her hair. John follows behind. Then they leave the room. That just leaves Dave and me to get dressed.

"Strange days, huh?" he whispers.

"Yeah," I whisper back.

After we're dressed we walk back into the living room. "Well, I guess we should be going," Dave says. "Thanks for dinner."

"You're welcome," Shirley says as we put on our coats and head for the door.

At the door Shirley puts her hand on my shoulder. "You're very nice people, but John and I are going to pray about this night; a night that Satan has dominated, and beg God for forgiveness. We will pray for you too.

When you leave, sin and temptation will be leaving with you, and that is good for the town. Safe travels to Chicago."

Dave and I look at each other and walk away. But in the car, we laugh the whole way home.

About The Authors

Jacqueline Applebee

Jacqueline Applebee is a black bisexual British woman, who breaks down barriers with smut. Jacqueline's stories have appeared in Clean Sheets, *Iridescence: Sensuous Shades of Lesbian Erotica*, *Best Women's Erotica 2008* and 2009, *Best Lesbian Erotica 2008* and many other anthologies. She also has two paranormal novellas that are scorching hot! Jacqueline's website is at Writing-In-Shadows.co.uk.

Neve Black

Neve Black has been writing since she can remember and opted for a degree in English Literature. She mostly enjoys writing about subjects that scratch the under-belly of society, thus her love of erotica. Her stories can be read in the on-line magazine Oysters and Chocolate, various anthologies and the eBook publisher Ravenous Romance which will include her first novel that comes out sometime in January 2009. Please feel free to read Neve's blog and or leave a comment at NeveBlack.com.

M. Christian

M.Christian is an acknowledged master of erotica with more than 300 stories in such anthologies as *Best American Erotica, Best Gay Erotica, Best Lesbian Erotica, Best Bisexual Erotica, Best Fetish Erotica*, and many, many other anthologies, magazines, and Web sites. He is the editor of 20 anthologies including the *Best S/M Erotica* series, *The Burning Pen, Guilty Pleasures*, and others. He is the author of the collections *Dirty Words, Speaking Parts, The Bachelor Machine*, and *Filthy;* and the novels *Running Dry, The Very Bloody Marys, Me2, Brushes*, and *Painted Doll*.

Amanda Earl

Amanda Earl's sexually explicit fiction appears in anthologies by Cleis Press, Alyson Books, Thunder's Mouth Press, & Carroll and Graf. On line you can find her recent smut at Unlikely 2.0, Lucrezia Magazine, and Lies With Occasional Truth at LWOT.

Jeremy Edwards

Jeremy Edwards is a pseudonymous sort of fellow whose efforts at spinning libido into literature have been widely published online (at Clean Sheets and other sites), as well as in numerous anthologies offered by Cleis Press, Phaze Books, and Xcite Books. His work was selected for the two most recent volumes in the *Mammoth Book of Best New Erotica* series. Meanwhile, out on the newsstand, Jeremy's stories have been seen in *Scarlet* and in *Forum* (UK). His first erotic novel will be unveiled soon.

Rowan Elizabeth

Brand new to the lifestyle, Rowan Elizabeth shares her first experience. Rowan's work can be found in *The Best of Best American Erotica 2008*, *Hustler*, and at Ruthie's Club.

Emerald

Emerald has been a writer since age seven, though her repertoire did not begin to include erotica until her early twenties. Her erotic fiction has been published or is forthcoming in anthologies such as *Swing!* edited by Jolie du Pré, *Tasting Her* and *Sex and Music* edited by Rachel Kramer Bussel, *G is for Games and K is for Kinky* edited by Alison Tyler, and *Best Women's Erotica 2006* edited by Violet Blue, as well as online at Good Vibrations Magazine, Oysters & Chocolate, and The Erotic Woman. Currently, she resides in suburban Maryland where she works as a webcam model and serves as an activist for reproductive freedom and sex workers' rights. More about Emerald can be found online at her website, The Green Light District, at TheGreenLightDistrict.org.

Michael Hemmingson

Michael Hemmingson's first feature film, "The Watermelon," will be released in 2009 by LightSong Films. His recent books include *How to Have an Affair and Other Instructions* (Borgo Press), *Zona Norte -Ethnography of Sex Workers in Tijuana and San Diego* (Cambridge Scholars), and *House of Dreams* (Blue Moon).

Jolene Hui

Jolene Hui (JoleneHui.com) is a writer of literary and erotic fiction and about anything else her fingers feel like typing. She's been known to write a horror column for *The Flesh Farm* and a hockey column for *Inside Hockey*. One of Tonto Books' first authors, her literary fiction has been published in their Tonto Short Stories, Tonto Christmas Stories, and More Tonto Short Stories anthologies. She's also been published by a variety of newspapers, magazines, websites, Cleis Press, Pretty Things Press and Alyson Books. She still holds onto her dream that she will one day be the mother of a Standard Poodle and frequently daydreams about cheesecake. She is based in Los Angeles.

Ashley Lister

Ashley Lister is the UK author of *SWINGERS: True Confessions from Today's Swinging Scene* and *SWINGERS: Female Confidential*. Aside from writing erotic fiction under a variety of pseudonyms, Ashley has also written many non-fiction articles on a broad range of topics. A regular columnist, reviewer and contributor at The Erotic Readers & Writers Association, examples of Ashley's work can be found at: Erotic Readers & Writers Association. Ashley's non-fiction has appeared in a wide range of magazines that include (among many others) *Forum*, *The International Journal of Erotica* and *Chapter & Verse*. Ashley's full-length fiction has been published by Nexus, Chimera and Silver Moon with shorter fiction appearing in anthologies edited by Maxim Jakubowski, Rachel Kramer Bussel and Mitzi Szereto.

Keeb Knight

Keeb Knight was born in London. He grew up in the cities of Detroit and Philadelphia. Currently living in Philly, he enjoys writing erotic, multicultural, urban, and romantic suspense stories. His story "Mandatory Overtime" was featured in Zane's Eroticanoir Anthology, *Caramel Flava*. He's currently working on two urban erotica novels. Visit him at KeebKnight.com.

Randall Lang

Randall Lang grew up in the tough coal fields of southwestern Pennsylvania where nothing came easily. It was a world of limited opportunity and few roles to follow. Dreams were quickly vanquished in the shadows of necessity and creativity was usually buried beneath an avalanche of cynicism. However, epiphanies come in all shapes, sizes, and in a wide range of locations. The dark, wet, often cold environment of the underground workplace can have the unexpected effect of freeing the mind to drift away from such a hostile world into one of burning desire, passionate kisses, soft touches, and the intense magnetism that draws men and women together. Randall Lang is the author of seven books of erotica published by Renaissance E-books and contributed to the first edition of *Midnight Raunch* as published by Midnight Showcase. His first full length mainstream erotic romance novel, *Magnificent Man* is being edited and should release before the end of 2008.

M. Millswan

M. Millswan is a cross-genre writer, best known outside of Erotica circles for the Sci-Fi bestseller, *Farlight* and the Horror novel series, *Evil Heights*. True world wide acclaim has come from the erotic short story, "Snap Shot," which remains an on-line number one favorite even after more than five years in publication. Other erotica titles of special note include the award-winning novel, *Rolling the Bones*, and recently published in paperback, the NIS novel, *Living in the State of Dreams*. Having owned and operated a white water lodge in the jungle of Costa Rica, he's also an avid blues guitarist with two CDs to his credit: *So Far* and *Lava Tooth*.

D. L. King

D. L. King is the publisher and editor of the review site, Erotica Revealed. She has just edited her first short story anthology, *Where the Girls Are: Urban Lesbian Erotica*, for Cleis Press. She has published two novels, *The Melinoe Project* and *The Art of Melinoe*, as eBooks. Some of her latest short stories can be found in anthologies such as *Best Lesbian Erotica '08*, *Yes, Sir: Erotic Stories of Female Submission*, *Yes, Ma'am: Erotic Stories of Male Submission*, *Frenzy: 60 Stories of Sudden Sex*, *Best Women's Erotica '09* and *Mammoth Book of Best New Erotica '08*.

Claudia Moss

Claudia Moss lives and writes in Atlanta, GA. The author of *DOLLY: The Memoirs of a High School Graduate*, her fiction has been published in *Longing, Lust, and Love: Black Lesbian Stories*, *The Hoot and Holler of the Owl*, Catalyst, Labrys, Black Romance, Jive, Venus, and *Black Issues Book Review* magazines. Visit Claudia Moss online at her sites; TheGolden-Goddess.blogspot.com and MySpace.com/TheSiren4U.

Alicia Night Orchid

A lawyer by training, a chef by taste, and a writer by necessity, Alicia Night Orchid's mainstream fiction has appeared in several literary journals under another name. Her erotic stories have appeared online at Cleansheets, Ruthie's Club, Sliptongue, Oysters and Chocolate, For the Girls, and the Erotica Readers and Writers' Association. Her story, "Savage Nights" took first prize in Desdmona's 2007 60's Contest. Another story "A Lover in the House of Spies" was runner up in the For the Girl's 2008 Fiction Contest. In May 2009 Alicia's story "Taste of Love" will be featured in Oysters and Chocolate's first print anthology to be published by NAL a division of Penguin Press, Oysters and Chocolate: Erotica of Every Flavor. Also, look for Alicia's story, "Sen-Sen," appearing in the anthology "Coming Together: Against the Odds," due out in June 2009 in both print and e-book.

Tawanna Sullivan

Tawanna Sullivan is the webmaster for Kuma, a website which encourages black lesbians to write and share erotica. Her work has appeared in *Longing, Lust, and Love: Black Lesbian Stories, Iridescence: Sensuous Shades of Lesbian Erotica, Purple Panties, Best Lesbian Erotica 2009* and *Spirited: Affirming the Soul and Black Gay/Lesbian Identity*. She lives in New Jersey with her civil union partner, Martina.

Rick R. Reed

Rick R. Reed's EPPIE-award-winning horror/suspense fiction has been referred to as "a harrowing ride through cutting-edge psychological horror" (Douglas Clegg, author of *The Attraction*) and "brutally honest" (*Fangoria*). His most recent books include *IM*, a thriller about a serial killer preying on gay men through Internet hook-up sites; *In the Blood*, a tragic vampire love story; *Deadly Vision*, about a small town single mom who begins having psychic visions into a series of murders of teenage girls in her small Ohio River town; *High Risk*, a sexy thriller about a bored, promiscuous housewife who brings home a very handsome—and very psychotic—stranger; *Orientation* (EPPIE 2009 winner, Best GLBT), a paranormal love story about reincarnation, love, and sexual orientation; and *Dead End Street*, a young adult horror novel. Published in Dell's acclaimed Abyss horror line, Reed's first two novels, *Obsessed* and *Penance* together sold more than 80,000 copies. Rick's short fiction has appeared in numerous anthologies and magazines. A collection of his short horror fiction, *Twisted: Tales of Obsession and Terror* was published in 2006. Rick lives in Seattle, WA with his partner and is at work on a new novel.

TreSart L. Sioux

TreSart L. Sioux has been writing for several years. She has seven published books with Renaissance and three more in the works. She is currently writing articles on health and sports. TreSart has been in the art scene for the past twenty years. Her media ranges from pen and ink, photography, erotic, animation and sculpting. She has traveled to Paris, Jamaica, and hiking in California to broaden her talent in photography and other areas.

Donna George Storey

Donna George Storey is the author of *Amorous Woman* (Neon/Orion), a semi-autobiographical tale of an American's steamy love affair with Japan. Her short fiction has been published in over ninety journals and anthologies, including *The Mile High Club: Plane Sex Stories, Do Not Disturb: Hotel Sex Stories, X: The Erotic Treasury*, and the last five volumes of *Best Women's Erotica* and *Mammoth Book of Best New Erotica*. She currently writes columns for the Erotica Readers and Writers Association: "Cooking up a Storey," about her favorite topics—delicious sex, well-crafted food, and mind-blowing writing and "Shameless Self-Promotion" about book promotion for erotica writers. Read more of her work at DonnaGeorgeStorey.com.

Karmen Red

Karmen Red is a freelance journalist and former full-time editor, with articles and essays published in diverse categories. Karmen's current focus is on erotica and erotic romance, with interests in antiques, mythology, fantasy, costume/fetishes, B&D, and bisexuality. She's presently working on a time travel romance novel. Inspiration for many stories grows from her love of world travel, and from an eclectic collection of erotic art and antiques. She explores life and collects with her husband, her ultimate hero. Contact her at karmenred34@yahoo.com.

Sage Vivant

Sage Vivant is the author of *Your Erotic Personality* and the original founder of Custom Erotica Source. Her short stories have been widely published and many of them can be heard on Playboy Radio's "Sexy Stories." She and partner M. Christian have co-edited several erotica anthologies, including *Confessions, Amazons, Garden of the Perverse*, and *The Best of Both Worlds: Bisexual Erotica*.

Beth Wylde

Beth Wylde writes what she likes to read, which includes a variety of genres and pairings. Her muse believes in equal opportunity plotting. Beth's books range in theme from paranormal to contemporary and in pairings from lesbian erotica to straight m/f as well as bisexual, menage and beyond. This year her work will be available in both e-book and print. When she isn't writing she can still be found in front of her computer typing, chatting or working on promo. Her first story was published in 2006 and her reviews have been top notch. Some of her most recent awards include; The Romance Erotica Connection's (REC) 2007 & 2008 F/F Author of the Year, REC's Best Gay Short Story (co-written with Cassandra Gold) and Lesbian Erotica's Best Lead Female Character. She was also nominated for the GLBT author of 2008 award from Love Romances Cafe (LRC). Beth loves to hear from readers and other writers. She can be reached at b.wylde@yahoo.com. For contest info, chat dates and new releases you can visit her at her website or her Yahoo group: BethWylde.com and groups.yahoo.com/group/bethwylde. Keep an eye out for more from this talented author in the upcoming year!

Lara Zielinsky

Lara Zielinsky is a relative newcomer to published fiction, erotica or otherwise. In 2007, her first novel, *Turning Point*, received the 2007 Lesbian Fiction Readers Choice Award. She was also a finalist for the 2008 Debut Author award from the Golden Crown Literary Society. Happily bisexual, she lives in Orlando with her husband and son. In the last year she has sold short stories to several anthologies, and reviews and articles have appeared in BBWN newsletter as well as a Canadian bisexuals' newsletter. Her second novel arrives in bookstores in December 2009. She also works as an editor for several publishers. You can read more about her many other projects and stories at her website: LZFiction.net.

About the Editor

Jolie du Pré (Joliedupre.com) is a full-time freelance writer. She is also an editor and author of erotica. Her stories have appeared in a variety of web sites, in eBook and in print anthologies including *Cream: The Best of ERWA* edited by Lisabet Sarai, *Best Lesbian Erotica 2007* edited by Tristan Taormino, *Best Erotica 2007* edited by Berbera and Hyde, *Purple Panties*, edited by Zane, among others.

Jolie is the editor of *Iridescence: Sensuous Shades of Lesbian Erotica*, published by Alyson Books. She is also the founder of GLBT Promo (GlbtPromoBlog.com), a promotional group for GLBT erotica and erotic romance. Her lesbian dating site is MeetHerHere.com.

Visit the SWING website at Swinganthology.com.

Acknowledgments

Thanks to Jim and Zetta for appreciating the vision I had for this book, and to Susan for lending the hand for the cover image.

Thanks to Robert, my husband and my best friend, for always being there for me. And thanks to all the readers, writers and publishers, across the globe, who support and enjoy erotica.

Other books by Logical-Lust

Messalina – Devourer of Men
By Zetta Brown

When life imitates art...

Eva Cavell is a woman with an embarrassing secret.
She is sexually frustrated and is convinced that her size and race intimidates men.
In an attempt to relieve her sexual tension, every Thursday Eva goes to a local movie theater and allows desperate strangers to fondle her in the dark. She allows no eye contact, no phone numbers—and definitely no names.
During one of her escapades, renowned artist, Jared Delaney, a smooth Southern gentleman with irresistible violet eyes, has Eva breaking her own rules. He has been watching Eva on her weekly visits and sees through her icy defence and straight through to the hot passion burning underneath.

...expect to be framed

Messing about in dark theaters isn't a good pastime for Eva. She is a tenure-track instructor at a private Denver college that is currently embroiled in a sex scandal and she is the youngest child of a prominent black family.
To add to her turmoil, Neil Hollister, Eva's classroom aide and former student, is a handsome, barely-legal frat brat whose interest in her is carnal rather than academic—and she's tempted.
Despite desperate attempts to maintain control, Eva's world is spiralling into chaos. As emotional pressures build inside her, an explosion is imminent. Will she ever be able to live her life how she wants and without shame?
The answer may lie with a woman who is bold and unashamed in her sexuality.
Can Eva be more like her? What would happen if she even tried?

__Messalina – Devourer of Men__ is available worldwide in paperback and digital (ebook) formats, direct from www.logical-lust.com, or from Amazon, Barnes & Noble, and all good retailers!

Future Perfect
A Collection of Fantastic Erotica
By Helen E. H. Madden

What if you made love to a woman at the end of the universe, only to discover she was devastating black hole? What if the archangel Gabriel fell in love with the Virgin Mary and never delivered the Annunciation? What if a female dominant saw the future . . . every time she had an orgasm? For years, speculative fiction has asked the question "What if . . .?" Now the tales of *Future Perfect* go one step beyond and speculate on the possibilities of the erotic.

From the distant future to a biblical past and everything in between, *Future Perfect* examines the role of sex in a fantastic world. The stories range from hard science fiction to urban fantasy, but through it all runs a thread of explicit sexuality that embraces a wide range of orientations and relationships. Whether presented as the force of cosmic creation or the deceitful lure of Satan, *Future Perfect* takes sex beyond the limits of the everyday to show it as the impetus for change on a universal scale.

So open the cover and leave the mundane behind. A world of "What if . . ." is waiting for you.

Future Perfect – A Collection of Fantastic Erotica is available worldwide in paperback and digital (ebook) formats, direct from www.logical-lust.com, or from Amazon, Barnes & Noble, and all good retailers!

Bittersweet

Stories of tainted desire
by Amber Hipple

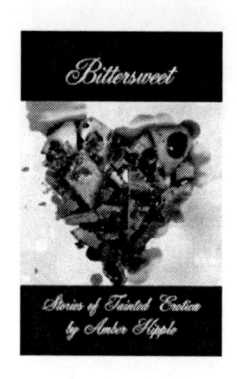

Not all sex is romance or fun. Sometimes there's desperation. Explore the deeper, darker aspects of love and want in "Bittersweet", Amber Hipple's intensely emotive debut collection of tainted erotica. Be moved by the cycle of wanting to be wanted and the pain of wanting too much. "Bittersweet" is a lesson in reality; it's what love and desire can be. Expect no "happy ever after" in these stories, but expect to be left wanting more.

Jim Brown, owner of Logical-Lust, says; *"Amber Hipple has come up with something quite out of the ordinary in 'Bittersweet'. Gone is the sugary-sweet romanticism and the happy-ever-after, to be replaced by the profound emotions and outpourings that are real in love and sex. You'll find your heart being wrenched apart by the yearnings and the despair of the characters, yet still be stirred and aroused by the sheer passion in the erotica she produces."*

BITTERSWEET by Amber Hipple, is released in both digital (ebook) and print formats, and will be available worldwide through www.logical-lust.com, Amazon, Barnes and Noble, and all good online retailers.

Crimson Succubus: The Demon Chronicles
By Carmine

"A few years back, I began receiving emailed submissions to the erotic literary ezine *Sauce*Box* from a writer known to me only as '*Carmine*'. These submissions were short pieces ('flash-fiction', if you will) detailing yet another 'Tale of the Crimson Succubus'. Each was a stand-alone jewel, horrible, cruel, fantastically, outrageously, graphically sexual, but also somehow (dare I say it . . . forgive me, Carmine) charming. I liked them very much and published every one that was sent.

"Now I find that some these short tales along with longer pieces concerning the 'adventures' of the Crimson Succubus, and a third section concerning a mythical nymph Mytoessa who also becomes involved with the succubus have been collected together in one place—a delightfully, tastefully disgusting book, **Tales of the Crimson Succubus, The Demon Chronicles** by Carmine.

"This person, Carmine, is one sick puppy, but one with adorable eyes and floppy ears. The tales involve much blood- and semen-letting, murder, torture, deception and pain, but at the same time, I often want to laugh and wish that the creatures would appear for real, in front of me, so that I could see with my own eyes and even touch (very, very carefully, mind you) these monsters formed from the primordial slime of all of our great cultural myths.

"And of course, like all myths, these tales speak to our deepest fears, and hopes and fantasies . . . perhaps to archetypes from times before even the written word, times long forgotten in consciousness but remembered in the collective genetic code. I don't know. Whatever. They're a great read, an exciting read and one that will tickle your nightmares and daydreams long after you've put this book down."

Guillermo Bosch, Editor: *Sauce*Box*, Ezine of Literary Erotica
Author of **Rain** and **The Passion of Muhammad Shakir**

<u>Crimson Succubus: The Demon Chronicles</u>is available worldwide in paperback and digital (ebook) formats, direct from www.logical-lust.com, or from Amazon, Barnes & Noble, and all good retailers!

Lightning Source UK Ltd.
Milton Keynes UK
UKOW051042060112

184866UK00001B/216/P